Case Studies in Contemporary Criticism

THOMAS MANN

Death in Venice

Case Studies in Contemporary Criticism

SERIES EDITOR: Ross C Murfin

Charlotte Brontë, *Jane Eyre*
EDITED BY Beth Newman, Southern Methodist University

Emily Brontë, *Wuthering Heights*
EDITED BY Linda H. Peterson, Yale University

Geoffrey Chaucer, *The Wife of Bath*
EDITED BY Peter G. Beidler, Lehigh University

Kate Chopin, *The Awakening*
EDITED BY Nancy A. Walker, Vanderbilt University

Joseph Conrad, *Heart of Darkness,* Second Edition
EDITED BY Ross C Murfin, Southern Methodist University

Charles Dickens, *Great Expectations*
EDITED BY Janice Carlisle, Tulane University

Thomas Hardy, *Tess of the d'Urbervilles*
EDITED BY John Paul Riquelme, Boston University

Nathaniel Hawthorne, *The Scarlet Letter*
EDITED BY Ross C Murfin, Southern Methodist University

Henry James, *The Turn of the Screw*
EDITED BY Peter G. Beidler, Lehigh University

James Joyce, *The Dead*
EDITED BY Daniel R. Schwarz, Cornell University

James Joyce, *A Portrait of the Artist as a Young Man*
EDITED BY R. B. Kershner, University of Florida

James Joyce, *A Companion to James Joyce's* Ulysses
EDITED BY Margot Norris, University of California, Irvine

William Shakespeare, *Hamlet*
EDITED BY Susanne L. Wofford, University of Wisconsin–Madison

Mary Shelley, *Frankenstein*
EDITED BY Johanna M. Smith, University of Texas at Arlington

Jonathan Swift, *Gulliver's Travels*
EDITED BY Christopher Fox, University of Notre Dame

Edith Wharton, *The House of Mirth*
EDITED BY Shari Benstock, University of Miami

Case Studies in Contemporary Criticism

SERIES EDITOR: Ross C Murfin, *Southern Methodist University*

THOMAS MANN
Death in Venice

Complete, Authoritative Text with Biographical and Historical Contexts, Critical History, and Essays from Five Contemporary Critical Perspectives

EDITED BY

Naomi Ritter
University of Missouri

Bedford Books

BOSTON   NEW YORK

For Bedford Books

President and Publisher: Charles H. Christensen
General Manager and Associate Publisher: Joan E. Feinberg
Managing Editor: Elizabeth M. Schaaf
Developmental Editor: Stephen A. Scipione
Assistant Managing Editor: John Amburg
Production Editor: Ara Salibian
Copyeditor: Barbara Sutton
Text Design: Sandra Rigney, The Book Department
Cover Design: Richard Emery Design, Inc.
Cover Art: Joseph Mallord William Turner, *The Riva degli Schiavoni,*
c. 1840 (detail). 217 × 318 mm. Watercolor. Ashmolean Museum,
Oxford.

For information, write: Bedford Books,
75 Arlington Street, Boston, MA 02116
(617–426–7440)

ISBN: 0–312–12002–8 (paperback)
ISBN: 0–312–21064–7 (hardcover)

Acknowledgments

"Death in Venice," from *Death in Venice* by Thomas Mann, translated
by David Luke. Translation copyright © 1988 by David Luke. Used by permission of Bantam Books, a division of Bantam Doubleday Dell Publishing
Group, Inc.

Robin Tobin, "Why Is Tadzio a Boy?" Reprinted by permission of the au-
thor. Adapted from "Why Is Tadzio a Boy? Perspectives on Homoeroticism in
Death in Venice." From *Death in Venice,* translated and edited by Clayton
Koelb. Copyright © 1944 by W. W. Norton & Company, Inc.

About the Series

Volumes in the Case Studies in Contemporary Criticism series provide college students with an entrée into the current critical and theoretical ferment in literary studies. Each volume reprints the complete text of a classic literary work and presents critical essays that approach the work from different theoretical perspectives, together with the editors' introductions to both the literary work and the critics' theoretical perspectives.

The volume editor of each Case Study has selected and prepared an authoritative text of the classic work, written an introduction to the work's biographical and historical contexts, and surveyed the critical responses to the work since its initial publication. Thus situated biographically, historically, and critically, the work is examined in five critical essays, each representing a theoretical perspective of importance to contemporary literary studies. These essays, prepared especially for undergraduates, show theory in praxis; whether written by established scholars or exceptional young critics, they demonstrate how current theoretical approaches can generate compelling readings of great literature.

As series editor, I have prepared introductions, with bibliographies, to the theoretical perspectives represented in the five critical essays. Each introduction presents the principal concepts of a particular theory in their historical context and discusses the major figures and key works that have influenced their formulation. It is my hope that these introductions will reveal to students that effective criticism is informed by a set of coherent assumptions, and will encourage them to recognize and examine their own assumptions about literature. After each introduction, a selective bibliography presents a partially annotated list of important works from the literature of the particular theoretical perspective, including the most recent and readily available editions and translations of the works cited in the introduction. Finally, I have compiled a glossary of key terms that recur in these volumes and in the discourse of contemporary theory and criticism. We hope that the Case Studies in Contemporary Criticism series will reaffirm the richness of its literary works, even as it introduces invigorating new ways to mine their apparently inexhaustible wealth.

Ross C Murfin
Series Editor
Southern Methodist University

About This Volume

This book features a translation by David Luke, first published by Bantam Books in 1988. At that time, the standard English translation was the British version by Helen Lowe-Porter, published by Secker in 1929. However, Knopf had already published Kenneth Burke's first American translation in 1925, and several more versions followed Lowe-Porter: Erich Heller (1970), Luke (1988), Clayton Koelb (1993), and Stanley Appelbaum (1995). The reasons Lowe-Porter's rendition stood unchallenged for forty years concern both her smoothly polished English and her professional relationship with Mann himself. Having consulted him regularly during her work, she gained his grudging but official approval: a startling fact, considering the many flawed passages and omissions that make Lowe-Porter's version simply inadequate. Another likely reason for the gap in time between her translation and Heller's is the difficulty of skillfully translating Mann's erudite prose. Indeed, his often convoluted syntax bewilders many native speakers of German. According to the latest translator, Stanley Appelbaum, "Mann's discourse can be 'as challenging for German readers as Henry James is for us.'"

As the essay on the novella's reception shows, recent criticism has dwelled on the psychoanalytic aspect of both Aschenbach and Mann. Rodney Symington updates this approach with his timely and original essay on the influence of Sigmund Freud and Jacques Lacan's revision of Freudian theory. Robert Tobin pursues one strand of the dense psychoanalytic fabric: the role that Mann's own culturally conditioned psychosexual nature played in the creation of Aschenbach and his story.

While these two approaches occupy the forefront of recent and current criticism on our text, the three other topics presented here offer equally valid and challenging means to interpretation. The area addressed by Lilian Furst, reader response, is not unknown to German criticism; indeed, its major contribution by Wolfgang Iser — *The Implied Reader* of 1974 and *The Art of Reading* of 1978 — has influenced a generation of American critics. However, Furst takes up an aspect of reader response still neglected by German critics: the questioning of the text's ethical basis and its impact on readers.

Russell Berman's essay on new history addresses some new aspects of what the text tells us about its time. Berman's original analysis helps us to articulate the delicate seam between fiction and history. It thereby alerts us to the interplay of life and art that traditional literary history has not often addressed. John Burt Foster Jr.'s essay explores some intriguing complexities posed by the various cultures impinging on our text. Naturally, his cultural approach implicitly assumes a premise like that of new history: namely, that our best understanding of historical cultures must include a study of determining factors neglected by traditional critical modes. For instance, Foster's attention to the Polish nationality of Tadzio breaks new ground for the criticism of *Death in Venice*. Likewise, and in a particularly apt way for this book, Foster discusses translation itself as a cultural phenomenon. While translation studies do exist, they do not typically treat the complex of cultural meanings that attach to the translation of a specific text.

Acknowledgments

My first debt of gratitude is to Ross Murfin and Steve Scipione, whose enthusiasm for this volume withstood years of deliberation and market research. Without their steady support the book would probably still exist only as my wistful idea. Other indispensable help came from Charles Christensen, Joan Feinberg, Elizabeth Schaaf, John Amburg, Laura Arcari, Maura Shea, and Ara Salibian.

Now that this volume is indeed reality, I have completed a personal circle that started with my first enthralled reading of the text as an undergraduate in 1959. Academics are a tenacious lot, but this project of deep immersion in the work has demanded almost forty years.

Although my first cicerone through the work, Mary Corcoran, has died, I still thank her for that seductive experience. Much later, when I was conceiving a critical edition, Hans Vaget and Kurt Ackermann gave valued information and encouragement. Jeffrey Berlin also gave his expertise and advice as generously as ever, as did that other Mann maven, Gerald Gillespie.

Of course the five contributors deserve the major credit for this venture's success. They all tailored their work to the particular demands of this series; they met our deadlines conscientiously; and they accepted graciously the suggestions of no less than three editors. For my part, warm thanks to all for tolerating my severe allergy to the passive voice and long sentences. Their patience in putting up with some inevitable delays was also exemplary. In short, one could not wish for more helpful colleagues.

Naomi Ritter

Contents

About the Series   v

About This Volume   vii

PART ONE
Death in Venice:
The Complete Text

Introduction: Biographical and Historical Contexts   3

The Complete Text   23

PART TWO
Death in Venice:
A Case Study in Contemporary Criticism

A Critical History of *Death in Venice*   91

Psychoanalytic Criticism and *Death in Venice*   110

What Is Psychoanalytic Criticism?   110
Psychoanalytic Criticism: A Selected Bibliography   122

A Psychoanalytic Perspective:
  RODNEY SYMINGTON, The Eruption of the Other: Psychoanalytic
  Approaches to *Death in Venice*   127

Reader-Response Criticism and *Death in Venice*   142

What Is Reader-Response Criticism?   142
Reader-Response Criticism: A Selected Bibliography   154
A Reader-Response Perspective:
  LILIAN R. FURST, The Potential Deceptiveness of Reading in *Death
  in Venice*   158

Cultural Criticism and *Death in Venice*   171

What Is Cultural Criticism?   171
Cultural Criticism: A Selected Bibliography   185
A Cultural Perspective:
  JOHN BURT FOSTER JR., Why Is Tadzio Polish? *Kultur* and
  Cultural Multiplicity in *Death in Venice*   192

Gender Criticism and *Death in Venice*   211

What Is Gender Criticism?   211
Gender Criticism: A Selected Bibliography   222
A Perspective on Gender and Sexuality:
  ROBERT TOBIN, The Life and Work of Thomas Mann: A Gay
  Perspective   225

The New Historicism and *Death in Venice*   245

What Is The New Historicism?   245
The New Historicism: A Selected Bibliography   258
A New Historicist Perspective:
  RUSSELL A. BERMAN, History and Community
  in *Death in Venice*   263

Glossary of Critical and Theoretical Terms   281

About the Contributors   294

Case Studies in Contemporary Criticism

THOMAS MANN

Death in Venice

PART ONE

Death in Venice:
The Complete Text

Introduction: Biographical and Historical Contexts

NATIONALISM AND THE WRITER'S SENSE OF PLACE

Perhaps the most striking fact about the year of Thomas Mann's birth, 1875, is that Germany itself was only four years old. If we assume that Mann had to be affected by national developments, then his arrival at this propitious moment in German history indeed determined his acute awareness of German nationalism. Out of some 300 local political units dating from the Holy Roman Empire, Otto von Bismarck had fashioned a nation-state in 1871. Among European lands, only Italy had awaited unity for a comparably long time; we can see the effects of this late political maturity in both nations' development of fascism.

However, in assessing the influence of national trends on Mann, we must compare it with the more palpable impact of his own local roots in the city of Lübeck. Mann clearly perceived himself as a proud son of this patriarchal city of the Hansa League, distinguished since the Middle Ages for its economic and political advancement. Mann's own family partook of this distinction, for he came from a long line of successful grain merchants. Moreover, his father's role as senator imprinted on Thomas the firm sense of civic duty and dignity that became quite problematic for the young writer. The 1903 autobiographical short story "Tonio Kröger" conveys the same tension that Mann himself felt in being both a staid North German and an imaginative artist. The poet Tonio Kröger, whose very name bespeaks his split Latin-German identity, resolves this conflict by a compromising acceptance of his endemically divided nature. But apparently this book did not settle the matter for Mann, for *Death in Venice* takes up the same problem in deeper tones and resolves it only with the writer's death. In "Tonio Kröger," Mann claimed "no problem in the world is more tormenting than the nature of the artist and its effect on humanity."

Mann's sensitivity to local ambience also played a role in his moving in 1893 from provincial northern Lübeck to sophisticated southern Munich, Germany's major city of artistic culture.[1] In specifying these two most significant places for Mann, we already note his tendency toward dichotomy: one of his constant themes concerns the polarity of north and south, commerce and culture, classic Prussian sobriety and romantic southern sensuality. The terms invented for these opposing qualities by Mann's admired forebear, Friedrich Nietzsche (1844–1900), are Apollonian and Dionysian. This classicist's revolutionary vision of Greek culture through the prism of these polar traits so imprinted *Death in Venice* that we may read it as a tragic verbal rendition of the inevitable conflict between these two massive cultural forces.

Nietzsche's dualistic notion of antiquity became a determining influence on Mann's general view of culture. Accordingly, the acute play of polarities in *Death in Venice* makes it as central to his oeuvre as the novels are. Several other reasons for the work's exemplary status emerge below: its rich breadth of source material, its brilliantly economical narration, its critical vision of European society, its trenchant character analysis. But generally, *Death in Venice* initiates us best into Mann's mature oeuvre because it offers his first novella-length yet major statement of abiding attitudes toward the relation of art to life — one of his essential subjects. The earlier stories collected in *Tristan*, especially "Tonio Kröger," had already broached the matter in 1903. Yet none of these works offers the later text's exquisitely organic conception, its lyric prose, or any hint of Mann's stylistic riches to come. *Buddenbrooks* of 1901 bespeaks Mann's early Platonic idea that the artist's physical, intellectual, and emotional condition brings moral de-

---

[1]Not accidentally, the protagonist of *Death in Venice*, Gustav von Aschenbach, also lives in Munich. Perhaps the most common coin of criticism on the novella is just this overlay of Mann's own biography and character on Aschenbach. Accordingly, all the following essays at least touch on this mirroring of the author in his protagonist.

cline. But that novel reflects the aura of naturalism too centrally to do justice to the author Mann would soon become. Its length may also daunt the beginning reader.

SOURCES IN BIOGRAPHY

Mann's early success proved as important as any other factor influencing his development. The death of his father in 1892 and the subsequent liquidation of the family business allowed young Thomas the independent means that most artists lack. Moreover, not many writers of twenty-six achieve national fame with a first novel, which is just what Mann did with the best-selling *Buddenbrooks*. By 1902, his family inheritance and the financial success of his early stories assured him the secure career that determined not only his productivity but even his attitudes. Undoubtedly Mann's own nature — cerebral, moralistic, proud, and self-assured — depended partly on genetic inheritance. Yet we see in his older brother and fellow writer Heinrich (1871–1950) a very different personality, one deeply marked by his relative lack of international acclaim.

In *Death in Venice* we see how success molds Aschenbach's character and behavior. The germ of the novella came from the life of the most renowned German author, Johann Wolfgang von Goethe (1749–1832), whose old-age love affair illumined for Mann the dangers of fame. The seventy-four-year-old poet fell in love with a young woman of seventeen, Ulrike von Levetzov, whom he had met at the spa Marienbad in 1823. This encounter resulted in the brilliant verse cycle *The Marienbad Elegies* of 1823. For Mann, the important fable behind the elegies concerned the loss of dignity occasioned by a late sexual passion. Although various experiences changed Mann's original plan into a story of homosexual love, this kernel of forbidden love remained a prime significance of Aschenbach's demise. As Mann stated in a letter of 1915, "The problem I had in mind particularly was that of the artist's dignity. I wanted to show something like the tragedy of greatness." Like Goethe, the aging Aschenbach falls in love hopelessly; indeed, this writer's crucial "adventure of the emotions" leaves him no viable identity, so he must die (37).

Beyond the forbidden love suggested by Goethe's Marienbad encounter, *Death in Venice* sprang from some other intricately interwoven sources. Both the dense integration of these sources and the breadth of their origins, ranging from Greek philology to Mann's study of epidemiology, make this text remarkable, both in his oeuvre and in European prewar literature. Thus, to understand the work in its fullest historical and authorial context, let us first consider its deep roots in Mann's literary development. Since 1905 he was musing on the Goethe-Aschenbach analogy, which not only changed into a story of homosexual love but gradually acquired several layers of reflection on Greek myth, personal experience, and psychology.

METHOD

Mann himself coined a formula for his literary method in *Death in Venice:* "myth plus psychology." (For the later echo of this phrase, see "A Critical History of *Death in Venice*" in Part Two.) We may understand this merging of source material by a comparison with Mann's contemporary and fellow modernist James Joyce (1882–1941). Joyce uses the name Dedalus to indicate the dangerously soaring ambitions of Stephen, his protagonist in *A Portrait of the Artist as a Young Man* (1916). Similarly, Mann constantly uses Greek philosophy and mythology to depict a modern artist whose final condition depends on both Greek aesthetics and that culture's ideal of homosexual love between an older man and a boy.

Even at first sight, Tadzio reminds Aschenbach of "Greek sculpture of the noblest period"; his long curls recall the famous *Greek Boy Extracting a Thorn,* and he bears "the head of Eros, with the creamy luster of Parian marble (216–17, 220). When Tadzio arrives late for breakfast, Aschenbach calls him "my little Phaeacian," alluding to the luxurious Phaeacian life described in Homer's *Odyssey* (8.249), which he then recites to himself: "Varied garments to wear, warm baths and restful reposing" (46). Other examples of the text's persistent classicizing recur in images of Dionysus, Apollo, Hermes, Hyacinth, Narcissus, Semele and Zeus, and Socrates and Phaedrus (231, 235, 260, 263). And aptly enough, the novella's climactic jungle dream recalls the hideous cannibal orgy in *The Bacchae* of Euripides (484–406 B.C.).

One of the most impressive examples of this mythologizing technique is what Aschenbach drinks — pomegranate juice and soda — during the portentous serenade of the Venetian street singers (248). Of course, Italians often drink this combination in warm weather, but in the context of this particular traveler's story, we must note Mann's allusion to its Greek forbear, the tale of Persephone, daughter of Demeter, goddess of the earth and fertility. Abducted and taken to the underworld of the dead by Hades, Persephone eats the seeds of a pomegranate. Like Eve's irresistible apple, this food brings a penalty that shapes history. Because Persephone had broken the fast of the dead in yielding to Hades' temptation to eat, she had to return to his dark realm of death for a third of the year. Indeed, only a special dispensation that Zeus granted Demeter allowed the wayward daughter to return to earth for the other two-thirds of the year. Accordingly, the myth explains seasonal change: Persephone's forced descent underground signifies winter; her fertilizing return to earth brings spring (Chevalier 766).

Aschenbach fits perfectly into this mythic symbolism. He, too, has felt driven southward, yielding to a force just as much beyond his control as Persephone's need to eat. Namely, the aging man can no longer resist the universal, instinctual human urge for that sensual gratification he has always repressed. He also goes to a sort of underworld — the infected Venice that brings death. And he, too, has eaten of forbidden fruit: not only the symbolic pomegranate, but also the actual overripe strawberries that probably infected him with cholera on his first day at the Lido. Furthermore, the pomegranate symbol implies an ironic reversal: its many seeds signify fertility, yet Mann associated homosexuality with sterility.[2]

This deeply literary motif of the pomegranate juice matters yet more for the reader. Namely, it demonstrates Mann's acutely economical means. In one deceptively simple symbol, he connotes the richly subconscious condition that determines Aschenbach's demise. Here lies a hallmark of the best possible writing, in which every detail, every sentence bears significance. Just as we grasp the organic necessity of a cell in a complex system, so we may intuit the importance of a tiny but dense detail in the literary work's coherence.

By interweaving myth in their fiction, both Joyce and Mann communicate the universality of their figures. Readers may understand and even identify with their characters just because they resonate in human history. Stephen as Joyce's mythic poet whose daring could prove suicidal, Aschenbach as a self-styled modern Socrates, and Tadzio as a Greek god don't just tell us there is nothing new under the sun. More important, they relate us all to myth, what Carl Jung (1875–1961) has labeled "the collective unconscious." Hence these authors

---

[2]A similar journalistic analogy to the Persephone myth appears in Shana Alexander's *Anyone's Daughter* (1979), an account of the hostage experience of Patty Hearst, an heiress kidnapped by terrorists. Alexander claims that, like Persephone, Hearst tasted the forbidden fruit of terrorism and, bonding with her captors, joined their Symbionese Liberation Army (161).

allow us to connect personally with the oldest, most universal sources of our culture.

Incidentally, *Death in Venice* relates further to Joyce's novel in that it renders a portrait of the artist as an *old* man. Actually we know only that Aschenbach is past fifty, as the story's first sentence tells us that he gained the honorary "von" title at that age. But the disgust Aschenbach feels at his gray hair and aging body shows that he perceives himself as old indeed. In the 1971 film *Death in Venice* directed by Luchino Visconti (1906–1976), Dirk Bogarde plays a decidedly older man, whose personal fussiness and uncertain, often halting movements convey the frailty of old age.

As for the quotient of specifically personal, rather than universal or mythic experience that helped to form this text, we must look at its immediate history. Mann started the writing as a diversion from other work that was proving difficult. Following the quite unsuccessful light novel *Royal Highness* in 1909, he turned to a more demanding project, intended as a pendant to "Tonio Kröger," his first novella-length allegory of the artist: *The Confessions of the Confidence Trickster Felix Krull.* This manuscript gave Mann such problems in 1911 that he dropped it for a while. Indeed, this parodic novel presented such a continuing challenge that, despite repeated attempts to finish it in the 1920s, it remained a fragment at Mann's death in 1954. Partly as distraction from this and other career worries, Mann and his wife vacationed in and near Venice in May and June of 1911. On May 18, Mann read an obituary for the composer Gustav Mahler (born 1860). This striking coincidence of the revered artist's death during Mann's Venetian holiday inspired him to give Aschenbach the facial features of the composer described at the end of chapter 2. Already on the first page, Mann signals the image of Mahler, who died at age fifty — just the age when Aschenbach had recently received his honorary name "von." Thus, by subtextually linking Aschenbach's age with Mahler's death on the novella's first page, Mann reinforces the message of the title: namely, that this work portrays another artist's final journey to death.

When Mann met Mahler in September of 1910 he described the composer as "a truly great man": rare praise from the demanding writer. So the sudden decision to contain his idea of Mahler within Aschenbach — despite the lack of psychological likeness — bespeaks Mann's prevailing sense that fame endangers an artist. More specifically, the link to Mahler's death at age fifty illuminates Mann's aim of addressing "the tragedy of greatness." The fifty-year-old "von" Aschenbach's very name bears the official evidence of his being what

Mann had already called himself in 1905, "a national factor." Hence Aschenbach was vulnerable to just the feeling of eminence that would bring eventual self-destruction. The 1905 diary entry that envisions a new work expresses Mann's fear of self-importance:

> I don't want to become a figure. [The danger lies in] a heightened self-respect, taking oneself too seriously. . . . I want to show the painful aberration of an artist who has enough talent to attain his ambitions, but lacks the maturity to master his success, which finally destroys him. (trans. mine)

Finally, showing that Mahler's aura hovers over *Death in Venice* from start to finish, a final echo of the composer resounds in the ending sentence, whose grave tone may reflect that of the obituary Mann had read. Visconti took Mann's hint of this similarity literally, for his film takes the daring liberty of turning the writer Aschenbach into Mahler himself.

So many aspects of the story came from Mann's own experience that in *A Sketch of My Life* (1930) he claimed, "nothing is invented in *Death in Venice*." An example of what he means is the actual outbreak of cholera in Venice in 1905, when Mann was on a nearby island. A more startling confirmation of Mann's life overlaying his fiction appeared in 1965, when a Polish baron, Wladyslaw Moes, identified himself as the boy whom Mann fictionalized in Tadzio.

At that time the Munich newspaper *Twen* published an article about Baron Moes, "I was Thomas Mann's Tadzio." Upon reading the Polish translation of *Death in Venice* in 1923, Moes had realized that he was indeed the boy on whom Mann had modeled Tadzio. Through the novella's Polish translator, Moes sent some old family photographs to Erika Mann, the author's daughter, in 1964. The article in *Twen* explains why the Moes family went to Venice: a doctor had recommended sea air for the boy's punctured lung. What better resort than Venice could they choose for everyone's delight? Wladyslaw's regimen duly appears in Mann's story, for Aschenbach notes Tadzio's late sleeping and carefully monitored exercise. Moes marveled at how faithfully Mann used the actual boy's striped linen suit, red tie, and blue jacket with gold buttons. The baron even identified his rough playmate, Jan Fudakowski, whose nickname "Jasio" echoes Mann's "Jaschiu." More surprisingly, Moes recalls the "old man" (though Mann was only thirty-five) who stared intently at him in the elevator. Apparently Jan also noticed the man watching them, and the two boys laughed about him (Hayman 250; Adair n.p.).

FREUD, PSYCHOLOGY, AND HOMOSEXUALITY

In a newspaper interview in 1925, Mann attributed specific ideas in his story to Sigmund Freud (1856–1939):

At least one of my works, the novella *Death in Venice*, came into being under the direct influence of Freud. Without him I would never have thought of treating this erotic theme; or I would certainly have treated it differently. If I may express myself in military terms, I would say that Freud's thesis represents a kind of general .offensive against the unconscious with the purpose of conquering it. It's true that as an artist I must confess I am not at all *satisfied* with Freud's ideas: I feel rather disconcerted and belittled by them. After all, Freud's ideas illuminate the artist like a beam of x-rays, to the point of damaging the secret of his creativity. (interview with *La Stampa*, in Beharriell 5)

What "disconcerted" Mann about Freud's theory of art was its claim that creativity depends on neurosis. However, judging by Mann's last, emphatically disturbing portrait of the composer Leverkühn in *Doctor Faustus*, he came to agree with Freud's unflattering analysis of the artist.

Of course Mann need not have read Freud in depth to be influenced by his ideas, for they had been current since at least 1900, when the pioneering *Interpretation of Dreams* appeared. Also, much of Freud's explication of mental states was not entirely new, for writers since antiquity had been analyzing their characters psychologically. Freud even pays his debt to *Oedipus Rex* (ca. 425 B.C.), by Sophocles (ca. 496–406? B.C.) in labeling the universal father-son rivalry "the Oedipus complex." Other familiar ideas that Freud brilliantly consolidated from various sources concern the link between art and mental illness, the explosive energy of the repressed libido, and the deep significance of dreams. We find all these traits in the lives and/or works of — just for instance — Georg Büchner (1813–1837), Henry Fuseli (1741–1825), Gérard de Nerval (1808–1855), Arthur Rimbaud (1854–1891), and Nietzsche.

Death in Venice reflects two major aspects of Freudian theory: the repression of libidinal drives, which Aschenbach has mastered, and the expression of his subconscious condition in the two crucial visions framing his "inner" story. Indicating the subconscious idea of travel itself, Aschenbach daydreams of a tropical swamp, replete with crouching tiger, just after seeing the exotic, strangely threatening man on his walk. Toward the end of his Venetian adventure, the distraught author dreams of a far more deadly jungle, containing a cannibal orgy ruled by "the Stranger-God." Both dreams encapsulate the Freudian longing for the ultimate erotic abandon in death. Neither the repression nor the symbolic dreams appear in Mann's earlier characters.

Aschenbach's many encounters with death figures also symbolize the Freudian subconscious death wish. Indeed, considering the ubiquity of death in this work, one might conclude that this morbidity sprang from Mann's fascination with the paradoxical longing for death in the very successful Aschenbach. Even Aschenbach's name — meaning "brook of ashes" — tells us what we already know from the title: this man is marked for death. But again, Freud was not the first to write of such subconscious wishes. In particular, Aschenbach's repressive reaction to seeing that first bizarre man at the mortuary chapel in Munich shows how he automatically shuts off disturbing unconscious perceptions. After more than a long paragraph's description of this man's eerie significance, the text tells us that Aschenbach turned and walked away: "A minute later he had put him out of his mind" (25). Considering the course of the story, we know that this foreboding figure has indeed nested symbolically in Aschenbach's unconscious death wish.

Aschenbach's adamant rejection of psychology is also significant. One of his stories appears as "an outbreak of disgust against an age undermined by psychology." The text proclaims the "writer's renunciation of all moral skepticism, of every kind of sympathy with the abyss; . . . his repudiation of the laxity of that compassionate principle which holds that to understand all is to forgive all" (32). Aschenbach's disgust probably pertains mainly to the adultery contained in the tale he reviles; a puritanical attitude toward all sexual matters typifies the disdain that Freud elicited from his many detractors.

One of the trenchant ironies of *Death in Venice* lies in Aschenbach's denial of his own needy psychological state. In believing that will alone can control his destiny, this artist goes precisely out of control. His experience of Venice and Tadzio releases just those instinctual drives that he has always suppressed; they finally emerge as uncontrollable passion. The symbol for this process appears in chapter 2, the clenched fist that an observer uses to describe Aschenbach: "'You see, Aschenbach has always lived like *this*' — and the speaker closed the fingers of his left hand tightly into a fist — 'and never like *this*' — and he let his open hand hang comfortably down along the back of the chair" (29). At the end of chapter 3, when Aschenbach sits "with his arms hanging limply down along the back of his chair," the reader may grasp an ironic reversal of "and never like *this*" (29). Such a verbal repetition of a phrase associated with a character is typical of Mann's literary leitmotiv, a stylistic means adopted from Richard Wagner's musical leitmotiv. In the story's final scene, the hand goes from limp to lifeless, completing the total inversion of Aschenbach's life. The dead hand of a corpse symbolizes his final condition with a perfectly circular irony.[3]

Regarding specifically what Mann called "the erotic motif" of *Death in Venice*, one can hardly exaggerate the significance of Aschenbach as the tragically repressed homosexual. The first clear sign of this condition appears on pp. 36–37, where Aschenbach sits on shipboard, reading the book of "a poet of plangent inspiration" who had earlier visited Venice. The "few lines of measured music" that Aschenbach recites to himself must come from August Graf von Platen (1796–1835), whose most famous work is the cycle *Venetian Sonnets* (1824). Moreover, because Platen is the best-known nineteenth-century German homosexual writer, Mann implies more than a literary kinship to Aschenbach. Mann also felt a personal link to Platen, about whom he wrote an admiring essay in 1930. Until all of his diaries had appeared by 1991, readers assumed that affinity pertained mainly to the literary and Venetian contexts; now we know Mann must have also identified with the plight of that earlier repressed homosexual artist.

As Robert Tobin's essay demonstrates, Aschenbach's story fits perfectly into the general European aesthetic tenor of its time. André Gide's comparable novel *The Immoralist* (1902) demonstrates the desperate identity crisis felt by many continental gay artists. The protagonist in *The Picture of Dorian Gray* (1891) by Oscar Wilde (1856–1900) is only the most familiar of many fictional figures who, like Aschenbach, serve partially as masks for their homosexual authors. Both the life and works of the French poet Jean Cocteau (1889–1963), the Russian symbolist writer Mikhail Kuzmin (1875–1936), the Russian dancer Vaslav Nijinsky (1890–1950), and the English authors W. H. Auden (1907–1973) and Osbert Sitwell (1892–1969) exemplify further how homoerotic attitudes pervaded European culture in the early years of the century.

---

[3]Mann attributed that image of the clenched fist to another writer's comment about their contemporary Hugo von Hofmannsthal, but its ultimate source may lie in Goethe's account of a singer he heard at Marienbad: her voice "unfolded" him, just as a clenched fist relaxes (Vaget 1984, 171–72).

DECADENCE AND ART: THE EUROPEAN CONTEXT

As early as *Buddenbrooks: The Decline of a Family* (1901), Mann developed the idea that art necessarily corrupts morality. This attitude had been around since Plato, who worried persistently about the harmful effects that artists might wreak on society. In particular, books 2, 3, and 4 of his *The Republic* (411–10? B.C.) attack poets as a pernicious influence on public morality. Plato cites Homer (ca. 700–800 B.C.) as the exemplary practitioner of ideal poetry, dedicated solely to the praise of famous heroes. Not only such didacticism but also a Platonic pessimistic view of art marks the demise of Aschenbach. In chapter 2, we read that his writing instructs schoolchildren, so he sees both his work and himself as truly exemplary. Yet in chapter 5, the Socratic discourse addressed to Phaedrus — imitating Plato's dialogue *Phaedrus* on the nature of beauty (ca. 360 B.C.) — claims just the opposite. It suggests that writers, lacking wisdom and dignity, cannot possibly uplift their readers: "We artists cannot tread the path of Beauty without Eros keeping company with us and appointing himself as our guide. . . . [H]ow can one be . . . an educator when one has been born with an incorrigible and natural tendency toward the abyss?" (205, 261). Mann's intent that this story demonstrate "the tragedy of greatness" shows that he recognized the possible threat posed by his own fame.

At the turn of the century, many European writers expressed a haunting awareness of cultural, social, and personal decadence. Indeed, broad social and moral decline became a major theme in such landmark European novels as *Against the Grain* (1884), by Joris Karl Huysmans (1848–1907), *Effi Briest* (1895), by Theodor Fontane (1819–1898); the multivolume *The Rougon-Macquarts* (1871–93) of Émile Zola (1840–1902); and Wilde's *The Picture of Dorian Gray*. Influential critical analysis came from the revered *Decline and Fall of the Roman Empire* (1776), by Edward Gibbon (1737–1794), and the popular tract of Max Nordau (1849–1923), *Degeneration* (1895), whence Nazi ideology derived many false assumptions about modern culture.

VENICE AS SYMBOLIC DECLINE

The turn of the century displayed two opposite tendencies simultaneously: both the hedonistic pleasure of "la belle epoque," the gay nineties, and a pessimistic anxiety about the inner corruption of that same glittering culture. These two conflicting emotional forces found resolution only in World War I (1914–18), which we may well consider the virtual end of the nineteenth century. External glory masking inner rottenness is indeed the narrator's ultimate verdict on Aschenbach: a condition mirrored tellingly by the crucial location of his story, Venice. That island of unique past economic and artistic fame, built on pilings in sand, tends to sink. Hence it has always represented a triumph of human ingenuity over the constantly threatening forces of nature. Analogously, Aschenbach has also conquered his frail constitution in producing a paradoxically strong body of work. In short, both Venice and Aschenbach have created, against all probability, a miracle of pure will. In this tight linkage of character and locus we note again the economy of Mann's conception. His title not only conveys the essence of the story's action; it also states the idea of a fatal mutual attraction between this city and death. Grasping fully the rich historical and aesthetic implications of this place, we know that Aschenbach must die there.

Another crucial tie between Aschenbach and Venice lies in the tradition of writers outside Italy, from Shakespeare onward, to associate Venice with moral corruption. Moreover, the organic ruin of a plague as a symbol of divine punishment for mysterious sins goes back to Oedipus. Mann's cholera penetrates Venice from the East, just as one cult of Dionysus invaded Greece. Here the text implies that Western-imperialist fear of a barbaric invasion that survives in our own culture's xenophobia toward immigrants from both the East and the South.

The association of the German poet Platen with Venice recalls the passion of many European artists, for whom this literally marvelous place connoted a shrine, a virtually sacred historical ground for the finest examples of European art, architecture, and music. A mere sample list of such artists includes Thomas Otway (1652–1685), Lord George Byron (1788–1824), Richard Wagner (1813–1883), Henry James (1843–1916), Gabriele d'Annunzio (1863–1938), Nietzsche, Maurice Barrès (1862–1923), and Hugo von Hofmannsthal (1874–1929). Igor Stravinsky (1882–1971) even insisted on burial in Venice's island graveyard, San Michele. As he requested, his grave lies beside that of his collaborator, the ballet impresario Serge Diaghilev (1872–1929). Both men obviously rejected their Russian birthplace in favor of their kindred locale, Venice. But no German writer is so closely associated with Venice as Platen. Mann's symbolic reference to him upon Aschenbach's arrival in Venice gives Platen only an evocative significance; the poet's primary relevance emerges in Mann's profound mirroring of Platen's sonnet "Tristan": "Whoever has beheld beauty /

Already belongs to death." One could hardly capture the essence of *Death in Venice* in a better capsule.

Moreover, the idea of fatal beauty goes well beyond Platen. Perhaps the first comparable poem is "La Belle Dame sans merci" (1425), by Alain Chartier (1385–1450). A rendition of the same title (1819) by John Keats (1795–1821) coins the romantic image of the deadly woman still known as "la femme fatale." In this respect, all four authors — Chartier, Keats, Platen, and Mann — build on a venerable tradition of coupling beauty with death (Daemmrich 103–5).

ARTISTIC CURRENTS

Mann grew up aesthetically in the era of naturalism, a literary movement whose proponents believed in biological and/or socioeconomic determinism. Naturalism's main practitioner, Émile Zola, had given massive expression to his and earlier positivists' belief in genetic decadence. In his many novels between 1871 and 1893, poverty and alcoholism, transmitted from one generation to the next, become as much an inevitable inheritance as the purely physical trait of blue eyes. Zola had virtually adopted the view that Hippolyte Taine (1828–1893) expressed in his famous capsule of forces determining character: heredity, time, and environment. Moreover, two other factors fostered the claim that industrialization brought inevitable social decline: the new discipline of sociology, named in 1838 by Auguste Comte (1798–1857), plus the racist pseudo-science promulgated by Arthur de Gobineau (1816–1882) and Otto Weininger (1880–1903).

In the 1890s, while naturalist attitudes declined, modernism grew. Perhaps Virginia Woolf (1882–1941) dated the change most radically in claiming that "in or about December, 1910, human character changed" (Woolf 320). At the very least, this pregnant sentence playfully implies the radically transformed assumptions about the human condition that modernist writers express in their challenging works. Examples of works suggesting such transformed assumptions are Franz Kafka's surrealistic *The Trial* (1916); the hermetically mysterious *Heart of Darkness* (1899), by Joseph Conrad (1857–1924); and the involuted *Remembrance of Things Past* (1913–22), by Marcel Proust (1871–1922). One notes immediately the difference from earlier styles of writing. The clear meaning of naturalist books, so welcoming for the reader, is yielding to the ambiguities of such densely textured novels as Joyce's *Ulysses* (1922) or Woolf's own *Orlando* (1928).

While Mann's prose retained its early mastery of the Goethean sovereign tone, it also gained some poetic traits typical of modernist writing. Two disparate and contrasting sentences in *Death in Venice* may demonstrate the simultaneous presence of naturalism and modernism: "It was from this marriage between hard-working, sober conscientiousness and darker, more fiery impulses that an artist, and indeed this particular kind of artist, had come into being" (28). This sentence enshrines Mann's most naturalistic concept of genetic mutation, first coined in *Buddenbrooks* and assumed regularly thereafter. Note the contrasting tone of this poetic sentence:

> And to behold this living figure, lovely and austere in its early masculinity, with dripping locks and beautiful as a young god, approaching out of the depths of the sky and the sea, rising and escaping from the elements — this sight filled the mind with mythical images, it was like a poet's tale from a primitive age, a tale of the origins of form and of the birth of the gods. (50)

This sentence renders a wholly unnaturalist integration of symbolism with the mythic lyrical imagery that Mann called "hymnic."

Other new aspects of this modernist style are trenchant, often critical analysis of both history and character; shifting narrative positions; and the piling up of overlaid images — rather like filmic montage. The most experimental modernist passages appear in the two Socratic speeches in chapters 3 and 5 (61–62, 85–86); the beginning of chapter 4, with an evocation of a Mediterranean seascape that shifts suddenly into German hexameter rhythm (57–58); and the final surrealistic dream (81–82). Furthermore, Mann's many foreboding death figures recall the blatantly symbolic imagery of Huysmans's *Against the Grain* more than any naturalist writing.

POLITICS AND PSYCHOHISTORY

Death in Venice, which may seem focused wholly on the aesthetic matter of how art relates to life, nonetheless bespeaks much of the political climate of 1911. The first sign of current events appears right in the second clause of the first sentence: "the year in which for months on end so grave a threat seemed to hang over the peace of Europe." While some critics read this phrase as a merely general reference to minor continental troubles in the years just before 1914, the most astute of them cite the actual diplomatic failure that Mann probably implied. During the summer of 1911, a widespread rumor of war developed from the crisis of Agidir, where the German navy threatened the French territorial claim to Morocco.

Mann's own politics displays a remarkable development: from the conservative aesthete indifferent to political activity described in *Thoughts of a Nonpolitical Man* (1918) to the writer fully committed to combating Nazi ideology in *Doctor Faustus* (1947). In this regard, Mann wrote that *Death in Venice* contains "sensitively seismographic elements" that show a "tension of the will and its morbidity immediately before the war." Indeed, the reader must notice the morbidity of this novella, whose plot, setting, and characters keep reiterating symbolically the ubiquity of death in both Aschenbach's external and inner worlds. Herein lies what recent literary critics call psychohistory: that is, the mirroring of characters' psychological states in events surrounding them.

Aschenbach's longing for death implies the imminent death of his culture, for he represents just that society. His life reflects the overstrained will — monarchic, imperialist, self-inflated — on the eve of the inevitable war. Mann sounds perhaps the most psychohistorical note in the implied comparison in chapter 2 of Aschenbach to Frederick the Great (1712–1786). Frederick's triumph over frail health pertains clearly to Aschenbach's own conquest of physical weakness. As Robert Tobin's essay notes, Mann also refers here to the persistent rumor of Frederick's homosexuality. But here I wish to stress only the death will of both such repressive natures and the cultures that have created them.

Aschenbach's Apollonian drive to rational form only *seems* to have mastered his irrational instinct for Dionysian passion. In this context we may recall Goethe's maxim that "Every great man is linked to his century by a weakness" (Goethe 628). This statement approximates Mann's claim: with a man as famous as Aschenbach, "there must be a hidden affinity, indeed a congruence, between the personal destiny of the author and the wider destiny of his generation" (30). In short, Aschenbach symbolizes the inevitable suicide of a civilization blinded to its inner corruption by its hubristic lust for power. Accordingly, the novella portends the death of that very middle-class "establishment" culture that the values in Aschenbach's work addressed so successfully. In this light, *Death in Venice* appears as a protest against what this society represented. Hence, even before his self-styled politicizing after the war, Mann was already battling mentally against the gods of his time.

MUSIC AND LITERATURE

One can hardly overstate the significance of music in Mann's thinking. Naturally, what he called "the paradigm of all art" had to appear in both the form and content of his work (Vaget 1978, 46). One of his early stories, "Tristan" (1903), shows Mann unabashedly under the spell of Wagner; his final novel, *Doctor Faustus* (1947), clearly opposes this hypnotic influence, for its antihero is a composer of demonic Wagnerian dimensions who symbolizes the fate of Germany under the Nazis. Most relevent for this volume is not the complex evolution of Mann's relation to Wagner, but rather his Wagner-induced fascination with the power of music itself.

Mann started to recognize what music would represent for him through the concerts of his childhood. But probably the crucial intellectual impact came from reading Nietzsche's new view of Greek culture, already hugely influential in Mann's time, *The Birth of Tragedy from the Spirit of Music* (1871). Mann's earliest writing shows the influence of Wagner's musical ideas, plus the thought of Nietzsche and Arthur Schopenhauer (1788–1860), the two German philosophers most linked to music. Mann also adopted from Wagner both the leitmotiv technique of characterizing and a lush, almost symphonic syntax. Perhaps the best example in *Death in Venice* appears in an evocation of the uniquely Wagnerian Liebestod (love-death), a longing for erotic death climaxed in Wagner's opera *Tristan und Isolde* (1865):

> Can there be anyone who has not had to overcome a fleeting sense of dread, a secret shudder of uneasiness, on stepping for the first time . . . into a Venetian gondola? How strange a vehicle it is, coming down unchanged from times of old romance, and so characteristically black, the way no other thing is black except a coffin — a vehicle evoking lawless adventures in the plashing stillness of night, and still more strongly evoking death itself, the bier, the dark obsequies, the last silent journey! . . . [T]he seat of such a boat, that armchair with its coffin-black lacquer and dull black upholstery, is the softest, the most voluptuous, most enervating seat in the world. (39)

Finally, we might consider an autobiographical link: just as Aschenbach writes a piece of fiction while watching Tadzio on the beach, so did Mann write the essay *About the Art of Richard Wagner* while in Venice in May of 1911. The manuscript of this essay, preserved in the Mann archive in Zurich, bears the letterhead of the Grand Hotel des Bains, Lido-Venice.

The young Mann felt awed by the emotional force in Wagner's music. Soon, however, like Wagner's earlier accolyte, Nietzsche, Mann turned against the effects of this music. Nietzsche found the starkly religious ethos of *Parsifal* intolerable; Mann became anxious about the ecstatic feelings that Wagner arouses. We sense this anxiety already in *Death in Venice*, in its Platonic horror at the artist's sensual, specifically erotic passion.

MANN'S HISTORICAL PLACE

In important ways — intellectually, socially, and to some extent aesthetically — Mann belongs more to the nineteenth century than to the twentieth, in which he lived most of his life. An avid reader of nineteenth-century fiction, Mann gleaned much from critical visions of society in the novels of Honoré de Balzac (1799–1850), Gustave Flaubert (1821–1880), Leo Tolstoy (1828–1910), and Ivan Turgenev (1818–1883). As for his own time, one need only compare the work of his German-writing contemporaries Rainer Maria Rilke, also born in 1875, and Franz Kafka, born in 1883, to note how little Mann shared with these two giants of twentieth-century literature. Mann's prose, delighting us by its brilliant clarity and prismatic complexity, owes much to the model for all German writers — *the* classic master, Goethe. Signs of Goethe's aura appear throughout *Death in Venice*, the first gracing Aschenbach's desk as two tall silver candlesticks, which also adorned Goethe's writing table (30).

Mann's acknowledged debt to Goethe may amount to that "anxiety of influence" famously postulated by Harold Bloom as the major link between literary masters and disciples. But Mann also developed the measured classic tone of his writing in novel directions. *Death in Venice* indeed exemplifies this change, for it ingeniously balances a sovereign, Apollonian narration with rhapsodic passages evoking Dionysian passion. Moreover, his shifts in narrative stance typify modernist experiment: a technique whose problematic effects Lilian Furst addresses in her reader-response essay in Part Two, "The Potential Deceptiveness of Reading in *Death in Venice*." Already in 1941 the critic Harry Levin compared Mann with Joyce as "an unchallenged master" of the modernist novel.

Thus we might follow Mann himself in considering his work transitional. From the earliest stories, bespeaking a vulnerable prewar innocence, to his somber assessment of Germany's disastrous world impact in *Doctor Faustus,* Mann reflects the era's hectic pace of historical, social, and cultural change. Accordingly, *Death in Venice* illuminates many factors that intersected both during the war and in its aftermath: the end of decadence, a contagious abandon of rationality, the demise of repressive Prussian mores, sexual liberation, and moral relativism. Along with all its verbal pleasures, the story offers a prismatic window on this historical landscape.

Naomi Ritter

WORKS CITED

Adair, Gilbert. "The Real Story of *Death in Venice.*" *Sunday Correspondent* (London), 8 April, 1990, n.p.

Alexander, Shana. *Anyone's Daughter.* New York: Viking, 1979.

Beharriell, Frederick J. "Never Without Freud: Freud's Influence on Mann." *Thomas Mann in Context: Papers of the Clark University Centennial Colloquium.* Ed. Kenneth Hughes. Worcester: Clark UP, 1978. 1–15.

Bloom, Harold. *The Anxiety of Influence: A Theory of Poetry.* Oxford: Oxford UP, 1973.

Chevalier, Jean, and Alain Gheerbrant. *A Dictionary of Symbols.* Oxford: Blackwell, 1994.

Daemmrich, Horst, and Ingrid Daemmrich. *Themes and Motifs in Western Literature: A Handbook.* Tübingen: Francke, 1987.

Freud, Sigmund. *Collected Papers.* Ed. James Strachey. 24 vols. London: Hogarth, 1953.

Gibbon, Edward. *The History of the Decline and Fall of the Roman Empire (1776–88).* Ed., abridged, and intro. Hugh Trevor-Roper. New York: Twayne, 1963.

Gide, André. *The Immoralist.* Trans. Richard Howard. New York: Vintage, 1970.

Goethe, Johann Wolfgang. *The Permanent Goethe.* Ed., trans., and intro. Thomas Mann. New York: Dial, 1948.

Hayman, Ronald. *Thomas Mann: A Biography.* New York: Scribner, 1995.

Huysmans, J.-K. *Against the Grain.* New York: Dover, 1969.

Mann, Thomas. *Diaries, 1918–21, 1933–39.* Ed. Hermann Kesten. Trans. Richard and Clara Winston. London: Clark, 1984.

————. *The Letters of Thomas Mann.* 2 vols. Sel. and trans. Richard and Clara Winston. London: Secker & Warburg, 1970.

Nietzsche, Friedrich. *The Birth of Tragedy: Basic Writings of Nietzsche.* Trans. Walter Kaufmann. New York: Modern Library, 1968. 1–144.

————. *The Portable Nietzsche.* Trans. Walter Kaufmann. Harmondsworth: Penguin, 1982.

Platen, August Graf von. *Selected Poems.* Trans. Edwin Morgan. West Linton, Scotland: Castlelaw P, 1978.

Plato. *Phaedrus.* Trans. Alexander Nehamas and Paul Woodruff. Indianapolis: Hackett, 1995.

————. *The Republic.* Trans. Robin Waterfield. Oxford: Oxford UP, 1993.

Timms, Edward. "*Death in Venice* as Psychohistory." In *Approaches to Teaching Mann's "Death in Venice" and Other Short Fiction,* ed. Jeffrey Berlin. New York: Modern Language Association, 1992. 134–39.

Vaget, Hans Rudolf. *Thomas Mann: Kommentar zu sämtlichen Erzählungen.* München: Winkler, 1984.

————. "George Lukacs, Thomas Mann, and the Modern Novel." *Thomas Mann in Context: Papers of the Clark University Centennial Colloquium.* Ed. Kenneth Hughes. Worcester: Clark UP, 1978.

Wilde, Oscar. *The Picture of Dorian Gray.* Ed. Donald Lawler. New York: Norton, 1988.

Woolf, Virginia. "Mr. Bennett and Mrs. Brown." In *Collected Essays,* vol. 1. London: Hogarth, 1967.

Death in Venice

1

On a spring afternoon in 19 —— , the year in which for months on end so grave a threat seemed to hang over the peace of Europe, Gustav Aschenbach, or von Aschenbach as he had been officially known since his fiftieth birthday, had set out from his apartment on the Prinzregentenstrasse in Munich to take a walk of some length by himself. The morning's writing had overstimulated him: his work had now reached a difficult and dangerous point which demanded the utmost care and circumspection, the most insistent and precise effort of will, and the productive mechanism in his mind — that *motus animi continuus* which according to Cicero is the essence of eloquence — had so pursued its reverberating rhythm that he had been unable to halt it even after lunch, and had missed the refreshing daily siesta which was now so necessary to him as he became increasingly subject to fatigue. And so, soon after taking tea, he had left the house hoping that fresh air and movement would set him to rights and enable him to spend a profitable evening.

It was the beginning of May, and after a succession of cold, wet weeks a premature high summer had set in. The Englischer Garten, although still only in its first delicate leaf, had been as sultry as in August, and at its city end full of traffic and pedestrians. Having made his way to the Aumeister along less and less frequented paths, Aschenbach had briefly surveyed the lively scene at the popular open-air restaurant, around which a few cabs and private carriages were standing; then, as the sun sank, he had started homeward across the open meadow beyond the park, and since he was now tired and a storm seemed to be brewing over Föhring, he had stopped by the Northern Cemetery to wait for the tram that would take him straight back to the city.

As it happened, there was not a soul to be seen at or near the tramstop. Not one vehicle passed along the Föhringer Chaussee or the paved Ungererstrasse on which solitary gleaming tramrails pointed toward Schwabing; nothing stirred behind the fencing of the stonemasons' yards, where crosses and memorial tablets and monuments, ready for sale, composed a second and untenanted burial ground; across the street, the mortuary chapel with its Byzantine styling stood silent in the glow of the westering day. Its facade, adorned with Greek crosses and brightly painted hieratic motifs, is also inscribed with symmetrically arranged texts in gilt lettering, selected scriptural passages about the life to come, such as: "They shall go in unto the dwelling-place of the Lord," or "May light perpetual shine upon them." The waiting Aschenbach had already been engaged for some minutes in the solemn pastime of deciphering the words and letting his mind wander in contemplation of the mystic meaning that suffused them, when he noticed something that brought him back to reality: in the portico of the chapel, above the two apocalyptic beasts that guard the steps leading up to it, a man was standing, a man whose slightly unusual appearance gave his thoughts an altogether different turn.

It was not entirely clear whether he had emerged through the bronze doors from inside the chapel or had suddenly appeared and mounted the steps from outside. Aschenbach, without unduly pondering the question, inclined to the former hypothesis. The man was moderately tall, thin, beardless and remarkably snub-nosed; he belonged to the red-haired type and had its characteristic milky, freckled complexion. He was quite evidently not of Bavarian origin; at all events he wore a straw hat with a broad straight brim which gave him an exotic air, as of someone who had come from distant parts. It is true that he also had the typical Bavarian rucksack strapped to his shoulders and wore a yellowish belted outfit of what looked like frieze, as well as carrying a gray rain-cape over his left forearm which was propped against his waist, and in his right hand an iron-pointed walking stick which he had thrust slantwise into the ground, crossing his feet and leaning his hip against its handle. His head was held high, so

that the Adam's apple stood out stark and bare on his lean neck where
it rose from the open shirt; and there were two pronounced vertical
furrows, rather strangely ill-matched to his turned-up nose, between
the colorless red-lashed eyes with which he peered sharply into the distance. There was thus — and perhaps the raised point of vantage on
which he stood contributed to this impression — an air of imperious
survey, something bold or even wild about his posture; for whether it
was because he was dazzled into a grimace by the setting sun or by
reason of some permanent facial deformity, the fact was that his lips
seemed to be too short and were completely retracted from his teeth,
so that the latter showed white and long between them, bared to the
gums.

Aschenbach's half absentminded, half inquisitive scrutiny of the
stranger had no doubt been a little less than polite, for he suddenly became aware that his gaze was being returned: the man was in fact staring at him so aggressively, so straight in the eye, with so evident an intention to make an issue of the matter and outstare him, that
Aschenbach turned away in disagreeable embarrassment and began to
stroll along the fence, casually resolving to take no further notice of
the fellow. A minute later he had put him out of his mind. But
whether his imagination had been stirred by the stranger's itinerant
appearance, or whether some other physical or psychological influence
was at work, he now became conscious, to his complete surprise, of an
extraordinary expansion of his inner self, a kind of roving restlessness,
a youthful craving for far-off places, a feeling so new or at least so long
unaccustomed and forgotten that he stood as if rooted, with his hands
clasped behind his back and his eyes to the ground, trying to ascertain
the nature and purport of his emotion.

It was simply a desire to travel; but it had presented itself as nothing less than a seizure, with intensely passionate and indeed hallucinatory force, turning his craving into vision. His imagination, still not at
rest from the morning's hours of work, shaped for itself a paradigm of
all the wonders and terrors of the manifold earth, of all that it was now
suddenly striving to envisage: he saw it, saw a landscape, a tropical
swampland under a cloud-swollen sky, moist and lush and monstrous,
a kind of primeval wilderness of islands, morasses and muddy alluvial
channels; far and wide around him he saw hairy palm-trunks thrusting
upward from rank jungles of fern, from among thick fleshy plants in
exuberant flower; saw strangely misshapen trees with roots that arched
through the air before sinking into the ground or into stagnant shadowy-green glassy waters where milk-white blossoms floated as big as

plates, and among them exotic birds with grotesque beaks stood
hunched in the shallows, their heads tilted motionlessly sideways; saw
between the knotted stems of the bamboo thicket the glinting eyes of
a crouching tiger; and his heart throbbed with terror and mysterious
longing. Then the vision faded; and with a shake of his head Aschenbach resumed his perambulation along the fencing of the gravestone
yards.

His attitude to foreign travel, at least since he had had the means
at his disposal to enjoy its advantages as often as he pleased, had always
been that it was nothing more than a necessary health precaution, to
be taken from time to time however disinclined to it one might be.
Too preoccupied with the tasks imposed upon him by his own sensibility and by the collective European psyche, too heavily burdened
with the compulsion to produce, too shy of distraction to have learned
how to take leisure and pleasure in the colorful external world, he had
been perfectly well satisfied to have no more detailed a view of the
earth's surface than anyone can acquire without stirring far from
home, and he had never even been tempted to venture outside Europe. This had been more especially the case since his life had begun
its gradual decline and his artist's fear of not finishing his task — the
apprehension that his time might run out before he had given the
whole of himself by doing what he had it in him to do — was no
longer something he could simply dismiss as an idle fancy; and during
this time his outward existence had been almost entirely divided between the beautiful city which had become his home and the rustic
mountain retreat he had set up for himself and where he passed his
rainy summers.

And sure enough, the sudden and belated impulse that had just
overwhelmed him very soon came under the moderating and corrective influence of common sense and of the self-discipline he had practiced since his youth. It had been his intention that the book to which
his life was at present dedicated should be advanced to a certain point
before he moved to the country, and the idea of a jaunt in the wide
world that would take him away from his work for months now
seemed too casual, too upsetting to his plans to be considered seriously. Nevertheless, he knew the reason for the unexpected temptation
only too well. This longing for the distant and the new, this craving
for liberation, relaxation and forgetfulness — it had been, he was
bound to admit, an urge to escape, to run away from his writing, away
from the humdrum scene of his cold, inflexible, passionate duty. True,
it was a duty he loved, and by now he had almost even learned to love

the enervating daily struggle between his proud, tenacious, tried and tested will and that growing weariness which no one must be allowed to suspect nor his finished work betray by any telltale sign of debility or lassitude. Nevertheless, it would be sensible, he decided, not to span the bow too far and willfully stifle a desire that had erupted in him with such vivid force. He thought of his work, thought of the passage at which he had again, today as yesterday, been forced to interrupt it — that stubborn problem which neither patient care could solve nor a decisive *coup de main* dispel. He reconsidered it, tried to break or dissolve the inhibition, and, with a shudder of repugnance, abandoned the attempt. It was not a case of very unusual difficulty, he was simply paralyzed by a scruple of distaste, manifesting itself as a perfectionistic fastidiousness which nothing could satisfy. Perfectionism, of course, was something which even as a young man he had come to see as the innermost essence of talent, and for its sake he had curbed and cooled his feelings; for he knew that feeling is apt to be content with high-spirited approximations and with work that falls short of supreme excellence. Could it be that the enslaved emotion was now avenging itself by deserting him, by refusing from now on to bear up his art on its wings, by taking with it all his joy in words, all his appetite for the beauty of form? Not that he was writing badly: it was at least the advantage of his years to be master of his trade, a mastery of which at any moment he could feel calmly confident. But even as it brought him national honor he took no pleasure in it himself, and it seemed to him that his work lacked that element of sparkling and joyful improvisation, that quality which surpasses any intellectual substance in its power to delight the receptive world. He dreaded spending the summer in the country, alone in that little house with the maid who prepared his meals and the servant who brought them to him; dreaded the familiar profile of the mountain summits and mountain walls which would once again surround his slow discontented toil. So what did he need? An interlude, some impromptu living, some *dolce far niente,* the invigoration of a distant climate, to make his summer bearable and fruitful. Very well then — he would travel. Not all that far, not quite to where the tigers were. A night in the wagon-lit and a siesta of three or four weeks at some popular holiday resort in the charming south . . .

Such were his thoughts as the tram clattered toward him along the Ungererstrasse, and as he stepped into it he decided to devote that evening to the study of maps and timetables. On the platform it occurred to him to look round and see what had become of the man in

the straw hat, his companion for the duration of this not inconsequen-
tial wait at a tram-stop. But the man's whereabouts remained a mystery, for he was no longer standing where he had stood, nor was he to
be seen anywhere else at the stop or in the tramcar itself.

2

The author of the lucid and massive prose-epic about the life of
Frederic of Prussia; the patient artist who with long toil had woven the
great tapestry of the novel called *Maya*, so rich in characters, gathering
so many human destinies together under the shadow of one idea; the
creator of that powerful tale entitled *A Study in Abjection*, which
earned the gratitude of a whole younger generation by pointing to the
possibility of moral resolution even for those who have plumbed the
depths of knowledge; the author (lastly but not least in this summary
enumeration of his maturer works) of that passionate treatise *Intellect
and Art* which in its ordering energy and antithetical eloquence has
led serious critics to place it immediately alongside Schiller's disquisition *On Naive and Reflective Literature:* in a word, Gustav Aschenbach, was born in L . . . , an important city in the province of Silesia,
as the son of a highly-placed legal official. His ancestors had been military officers, judges, government administrators; men who had spent
their disciplined, decently austere life in the service of the king and the
state. A more inward spirituality had shown itself in one of them who
had been a preacher; a strain of livelier, more sensuous blood had entered the family in the previous generation with the writer's mother,
the daughter of a director of music from Bohemia. Certain exotic
racial characteristics in his external appearance had come to him from
her. It was from this marriage between hard-working, sober conscientiousness and darker, more fiery impulses that an artist, and indeed this
particular kind of artist, had come into being.
　　With his whole nature intent from the start upon fame, he had displayed not exactly precocity, but a certain decisiveness and personal
trenchancy in his style of utterance, which at an early age made him
ripe for a life in the public eye and well suited to it. He had made a
name for himself when he had scarcely left school. Ten years later he
had learned to perform, at his writing desk, the social and administrative duties entailed by his reputation; he had learned to write letters
which, however brief they had to be (for many claims beset the successful man who enjoys the confidence of the public), would always

contain something kindly and pointed. By the age of forty he was obliged, wearied though he might be by the toils and vicissitudes of his real work, to deal with a daily correspondence that bore postage-stamps from every part of the globe.

His talent, equally remote from the commonplace and from the excentric, had a native capacity both to inspire confidence in the general public and to win admiration and encouragement from the discriminating connoisseur. Ever since his boyhood the duty to achieve — and to achieve exceptional things — had been imposed on him from all sides, and thus he had never known youth's idleness, its carefree negligent ways. When in his thirty-fifth year he fell ill in Vienna, a subtle observer remarked of him on a social occasion: "You see, Aschenbach has always only lived like *this*" — and the speaker closed the fingers of his left hand tightly into a fist — "and never like *this*" — and he let his open hand hang comfortably down along the back of the chair. It was a correct observation; and the morally courageous aspect of the matter was that Aschenbach's native constitution was by no means robust, and that the constant harnessing of his energies was something to which he had been called, but not really born.

As a young boy, medical advice and care had made school attendance impossible and obliged him to have his education at home. He had grown up by himself, without companions, and had nevertheless had to recognize in good time that he belonged to a breed not seldom talented, yet seldom endowed with the physical basis which talent needs if it is to fulfill itself — a breed that usually gives of its best in youth, and in which the creative gift rarely survives into mature years. But he would "stay the course" — it was his favorite motto, he saw his historical novel about Frederic the Great as nothing if not the apotheosis of this, the king's word of command, *"durchhalten!"* which to Aschenbach epitomized a manly ethos of suffering action. And he dearly longed to grow old, for it had always been his view that an artist's gift can only be called truly great and wide-ranging, or indeed truly admirable, if it has been fortunate enough to bear characteristic fruit at all the stages of human life.

They were not broad, the shoulders on which he thus carried the tasks laid upon him by his talent; and since his aims were high, he stood in great need of discipline — and discipline, after all, was fortunately his inborn heritage on his father's side. At the age of forty or fifty, and indeed during those younger years in which other men live prodigally and dilettantishly, happily procrastinating the execution of great plans, Aschenbach would begin his day early by dashing cold

water over his chest and back, and then, with two tall wax candles in
silver candlesticks placed at the head of his manuscript, he would offer
up to art, for two or three ardently conscientious morning hours, the
strength he had gathered during sleep. It was a pardonable error, indeed it was one that betokened as nothing else could the triumph of
his moral will, that uninformed critics should mistake the great world
of *Maya*, or the massive epic unfolding of Frederic's life, for the product of solid strength and long stamina, whereas in fact they had been
built up to their impressive size from layer upon layer of daily opuscula, from a hundred or a thousand separate inspirations; and if they
were indeed so excellent, wholly and in every detail, it was only because their creator, showing that same constancy of will and tenacity of
purpose as had once conquered his native Silesia, had held out for
years under the pressure of one and the same work, and had devoted
to actual composition only his best and worthiest hours.

For a significant intellectual product to make a broad and deep immediate appeal, there must be a hidden affinity, indeed a congruence,
between the personal destiny of the author and the wider destiny of
his generation. The public does not know why it grants the accolade
of fame to a work of art. Being in no sense connoisseurs, readers imagine they perceive a hundred good qualities in it which justify their admiration; but the real reason for their applause is something imponderable, a sense of sympathy. Hidden away among Aschenbach's
writings was a passage directly asserting that nearly all the great things
that exist owe their existence to a defiant despite: it is despite grief and
anguish, despite poverty, loneliness, bodily weakness, vice and passion
and a thousand inhibitions, that they have come into being at all. But
this was more than an observation, it was an experience, it was positively the formula of his life and his fame, the key to his work; is it surprising then that it was also the moral formula, the outward gesture, of
his work's most characteristic figures?

The new hero-type favored by Aschenbach, and recurring in his
books in a multiplicity of individual variants, had already been remarked upon at an early stage by a shrewd commentator, who had described his conception as that of "an intellectual and boyish manly
virtue, that of a youth who clenches his teeth in proud shame and
stands calmly on as the swords and spears pass through his body."
That was well put, perceptive and precisely true, for all its seemingly
rather too passive emphasis. For composure under the blows of fate,
grace in the midst of torment — this is not only endurance: it is an active achievement, a positive triumph, and the figure of Saint Sebastian

is the most perfect symbol if not of art in general, then certainly of the kind of art here in question. What did one see if one looked in any depth into the world of this writer's fiction? Elegant self-control concealing from the world's eyes until the very last moment a state of inner disintegration and biological decay; sallow ugliness, sensuously marred and worsted, which nevertheless is able to fan its smouldering concupiscence to a pure flame, and even to exalt itself to mastery in the realm of beauty; pallid impotence, which from the glowing depths of the spirit draws strength to cast down a whole proud people at the foot of the Cross and set its own foot upon them as well; gracious poise and composure in the empty austere service of form; the false, dangerous life of the born deceiver, his ambition and his art which lead so soon to exhaustion — to contemplate all these destinies, and many others like them, was to doubt if there is any other heroism at all but the heroism of weakness. In any case, what other heroism could be more in keeping with the times? Gustav Aschenbach was the writer who spoke for all those who work on the brink of exhaustion, who labor and are heavy-laden, who are worn out already but still stand upright, all those moralists of achievement who are slight of stature and scanty of resources, but who yet, by some ecstasy of the will and by wise husbandry, manage at least for a time to force their work into a semblance of greatness. There are many such, they are the heroes of our age. And they all recognized themselves in his work, they found that it confirmed them and raised them on high and celebrated them; they were grateful for this, and they spread his name far and wide.

He had been young and raw with the times: ill advised by fashion, he had publicly stumbled, blundered, made himself look foolish, offended in speech and writing against tact and balanced civility. But he had achieved dignity, that goal toward which, as he declared, every great talent is innately driven and spurred; indeed it can be said that the conscious and defiant purpose of his entire development had been, leaving all the inhibitions of skepticism and irony behind him, an ascent to dignity.

Lively, clear-outlined, intellectually undemanding presentation is the delight of the great mass of the middle-class public, but passionate radical youth is interested only in problems: and Aschenbach had been as problematic and as radical as any young man ever was. He had been in thrall to intellect, had exhausted the soil by excessive analysis and ground up the seed corn of growth; he had uncovered what is better kept hidden, made talent seem suspect, betrayed the truth about art — indeed, even as the sculptural vividness of his descriptions was giving pleasure to his more naive devotees and lifting their minds and hearts, he, this same youthful artist, had fascinated twenty-year-olds with his breathtaking cynicisms about the questionable nature of art and of the artist himself.

But it seems that there is nothing to which a noble and active mind more quickly becomes inured than that pungent and bitter stimulus, the acquisition of knowledge; and it is very sure that even the most gloomily conscientious and radical sophistication of youth is shallow by comparison with Aschenbach's profound decision as a mature master to repudiate knowledge as such, to reject it, to step over it with head held high — in the recognition that knowledge can paralyze the will, paralyze and discourage action and emotion and even passion, and rob all these of their dignity. How else is the famous short story *A Study in Abjection* to be understood but as an outbreak of disgust against an age indecently undermined by psychology and represented by the figure of that spiritless, witless semiscoundrel who cheats his way into a destiny of sorts when, motivated by his own ineptitude and depravity and ethical whimsicality, he drives his wife into the arms of a callow youth — convinced that his intellectual depths entitle him to behave with contemptible baseness? The forthright words of condemnation which here weighed vileness in the balance and found it wanting — they proclaimed their writer's renunciation of all moral skepticism, of every kind of sympathy with the abyss; they declared his repudiation of the laxity of that compassionate principle which holds that to understand all is to forgive all. And the development that was here being anticipated, indeed already taking place, was that "miracle of reborn naiveté" to which, in a dialogue written a little later, the author himself had referred with a certain mysterious emphasis. How strange these associations! Was it an intellectual consequence of this "rebirth," of this new dignity and rigor, that, at about the same time, his sense of beauty was observed to undergo an almost excessive resurgence, that his style took on the noble purity, simplicity and symmetry that were to set upon all his subsequent works that so evident and evidently intentional stamp of the classical master? And yet: moral resoluteness at the far side of knowledge, achieved in despite of all corrosive and inhibiting insight — does this not in its turn signify a simplification, a morally simplistic view of the world and of human psychology, and thus also a resurgence of energies that are evil, forbidden, morally impossible? And is form not two-faced? Is it not at one and the same time moral and immoral — moral as the product and expression of discipline, but immoral and even antimoral inasmuch as it houses within itself an innate moral indifference, and indeed essentially strives for nothing less than to bend morality under its proud and absolute scepter?

Be that as it may! A development is a destiny; and one that is accompanied by the admiration and mass confidence of a wide public must inevitably differ in its course from one that takes place far from the limelight and from the commitments of fame. Only the eternal intellectual vagrant is bored and prompted to mockery when a great talent grows out of its libertinistic chrysalis-stage, becomes an expressive representative of the dignity of mind, takes on the courtly bearing of that solitude which has been full of hard, uncounseled, self-reliant sufferings and struggles, and has achieved power and honor among men. And what a game it is too, how much defiance there is in it and how much satisfaction, this self-formation of a talent! As time passed, Gustav Aschenbach's presentations took on something of an official air, of an educator's stance; his style in later years came to eschew direct audacities, new and subtle nuances, it developed toward the exemplary and definitive, the fastidiously conventional, the conservative and formal and even formulaic; and as tradition has it of Louis XIV, so Aschenbach as he grew older banned from his utterance every unrefined word. It was at this time that the education authority adopted selected pages from his works for inclusion in the prescribed school readers. And when a German ruler who had just come to the throne granted personal nobilitation to the author of *Frederic of Prussia* on his fiftieth birthday, he sensed the inner appropriateness of this honor and did not decline it.

After a few restless years of experimental living in different places, he soon chose Munich as his permanent home and lived there in the kind of upper-bourgeois status which is occasionally the lot of certain intellectuals. The marriage which he had contracted while still young with the daughter of an academic family had been ended by his wife's death after a short period of happiness. She had left him a daughter, now already married. He had never had a son.

Gustav von Aschenbach was of rather less than average height, dark and clean-shaven. His head seemed a little too large in proportion to his almost delicate stature. His brushed-back hair, thinning at the top, very thick and distinctly gray over the temples, framed a high, deeply lined, scarred-looking forehead. The bow of a pair of gold spectacles with rimless lenses cut into the base of his strong, nobly curved nose. His mouth was large, often relaxed, often suddenly narrow and tense; the cheeks were lean and furrowed, the well-formed chin slightly cleft. Grave visitations of fate seemed to have passed over this head, which usually inclined to one side with an air of suffering. And yet it was art that had here performed that fashioning of the physiognomy which is usually the work of a life full of action and stress. The flashing exchanges of the dialogue between Voltaire and the king on the subject of war had been born behind that brow; these eyes that looked so wearily and deeply through their glasses had seen the bloody inferno of the Seven Years War sick bays. Even in a personal sense, after all, art is an intensified life. By art one is more deeply satisfied and more rapidly used up. It engraves on the countenance of its servant the traces of imaginary and intellectual adventures, and even if he has outwardly existed in cloistral tranquillity, it leads in the long term to overfastidiousness, overrefinement, nervous fatigue and overstimulation, such as can seldom result from a life full of the most extravagant passions and pleasures.

3

Mundane and literary business of various kinds delayed Aschenbach's eagerly awaited departure until about a fortnight after that walk in Munich. Finally he gave instructions that his country house was to be made ready for occupation in four weeks' time, and then, one day between the middle and end of May, he took the night train to Trieste, where he stayed only twenty-four hours, embarking on the following morning for Pola.

What he sought was something strange and random, but in a place easily reached, and accordingly he took up his abode on an Adriatic island which had been highly spoken of for some years: a little way off the Istrian coast, with colorful ragged inhabitants speaking a wild unintelligible dialect, and picturesque fragmented cliffs overlooking the open sea. But rain and sultry air, a self-enclosed provincial Austrian hotel clientele, the lack of that restful intimate contact with the sea which can only be had on a gentle, sandy coast, filled him with vexation and with a feeling that he had not yet come to his journey's end. He was haunted by an inner impulse that still had no clear direction; he studied shipping timetables, looked up one place after another — and suddenly his surprising yet at the same time self-evident destination stared him in the face. If one wanted to travel overnight to somewhere incomparable, to a fantastic mutation of normal reality, where did one go? Why, the answer was obvious. What was he doing here?

He had gone completely astray. *That* was where he had wanted to travel. He at once gave notice of departure from his present, mischosen stopping place. Ten days after his arrival on the island, in the early morning mist, a rapid motor-launch carried him and his luggage back over the water to the naval base, and here he landed only to re-embark immediately, crossing the gangway onto the damp deck of a ship that was waiting under steam to leave for Venice.

It was an ancient Italian boat, out of date and dingy and black with soot. Aschenbach was no sooner aboard than a grubby hunchbacked seaman, grinning obsequiously, conducted him to an artificially lit cavelike cabin in the ship's interior. Here, behind a table, with his cap askew and a cigarette end in the corner of his mouth, sat a goat-bearded man with the air of an old-fashioned circus director and a slick caricatured business manner, taking passengers' particulars and issuing their tickets. "To Venice!" he exclaimed, echoing Aschenbach's request, and extending his arm he pushed his pen into some coagulated leftover ink in a tilted inkstand. "One first class to Venice. Certainly, sir!" He scribbled elaborately, shook some blue sand from a box over the writing and ran it off into an earthenware dish, then folded the paper with his yellow bony fingers and wrote on it again. "A very happily chosen destination!" he chattered as he did so. "Ah, Venice! A splendid city! A city irresistibly attractive to the man of culture, by its history no less than by its present charms!" There was something hypnotic and distracting about the smooth facility of his movements and the glib empty talk with which he accompanied them, almost as if he were anxious that the traveler might have second thoughts about his decision to go to Venice. He hastily took Aschenbach's money and with the dexterity of a croupier dropped the change on the stained tablecloth. *"Buon divertimento, signore,"* he said, bowing histrionically. "It is an honor to serve you . . . Next, please, gentlemen!" he exclaimed with a wave of the arm, as if he were doing a lively trade, although in fact there was no one else there to be dealt with. Aschenbach returned on deck.

Resting one elbow on the handrail, he watched the idle crowd hanging about the quayside to see the ship's departure, and watched the passengers who had come aboard. Those with second-class tickets were squatting, men and women together, on the forward deck, using boxes and bundles as seats. The company on the upper deck consisted of a group of young men, probably shop or office workers from Pola, a high-spirited party about to set off on an excursion to Italy. They were making a considerable exhibition of themselves and their enterprise,

chattering, laughing, fatuously enjoying their own gesticulations, leaning overboard and shouting glibly derisive ribaldries at their friends on
the harbor-side street, who were hurrying about their business with
briefcases under their arms and waved their sticks peevishly at the holi-
day-makers. One of the party, who wore a light yellow summer suit of
extravagant cut, a scarlet necktie and a rakishly tilted Panama hat, was
the most conspicuous of them all in his shrill hilarity. But as soon as
Aschenbach took a slightly closer look at him, he realized with a kind
of horror that the man's youth was false. He was old, there was no
mistaking it. There were wrinkles round his eyes and mouth. His
cheeks' faint carmine was rouge, the brown hair under his straw hat
with its colored ribbon was a wig, his neck was flaccid and scrawny, his
small stuck-on moustache and the little imperial on his chin were
dyed; his yellowish full complement of teeth, displayed when he
laughed, were a cheap artificial set, and his hands, with signet rings on
both index fingers, were those of an old man. With a spasm of distaste
Aschenbach watched him as he kept company with his young friends.
Did they not know, did they not notice that he was old, that he had
no right to be wearing foppish and garish clothes like theirs, no right
to be acting as if he were one of them? They seemed to be tolerating
his presence among them as something habitual and to be taken for
granted, they treated him as an equal, reciprocated without embarrassment when he teasingly poked them in the ribs. How was this possible? Aschenbach put his hand over his forehead and closed his eyes,
which were hot from too little sleep. He had a feeling that something
not quite usual was beginning to happen, that the world was undergo-
ing a dreamlike alienation, becoming increasingly deranged and
bizarre, and that perhaps this process might be arrested if he were to
cover his face for a little and then take a fresh look at things. But at
that moment he had the sensation of being afloat, and starting up in
irrational alarm, he noticed that the dark heavy hulk of the steamer
was slowly parting company with the stone quayside. Inch by inch, as
the engine pounded and reversed, the width of the dirty glinting water
between the hull and the quay increased, and after clumsy maneuver-
ings the ship turned its bows toward the open sea. Aschenbach crossed
to the starboard side, where the hunchback had set up a deck chair for
him and a steward in a grease-stained frock coat offered his services.

The sky was gray, the wind damp. The port and the islands had
been left behind, and soon all land was lost to view in the misty
panorama. Flecks of sodden soot drifted down on the washed deck,

which never seemed to get dry. After only an hour an awning was set
up, as it was beginning to rain.

Wrapped in his overcoat, a book lying on his lap, the traveler
rested, scarcely noticing the hours as they passed him by. It had
stopped raining; the canvas shelter was removed. The horizon was
complete. Under the turbid dome of the sky the desolate sea surrounded him in an enormous circle. But in empty, unarticulated space
our mind loses its sense of time as well, and we enter the twilight of
the immeasurable. As Aschenbach lay there, strange and shadowy figures, the foppish old man, the goat-bearded purser from the ship's interior, passed with uncertain gestures and confused dream-words
through his mind, and he fell asleep.

At midday he was requested to come below for luncheon in the
long, narrow dining saloon, which ended in the doors to the sleeping
berths; here he ate at the head of the long table, at the other end of
which the group of apprentices, with the old man among them, had
been quaffing since ten o'clock with the good-humored ship's captain.
The meal was wretched and he finished it quickly. He needed to be
back in the open air, to look at the sky: perhaps it would clear over
Venice.

It had never occurred to him that this would not happen, for the
city had always received him in its full glory. But the sky and the sea
remained dull and leaden, from time to time misty rain fell, and he resigned himself to arriving by water in a different Venice, one he had
never encountered on the landward approach. He stood by the fore-
mast, gazing into the distance, waiting for the sight of land. He recalled that poet of plangent inspiration who long ago had seen the
cupolas and bell-towers of his dream rise before him out of these same
waters; inwardly he recited a few lines of the measured music that had
been made from that reverence and joy and sadness, and effortlessly
moved by a passion already shaped into language, he questioned his
grave and weary heart, wondering whether some new inspiration and
distraction, some late adventure of the emotions, might yet be in store
for him on his leisured journey.

And now, on his right, the flat coastline rose above the horizon,
the sea came alive with fishing vessels, the island resort appeared: the
steamer left it on its port side, glided at half speed through the narrow
channel named after it, entered the lagoon, and presently, near some
shabby miscellaneous buildings, came to a complete halt, as this was
where the launch carrying the public health inspector must be awaited.

An hour passed before it appeared. One had arrived and yet not arrived; there was no hurry, and yet one was impelled by impatience.
The young men from Pola had come on deck, no doubt also patriotically attracted by the military sound of bugle calls across the water
from the direction of the Public Gardens; and elated by the Asti they
had drunk, they began cheering the *bersaglieri* as they drilled there in
the park. But the dandified old man, thanks to his spurious fraterniza-
tion with the young, was now in a condition repugnant to behold. His
old head could not carry the wine as his sturdy youthful companions
had done, and he was lamentably drunk. Eyes glazed, a cigarette between his trembling fingers, he stood swaying, tilted to and fro by inebriation and barely keeping his balance. Since he would have fallen at
his first step he did not dare move from the spot, and was nevertheless
full of wretched exuberance, clutching at everyone who approached
him, babbling, winking, sniggering, lifting his ringed and wrinkled
forefinger as he uttered some bantering inanity, and licking the corners
of his mouth with the tip of his tongue in a repellently suggestive way.
Aschenbach watched him with frowning disapproval, and once more a
sense of numbness came over him, a feeling that the world was somehow, slightly yet uncontrollably, sliding into some kind of bizarre and
grotesque derangement. It was a feeling on which, to be sure, he was
unable to brood further in present circumstances, for at this moment
the thudding motion of the engine began again, and the ship, having
stopped short so close to its destination, resumed its passage along the
San Marco Canal.

Thus it was that he saw it once more, that most astonishing of all
landing places, that dazzling composition of fantastic architecture
which the Republic presented to the admiring gaze of approaching
seafarers: the unburdened splendor of the Ducal Palace, the Bridge of
Sighs, the lion and the saint on their two columns at the water's edge,
the magnificently projecting side wing of the fabulous basilica, the
vista beyond it of the gate tower and the Giants' Clock; and as he contemplated it all he reflected that to arrive in Venice by land, at the station, was like entering a palace by a back door: that only as he was now
doing, only by ship, over the high sea, should one come to this most
extraordinary of cities.

The engine stopped, gondolas pressed alongside, the gangway was
let down, customs officers came on board and perfunctorily discharged
their duties; disembarkation could begin. Aschenbach indicated that
he would like a gondola to take him and his luggage to the stopping
place of the small steamboats that ply between the city and the Lido,

since he intended to stay in a hotel by the sea. His wishes were approved, his orders shouted down to water level, where the gondoliers were quarreling in Venetian dialect. He was still prevented from leaving the ship, held up by his trunk which at that moment was being laboriously dragged and maneuvered down the ladderlike gangway; and thus, for a full minute or two, he could not avoid the importunate attentions of the dreadful old man, who on some obscure drunken impulse felt obliged to do this stranger the parting honors. "We wish the signore a most enjoyable stay!" he bleated, bowing and scraping. "We hope the signore will not forget us! *Au revoir, excusez* and *bon jour*, your Excellency!" He drooled, he screwed up his eyes, licked the corners of his mouth, and the dyed imperial on his senile underlip reared itself upward. "Our compliments," he driveled, touching his lips with two fingers, "our compliments to your sweetheart, to your most charming, beautiful sweetheart . . . " And suddenly the upper set of his false teeth dropped half out of his jaw. Aschenbach was able to escape. "Your sweetheart, your pretty sweetheart!" he heard from behind his back, in gurgling, cavernous, encumbered tones, as he clung to the rope railing and descended the gangway.

Can there be anyone who has not had to overcome a fleeting sense of dread, a secret shudder of uneasiness, on stepping for the first time or after a long interval of years into a Venetian gondola? How strange a vehicle it is, coming down unchanged from times of old romance, and so characteristically black, the way no other thing is black except a coffin — a vehicle evoking lawless adventures in the plashing stillness of night, and still more strongly evoking death itself, the bier, the dark obsequies, the last silent journey! And has it been observed that the seat of such a boat, that armchair with its coffin-black lacquer and dull black upholstery, is the softest, the most voluptuous, most enervating seat in the world? Aschenbach became aware of this when he had settled down at the gondolier's feet, sitting opposite his luggage, which was neatly assembled at the prow. The oarsmen were still quarreling; raucously, unintelligibly, with threatening gestures. But in the peculiar silence of this city of water their voices seemed to be softly absorbed, to become bodiless, dissipated above the sea. It was sultry here in the harbor. As the warm breath of the sirocco touched him, as he leaned back on cushions over the yielding element, the traveler closed his eyes in the enjoyment of this lassitude as sweet as it was unaccustomed. It will be a short ride, he thought; if only it could last forever! In a gently swaying motion he felt himself gliding away from the crowd and the confusion of voices.

How still it was growing all round him! There was nothing to be heard except the plashing of the oar, the dull slap of the wave against the boat's prow where it rose up steep and black and armed at its tip like a halberd, and a third sound also: that of a voice speaking and murmuring — it was the gondolier, whispering and muttering to himself between his teeth, in intermittent grunts pressed out of him by the labor of his arms. Aschenbach looked up and noticed with some consternation that the lagoon was widening round him and that his gondola was heading out to sea. It was thus evident that he must not relax too completely, but give some attention to the proper execution of his instructions.

"Well! To the *vaporetto* stop!" he said, half turning round. The muttering ceased, but no answer came.

"I said to the *vaporetto* stop!" he repeated, turning round completely and looking up into the face of the gondolier, who was standing behind him on his raised deck, towering between him and the pale sky. He was a man of displeasing, indeed brutal appearance, wearing blue seaman's clothes, with a yellow scarf round his waist and a shapeless, already fraying straw hat tilted rakishly on his head. To judge by the cast of his face and the blond curling moustache under his snub nose, he was quite evidently not of Italian origin. Although rather slightly built, so that one would not have thought him particularly well suited to his job, he plied his oar with great energy, putting his whole body into every stroke. Occasionally the effort made him retract his lips and bare his white teeth. With his reddish eyebrows knitted, he stared right over his passenger's head as he answered peremptorily, almost insolently:

"You are going to the Lido."

Aschenbach replied:

"Of course. But I only engaged this gondola to row me across to San Marco. I wish to take the *vaporetto*."

"You cannot take the *vaporetto*, signore."

"And why not?"

"Because the *vaporetto* does not carry luggage."

That was correct, as Aschenbach now remembered. He was silent. But the man's abrupt, presumptuous manner, so uncharacteristic of the way foreigners were usually treated in this country, struck him as unacceptable. He said:

"That is my business. I may wish to deposit my luggage. Will you kindly turn round."

There was silence. The oar plashed, the dull slap of the water against the bow continued, and the talking and muttering began again: the gondolier was talking to himself between his teeth. What was to be done? Alone on the sea with this strangely contumacious, uncannily resolute fellow, the traveler could see no way of compelling him to obey his instructions. And in any case, how luxurious a rest he might have here if he simply accepted the situation! Had he not wished the trip were longer, wished it to last forever? It was wisest to let things take their course, and above all it was very agreeable to do so. A magic spell of indolence seemed to emanate from his seat, from this low black-upholstered armchair, so softly rocked by the oarstrokes of the high-handed gondolier behind him. The thought that he had perhaps fallen into the hands of a criminal floated dreamily across Aschenbach's mind — powerless to stir him to any active plan of self-defence. There was the more annoying possibility that the whole thing was simply a device for extorting money from him. A kind of pride or sense of duty, a recollection, so to speak, that there are precautions to be taken against such things, impelled him to make one further effort. He asked:

"What is your charge for the trip?"

And looking straight over his head, the gondolier answered:

"You will pay, signore."

The prescribed retort to this was clear enough. Aschenbach answered mechanically:

"I shall pay nothing, absolutely nothing, if you take me where I do not want to go."

"The signore wants to go to the Lido."

"But not with you."

"I can row you well."

True enough, thought Aschenbach, relaxing. True enough, you will row me well. Even if you are after my cash and dispatch me to the house of Hades with a blow of your oar from behind, you will have rowed me well.

But nothing of the sort happened. He was even provided with company: a boat full of piratical musicians, men and women singing to the guitar or mandolin, importunately traveling hard alongside the gondola and for the foreigner's benefit filling the silence of the waters with mercenary song. Aschenbach threw some money into the outheld hat, whereupon they fell silent and moved off. And the gondolier's muttering became audible again, as in fits and starts he continued his self-colloquy.

And so in due course one arrived, bobbing about in the wake of a *vaporetto* bound for the city. Two police officers, with their hands on their backs, were pacing up and down the embankment and looking out over the lagoon. Aschenbach stepped from the gondola onto the gangway, assisted by the old man with a boat hook who turns up for this purpose at every landing stage in Venice; and having run out of small change, he walked across to the hotel opposite the pier, intending to change money and pay off the oarsman with some suitable gratuity. He was served at the hall desk, and returned to the landing stage to find his luggage loaded onto a trolley on the embankment: the gondola and the gondolier had vanished.

"He cleared off," said the old man with the boat hook. "A bad man, a man without a licence, signore. He is the only gondolier who has no licence. The others telephoned across to us. He saw the police waiting for him. So he cleared off."

Aschenbach shrugged his shoulders.

"The signore has had a free trip," said the old man, holding out his hat. Aschenbach threw coins into it. He directed that his luggage should be taken to the Hotel des Bains, and followed the trolley along the avenue, that white-blossoming avenue, bordered on either side by taverns and bazaars and guesthouses, which runs straight across the island to the beach.

He entered the spacious hotel from the garden terrace at the back, passing through the main hall and the vestibule to the reception office. As his arrival had been notified in advance, he was received with obsequious obligingness. A manager, a soft-spoken, flatteringly courteous little man with a black moustache and a frock coat of French cut, accompanied him in the lift to the second floor and showed him to his room, an agreeable apartment with cherry-wood furniture, strongly scented flowers put out to greet him, and a view through tall windows to the open sea. He went and stood by one of them when the manager had withdrawn, and as his luggage was brought in behind him and installed in the room, he gazed out over the beach, uncrowded at this time of the afternoon, and over the sunless sea which was at high tide, its long low waves beating with a quiet regular rhythm on the shore.

The observations and encounters of a devotee of solitude and silence are at once less distinct and more penetrating than those of the sociable man; his thoughts are weightier, stranger, and never without a tinge of sadness. Images and perceptions which might otherwise be easily dispelled by a glance, a laugh, an exchange of comments, concern him unduly, they sink into mute depths, take on significance, become experiences, adventures, emotions. The fruit of solitude is originality, something daringly and disconcertingly beautiful, the poetic creation. But the fruit of solitude can also be the perverse, the disproportionate, the absurd and the forbidden. And thus the phenomena of his journey to this place, the horrible old made-up man with his maudlin babble about a sweetheart, the illicit gondolier who had been done out of his money, were still weighing on the traveler's mind. Without in any way being rationally inexplicable, without even really offering food for thought, they were nevertheless, as it seemed to him, essentially strange, and indeed it was no doubt this very paradox that made them disturbing. In the meantime he saluted the sea with his gaze and rejoiced in the knowledge that Venice was now so near and accessible. Finally he turned round, bathed his face, gave the room maid certain instructions for the enhancement of his comfort, and then had himself conveyed by the green-uniformed Swiss lift attendant to the ground floor.

He took tea on the front terrace, then went down to the esplanade and walked some way along it in the direction of the Hotel Excelsior. When he returned, it was already nearly time to be changing for dinner. He did so in his usual leisurely and precise manner, for it was his custom to work when performing his toilet; despite this, he arrived a little early in the hall, where he found a considerable number of the hotel guests assembled, unacquainted with each other and affecting a studied mutual indifference, yet all united in expectancy by the prospect of their evening meal. He picked up a newspaper from the table, settled down in a leather armchair and took stock of the company, which differed very agreeably from what he had encountered at his previous hotel.

A large horizon opened up before him, tolerantly embracing many elements. Discreetly muted, the sounds of the major world languages mingled. Evening dress, that internationally accepted uniform of civilization, imparted a decent outward semblance of unity to the wide variations of mankind here represented. One saw the dry elongated visages of Americans, many-membered Russian families, English ladies, German children with French nurses. The Slav component seemed to predominate. In his immediate vicinity he could hear Polish being spoken.

It was a group of adolescent and barely adult young people, sitting round a cane table under the supervision of a governess or companion: three young girls, of fifteen to seventeen as it seemed, and a long-haired boy of about fourteen. With astonishment Aschenbach noticed that the boy was entirely beautiful. His countenance, pale and gracefully reserved, was surrounded by ringlets of honey-colored hair, and with its straight nose, its enchanting mouth, its expression of sweet and divine gravity, it recalled Greek sculpture of the noblest period; yet despite the purest formal perfection, it had such unique personal charm that he who now contemplated it felt he had never beheld, in nature or in art, anything so consummately successful. What also struck him was an obvious contrast of educational principles in the way the boy and his sisters were dressed and generally treated. The system adopted for the three girls, the eldest of whom could be considered to be grown-up, was austere and chaste to the point of disfigurement. They all wore exactly the same slate-colored half-length dresses, sober and of a deliberately unbecoming cut, with white turnover collars as the only relieving feature, and any charm of figure they might have had was suppressed and negated from the outset by this cloistral uniform. Their hair, smoothed and stuck back firmly to their heads, gave their faces a nunlike emptiness and expressionlessness. A mother was clearly in charge here; and it had not even occurred to her to apply to the boy the same pedagogic strictness as she thought proper for the girls. In his life, softness and tenderness were evidently the rule. No one had ever dared to cut short his beautiful hair; like that of the *Boy Extracting a Thorn* it fell in curls over his forehead, over his ears, and still lower over his neck. The English sailor's suit, with its full sleeves tapering down to fit the fine wrists of his still childlike yet slender hands, and with its lanyards and bows and embroideries, enhanced his delicate shape with an air of richness and indulgence. He was sitting, in semiprofile to Aschenbach's gaze, with one foot in its patent leather shoe advanced in front of the other, with one elbow propped on the arm of his basket chair, with his cheek nestling against the closed hand, in a posture of relaxed dignity, without a trace of the almost servile stiffness to which his sisters seemed to have accustomed themselves. Was he in poor health? For his complexion was white as ivory against the dark gold of the surrounding curls. Or was he simply a pampered favorite child, borne up by the partiality of a capricious love? Aschenbach was inclined to think so. Inborn in almost every artistic nature is a luxuriant, treacherous bias in favor of the injustice that creates beauty, a tendency to sympathize with aristocratic preference and pay it homage.

A waiter circulated and announced in English that dinner was served. Gradually the company disappeared through the glass door into the dining room. Latecomers passed, coming from the vestibule or the lifts. The service of dinner had already begun, but the young

Poles were still waiting round their cane table, and Aschenbach, comfortably ensconced in his deep armchair, and additionally having the spectacle of beauty before his eyes, waited with them.

The governess, a corpulent and rather unladylike, red-faced little woman, finally gave the signal for them to rise. With arched brows she pushed back her chair and bowed as a tall lady, dressed in silvery gray and very richly adorned with pearls, entered the hall. This lady's attitude was cool and poised, her lightly powdered coiffure and the style of her dress both had that simplicity which is the governing principle of taste in circles where piety is regarded as one of the aristocratic values. In Germany she might have been the wife of a high official. The only thing that did give her appearance a fantastic and luxurious touch was her jewelry, which was indeed beyond price, consisting of earrings as well as a very long three-stranded necklace of gently shimmering pearls as big as cherries.

The brother and sisters had quickly risen to their feet. They bowed over their mother's hand to kiss it, while she, with a restrained smile on her well-maintained but slightly weary and angular face, looked over their heads and addressed a few words in French to the governess. Then she walked toward the glass door. Her children followed her: the girls in order of age, after them the governess, finally the boy. For some reason or other he turned round before crossing the threshold, and as there was now no one else in the hall, his strangely twilight-gray eyes met those of Aschenbach, who with his paper in his lap, lost in contemplation, had been watching the group leave.

What he had seen had certainly not been remarkable in any particular. One does not go in to table before one's mother, they had waited for her, greeted her respectfully, and observed normal polite precedence in entering the dining room. But this had all been carried out with such explicitness, with such a strongly accented air of discipline, obligation and self-respect, that Aschenbach felt strangely moved. He lingered for another few moments, then he too crossed into the dining room and had himself shown to his table — which, as he noticed with a brief stirring of regret, was at some distance from that of the Polish family.

Tired and yet intellectually stimulated, he beguiled the long and tedious meal with abstract and indeed transcendental reflections. He meditated on the mysterious combination into which the canonical and the individual must enter for human beauty to come into being, proceeded from this point to general problems of form and art, and concluded in the end that his thoughts and findings resembled certain seemingly happy inspirations that come to us in dreams, only to be recognized by the sober senses as completely shallow and worthless. After dinner he lingered for a while, smoking and sitting and walking about, in the evening fragrance of the hotel garden, then retired early and passed the night in sleep which was sound and long, though dream images enlivened it from time to time.

Next day the weather did not seem to be improving. The wind was from landward. Under a pallid overcast sky the sea lay sluggishly still and shrunken-looking, with the horizon in prosaic proximity and the tide so far out that several rows of long sandbars lay exposed. When Aschenbach opened his window, he thought he could smell the stagnant air of the lagoon.

Vexation overcame him. The thought of leaving occurred to him then and there. Once before, years ago, after fine spring weeks, this same weather had come on him here like a visitation, and so adversely affected his health that his departure from Venice had been like a precipitate escape. Were not the same symptoms now presenting themselves again, that unpleasant feverish sensation, the pressure in the temples, the heaviness in the eyelids? To move elsewhere yet again would be tiresome; but if the wind did not change, then there was no question of his staying here. As a precaution he did not unpack completely. At nine he breakfasted in the buffet between the hall and the main restaurant which was used for serving breakfast.

The kind of ceremonious silence prevailed here which a large hotel always aims to achieve. The serving waiters moved about noiselessly. A clink of crockery, a half-whispered word, were the only sounds audible. In one corner, obliquely opposite the door and two tables away from his own, Aschenbach noticed the Polish girls with their governess. Perched very upright, their ash-blond hair newly brushed and with reddened eyes, in stiff blue linen dresses with little white turnover collars and cuffs, they sat there passing each other a jar of preserves. They had almost finished their breakfast. The boy was missing.

Aschenbach smiled. Well, my little Phaeacian! he thought. You seem, unlike these young ladies, to enjoy the privilege of sleeping your fill. And with his spirits suddenly rising, he recited to himself the line: "Varied garments to wear, warm baths and restful reposing."

He breakfasted unhurriedly, received some forwarded mail from the porter who came into the breakfast room with his braided cap in hand, and opened a few letters as he smoked a cigarette. Thus it happened that he was still present to witness the entry of the lie-abed they were waiting for across the room.

He came through the glass door and walked in the silence obliquely across the room to his sisters' table. His walk was extraordinarily graceful, in the carriage of his upper body, the motion of his knees, the placing of his white-shod foot; it was very light, both delicate and proud, and made still more beautiful by the childlike modesty with which he twice, turning his head toward the room, raised and lowered his eyes as he passed. With a smile and a murmured word in his soft liquescent language, he took his seat; and now especially, as his profile was exactly turned to the watching Aschenbach, the latter was again amazed, indeed startled, by the truly godlike beauty of this human creature. Today the boy was wearing a light casual suit of blue and white-striped linen material with a red silk breast-knot, closing at the neck in a simple white stand-up collar. But on this collar — which did not even match the rest of the suit very elegantly — there, like a flower in bloom, his head was gracefully resting. It was the head of Eros, with the creamy luster of Parian marble, the brows fine-drawn and serious, the temples and ear darkly and softly covered by the neat right-angled growth of the curling hair.

Good, good! thought Aschenbach, with that cool professional approval in which artists confronted by a masterpiece sometimes cloak their ecstasy, their rapture. And mentally he added: Truly, if the sea and the shore did not await me, I should stay here as long as you do! But as it was, he went, went through the hall accompanied by the courteous attentions of the hotel staff, went down over the great terrace and straight along the wooden passageway to the enclosed beach reserved for hotel guests. Down there, a barefooted old man with linen trousers, sailor's jacket and straw hat functioned as bathing attendant: Aschenbach had himself conducted by him to his reserved beach cabin, had his table and chair set up on the sandy wooden platform in front of it, and made himself comfortable in the deck chair which he had drawn further out toward the sea onto the wax-yellow sand.

The scene on the beach, the spectacle of civilization taking its carefree sensuous ease at the brink of the element, entertained and delighted him as much as ever. Already the gray shallow sea was alive with children wading, with swimmers, with assorted figures lying on the sandbars, their crossed arms under their heads. Others were rowing little keelless boats painted red and blue, and capsizing with shrieks of laughter. In front of the long row of *capanne,* with their platforms like little verandahs to sit on, there was animated play and leisurely sprawling repose, there was visiting and chattering, there was punctil-

ious morning elegance as well as unabashed nakedness contentedly enjoying the liberal local conventions. Further out, on the moist firm
sand, persons in white bathing robes, in loose-fitting colorful shirtwear
wandered to and fro. On the right, a complicated sand castle built by
children was bedecked by flags in all the national colors. Vendors of
mussels, cakes and fruit knelt to display their wares. On the left, in
front of one of the huts in the row that was set at right angles to the
others and to the sea, forming a boundary to the beach at this end, a
Russian family was encamped: men with beards and big teeth, overripe
indolent women, a Baltic spinster sitting at an easel and with exclama-
tions of despair painting the sea, two good-natured hideous children,
an old nanny in a headcloth who behaved in the caressingly deferential
manner of the born serf. There they all were, gratefully enjoying their
lives, tirelessly shouting the names of their disobediently romping children, mustering a few Italian words to joke at length with the amusing
old man who sold them sweets, kissing each other on the cheeks and
caring not a jot whether anyone was watching their scene of human
solidarity.

Well, I shall stay, thought Aschenbach. What better place could I
find? And with his hands folded in his lap, he let his eyes wander in the
wide expanse of the sea, let his gaze glide away, dissolve and die in the
monotonous haze of this desolate emptiness. There were profound
reasons for his attachment to the sea: he loved it because as a hard-
working artist he needed rest, needed to escape from the demanding
complexity of phenomena and lie hidden on the bosom of the simple
and tremendous; because of a forbidden longing deep within him that
ran quite contrary to his life's task and was for that very reason seductive, a longing for the unarticulated and immeasurable, for eternity, for
nothingness. To rest in the arms of perfection is the desire of any man
intent upon creating excellence; and is not nothingness a form of perfection? But now, as he mused idly on such profound matters, the horizontal line of the sea's shore was suddenly intersected by a human figure, and when he had retrieved his gaze from limitless immensity and
concentrated it again, he beheld the beautiful boy, coming from the
left and walking past him across the sand. He walked barefoot, ready
for wading, his slender legs naked to above the knees; his pace was
leisured, but as light and proud as if he had long been used to going
about without shoes. As he walked he looked round at the projecting
row of huts: but scarcely had he noticed the Russian family, as it sat
there in contented concord and going about its natural business, than
a storm of angry contempt gathered over his face. He frowned darkly,

his lips pouted, a bitter grimace pulled them to one side and distorted his cheek; his brows were contracted in so deep a scowl that his eyes seemed to have sunk right in under their pressure, glaring forth a black message of hatred. He looked down, looked back again menacingly, then made with one shoulder an emphatic gesture of rejection as he turned his back and left his enemies behind him.

A kind of delicacy or alarm, something like respect and embarrassment, moved Aschenbach to turn away as if he had seen nothing; for no serious person who witnesses a moment of passion by chance will wish to make any use, even privately, of what he has observed. But he was at one and the same time entertained and moved, that is to say he was filled with happiness. Such childish fanaticism, directed against so harmless a piece of good-natured living — it gave a human dimension to mute divinity, it made a statuesque masterpiece of nature, which had hitherto merely delighted the eyes, seem worthy of a profounder appreciation as well; and it placed the figure of this adolescent, remarkable already by his beauty, in a context which enabled one to take him seriously beyond his years.

With his head still averted, Aschenbach listened to the boy's voice, his high, not very strong voice, as he called out greetings to his playmates working at the sand castle, announcing his arrival when he was still some way from them. They answered, repeatedly shouting his name or a diminutive of his name, and Aschenbach listened for this with a certain curiosity, unable to pick up anything more precise than two melodious syllables that sounded something like "Adgio" or still oftener "Adgiu," called out with a long *u* at the end. The sound pleased him, he found its euphony befitting to its object, repeated it quietly to himself and turned again with satisfaction to his letters and papers.

With his traveling writing-case on his knees, he took out his fountain pen and began to deal with this and that item of correspondence. But after no more than a quarter of an hour he felt that it was a great pity to turn his mind away like this from the present situation, this most enjoyable of all situations known to him, and to miss the experience of it for the sake of an insignificant activity. He threw his writing materials aside, he returned to the sea; and before long, his attention attracted by the youthful voices of the sand castle builders, he turned his head comfortably to the right against the back of his chair, to investigate once more the whereabouts and doings of the excellent Adgio.

His first glance found him; the red breast-knot was unmistakable.

He and some others were busy laying an old plank as a bridge across the damp moat of the sand castle, and he was supervising this work, calling out instructions and motioning with his head. With him were about ten companions, both boys and girls, of his age and some of them younger, all chattering together in tongues, in Polish, in French and even in Balkan idioms. But it was his name that was most often heard. It was obvious that he was sought after, wooed, admired. One boy in particular, a Pole like him, a sturdy young fellow whom they called something like "Jashu," with glossy black hair and wearing a linen belted suit, seemed to be his particular vassal and friend. When the work on the sand castle ended for the time being, they walked along the beach with their arms round each other, and the boy they called "Jashu" kissed his beautiful companion.

Aschenbach was tempted to shake his finger at him. "But I counsel you, Critobulus," he thought with a smile, "to go traveling for a year! You will need that much time at least before you are cured." And he then breakfasted on some large, fully ripe strawberries which he bought from a vendor. It had grown very warm, although the sun was unable to break through the sky's layer of cloud. Even as one's senses enjoyed the tremendous and dizzying spectacle of the sea's stillness, lassitude paralyzed the mind. To the mature and serious Aschenbach it seemed an appropriate, fully satisfying task and occupation for him to guess or otherwise ascertain what name this could be that sounded approximately like "Adgio." And with the help of a few Polish recollections he established that what was meant must be "Tadzio," the abbreviation of "Tadeusz" and changing in the vocative to "Tadziu."

Tadzio was bathing. Aschenbach, who had lost sight of him, identified his head and his flailing arm far out to sea; for the water was evidently still shallow a long way out. But already he seemed to be giving cause for alarm, already women's voices were calling out to him from the bathing huts, again shrieking this name which ruled the beach almost like a rallying-cry, and which with its soft consonants, its long-drawn-out *u*-sound at the end, had both a sweetness and a wildness about it: "Tadziu! Tadziu!" He returned, he came running, beating the resisting water to foam with his feet, his head thrown back, running through the waves. And to behold this living figure, lovely and austere in its early masculinity, with dripping locks and beautiful as a young god, approaching out of the depths of the sky and the sea, rising and escaping from the elements — this sight filled the mind with mythical images, it was like a poet's tale from a primitive age, a tale of the origins of form and of the birth of the gods. Aschenbach listened with closed eyes to this song as it began its music deep within him, and once again he reflected that it was good to be here and that here he would stay.

Later on, Tadzio lay in the sand resting from his bathe, wrapped in his white bathing robe which he had drawn through under his right shoulder, and cradling his head on his naked arm; and even when Aschenbach was not watching him but reading a few pages in his book, he almost never forgot that the boy was lying there, and that he need only turn his head slightly to the right to have the admired vision again in view. It almost seemed to him that he was sitting here for the purpose of protecting the half-sleeping boy — busy with doings of his own and yet nevertheless constantly keeping watch over this noble human creature there on his right, only a little way from him. And his heart was filled and moved by a paternal fondness, the tender concern by which he who sacrifices himself to beget beauty in the spirit is drawn to him who possesses beauty.

After midday he left the beach, returned to the hotel and took the lift up to his room. Here he spent some time in front of the looking glass studying his gray hair, his weary sharp-featured face. At that moment he thought of his fame, reflected that many people recognized him on the streets and would gaze at him respectfully, saluting the unerring and graceful power of his language — he recalled all the external successes he could think of that his talent had brought him, even calling to mind his elevation to the nobility. Then he went down to the restaurant and took lunch at his table. When he had finished and was entering the lift again, a group of young people who had also just been lunching crowded after him into the hovering cubicle, and Tadzio came with them. He stood quite near Aschenbach, so near that for the first time the latter was not seeing him as a distant image, but perceiving and taking precise cognizance of the details of his humanity. The boy was addressed by someone, and as he replied, with an indescribably charming smile, he was already leaving the lift again as it reached the first floor, stepping out backward with downcast eyes. The beautiful are modest, thought Aschenbach, and began to reflect very intensively on why this should be so. Nevertheless, he had noticed that Tadzio's teeth were not as attractive as they might have been: rather jagged and pale, lacking the luster of health and having that peculiar brittle transparency that is sometimes found in cases of anemia. "He's very delicate, he's sickly," thought Aschenbach, "he'll probably not live to grow old." And he made no attempt to explain to himself a certain feeling of satisfaction or relief that accompanied this thought.

He spent two hours in his room, and in mid-afternoon took the *vaporetto* across the stale-smelling lagoon to Venice. He got out at San Marco, took tea on the Piazza, and then, in accordance with the daily program he had adopted for his stay here, set off on a walk through the streets. But it was this walk that brought about a complete change in his mood and intentions.

An unpleasant sultriness pervaded the narrow streets; the air was so thick that the exhalations from houses and shops and hot food stalls, the reek of oil, the smell of perfume and many other odors hung about in clouds instead of dispersing. Cigarette smoke lingered and was slow to dissipate. The throng of people in the alleyways annoyed him as he walked instead of giving him pleasure. The further he went, the more overwhelmingly he was afflicted by that appalling condition sometimes caused by a combination of the sea air with the sirocco, a condition of simultaneous excitement and exhaustion. He began to sweat disagreeably. His eyes faltered, his chest felt constricted, he was feverish, the blood throbbed in his head. He fled from the crowded commercial thoroughfares, over bridges, into the poor quarters. There he was besieged by beggars, and the sickening stench from the canals made it difficult to breathe. In a silent square, one of those places in the depths of Venice that seem to have been forgotten and put under a spell, he rested on the edge of a fountain, wiped the sweat from his forehead and realized that he would have to leave.

For the second time, and this time definitively, it had become evident that this city, in this state of the weather, was extremely injurious to him. To stay on willfully would be contrary to good sense, the prospect of a change in the wind seemed quite uncertain. He must make up his mind at once. To return straight home was out of the question. Neither his summer nor his winter quarters were ready to receive him. But this was not the only place with the sea and a beach, and elsewhere they were to be had without the harmful additional ingredient of this lagoon with its mephitic vapors. He remembered a little coastal resort not far from Trieste which had been recommended to him. Why not go there? And he must do so without delay, if it was to be worthwhile changing to a different place yet again. He declared himself resolved and rose to his feet. At the next gondola stop he took a boat and had himself conveyed back to San Marco through the murky labyrinth of canals, under delicate marble balconies flanked with carved lions, round the slimy stone corners of buildings, past the mournful facades of *palazzi* on which boards bearing the names of commercial enterprises were mirrored in water where refuse bobbed up and down. He had some trouble getting to his destination, as the gondolier was in league with lace factories and glassworks and tried to land him at every place where he might view the wares and make a purchase; and whenever this bizarre journey through Venice might have cast its spell on him, he was effectively and irksomely disenchanted by the cutpurse mercantile spirit of the sunken queen of the Adriatic.

Back in the hotel, before he had even dined, he notified the office that unforeseen circumstances obliged him to leave on the following morning. Regret was expressed, his bill was settled. He took dinner and spent the warm evening reading newspapers in a rocking chair on the back terrace. Before going to bed he packed completely for departure.

He slept fitfully, troubled by his impending further journey. When he opened his windows in the morning, the sky was still overcast, but the air seemed fresher, and — he began even now to regret his decision. Had he not given notice too impulsively, had it not been a mistake, an action prompted by a mere temporary indisposition? If only he had deferred it for a little, if only, without giving up so soon, he had taken a chance on acclimatizing himself to Venice or waiting for the wind to change, then he would now have before him not the hurry and flurry of a journey, but a morning on the beach like that of the previous day. Too late. What he had wanted yesterday he must go on wanting now. He got dressed and took the lift down to breakfast at eight o'clock.

When he entered the breakfast room it was still empty of guests. A few came in as he was sitting waiting for what he had ordered. As he sipped his tea he saw the Polish girls arrive with their companion: strict and matutinal, with reddened eyes, they proceeded to their table in the window corner. Shortly after this the porter approached with cap in hand and reminded him that it was time to leave. The motor coach was standing ready to take him and other passengers to the Hotel Excelsior, from which point the motor launch would convey the ladies and gentlemen through the company's private canal and across to the station. Time is pressing, signore. — In Aschenbach's opinion time was doing nothing of the sort. There was more than an hour till his train left. He found it extremely annoying that hotels should make a practice of getting their departing clients off the premises unnecessarily early, and indicated to the porter that he wished to have his breakfast in peace. The man hesitantly withdrew, only to reappear five minutes later. It was impossible, he said, for the automobile to wait any longer.

Aschenbach retorted angrily that in that case it should leave, and take his trunk with it. He himself would take the public steamboat when it was time, and would they kindly leave it to him to deal with the problem of his own departure. The hotel servant bowed. Aschenbach, glad to have fended off these tiresome admonitions, finished his breakfast unhurriedly, and even got the waiter to hand him a newspaper. It was indeed getting very late by the time he rose. It so happened that at that same moment Tadzio entered through the glass door.

As he walked to his family's table his path crossed that of the departing guest. Meeting this gray-haired gentleman with the lofty brow, he modestly lowered his eyes, only to raise them again at once in his enchanting way, in a soft and full glance; and then he had passed. Good-bye, Tadzio! thought Aschenbach. How short our meeting was. And he added, actually shaping the thought with his lips and uttering it aloud to himself, as he normally never did: "May God bless you!" — He then went through the routine of departure, distributed gratuities, received the parting courtesies of the soft-spoken little manager in the French frock coat, and left the hotel on foot as he had come, walking along the white-blossoming avenue with the hotel servant behind him carrying his hand luggage, straight across the island to the *vaporetto* landing stage. He reached it, he took his seat on board — and what followed was a voyage of sorrow, a grievous passage that plumbed all the depths of regret.

It was the familiar trip across the lagoon, past San Marco, up the Grand Canal. Aschenbach sat on the semicircular bench in the bows, one arm on the railing, shading his eyes with his hand. The Public Gardens fell away astern, the Piazzetta revealed itself once more in its princely elegance and was left behind, then came the great flight of the *palazzi*, with the splendid marble arch of the Rialto appearing as the waterway turned. The traveler contemplated it all, and his heart was rent with sorrow. The atmosphere of the city, this slightly moldy smell of sea and swamp from which he had been so anxious to escape — he breathed it in now in deep, tenderly painful drafts. Was it possible that he had not known, had not considered how deeply his feelings were involved in all these things? What had been a mere qualm of compunction this morning, a slight stirring of doubt as to the wisdom of his behavior, now became grief, became real suffering, an anguish of the soul, so bitter that several times it brought tears to his eyes, and which as he told himself he could not possibly have foreseen. What he found so hard to bear, what was indeed at times quite unendurable, was evidently the thought that he would never see Venice again, that this was a parting forever. For since it had become clear for a second time that this city made him ill, since he had been forced a second time to leave it precipitately, he must of course from now on regard it as an impossible and forbidden place to which he was not suited, and which it would be senseless to attempt to revisit. Indeed, he felt that if he left now, shame and pride must prevent him from ever setting eyes again on this beloved city which had twice physically defeated him; and this contention between his soul's desire and his physical capacities suddenly seemed to the aging Aschenbach so grave and important, the bodily inadequacy so shameful, so necessary to overcome at all costs, that he could not understand the facile resignation with which he had decided yesterday, without any serious struggle, to tolerate that inadequacy and to acknowledge it.

In the meantime the *vaporetto* was approaching the station, and Aschenbach's distress and sense of helplessness increased to the point of distraction. In his torment he felt it to be impossible to leave and no less impossible to turn back. He entered the station torn by this acute inner conflict. It was very late, he had not a moment to lose if he was to catch his train. He both wanted to catch it and wanted to miss it. But time was pressing, lashing him on; he hurried to get his ticket, looking round in the crowded concourse for the hotel company's employee who would be on duty here. The man appeared and informed him that his large trunk had been sent off as registered baggage. Sent off already? Certainly — to Como. To Como? And from hasty comings and goings, from angry questions and embarrassed replies, it came to light that the trunk, before even leaving the luggage room in the Hotel Excelsior, had been put with some quite different baggage and dispatched to a totally incorrect address.

Aschenbach had some difficulty preserving the facial expression that would be the only comprehensible one in these circumstances. A wild joy, an unbelievable feeling of hilarity, shook him almost convulsively from the depths of his heart. The hotel employee rushed to see if it was still possible to stop the trunk, and needless to say returned without having had any success. Aschenbach accordingly declared that he was not prepared to travel without his luggage, that he had decided to go back and wait at the Hotel des Bains for the missing article to turn up again. Was the company's motor launch still at the station? The man assured him that it was waiting immediately outside. With Italian eloquence he prevailed upon the official at the ticket office to take back Aschenbach's already purchased ticket. He swore that telegrams would be sent, that nothing would be left undone and no effort spared to get the trunk back in no time at all — and thus it most strangely came about that the traveler, twenty minutes after arriving at the station, found himself back on the Grand Canal and on his way back to the Lido.

How unbelievably strange an experience it was, how shaming, how like a dream in its bizarre comedy: to be returning, by a quirk of fate, to places from which one has just taken leave forever with the deepest sorrow — to be sent back and to be seeing them again within the hour! With spray tossing before its bows, deftly and entertainingly tacking to and fro between gondolas and *vaporetti*, the rapid little boat darted toward its destination, while its only passenger sat concealing under a mask of resigned annoyance the anxiously exuberant excitement of a truant schoolboy. From time to time he still inwardly shook with laughter at this mishap, telling himself that even a man born under a lucky star could not have had a more welcome piece of ill luck. There would be explanations to be given, surprised faces to be confronted — and then, as he told himself, everything would be well again, a disaster would have been averted, a grievous mistake corrected, and everything he thought he had turned his back on for good would lie open again for him to enjoy, would be his for as long as he liked . . . And what was more, did the rapid movement of the motor launch deceive him, or was there really now, to crown all else, a breeze blowing from the sea?

The bow waves dashed against the concrete walls of the narrow canal that cuts across the island to the Hotel Excelsior. There a motor omnibus was waiting for the returning guest and conveyed him along the road above the rippling sea straight to the Hotel des Bains. The little manager with the moustache and the fancily-cut frock coat came down the flight of steps to welcome him.

In softly flattering tones he expressed regret for the incident, described it as highly embarrassing for himself and for the company, but emphatically endorsed Aschenbach's decision to wait here for his luggage. His room, to be sure, had been relet, but another, no less comfortable, was immediately at his disposal. *"Pas de chance, monsieur!"* said the Swiss lift-attendant as they glided up. And thus the fugitive was once more installed in a room situated and furnished almost exactly like the first.

Exhausted and numbed by the confusion of this strange morning, he had no sooner distributed the contents of his hand luggage about the room than he collapsed into a reclining chair at the open window. The sea had turned pale green, the air seemed clearer and purer, the beach with its bathing cabins and boats more colorful, although the sky was still gray. Aschenbach gazed out, his hands folded in his lap, pleased to be here again but shaking his head with displeasure at his irresolution, his ignorance of his own wishes. Thus he sat for about an hour, resting and idly daydreaming. At midday he caught sight of Tadzio in his striped linen suit with the red breast-knot, coming from the sea, through the beach barrier and along the boarded walks back to the hotel. From up here at his window Aschenbach recognized him at once, before he had even looked at him properly, and some such thought came to him as: Why, Tadzio, there you are again too! But at the same instant he felt that casual greeting die on his lips, stricken dumb by the truth in his heart — he felt the rapturous kindling of his blood, the joy and the anguish of his soul, and realized that it was because of Tadzio that it had been so hard for him to leave.

He sat quite still, quite unseen at his high vantage point, and began to search his feelings. His features were alert, his eyebrows rose, an attentive, intelligently inquisitive smile parted his lips. Then he raised his head, and with his arms hanging limply down along the back of his chair, described with both of them a slowly rotating and lifting motion, the palms of his hands turning forward, as if to sketch an opening and outspreading of the arms. It was a gesture that gladly bade welcome, a gesture of calm acceptance.

4

Now day after day the god with the burning cheeks soared naked, driving his four fire-breathing steeds through the spaces of heaven, and now, too, his yellow-gold locks fluttered wide in the outstorming east wind. Silk-white radiance gleamed on the slow-swelling deep's vast waters. The sand glowed. Under the silvery quivering blue of the ether, rust-colored awnings were spread out in front of the beach cabins, and one spent the morning hours on the sharply defined patch of shade they provided. But exquisite, too, was the evening, when the plants in the park gave off a balmy fragrance, and the stars on high moved through their dance, and the softly audible murmur of the night-surrounded sea worked its magic on the soul. Such an evening carried with it the delightful promise of a new sunlit day of leisure easily ordered, and adorned with countless close-knit possibilities of charming chance encounter.

The guest whom so convenient a mishap had detained here was very far from seeing the recovery of his property as a reason for yet another departure. For a couple of days he had had to put up with some privations and appear in the main dining room in his traveling clothes. Then, when finally the errant load was once more set down in his room, he unpacked completely and filled the cupboards and drawers with his possessions, resolving for the present to set no time limit on his stay; he was glad now to be able to pass his hours on the beach in a tussore suit and to present himself again in seemly evening attire at the dinner table.

The lulling rhythm of this existence had already cast its spell on him; he had been quickly enchanted by the indulgent softness and splendor of this way of life. What a place this was indeed, combining the charms of a cultivated seaside resort in the south with the familiar ever-ready proximity of the strange and wonderful city! Aschenbach did not enjoy enjoying himself. Whenever and wherever he had to stop work, have a breathing space, take things easily, he would soon find himself driven by restlessness and dissatisfaction — and this had been so in his youth above all — back to his lofty travail, to his stern and sacred daily routine. Only this place bewitched him, relaxed his will, gave him happiness. Often in the forenoon, under the awning of his hut, gazing dreamily at the blue of the southern sea, or on a mild night perhaps, reclining under a star-strewn sky on the cushions of a gondola that carried him back to the Lido from the Piazza where he had long lingered — and as the bright lights, the melting sounds of the serenade dropped away behind him — often he recalled his country house in the mountains, the scene of his summer labors, where the low clouds would drift through his garden, violent evening thunderstorms would put out all the lights, and the ravens he fed would take refuge in the tops of the pine trees. Then indeed he would feel he had been snatched away now to the Elysian land, to the ends of the earth, where lightest of living is granted to mortals, where no snow is nor winter, no storms and no rain downstreaming, but where Oceanus ever causes a gentle cooling breeze to ascend, and the days flow past in blessed idleness, with no labor or strife, for to the sun alone and its feasts they are all given over.

Aschenbach saw much of the boy Tadzio, he saw him almost constantly; in a confined environment, with a common daily program, it was natural for the beautiful creature to be near him all day, with only brief interruptions. He saw him and met him everywhere: in the ground floor rooms of the hotel, on their cooling journeys by water to the city and back, in the sumptuous Piazza itself, and often elsewhere from time to time, in alleys and byways, when chance had played a part. But it was during the mornings on the beach above all, and with the happiest regularity, that he could devote hours at a time to the contemplation and study of this exquisite phenomenon. Indeed, it was precisely this ordered routine of happiness, this equal daily repetition of favorable circumstances, that so filled him with contentment and zest for life, that made this place so precious to him, that allowed one sunlit day to follow another in such obligingly endless succession.

He rose early, as he would normally have done under the insistent compulsion of work, and was down at the beach before most of the other guests, when the sun's heat was still gentle and the sea lay dazzling white in its morning dreams. He greeted the barrier attendant affably, exchanged familiar greetings also with the barefooted, white-bearded old man who had prepared his place for him, spread the brown awning and shifted the cabin furniture out to the platform where Aschenbach would settle down. Three hours or four were then his, hours in which the sun would rise to its zenith and to terrible power, hours in which the sea would turn a deeper and deeper blue, hours in which he would be able to watch Tadzio.

He saw him coming, walking along from the left by the water's edge, saw him from behind as he emerged between the cabins, or indeed would sometimes look up and discover, gladdened and startled, that he had missed his arrival and that the boy was already there, already in the blue and white bathing costume which now on the beach was his sole attire. There he would be, already busy with his customary activities in the sun and the sand — this charmingly trivial, idle yet ever-active life that was both play and repose, a life of sauntering, wading, digging, snatching, lying about and swimming, under the watchful eyes and at the constant call of the women on their platform, who with their high-pitched voices would cry out his name: "Tadziu! Tadziu!" and to whom he would come running with eager gesticulation, to tell them what he had experienced, to show them what he had found, what he had caught: jellyfish, little seahorses, and mussels, and crabs that go sideways. Aschenbach understood not a word of what he said, and commonplace though it might be, it was liquid melody in his ears. Thus the foreign sound of the boy's speech exalted it to music, the sun in its triumph shed lavish brightness all over him, and the sublime perspective of the sea was the constant contrasting background against which he appeared.

Soon the contemplative beholder knew every line and pose of that noble, so freely displayed body, he saluted again with joy each already familiar perfection, and there was no end to his wonder, to the delicate

delight of his senses. The boy would be summoned to greet a guest
who was making a polite call on the ladies in their cabin; he would run
up, still wet perhaps from the sea, throw back his curls, and as he held
out his hand, poised on one leg with the other on tiptoe, he had an
enchanting way of turning and twisting his body, gracefully expectant,
charmingly shamefaced, seeking to please because good breeding required him to do so. Or he would be lying full-length, his bathing
robe wrapped round his chest, his finely chiseled arm propped on the
sand, his hand cupping his chin; the boy addressed as "Jashu" would
squat beside him caressing him, and nothing could be more bewitching than the way the favored Tadzio, smiling with his eyes and lips,
would look up at this lesser and servile mortal. Or he would be standing at the edge of the sea, alone, some way from his family, quite near
Aschenbach, standing upright with his hands clasped behind his neck,
slowly rocking to and fro on the balls of his feet and dreamily gazing
into the blue distance, while little waves ran up and bathed his toes.
His honey-colored hair nestled in ringlets at his temples and at the
back of his neck, the sun gleamed in the down on his upper spine, the
subtle outlining of his ribs and the symmetry of his breast stood out
through the scanty covering of his torso, his armpits were still as
smooth as those of a statue, the hollows of his knees glistened and
their bluish veins made his body seem composed of some more
translucent material. What discipline, what precision of thought was
expressed in that outstretched, youthfully perfect physique! And yet
the austere pure will that had here been darkly active, that had succeeded in bringing this divine sculptured shape to light — was it not
well known and familiar to Aschenbach as an artist? Was it not also active in him, in the sober passion that filled him as he set free from the
marble mass of language that slender form which he had beheld in the
spirit, and which he was presenting to mankind as a model and mirror
of intellectual beauty?
    A model and mirror! His eyes embraced that noble figure at the
blue water's edge, and in rising ecstasy he felt he was gazing on Beauty
itself, on Form as a thought of God, on the one and pure perfection
which dwells in the spirit and of which a human image and likeness
had here been lightly and graciously set up for him to worship. Such
was his emotional intoxication; and the aging artist welcomed it un-
hesitatingly, even greedily. His mind was in labor, its store of culture
was in ferment, his memory threw up thoughts from ancient tradition
which he had been taught as a boy, but which had never yet come
alive in his own fire. Had he not read that the sun turns our attention

from spiritual things to the things of the senses? He had read that it so numbs and bewitches our intelligence and memory that the soul, in its joy, quite forgets its proper state and clings with astonished admiration to that most beautiful of all the things the sun shines upon: yes, that only with the help of a bodily form is the soul then still able to exalt itself to a higher vision. That Cupid, indeed, does as mathematicians do, when they show dull-witted children tangible images of the pure Forms: so too the love god, in order to make spiritual things visible, loves to use the shapes and colors of young men, turning them into instruments of Recollection by adorning them with all the reflected splendor of Beauty, so that the sight of them will truly set us on fire with pain and hope.

Such were the thoughts the god inspired in his enthusiast, such were the emotions of which he grew capable. And a delightful vision came to him, spun from the sea's murmur and the glittering sunlight. It was the old plane tree not far from the walls of Athens — that place of sacred shade, fragrant with chaste-tree blossoms, adorned with sacred statues and pious gifts in honor of the nymphs and of Acheloüs. The stream trickled crystal clear over smooth pebbles at the foot of the great spreading tree; the crickets made their music. But on the grass, which sloped down gently so that one could hold up one's head as one lay, there reclined two men, sheltered here from the heat of the noonday: one elderly and one young, one ugly and one beautiful, the wise beside the desirable. And Socrates, wooing him with witty compliments and jests, was instructing Phaedrus on desire and virtue. He spoke to him of the burning tremor of fear which the lover will suffer when his eye perceives a likeness of eternal Beauty; spoke to him of the lusts of the profane and base who cannot turn their eyes to Beauty when they behold its image and are not capable of reverence; spoke of the sacred terror that visits the noble soul when a godlike countenance, a perfect body appears to him — of how he trembles then and is beside himself and hardly dares look at the possessor of beauty, and reveres him and would even sacrifice to him as to a graven image, if he did not fear to seem foolish in the eyes of men. For Beauty, dear Phaedrus, only Beauty is at one and the same time divinely desirable and visible: it is, mark well, the only form of the spiritual that we can receive with our senses and endure with our senses. For what would become of us if other divine things, if Reason and Virtue and Truth were to appear to us sensuously? Should we not perish in a conflagration of love, as once upon a time Semele did before Zeus? Thus Beauty is the lover's path to the spirit — only the path, only a means, little Phaedrus . . . And then he uttered the subtlest thing of all, that sly wooer: he who loves, he said, is more divine than the beloved, because the god is in the former, but not in the latter — this, the tenderest perhaps and the most mocking thought ever formulated, a thought alive with all the mischievousness and most secret voluptuousness of the heart.

The writer's joy is the thought that can become emotion, the emotion that can wholly become a thought. At that time the solitary Aschenbach took possession and control of just such a pulsating thought, just such a precise emotion: namely, that Nature trembles with rapture when the spirit bows in homage before Beauty. He suddenly desired to write. Eros indeed, we are told, loves idleness and is born only for the idle. But at this point of Aschenbach's crisis and visitation his excitement was driving him to produce. The occasion was almost a matter of indifference. An inquiry, an invitation to express a personal opinion on a certain important cultural problem, a burning question of taste, had been circulated to the intellectual world and had been forwarded to him on his travels. The theme was familiar to him, it was close to his experience; the desire to illuminate it in his own words was suddenly irresistible. And what he craved, indeed, was to work on it in Tadzio's presence, to take the boy's physique for a model as he wrote, to let his style follow the lineaments of this body which he saw as divine, and to carry its beauty on high into the spiritual world, as the eagle once carried the Trojan shepherd boy up into the ether. Never had he felt the joy of the word more sweetly, never had he known so clearly that Eros dwells in language, as during those perilously precious hours in which, seated at his rough table under the awning, in full view of his idol and with the music of his voice in his ears, he used Tadzio's beauty as a model for his brief essay — that page and a half of exquisite prose which with its limpid nobility and vibrant controlled passion was soon to win the admiration of many. It is as well that the world knows only a fine piece of work and not also its origins, the conditions under which it came into being; for knowledge of the sources of an artist's inspiration would often confuse readers and shock them, and the excellence of the writing would be of no avail. How strange those hours were! How strangely exhausting that labor! How mysterious this act of intercourse and begetting between a mind and a body! When Aschenbach put away his work and left the beach, he felt worn out, even broken, and his conscience seemed to be reproaching him as if after some kind of debauch.

On the following morning, just as he was leaving the hotel, he noticed from the steps that Tadzio, already on his way to the sea — and alone — was just approaching the beach barrier. The wish to use this opportunity, the mere thought of doing so, and thereby lightly, lightheartedly, making the acquaintance of one who had unknowingly so exalted and moved him: the thought of speaking to him, of enjoying his answer and his glance — all this seemed natural, it was the irresistibly obvious thing to do. The beautiful boy was walking in a leisurely fashion, he could be overtaken, and Aschenbach quickened his pace. He reached him on the boarded way behind the bathing cabins, he was just about to lay his hand on his head or his shoulder, and some phrase or other, some friendly words in French were on the tip of his tongue — when he felt his heart, perhaps partly because he had been walking fast, hammering wildly inside him, felt so breathless that he would only have been able to speak in a strangled and trembling voice. He hesitated, struggled to control himself, then was suddenly afraid that he had already been walking too long close behind the beautiful boy, afraid that Tadzio would notice this, that he would turn and look at him questioningly; he made one more attempt, failed, gave up, and hurried past with his head bowed.

Too late! he thought at that moment. Too late! But was it too late? This step he had failed to take would very possibly have been all to the good, it might have had a lightening and gladdening effect, led perhaps to a wholesome disenchantment. But the fact now seemed to be that the aging lover no longer wished to be disenchanted, that the intoxication was too precious to him. Who shall unravel the mystery of an artist's nature and character! Who shall explain the profound instinctual fusion of discipline and dissoluteness on which it rests! For not to be able to desire wholesome disenchantment is to be dissolute. Aschenbach was no longer disposed to self-criticism; taste, the intellectual mold of his years, self-respect, maturity and late simplicity all disinclined him to analyze his motives and decide whether what had prevented him from carrying out his intention had been a prompting of conscience or a disreputable weakness. He was confused, he was afraid that someone, even if only the bathing attendant, might have witnessed his haste and his defeat; he was very much afraid of exposure to ridicule. For the rest, he could not help inwardly smiling at his comic-sacred terror. "Crestfallen," he thought, "spirits dashed, like a frightened cock hanging its wings in a fight! Truly this is the god who at the sight of the desired beauty so breaks our courage and dashes our pride so utterly to the ground . . ." He toyed with the theme, gave rein to his enthusiasm, plunged into emotions he was too proud to fear.

He was no longer keeping any tally of the leisure time he had allowed himself; the thought of returning home did not even occur to him. He had arranged for ample funds to be made available to him here. His one anxiety was that the Polish family might leave; but he had surreptitiously learned, by a casual question to the hotel barber, that these guests had begun their stay here only very shortly before he had arrived himself. The sun was browning his face and hands, the stimulating salty breeze heightened his capacity for feeling, and whereas formerly, when sleep or food or contact with nature had given him any refreshment, he would always have expended it completely on his writing, he now, with high-hearted prodigality, allowed all the daily revitalization he was receiving from the sun and leisure and sea air to burn itself up in intoxicating emotion.

He slept fleetingly; the days of precious monotony were punctuated by brief, happily restless nights. To be sure, he would retire early, for at nine o'clock, when Tadzio had disappeared from the scene, he judged his day to be over. But at the first glint of dawn a pang of tenderness would startle him awake, his heart would remember its adventure, he could bear his pillows no longer, he would get up, and lightly wrapped against the early morning chill he would sit down at the open window to wait for the sunrise. His soul, still fresh with the solemnity of sleep, was filled with awe by this wonderful event. The sky, the earth and the sea still wore the glassy paleness of ghostly twilight; a dying star still floated in the void. But a murmur came, a winged message from dwelling places no mortal may approach, that Eos was rising from her husband's side; and now it appeared, that first sweet blush at the furthest horizon of the sky and sea, which heralds the sensuous disclosure of creation. The goddess approached, that ravisher of youth, who carried off Cleitus and Cephalus and defied the envy of all the Olympians to enjoy the love of the beautiful Orion. A scattering of roses began, there at the edge of the world, an ineffably lovely shining and blossoming: childlike clouds, transfigured and transparent with light, hovered like serving *amoretti* in the vermilion and violet haze; crimson light fell across the waves, which seemed to be washing it landward; golden spears darted from below into the heights of heaven, the gleam became a conflagration, noiselessly and with overwhelming divine power the glow and the fire and the blazing flames reared upward, and the sacred steeds of the goddess's brother Helios, tucking their hooves, leapt above the earth's round surface. With the splendor of the god irradiating him, the lone watcher sat; he closed his eyes and let the glory kiss his eyelids. Feelings he had had long ago, early and precious dolors of the heart, which had died out in his life's austere service and were now, so strangely transformed, returning to him —

he recognized them with a confused and astonished smile. He meditated, he dreamed, slowly a name shaped itself on his lips, and still smiling, with upturned face, his hands folded in his lap, he fell asleep in his chair once more.

With such fiery ceremony the day began, but the rest of it, too, was strangely exalted and mythically transformed. Where did it come from, what was its origin, this sudden breeze that played so gently and speakingly around his temples and ears, like some higher insufflation? Innumerable white fleecy clouds covered the sky, like the grazing flocks of the gods. A stronger wind rose, and the horses of Poseidon reared and ran; his bulls too, the bulls of the blue-haired sea god, roared and charged with lowered horns. But among the rocks and stones of the more distant beach the waves danced like leaping goats. A sacred, deranged world, full of Panic life, enclosed the enchanted watcher, and his heart dreamed tender tales. Sometimes, as the sun was sinking behind Venice, he would sit on a bench in the hotel park to watch Tadzio, dressed in white with a colorful sash, at play on the rolled gravel tennis court; and in his mind's eye he was watching Hyacinthus, doomed to perish because two gods loved him. He could even feel Zephyr's grievous envy of his rival, who had forgotten his oracle and his bow and his zither to be forever playing with the beautiful youth; he saw the discus, steered by cruel jealousy, strike the lovely head; he himself, turning pale too, caught the broken body in his arms, and the flower that sprang from that sweet blood bore the inscription of his undying lament.

Nothing is stranger, more delicate, than the relationship between people who know each other only by sight — who encounter and observe each other daily, even hourly, and yet are compelled by the constraint of convention or by their own temperament to keep up the pretense of being indifferent strangers, neither greeting nor speaking to each other. Between them is uneasiness and overstimulated curiosity, the nervous excitement of an unsatisfied, unnaturally suppressed need to know and to communicate; and above all, too, a kind of strained respect. For man loves and respects his fellow man for as long as he is not yet in a position to evaluate him, and desire is born of defective knowledge.

It was inevitable that some kind of relationship and acquaintance should develop between Aschenbach and the young Tadzio, and with a surge of joy the older man became aware that his interest and attention were not wholly unreciprocated. Why, for example, when the beautiful creature appeared in the morning on the beach, did he now never use the boarded walk behind the bathing cabins, but always take the front way, through the sand, passing Aschenbach's abode and often passing unnecessarily close to him, almost touching his table or his chair, as he sauntered toward the cabin where his family sat? Was this the attraction, the fascination exercised by a superior feeling on its tender and thoughtless object? Aschenbach waited daily for Tadzio to make his appearance and sometimes pretended to be busy when he did so, letting the boy pass him seemingly unnoticed. But sometimes, too, he would look up, and their eyes would meet. They would both be deeply serious when this happened. In the cultured and dignified countenance of the older man, nothing betrayed an inner emotion; but in Tadzio's eyes there was an inquiry, a thoughtful questioning, his walk became hesitant, he looked at the ground, looked sweetly up again, and when he had passed, something in his bearing seemed to suggest that only good breeding restrained him from turning to look back.

But once, one evening, it was different. The Poles and their governess had been absent from dinner in the main restaurant — Aschenbach had noticed this with concern. After dinner, very uneasy about where they might be, he was walking in evening dress and a straw hat in front of the hotel, at the foot of the terrace, when suddenly he saw the nunlike sisters appearing with their companion, in the light of the arc lamps, and four paces behind them was Tadzio. Obviously they had come from the *vaporetto* pier, having for some reason dined in the city. The crossing had been chilly perhaps; Tadzio was wearing a dark blue reefer jacket with gold buttons and a naval cap to match. The sun and sea air never burned his skin, it was marble-pale as always; but today he seemed paler than usual, either because of the cool weather or in the blanching moonlight of the lamps. His symmetrical eyebrows stood out more sharply, his eyes seemed much darker. He was more beautiful than words can express, and Aschenbach felt, as so often already, the painful awareness that language can only praise sensuous beauty, but not reproduce it.

He had not been prepared for the beloved encounter, it came unexpectedly, he had not had time to put on an expression of calm and dignity. Joy no doubt, surprise, admiration, were openly displayed on his face when his eyes met those of the returning absentee — and in that instant it happened that Tadzio smiled: smiled at him, speakingly, familiarly, enchantingly and quite unabashed, with his lips parting slowly as the smile was formed. It was the smile of Narcissus as he bows his head over the mirroring water, that profound, fascinated, protracted smile with which he reaches out his arms toward the reflection of his own beauty — a very slightly contorted smile, contorted by the hopelessness of his attempt to kiss the sweet lips of his shadow; a smile that was provocative, curious and imperceptibly troubled, bewitched and bewitching.

He who had received this smile carried it quickly away with him like a fateful gift. He was so deeply shaken that he was forced to flee the lighted terrace and the front garden and hurry into the darkness of the park at the rear. Words struggled from his lips, strangely indignant and tender reproaches: "You mustn't smile like that! One mustn't, do you hear, mustn't smile like that at anyone!" He sank down on one of the seats, deliriously breathing the nocturnal fragrance of the flowers and trees. And leaning back, his arms hanging down, overwhelmed, trembling, shuddering all over, he whispered the standing formula of the heart's desire — impossible here, absurd, depraved, ludicrous and sacred nevertheless, still worthy of honor even here: "I love you!"

5

During the fourth week of his stay at the Lido Gustav von Aschenbach began to notice certain uncanny developments in the outside world. In the first place it struck him that as the height of the season approached, the number of guests at his hotel was diminishing rather than increasing, and in particular that the German language seemed to be dying away into silence all round him, so that in the end only foreign sounds fell on his ear at table and on the beach. Then one day the hotel barber, whom he visited frequently now, let slip in conversation a remark that aroused his suspicions. The man had mentioned a German family who had just left after only a brief stay, and in his chattering, flattering manner he added: "But you are staying on, signore; you are not afraid of the sickness." Aschenbach looked at him. "The sickness?" he repeated. The fellow stopped his talk, pretended to be busy, had not heard the question. And when it was put to him again more sharply, he declared that he knew nothing and tried with embarrassed loquacity to change the subject.

That was at midday. In the afternoon, with the sea dead calm and the sun burning, Aschenbach crossed to Venice, for he was now driven by a mad compulsion to follow the Polish boy and his sisters, having seen them set off toward the pier with their companion. He did not find his idol at San Marco. But at tea, sitting at his round wrought-iron table on the shady side of the Piazza, he suddenly scented in the air a peculiar aroma, one which it now seemed to him he had been noticing for days without really being conscious of it — a sweetish, medicinal smell that suggested squalor and wounds and suspect cleanliness. He scrutinized it, pondered and identified it, finished his tea and left the Piazza at the far end opposite the basilica. In the narrow streets the smell was stronger. At corners, printed notices had been pasted up in which the civic authorities, with fatherly concern, gave warning to the local population that since certain ailments of the gastric system were normal in this weather, they should refrain from eating oysters and mussels and indeed from using water from the canals. The euphemistic character of the announcement was obvious. Groups of people were standing about silently on bridges or in squares, and the stranger stood among them, brooding and scenting the truth.

He found a shopkeeper leaning against his vaulted doorway, surrounded by coral necklaces and trinkets made of imitation amethyst, and asked him about the unpleasant smell. The man looked him over with heavy eyes, and hastily gathered his wits. "A precautionary measure, signore," he answered, gesticulating. "The police have laid down regulations, and quite right too, it must be said. This weather is oppressive, the sirocco is not very wholesome. In short, the signore will understand — an exaggerated precaution no doubt . . ." Aschenbach thanked him and walked on. Even on the *vaporetto* taking him back to the Lido he now noticed the smell of the bactericide.

Back at the hotel, he went at once to the table in the hall where the newspapers were kept, and carried out some research. In the foreign papers he found nothing. Those in his own language mentioned rumors, quoted contradictory statistics, reported official denials and questioned their veracity. This explained the withdrawal of the German and Austrian clientele. Visitors of other nationalities evidently knew nothing, suspected nothing, still had no apprehensions. "They want it kept quiet!" thought Aschenbach in some agitation, throwing the newspapers back on the table. "They're hushing this up!" But at the same time his heart filled with elation at the thought of the adventure in which the outside world was about to be involved. For to passion, as to crime, the assured everyday order and stability of things is not opportune, and any weakening of the civil structure, any chaos and disaster afflicting the world, must be welcome to it, as offering a vague hope of turning such circumstances to its advantage. Thus Aschenbach felt an obscure sense of satisfaction at what was going on in the dirty alleyways of Venice, cloaked in official secrecy — this guilty secret of the city, which merged with his own innermost secret and which it was also so much in his own interests to protect. For in his enamored state his one anxiety was that Tadzio might leave, and he realized with a kind of horror that he would not be able to go on living if that were to happen.

Lately he had not been content to owe the sight and proximity of the beautiful boy merely to daily routine and change: he had begun pursuing him, following him obtrusively. On Sunday, for example, the Poles never appeared on the beach; he rightly guessed that they were attending mass in San Marco, and hastened to the church himself. There, stepping from the fiery heat of the Piazza into the golden twilight of the sanctuary, he would find him whom he had missed, bowed over a prie-dieu and performing his devotions. Then he would stand in the background, on the cracked mosaic floor, amid a throng of people kneeling, murmuring and crossing themselves, and the massive magnificence of the oriental temple would weigh sumptuously on his senses. At the front, the ornately vested priest walked to and fro, doing his business and chanting. Incense billowed up, clouding the feeble flames of the altar candles, and with its heavy, sweet sacrificial odor another seemed to mingle: the smell of the sick city. But through the vaporous dimness and the flickering lights Aschenbach saw the boy, up there at the front, turn his head and seek him with his eyes until he found him.

Then, when the great doors were opened and the crowd streamed out into the shining Piazza swarming with pigeons, the beguiled lover would hide in the antebasilica, he would lurk and lie in wait. He would see the Poles leave the church, see the brother and sisters take ceremonious leave of their mother, who would then set off home, turning toward the Piazzetta; he would observe the boy, the cloistral sisters and the governess turn right and walk through the clock tower gateway into the Merceria, and after letting them get a little way ahead he would follow them — follow them furtively on their walk through Venice. He had to stop when they lingered, had to take refuge in hot food stalls and courtyards to let them pass when they turned round; he would lose them, search for them frantically and exhaustingly, rushing over bridges and along filthy culs-de-sac, and would then have to endure minutes of mortal embarrassment when he suddenly saw them coming toward him in a narrow passageway where no escape was possible. And yet one cannot say that he suffered. His head and his heart were drunk, and his steps followed the dictates of that dark god whose pleasure it is to trample man's reason and dignity underfoot.

Presently, somewhere or other, Tadzio and his family would take a gondola, and while they were getting into it Aschenbach, hiding behind a fountain or the projecting part of a building, would wait till they were a little way from the shore and then do the same. Speaking hurriedly and in an undertone, he would instruct the oarsman, promising him a large tip, to follow that gondola ahead of them that was just turning the corner, to follow it at a discreet distance; and a shiver would run down his spine when the fellow, with the roguish compliance of a pander, would answer him in the same tone, assuring him that he was at his service, entirely at his service.

Thus he glided and swayed gently along, reclining on soft black cushions, shadowing that other black, beaked craft, chained to its pursuit by his infatuation. Sometimes he would lose sight of it and become distressed and anxious, but his steersman, who seemed to be well practiced in commissions of this kind, would always know some cunning maneuver, some side-canal or short cut that would again bring Aschenbach in sight of what he craved. The air was stagnant and malodorous, the sun burned oppressively through the haze that had turned the sky to the color of slate. Water lapped against wood and stone. The gondolier's call, half warning and half greeting, was answered from a distance out of the silent labyrinth, in accordance with some strange convention. Out of little overhead gardens unbelliferous blossoms spilled over and hung down the crumbling masonry, white and purple and almond scented. Moorish windows were mirrored in the murky water. The marble steps of a church dipped below the surface; a beggar squatted on them, protesting his misery, holding out his hat and showing the whites of his eyes as if he were blind; an antiques dealer beckoned to them with crawling obsequiousness as they passed his den, inviting them to stop and be swindled. This was Venice, the flattering and suspect beauty — this city, half fairy tale and half tourist trap, in whose insalubrious air the arts once rankly and voluptuously blossomed, where composers have been inspired to lulling tones of somniferous eroticism. Gripped by his adventure, the traveler felt his eyes drinking in this sumptuousness, his ears wooed by these melodies; he remembered, too, that the city was stricken with sickness and concealing it for reasons of cupidity, and he peered around still more wildly in search of the gondola that hovered ahead.

So it was that in his state of distraction he could no longer think of anything or want anything except this ceaseless pursuit of the object that so inflamed him: nothing but to follow him, to dream of him when he was not there, and after the fashion of lovers to address tender words to his mere shadow. Solitariness, the foreign environment, and the joy of an intoxication of feeling that had come to him so late and affected him so profoundly — all this encouraged and persuaded him to indulge himself in the most astonishing ways: as when it had happened that late one evening, returning from Venice and reaching the first floor of the hotel, he had paused outside the boy's bedroom door, leaning his head against the doorframe in a complete drunken ecstasy, and had for a long time been unable to move from the spot, at the risk of being surprised and discovered in this insane situation.

Nevertheless, there were moments at which he paused and half came to his senses. Where is this leading me! he would reflect in consternation at such moments. Where was it leading him! Like any man whose natural merits move him to take an aristocratic interest in his origins, Aschenbach habitually let the achievements and successes of his life remind him of his ancestors, for in imagination he could then feel sure of their approval, of their satisfaction, of the respect they could not have withheld. And he thought of them even here and now, entangled as he was in so impermissible an experience, involved in such exotic extravagances of feeling; he thought, with a sad smile, of their dignified austerity, their decent manliness of character. What would they say? But for that matter, what would they have said about his entire life, a life that had deviated from theirs to the point of degeneracy, this life of his in the compulsive service of art, this life about which he himself, adopting the civic values of his forefathers, had once let fall such mocking observations — and which nevertheless had essentially been so much like theirs! He too had served, he too had been a soldier and a warrior, like many of them: for art was a war, an exhausting struggle, it was hard these days to remain fit for it for long. A life of self-conquest and of defiant resolve, an astringent, steadfast and frugal life which he had turned into the symbol of that heroism for delicate constitutions, that heroism so much in keeping with the times — surely he might call this manly, might call it courageous? And it seemed to him that the kind of love that had taken possession of him did, in a certain way, suit and befit such a life. Had it not been highly honored by the most valiant of peoples, indeed had he not read that in their cities it had flourished by inspiring valorous deeds? Numerous warrior-heroes of olden times had willingly borne its yoke, for there was no kind of abasement that could be reckoned as such if the god had imposed it; and actions that would have been castigated as signs of cowardice had their motives been different, such as falling to the ground in supplication, desperate pleas and slavish demeanor — these were accounted no disgrace to a lover, but rather won him still greater praise.

Such were the thoughts with which love beguiled him, and thus he sought to sustain himself, to preserve his dignity. But at the same time he kept turning his attention, inquisitively and persistently, to the disreputable events that were evolving in the depths of Venice, to that adventure of the outside world which darkly mingled with the adventure of his heart, and which nourished his passion with vague and lawless hopes. Obstinately determined to obtain new and reliable information about the status and progress of the malady, he would sit in the city's coffee houses searching through the German newspapers, which several days ago had disappeared from the reading table in the hotel foyer. They carried assertions and retractions by turns. The number of cases, the number of deaths, was said to be twenty, or forty, or a hundred and more, such reports being immediately followed by statements flatly denying the outbreak of an epidemic, or at least reducing it to a few quite isolated cases brought in from outside the city. Scattered here and there were warning admonitions, or protests against the dangerous policy being pursued by the Italian authorities. There was no certainty to be had.

The solitary traveler was nevertheless conscious of having a special claim to participation in this secret, and although excluded from it, he took a perverse pleasure in putting embarrassing questions to those in possession of the facts, and thus, since they were pledged to silence, forcing them to lie to him directly. One day, at luncheon in the main dining room, he interrogated the hotel manager in this fashion, the soft-footed little man in the French frock coat who was moving around among the tables supervising the meal and greeting the clients, and who also stopped at Aschenbach's table for a few words of conversation. Why, in fact, asked his guest in a casual and nonchalant way, why on earth had they begun recently to disinfect Venice? — "It is merely a police measure, sir," answered the trickster, "taken in good time, as a safeguard against various disagreeable public health problems that might otherwise arise from this sultry and exceptionally warm weather — a precautionary measure which it is their duty to take." — "Very praiseworthy of the police," replied Aschenbach; and after exchanging a few meteorological observations with him the manager took his leave.

On the very same day, in the evening after dinner, it happened that • a small group of street singers from the city gave a performance in the front garden of the hotel. They stood by one of the iron arc lamp standards, two men and two women, their faces glinting white in the glare, looking up at the great terrace where the hotel guests sat over their coffee and cooling drinks, resigned to watching this exhibition of folk culture. The hotel staff, the lift boys, waiters, office employees, had come out to listen in the hall doorways. The Russian family, eager to savor every pleasure, had had cane chairs put out for them down in the garden in order to be nearer the performers and were contentedly sitting there in a semicircle. Behind her master and mistress, in a turban-like headcloth, stood their aged serf.

The beggar virtuosi were playing a mandolin, a guitar, a harmonica and a squeaking fiddle. Instrumental developments alternated with vocal numbers, as when the younger of the women, shrill and squawky of voice, joined the tenor with his sweet falsetto notes in an ardent love duet. But the real talent and leader of the ensemble was quite evidently the other man, the one who had the guitar and was a kind of buffo-baritone character, with hardly any voice but with a mimic gift and remarkable comic verve. Often he would detach himself from the rest of the group and come forward, playing his large instrument and gesticulating, toward the terrace, where his pranks were rewarded with encouraging laughter. The Russians in their parterre seats took special delight in all this southern vivacity, and their plaudits and admiring shouts led him on to ever further and bolder extravagances.

Aschenbach sat by the balustrade, cooling his lips from time to time with the mixture of pomegranate juice and soda water that sparkled ruby-red in the glass before him. His nervous system greedily drank in the jangling tones, for passion paralyzes discrimination and responds in all seriousness to stimuli which the sober senses would either treat with humorous tolerance or impatiently reject. The antics of the mountebank had distorted his features into a rictus-like smile which he was already finding painful. He sat on with a casual air, but inwardly he was utterly engrossed; for six paces from him Tadzio was leaning against the stone parapet.

There he stood, in the white belted suit he occasionally put on for dinner, in a posture of innate and inevitable grace, his left forearm on the parapet, his feet crossed, his right hand on the supporting hip; and he was looking down at the entertainers with an expression that was scarcely a smile, merely one of remote curiosity, a polite observation of the spectacle. Sometimes he straightened himself, stretching his chest, and with an elegant movement of both arms drew his white tunic down through his leather belt. But sometimes, too, and the older man noticed it with a mind-dizzying sense of triumph as well as with terror, he would turn his head hesitantly and cautiously, or even quickly and suddenly as if to gain the advantage of surprise, and look over his left shoulder to where his lover was sitting. Their eyes did not meet, for an ignominious apprehension was forcing the stricken man to keep his looks anxiously in check. Behind them on the terrace sat the women who watched over Tadzio, and at the point things had now reached, the enamored Aschenbach had reason to fear that he had attracted attention and aroused suspicion. Indeed, he had several times, on the beach, in the hotel foyer, and on the Piazza San Marco, been frozen with alarm to notice that Tadzio was being called away if he was near him, that they were taking care to keep them apart — and although his pride writhed in torments it had never known under the appalling insult that this implied, he could not in conscience deny its justice.

In the meantime the guitarist had begun a solo to his own accompaniment, a song in many stanzas which was then a popular hit all over Italy, and which he managed to perform in a graphic and dramatic manner, with the rest of his troupe joining regularly in the refrain. He was a lean fellow, thin and cadaverous in the face as well, standing there on the gravel detached from his companions, with a shabby felt hat on the back of his head and a quiff of his red hair bulging out under the brim, in a posture of insolent bravado; strumming and thrumming on his instrument, he tossed his pleasantries up to the terrace in a vivid *parlando,* enacting it all so strenuously that the veins swelled on his forehead. He was quite evidently not of Venetian origin, but rather of the Neapolitan comic type, half pimp, half actor, brutal and bold-faced, dangerous and entertaining. The actual words of his song were merely foolish, but in his presentation, with his grimaces and bodily movements, his way of winking suggestively and lasciviously licking the corner of his mouth, it had something indecent and vaguely offensive about it. Though otherwise dressed in urban fashion he wore a sports shirt, out of the soft collar of which his skinny neck projected, displaying a remarkably large and naked Adam's apple. His pallid snub-nosed face, the features of which gave little clue to his age, seemed to be lined with contortions and vice, and the grinning of his mobile mouth was rather strangely ill-matched to the two deep furrows that stood defiantly, imperiously, almost savagely, between his reddish brows. But what really fixed the solitary Aschenbach's deep attention on him was his observation that this suspect figure seemed to be carrying his own suspect atmosphere about with him as well. For every time the refrain was repeated the singer would perform, with much grimacing and wagging of his hand as if in greeting, a grotesque march round the scene, which brought him immediately below where Aschenbach sat; and every time this happened a stench of carbolic from his clothes or his body drifted up to the terrace.

Having completed his ballad he began to collect money. He started with the Russians, who were seen to give generously, and then came up the steps. Saucy as his performance had been, up here he was humility itself. Bowing and scraping, he crept from table to table, and a sly obsequious grin bared his prominent teeth, although the two fur-rows still stood threateningly between his red eyebrows. The spectacle of this alien being gathering in his livelihood was viewed with curiosity and not a little distaste; one threw coins with the tips of one's finger into the hat, which one took care not to touch. Removal of the physical distance between the entertainer and decent folk always causes, however great one's pleasure has been, a certain embarrassment. He sensed this, and sought to make amends by cringing. He approached Aschenbach, and with him came the smell, which no one else in the company appeared to have noticed.

"Listen to me!" said the solitary traveler in an undertone and al-most mechanically. "Venice is being disinfected. Why?" — The come-dian answered hoarsely: "Because of the police! It's the regulations, signore, when it's so hot and when there's sirocco. The sirocco is op-pressive. It is not good for the health . . ." He spoke in a tone of sur-prise that such a question could be asked, and demonstrated, with his outspread hand how oppressive the sirocco was. — "So there is no sickness in Venice?" asked Aschenbach very softly and between his teeth. — The clown's muscular features collapsed into a grimace of comic helplessness. "A sickness? But what sickness? Is the sirocco a sickness? Is our police a sickness perhaps? The signore is having his lit-tle joke! A sickness! Certainly not, signore! A preventive measure, you must understand, a police precaution against the effects of the oppres-sive weather . . . " He gesticulated. "Very well," said Aschenbach briefly, still without raising his voice, and quickly dropped an unduly large coin into the fellow's hat. Then he motioned him with his eyes to clear off. The man obeyed, grinning and bowing low. But he had not even reached the steps when two hotel servants bore down on him, and with their faces close to his subjected him to a whispered cross examination. He shrugged, gave assurances, swore that he had been discreet; it was obvious. Released, he returned to the garden, and after a brief consultation with his colleagues under the arc lamp he came forward once more, to express his thanks in a parting number.

It was a song that Aschenbach could not remember ever having heard before; a bold hit in an unintelligible dialect, and having a laughing refrain in which the rest of the band regularly and loudly joined. At this point both the words and the instrumental accompaniment stopped, and nothing remained except a burst of laughter, to some extent rhythmically ordered but treated with a high degree of naturalism, the soloist in particular showing great talent in his lifelike rendering of it. With artistic distance restored between himself and the spectators, he had recovered all his impudence, and the simulated laughter which he shamelessly directed at the terrace was a laughter of mockery. Even before the end of the articulated part of each stanza he would pretend to be struggling with an irresistible impulse of hilarity. He would sob, his voice would waver, he would press his hand against his mouth and hunch his shoulders, till at the proper moment the laughter would burst out of him, exploding in a wild howl, with such authenticity that it was infectious and communicated itself to the audience, so that a wave of objectless and merely self-propagating merriment swept over the terrace as well. And precisely this seemed to redouble the singer's exuberance. He bent his knees, slapped his thighs, held his sides, he nearly burst with what was now no longer laughing but shrieking; he pointed his finger up at the guests, as if that laughing company above him were itself the most comical thing in the world, and in the end they were all laughing, everyone in the garden and on the verandah, the waiters and the lift boys and the house servants in the doorways.

Aschenbach reclined in his chair no longer, he was sitting bolt upright as if trying to fend off an attack or flee from it. But the laughter, the hospital smell drifting toward him, and the nearness of the beautiful boy, all mingled for him into an immobilizing nightmare, an unbreakable and inescapable spell that held his mind and senses captive. In the general commotion and distraction he ventured to steal a glance at Tadzio, and as he did so he became aware that the boy, returning his glance, had remained no less serious than himself, just as if he were regulating his attitude and expression by those of the older man, and as if the general mood had no power over him while Aschenbach kept aloof from it. There was something so disarming and overwhelmingly moving about this childlike submissiveness, so rich in meaning, that the gray-haired lover could only with difficulty restrain himself from burying his face in his hands. He had also had the impression that the way Tadzio from time to time drew himself up with an intake of breath was like a kind of sighing, as if from a constriction of the chest.

"He's sickly, he'll probably not live long," he thought again, with that sober objectivity into which the drunken ecstasy of desire sometimes strangely escapes; and his heart was filled at one and the same time with pure concern on the boy's behalf and with a certain wild satisfaction.

In the meantime the troupe of Venetians had finished their performance and were leaving. Applause accompanied them, and their leader took care to embellish even his exit with comical pranks. His bowing and scraping and hand-kissing amused the company, and so he redoubled them. When his companions were already outside, he put on yet another act of running backward and painfully colliding with a lamppost, then hobbling to the gate apparently doubled up in agony. When he got there however, he suddenly discarded the mask of comic underdog, uncoiled like a spring to his full height, insolently stuck out his tongue at the hotel guests on the terrace and slipped away into the darkness. The company was dispersing; Tadzio had left the balustrade some time ago. But the solitary Aschenbach, to the annoyance of the waiters, sat on and on at his little table over his unfinished pomegranate drink. The night was advancing, time was ebbing away. In his parents' house, many years ago, there had been an hourglass — he suddenly saw that fragile symbolic little instrument as clearly as if it were standing before him. Silently, subtly, the rust-red sand trickled through the narrow glass aperture, dwindling away out of the upper vessel, in which a little whirling vortex had formed.

On the very next day, in the afternoon, Aschenbach took a further step in his persistent probing of the outside world, and this time his success was complete. What he did was to enter the British travel agency just off the Piazza San Marco, and after changing some money at the cash desk, he put on the look of a suspicious foreigner and addressed his embarrassing question to the clerk who had served him. The clerk was a tweed-clad Englishman, still young, with his hair parted in the middle, his eyes close set, and having that sober, honest demeanor which makes so unusual and striking an impression amid the glib knaveries of the south. "No cause for concern, sir," he began. "An administrative measure, nothing serious. They often issue directives of this kind, as a precaution against the unhealthy effects of the heat and the sirocco . . ." But raising his blue eyes he met those of the stranger, which were looking wearily and rather sadly at his lips, with an expression of slight contempt. At this the Englishman colored. "That is," he continued in an undertone and with some feeling, "the official explanation, which the authorities here see fit to stick to. I can tell you that there is rather more to it than that." And then, in his straightforward comfortable language, he told Aschenbach the truth.

For several years now, Asiatic cholera had been showing an increased tendency to spread and migrate. Originating in the sultry morasses of the Ganges delta, rising with the mephitic exhalations of that wilderness of rank useless luxuriance, that primitive island jungle shunned by man, where tigers crouch in the bamboo thickets, the pestilence had raged with unusual and prolonged virulence all over northern India; it had struck eastward into China, westward into Afghanistan and Persia, and following the main caravan routes, it had borne its terrors to Astrakhan and even to Moscow. But while Europe trembled with apprehension that from there the specter might advance and arrive by land, it had been brought by Syrian traders over the sea; it had appeared almost simultaneously in several Mediterranean ports, raising its head in Toulon and Malaga, showing its face repeatedly in Palermo and Naples, and taking a seemingly permanent hold all over Calabria and Apulia. The northern half of the peninsula had still been spared. But in the middle of May this year, in Venice, the dreadful comma-bacilli had been found on one and the same day in the emaciated and blackened corpses of a ship's hand and of a woman who sold greengroceries. The two cases were hushed up. But a week later there were ten, there were twenty and then thirty, and they occurred in different quarters of the city. A man from a small provincial town in Austria who had been taking a few days' holiday in Venice died with unmistakable symptoms after returning home, and that was why the first rumors of a Venetian outbreak had appeared in German newspapers. The city authorities replied with a statement that the public health situation in Venice had never been better, and at the same time adopted the most necessary preventive measures. But the taint had probably now passed into foodstuffs, into vegetables or meat or milk; for despite every denial and concealment, the mortal sickness went on eating its way through the narrow little streets, and with the premature summer heat warming the water in the canals, conditions for the spread of infection were particularly favorable. It even seemed as if the pestilence had undergone a renewal of its energy, as if the tenacity and fertility of its pathogens had redoubled. Cases of recovery were rare; eighty percent of the victims died, and they died in a horrible manner, for the sickness presented itself in an extremely acute form and was frequently of the so-called "dry" type, which is the most dangerous of all. In this condition the body could not even evacuate the massive fluid lost from the blood-vessels. Within a few hours the patient would become dehydrated, his blood would thicken like pitch and he would suffocate with convulsions and hoarse cries. He was lucky if, as sometimes happened, the disease took the form of a slight malaise followed by a deep coma from which one never, or scarcely at all, regained consciousness. By the beginning of June the isolation wards in the Ospedale Civile were quietly filling, the two orphanages were running out of accommodation, and there was a gruesomely brisk traffic between the quayside of the Fondamente Nuove and the cemetery island of San Michele. But fear of general detriment to the city, concern for the recently opened art exhibition in the Public Gardens, consideration of the appalling losses which panic and disrepute would inflict on the hotels, on the shops, on the whole nexus of the tourist trade, proved stronger in Venice than respect for the truth and for international agreements; it was for this reason that the city authorities obstinately adhered to their policy of concealment and denial. The city's chief medical officer, a man of high repute, had resigned from his post in indignation and had been quietly replaced by a more pliable personality. This had become public knowledge; and such corruption in high places, combined with the prevailing insecurity, the state of crisis into which the city had been plunged by the death that walked its streets, led at the lower social levels to a certain breakdown of moral standards, to an activation of the dark and antisocial forces, which manifested itself in intemperance, shameless license and growing criminality. Drunkenness in the evenings became noticeably more frequent; thieves and ruffians, it was said, were making the streets unsafe at night; there were repeated robberies and even murders, for it had already twice come to light that persons alleged to have died of the plague had in fact been poisoned by their own relatives; and commercial vice now took on obtrusive and extravagant forms which had hitherto been unknown in this area and indigenous only to southern Italy or oriental countries.

The Englishman's narrative conveyed the substance of all this to Aschenbach. "You would be well advised, sir," he concluded, "to leave today rather than tomorrow. The imposition of quarantine can be expected any day now." — "Thank you," said Aschenbach, and left the office.

The Piazza was sunless and sultry. Unsuspecting foreigners were sitting at the cafés, or standing in front of the church with pigeons completely enveloping them, watching the birds swarm and beat their wings and push each other out of the way as they snatched with their beaks at the hollow hands offering them grains of maize. Feverish with excitement, triumphant in his possession of the truth, yet with a taste

of disgust on his tongue and a fantastic horror in his heart, the solitary
traveler paced up and down the flagstones of the magnificent precinct.
He was considering a decent action which would cleanse his conscience. Tonight, after dinner, he might approach the lady in the pearls
and address her with words which he now mentally rehearsed:
"Madam, allow me as a complete stranger to do you a service, to warn
you of something which is being concealed from you for reasons of
self-interest. Leave here at once with Tadzio and your daughters!
Venice is plague-stricken." He might then lay his hand in farewell on
the head of a mocking deity's instrument, turn away and flee from this
quagmire. But at the same time he sensed an infinite distance between
himself and any serious resolve to take such a step. It would lead him
back to where he had been, give him back to himself again; but to
one who is beside himself, no prospect is so distasteful as that of self-
recovery. He remembered a white building adorned with inscriptions
that glinted in the evening light, suffused with mystic meaning in
which his mind had wandered; remembered then that strange itinerant
figure who had wakened in him, in his middle age, a young man's
longing to rove to far-off and strange places; and the thought of returning home, of levelheadedness and sobriety, of toil and mastery,
filled him with such repugnance that his face twisted into an expression of physical nausea. "They want it kept quiet!" he whispered vehe-
mently. And: "I shall say nothing!" The consciousness of his complicity in the secret, of his share in the guilt, intoxicated him as small
quantities of wine intoxicate a weary brain. The image of the stricken
and disordered city, hovering wildly before his mind's eye, inflamed
him with hopes that were beyond comprehension, beyond reason and
full of monstrous sweetness. What, compared with such expectations,
was that tender happiness of which he had briefly dreamed a few moments ago? What could art and virtue mean to him now, when he
might reap the advantages of chaos? He said nothing, and stayed on.

That night he had a terrible dream, if dream is the right word for a
bodily and mental experience which did indeed overtake him during
deepest sleep, in complete independence of his will and with complete
sensuous vividness, but with no perception of himself as present and
moving about in any space external to the events themselves; rather,
the scene of the events was his own soul, and they irrupted into it from
outside, violently defeating his resistance — a profound, intellectual
resistance — as they passed through him, and leaving his whole being,
the culture of a lifetime, devastated and destroyed.

It began with fear, fear and joy and a horrified curiosity about what was to come. It was night, and his senses were alert; for from far off a hubbub was approaching, an uproar, a compendium of noise, a clangor and blare and dull thundering, yells of exultation and a particular howl with a long-drawn-out *u* at the end — all of it permeated and dominated by a terrible sweet sound of flute music: by deep-warbling, infamously persistent, shamelessly clinging tones that bewitched the innermost heart. Yet he was aware of a word, an obscure word, but one that gave a name to what was coming; *"the stranger-god!"* There was a glow of smoky fire: in it he could see a mountain landscape, like the mountains round his summer home. And in fragmented light, from wooded heights, between tree trunks and mossy boulders, it came tumbling and whirling down: a human and animal swarm, a raging rout, flooding the slope with bodies, with flames, with tumult and frenzied dancing. Women, stumbling on the hide garments that fell too far about them from the waist, held up tambourines and moaned as they shook them above their thrown-back heads; they swung blazing torches, scattering the sparks, and brandished naked daggers; they carried snakes with flickering tongues which they had seized in the middle of the body, or they bore up their own breasts in both hands, shrieking as they did so. Men with horns over their brows, hairy-skinned and girdled with pelts, bowed their necks and threw up their arms and thighs, clanging brazen cymbals and beating a furious tattoo on drums, while smooth-skinned boys prodded goats with leafy staves, clinging to their horns and yelling with delight as the leaping beasts dragged them along. And the god's enthusiasts howled out the cry with the soft consonants and long-drawn-out final *u*, sweet and wild both at once, like no cry that was ever heard: here it was raised, belled out into the air as by rutting stags, and there they threw it back with many voices, in ribald triumph, urging each other on with it to dancing and tossing of limbs, and never did it cease. But the deep, enticing flute music mingled irresistibly with everything. Was it not also enticing him, the dreamer who experienced all this while struggling not to, enticing him with shameless insistence to the feast and frenzy of the uttermost surrender? Great was his loathing, great his fear, honorable his effort of will to defend to the last what was his and protect it against the Stranger, against the enemy of the composed and dignified intellect. But the noise, the howling grew louder, with the echoing cliffs reiterating it: it increased beyond measure, swelled up to an enrapturing madness. Odors besieged the mind, the pungent reek of the

goats, the scent of panting bodies and an exhalation as of staling waters, with another smell, too, that was familiar: that of wounds and
wandering disease. His heart throbbed to the drumbeats, his brain
whirled, a fury seized him, a blindness, a dizzying lust, and his soul
craved to join the round-dance of the god. The obscene symbol,
wooden and gigantic, was uncovered and raised on high: and still
more unbridled grew the howling of the rallying-cry. With foaming
mouths they raged, they roused each other with lewd gestures and li-
centious hands, laughing and moaning they thrust the prods into each
other's flesh and licked the blood from each other's limbs. But the
dreamer now was with them and in them, he belonged to the Stranger-
God. Yes, they were himself as they flung themselves, tearing and slay-
ing, on the animals and devoured steaming gobbets of flesh, they were
himself as an orgy of limitless coupling, in homage to the god, began
on the trampled, mossy ground. And his very soul savored the lascivi-
ous delirium of annihilation.

  Out of this dream the stricken man woke unnerved, shattered and
powerlessly enslaved to the daemon-god. He no longer feared the observant eyes of other people; whether he was exposing himself to their
suspicions he no longer cared. In any case they were running away,
leaving Venice; many of the bathing cabins were empty now, there
were great gaps in the clientele at dinner, and in the city one scarcely
saw any foreigners. The truth seemed to have leaked out, and however
tightly the interested parties closed ranks, panic could no longer be
stemmed. But the lady in the pearls stayed on with her family, either
because the rumors were not reaching her or because she was too
proud and fearless to heed them. Tadzio stayed on; and to Aschenbach, in his beleaguered state, it sometimes seemed that all these un-
wanted people all round him might flee from the place or die, that
every living being might disappear and leave him alone on this island
with the beautiful boy — indeed, as he sat every morning by the sea
with his gaze resting heavily, recklessly, incessantly on the object of his
desire, or as he continued his undignified pursuit of him in the
evenings along streets in which the disgusting mortal malady wound
its underground way, then indeed monstrous things seemed full of
promise to him, and the moral law no longer valid.

  Like any other lover, he desired to please and bitterly dreaded that he
might fail to do so. He added brightening and rejuvenating touches to
his clothes, he wore jewelery and used scent, he devoted long sessions to
his toilet several times a day, arriving at table elaborately attired and full
of excited expectation. As he beheld the sweet youthful creature who

had so entranced him he felt disgust at his own aging body, the sight of his gray hair and sharp features filled him with a sense of shame and hopelessness. He felt a compulsive need to refresh and restore himself physically; he paid frequent visits to the hotel barber.

Cloaked in a hairdressing gown, leaning back in the chair as the chatterer's hands tended him, he stared in dismay at his reflection in the looking glass.

"Gray," he remarked with a wry grimace.

"A little," the man replied. "And the reason? A slight neglect, a slight lack of interest in outward appearances, very understandable in persons of distinction, but not altogether to be commended, especially as one would expect those very persons to be free from prejudice about such matters as the natural and the artificial. If certain people who profess moral disapproval of cosmetics were to be logical enough to extend such rigorous principles to their teeth, the result would be rather disgusting. After all, we are only as old as we feel in our minds and hearts, and sometimes gray hair is actually further from the truth than the despised corrective would be. In your case, signore, one has a right to the natural color of one's hair. Will you permit me simply to give your color back to you?"

"How so?" asked Aschenbach.

Whereupon the eloquent tempter washed his client's hair in two kinds of water, one clear and one dark; and his hair was as black as when he had been young. Then he folded it into soft waves with the curling tongs, stepped back and surveyed his handiwork.

"Now the only other thing," he said, "would be just to freshen up the signore's complexion a little."

And like a craftsman unable to finish, unable to satisfy himself, he passed busily and indefatigably from one procedure to another. Aschenbach, reclining comfortably, incapable of resistance, filled rather with exciting hopes by what was happening, gazed at the glass and saw his eyebrows arched more clearly and evenly, the shape of his eyes lengthened, their brightness enhanced by a slight underlining of the lids; saw below them a delicate carmine come to life as it was softly applied to skin that had been brown and leathery; saw his lips that had just been so pallid now burgeoning cherry-red; saw the furrows on his cheeks, round his mouth, the wrinkles by his eyes, all vanishing under face cream and an aura of youth — with beating heart he saw himself as a young man in his earliest bloom. The cosmetician finally declared himself satisfied, with the groveling politeness usual in such people, by profusely thanking the client he had served. "An insignificant adjust-

ment, signore," he said as he gave a final helping hand to Aschenbach's outward appearance. "Now the signore can fall in love as soon
as he pleases." And the spellbound lover departed, confused and timo-
rous but happy as in a dream. His necktie was scarlet, his broad-
brimmed straw hat encircled with a many-colored ribbon.

A warm gale had blown up; it rained little and lightly, but the air
was humid and thick and filled with smells of decay. The ear was beset
with fluttering, flapping and whistling noises, and to the fevered devotee, sweating under his makeup, it seemed that a vile race of wind
demons was disporting itself in the sky, malignant sea birds that churn
up and gnaw and befoul a condemned man's food. For the sultry
weather was taking away his appetite, and he could not put aside the
thought that what he ate might be tainted with infection.

One afternoon, dogging Tadzio's footsteps, Aschenbach had
plunged into the confused network of streets in the depths of the sick
city. Quite losing his bearings in this labyrinth of alleys, narrow water-
ways, bridges and little squares that all looked so much like each other,
not sure now even of the points of the compass, he was intent above
all on not losing sight of the vision he so passionately pursued. Ignominious caution forced him to flatten himself against walls and hide
behind the backs of people walking in front of him; and for a long
time he was not conscious of the weariness, the exhaustion that emotion and constant tension had inflicted on his body and mind. Tadzio
walked behind his family; he usually gave precedence in narrow passages to his attendant and his nunlike sisters, and as he strolled along
by himself he sometimes turned his head and glanced over his shoulder with his strange twilight-gray eyes, to ascertain that his lover was
still following him. He saw him, and did not give him away. Drunk
with excitement as he realized this, lured onward by those eyes, helpless in the leading strings of his mad desire, the infatuated Aschenbach
stole upon the trail of his unseemly hope — only to find it vanish from
his sight in the end. The Poles had crossed a little humpbacked bridge;
the height of the arch hid them from their pursuer, and when in his
turn he reached the top of it, they were no longer to be seen. He
looked frantically for them in three directions, straight ahead and to
left and right along the narrow, dirty canal-side, but in vain. Unnerved
and weakened, he was compelled to abandon his search.

His head was burning, his body was covered with sticky sweat, his
neck quivered, a no longer endurable thirst tormented him; he looked
round for something, no matter what, that would instantly relieve it.
At a little greengrocer's shop he bought some fruit, some overripe soft

strawberries, and ate some of them as he walked. A little square, one that seemed to have been abandoned, to have been put under a spell, opened up in front of him: he recognized it, he had been here, it was where he had made that vain decision weeks ago to leave Venice. On the steps of the well in its center he sank down and leaned his head against the stone rim. The place was silent, grass grew between the cobblestones, garbage was lying about. Among the dilapidated houses of uneven height all round him there was one that looked like a *palazzo*, with Gothic windows that now had nothing behind them, and little lion balconies. On the ground floor of another there was a chemist's shop. From time to time warm gusts of wind blew the stench of carbolic across to him.

There he sat, the master, the artist who had achieved dignity, the author of *A Study in Abjection,* he who in such paradigmatically pure form had repudiated intellectual vagrancy and the murky depths, who had proclaimed his renunciation of all sympathy with the abyss, who had weighed vileness in the balance and found it wanting; he who had risen so high, who had set his face against his own sophistication, grown out of all his irony, and taken on the commitments of one whom the public trusted; he, whose fame was official, whose name had been ennobled, and on whose style young boys were taught to model their own — there he sat, with his eyelids closed, with only an occasional mocking and rueful sideways glance from under them which he hid again at once; and his drooping, cosmetically brightened lips shaped the occasional word of the discourse his brain was delivering, his half-asleep brain with its tissue of strange dream-logic.

"For Beauty, Phaedrus, mark well! only Beauty is at one and the same time divine and visible, and so it is indeed the sensuous lover's path, little Phaedrus, it is the artist's path to the spirit. But do you believe, dear boy, that the man whose path to the spiritual passes through the senses can ever achieve wisdom and true manly dignity? Or do you think (I leave it to you to decide) that this is a path of dangerous charm, very much an errant and sinful path which must of necessity lead us astray? For I must tell you that we artists cannot tread the path of Beauty without Eros keeping company with us and appointing himself as our guide; yes, though we may be heroes in our fashion and disciplined warriors, yet we are like women, for it is passion that exalts us, and the longing of our soul must remain the longing of a lover — that is our joy and our shame. Do you see now perhaps why we writers can be neither wise nor dignified? That we necessarily go astray, necessarily remain dissolute emotional adventur-

ers? The magisterial poise of our style is a lie and a farce, our fame and
social position are an absurdity, the public's faith in us is altogether
ridiculous, the use of art to educate the nation and its youth is a reprehensible undertaking which should be forbidden by law. For how can
one be fit to be an educator when one has been born with an incorrigible and natural tendency toward the abyss? We try to achieve dignity
by repudiating that abyss, but whichever way we turn we are subject to
its allurement. We renounce, let us say, the corrosive process of knowledge — for knowledge, Phaedrus, has neither dignity nor rigor: it is all
insight and understanding and tolerance, uncontrolled and formless; it
sympathizes with the abyss, it *is* the abyss. And so we reject it res-
olutely, and henceforth our pursuit is of Beauty alone, of Beauty which
is simplicity, which is grandeur and a new kind of rigor and a second
naiveté, of Beauty which is Form. But form and naiveté, Phaedrus,
lead to intoxication and lust; they may lead a noble mind into terrible
criminal emotions, which his own fine rigor condemns as infamous;
they lead, they too lead, to the abyss. I tell you, that is where they lead
us writers; for we are not capable of self-exaltation, we are merely capable of self-debauchery. And now I shall go, Phaedrus, and you shall
stay here; and leave this place only when you no longer see me."

A few days later Gustav von Aschenbach, who had been feeling un-
well, left the Hotel des Bains at a later morning hour than usual. He was
being attacked by waves of dizziness, only half physical, and with them
went an increasing sense of dread, a feeling of hopelessness and point-
lessness, though he could not decide whether this referred to the external world or to his personal existence. In the foyer he saw a large quan-
tity of luggage standing ready for dispatch, asked one of the doormen
which guests were leaving, and was given in reply the aristocratic Polish
name which he had inwardly been expecting to hear. As he received the
information there was no change in his ravaged features, only that slight
lift of the head with which one casually notes something one did not
need to know. He merely added the question: "When?" and was told:
"After lunch." He nodded and went down to the sea.

It was a bleak spectacle there. Tremors gusted outward across the
water between the beach and the first long sandbar, wrinkling its wide
flat surface. An autumnal, out-of-season air seemed to hang over the
once so colorful and populous resort, now almost deserted, with litter
left lying about on the sand. An apparently abandoned camera stood
on its tripod at the edge of the sea, and the black cloth over it fluttered
and flapped in the freshening breeze.

Tadzio, with the three or four playmates he still had, was walking about on the right in front of his family's bathing cabin; and reclining in his deck chair with a rug over his knees, about midway between the sea and the row of cabins, Aschenbach once more sat watching him. The boys' play was unsupervised, as the women were probably busy with travel preparations; it seemed to be unruly and degenerating into roughness. The sturdy boy he had noticed before, the one in the belted suit with glossy black hair who was addressed as "Jashu," had been angered and blinded by some sand thrown into his face: he forced Tadzio to a wrestling match, which soon ended in the downfall of the less muscular beauty. But as if in this hour of leave-taking the submissiveness of the lesser partner had been transformed into cruel brutality, as if he were now bent on revenge for his long servitude, the victor did not release his defeated friend even then, but knelt on his back and pressed his face into the sand so hard and so long that Tadzio, breathless from the fight in any case, seemed to be on the point of suffocation. His attempts to shake off the weight of his tormentor were convulsive; they stopped altogether for moments on end and became a mere repeated twitching. Appalled, Aschenbach was about to spring to the rescue when the bully finally released his victim. Tadzio, very pale, sat up and went on sitting motionless for some minutes, propped on one arm, his hair tousled and his eyes darkening. Then he stood right up and walked slowly away. His friends called to him, laughingly at first, then anxiously and pleadingly; he took no notice. The dark-haired boy, who had no doubt been seized at once by remorse at having gone so far, ran after him and tried to make up the quarrel. A jerk of Tadzio's shoulder rejected him. Tadzio walked on at an angle down to the water. He was barefooted and wearing his striped linen costume with the red bow.

At the edge of the sea he lingered, head bowed, drawing figures in the wet sand with the point of one foot, then walked into the shallow high water, which at its deepest point did not even wet his knees; he waded through it, advancing easily, and reached the sandbar. There he stood for a moment looking out into the distance and then, moving left, began slowly to pace the length of this narrow strip of unsubmerged land. Divided from the shore by a width of water, divided from his companions by proud caprice, he walked, a quite isolated and unrelated apparition, walked with floating hair out there in the sea, in the wind, in front of the nebulous vastness. Once more he stopped to survey the scene. And suddenly, as if prompted by a memory, by an impulse, he turned at the waist, one hand on his hip, with an enchanting twist of the body, and looked back over his shoulder at the beach. There the watcher sat, as he had sat once before when those twilight-gray eyes, looking back at him then from that other threshold, had for the first time met his. Resting his head on the back of his chair, he had slowly turned it to follow the movements of the walking figure in the distance; now he lifted it toward this last look; then it sank down on his breast, so that his eyes stared up from below, while his face wore the inert, deep-sunken expression of profound slumber. But to him it was as if the pale and lovely soul-summoner out there were smiling to him, beckoning to him; as if he loosed his hand from his hip and pointed outward, hovering ahead and onward, into an immensity rich with unutterable expectation. And as so often, he set out to follow him.

Minutes passed, after he had collapsed sideways in his chair, before anyone hurried to his assistance. He was carried to his room. And later that same day the world was respectfully shocked to receive the news of his death.

PART TWO

Death in Venice:
A Case Study in
Contemporary Criticism

A Critical History
of *Death in Venice*

CONTEMPORARY CRITICISM

When *Death in Venice* appeared in two segments in the October and November 1912 issues of the literary magazine *Die Neue Rundschau*, it prompted some predictable controversy. Mann expected that the book would probably offend both moralistic critics, who would condemn any literary depiction of homoerotic love, and homosexuals themselves, who would object to the book's ultimately negative view of Aschenbach. Indeed, the well-known gay poet Stefan George (1868–1933) could not accept the story's association of sexual love between men with disease. Here indeed lies a characteristic idea for Mann, whose later essay "On Marriage" (1925) paraphrased the link that *Death in Venice* makes between homosexuality and death: "Virtue and morality are the stuff of life, nothing other than a categorical imperative, the command to live — while all aestheticism is of a pessimistic-orgiastic nature, in short: the stuff of death. That all artistry is susceptible to such an abyss is all too certain."

In this essay, Mann equated "virtue and morality" with heterosexual marriage, and "aestheticism" with homosexual artists. He seemed to see in gay love only a narcissistic death wish. Yet, confusingly enough, he also insisted in his diaries that *his* particular "abstract" homoerotic desire represented a healthier instinct than his far more

powerful drive for a bourgeois family. However, regardless of how
Mann judged sexual love between men, the criticism of this story has
assumed just what George decried: its implicit equating of homosexuality with death.

Predictable attacks came from conservative critics. A personal critique of Mann himself appeared in the respected Berlin newspaper
Pan, as its literary critic Alfred Kerr had long nursed a petty personal
hostility toward Mann. Kerr carped that Mann was still writing about
poets, although he himself was a mere writer. (Many intellectual Germans, including Mann himself, considered lyric poetry the ultimate literary genre and prose an inferior form.) More significantly, Kerr
claimed that the novella had made gay love acceptable to middle-class
readers. Such puritanical reactions dogged the work right up to
Mann's death, for in 1954 the journalist Jürgen Ernestus called it
"perverted" and "irresponsible." Mann countered that the story could
not be immoral, for it represented "a confession, the product of a
thinking conscience and a pessimistic love of truth" (Reed 1994, 18).
He meant that his morally honest portrait of the repressed homosexual
artist transcends any supposed authorial defense of that artist. Interestingly, no critic has explored the clearly autobiographical meaning of
this "confession" until recently.

Early negative reviewers focused on the work's two most obvious
aspects: its "decadent" subject and its architectonic style. Some formalist critics admired the acutely analytic prose but stressed its
Flaubertian ironic coldness. Others decried the mere presentation of
an acclaimed national artist as a repressed and finally pitiable homosexual. Surprisingly, D. H. Lawrence covered both these negative reactions in a review of 1913. He saw Mann as "a last too-sick disciple of
Flaubert in his derivative treatment of the conflict between life and
art." Generally, too, Lawrence found that Mann's style suffered from
the typically German "craving for form." He called the style lifeless:
"Even while [Mann] has a rhythm in style, . . . yet his work has
none of the rhythm of a living thing" (Vaget 1984, 195). As for the
work's content, Lawrence called it "unwholesome"; quite a paradoxical reaction from one whose own work received similar prudish objec-
tions.

Lawrence's critique of the text's lifelessness recalls an old argument
in German criticism inspired by the dichtomy between "art" and "life"
posited by Friedrich Schiller (1759–1805). In his classic essay *Über
Naïve und Sentimentalische Dichtung (About Naïve and Reflective Poetry,* 1795), Schiller characterized himself as the cerebral, brooding

type of artist — the type we call Romantic — and his fellow poet Johann Wolfgang von Goethe (1749–1832) as the naive, untroubled type we call classic. Schiller claimed that Goethe, like the Greeks, lived and wrote spontaneously, out of his closeness to ordinary experience. By contrast, Schiller found that his own work sprang from mental detachment, what we would call an alienation from nature, both human and physical. Accordingly, German criticism has long drawn on this basic polarity between art and life. And because much of Mann's work assumes this opposition, discussions of how he treats it are staple fare in most Mann criticism.

Positive reviews of *Death in Venice* also came quickly. Oswald Bruell called Mann "the German Flaubert," in regard to both the text's self-critical overlay of autobiography on fiction and its exquisitely polished language. Bruell anticipates two major strands of criticism that later developed around the novella: namely, the exploration of psychological or psychoanalytic ties between Mann and Aschenbach and an analysis of Mann's meticulously crafted, rhythmic prose.

A third important strand pursued by contemporary reviewers concerns the story's veiled reference to its political background, Europe on the eve of World War I. Indeed, the most significant prewar criticism discusses the story's implicit foreshadowing of political crisis. Early reviewers saw that Aschenbach's fated death pointed to the equally inevitable demise of Kaiser Wilhelm's — actually Otto von Bismarck's — Prussian empire. Heinrich Mann, Thomas's older brother and another writer, compared the novella's hints at the corrupt empire's collapse with those in Émile Zola's novels of the 1860s, which heralded the end of the French empire.

Another influential critic, Ernst Heilborn, aptly titled his review "An Orgy of Dying," for he coupled the specific gradual process of Aschenbach's decline with Venice's parallel agony of cholera. Heilborn's metaphoric reading of personal death as an expression of ruinous social forces reflects the consciousness of a nation facing war. And when war broke out, even soldiers at the front found in Aschenbach's life an inspiring heroic struggle against death. Reporting information from the Berlin military office that distributed books at the front, Franz Leppmann claimed that soldiers read the story "with mounting awe." Now we find Aschenbach hardly worthy of such a reception, but obviously historical conditions allowed readers to take from the work just the message they needed.

In the "overripeness" surrounding Aschenbach — think of those strawberries that infected him — Anton Kuh saw a climactic anticipation of "the first thunderclap of war": Here lies "the turning point in German literature between peace and war." In this sociopolitical context, Mann told a friend in 1919, "a nation in which such a novella was not only written but also acclaimed perhaps needs a war." Such ominous views were not unusual before the war, for many European intellectuals believed that the decadent culture they inherited from the fin-de-siècle needed a violent purging. Later the political reading of *Death in Venice* became broadly cultural; in 1971 the Hungarian Marxist literary critic Georg Lukács claimed that *Death in Venice* had prepared "a tragically ironic downfall" for "the Prussian ethos" (Harpprecht 349).

The sum of about forty contemporary reviews is largely appreciative, with only five clearly negative. The reasons for both types of reception tell us much — not only about the book itself but also about the aesthetic and cultural values of the era. For instance, the prewar critics praised mainly the story's stylistic perfection. Such a focus on formal concerns encouraged readers to overlook the story's psychosexual core. But it also bespeaks the formalism that had characterized one strand of German literary criticism since the nineteenth century. Moreover, the reviewers' obvious susceptibility to the neoclassical aura that Mann invoked reveals their wish to root the new century's literature in Germany's own classical tradition of Goethe: perhaps a sign of their resistance to inevitable impending changes.

The prewar critics also show an interest typical of the time in admiring Mann's masterful psychological study of the acclaimed yet inwardly vulnerable author. Without the background of Sigmund Freud's psychoanalytic theory, itself an outgrowth of positivist and naturalist ideas of psychological determination, they would probably have shown less sensitivity to Aschenbach as conditioned by cultural factors. For instance, Eduard Korrodi praised Mann's poignant portrait of the suffering artist as "a holy St Sebastian of art" (Vaget 1984, 192). Such an analysis captures well Mann's own view of the famous writer condemned by his self-denial. Kurt Martens even combined the excellence of the work's formal and psychological aspects to portray Mann's achievement as heroic: "Here for the first time Mann conquered a mountainous challenge, just the type of task that only he would set himself and accomplish brilliantly. And what did he create? Psychology as literature, the recognition of a subjective peculiarity as an objective portrait of the soul" (Vaget 1984, 192; my translations).

Mann's own authorial persona also colored some of the work's early reception. In his characteristically autocratic manner, he constantly tried, with some success, to manipulate the novella's reviews. His letters and diaries show that, particularly in the years right after publication, he tracked criticism with a determination bordering on paranoia. He expressed bitter rancor at negative reviews; for positive ones he often thanked the critic personally. Sometimes he tried to influence the story's reception by supplying critics with his own interpretation.

POSTWAR CRITICISM

Only in the 1930s did the literature on Mann develop significantly. From this point onward we may categorize seven broad areas of study in the major reception: (1) the links to Greek myth and culture, (2) the historical/political aspect, (3) influence study, (4) style (language, structure, tone — featuring irony and parody — and narratology), (5) major themes, (6) comparison to other authors' works, and (7) psychology/psychoanalysis. A massive body of scholarship has developed from these seven fields, but perhaps the most steadily fruitful has been the psychological analysis of Aschenbach as an artist, as a product and victim of his North German culture, and as a repressed homosexual. The newer critical approaches, particularly new history and cultural criticism, explore manifold aspects of the society that both created and destroyed Aschenbach. As recently as 1984, the major Mann scholar Hans Rudolf Vaget claimed that interpreters pursuing sociohistorical approaches could do little with *Death in Venice*. So we see how significantly these new approaches have expanded the critical literature.

From Myth to Psychology

Because a chronological account of the major criticism will quickly lead us to the leading area, psychology, let us start with the first important review by Josef Hofmiller in 1913. His article in *Merkur*, exploring Mann's sources, demonstrated his huge intellectual debt to Greek mythology and culture. Hofmiller and several other contemporary and later critics formed a small school for tracing specific phrases in the text to passages in Homer, Virgil, and Plato. One of the most researched and discussed such phrases is the Latin one appearing in the story's first paragraph, *motus animi continuus,* "continuous motion of the spirit," which the narrator erroneously attributes to Cicero. The latest and most original interpretation of the phrase comes from

Robert Tobin, who reads it as referring to Aschenbach's sexual energy. Most of the scholars of Mann's classical sources showed that his portrait of Aschenbach as a neoclassical homosexual writer departed significantly from authentic Platonic/Socratic concepts of love and beauty. While the aura of Platonic Greek culture pervades the story, Mann's use of antique sources is anything but slavish.

In an acclaimed article of 1956, "Myth and Psychology: A Stylistic Analysis of *Death in Venice*," André von Gronicka discussed Mann's characteristic "bifocal vision," in which two dense layers of meaning — psychological and mythic — mutually nourish each other. In the realm of psychology, von Gronicka places the text's generally realistic rendering of daily experience, from Aschenbach's initial stroll to his death in a beach chair. Von Gronicka demonstrates Mann's uncanny gift for imbuing such quotidian events with deeply significant mythic echoes. For instance, the redheaded stranger in Munich is both an odd-looking tourist and the devil incarnate — a surreal harbinger of Aschenbach's fate. Similarly, Tadzio represents both a beautiful blond youth and the demigods Eros, Narcissus, Pan, and Hermes.

In 1965, Isadore Traschen's impressive article "The Uses of Myth in *Death in Venice*" showed crucial links between Mann's mythologizing and Aschenbach's psyche. Traschen noticed that Aschenbach's fateful journey to self-awareness closely parallels the anthropologist Joseph Campbell's account of the three-part "monomyth" of the hero's adventure. In his famous *The Hero with a Thousand Faces* (1949), Campbell traced the Greek mythological hero's quest through the phases of Departure, Initiation, and Return. In comparing this pattern to Aschenbach's adventure, we note immediately that he does not return. His ironically failed flight, marking the story's midpoint in chapter 3, seals his fate as an inevitable death in Venice. Hence Traschen reads Mann's treatment of the monomyth as thoroughly parodic.

A major example of such parody is Mann's treatment of the hero's Road of Trials, which begins the Initiation phase. Like Odysseus, Theseus, and Hercules, Aschenbach embarks on a voyage to the underworld; his trip starts when the menacing gondolier ferries him across the canal, just as the demigod Charon took the mythological figures across the Styx river into Hades. (In his *Aeneid*, Virgil portrays Charon as "squalid and malign," traits that reappear in Mann's boatman.) Traschen locates the parody in this scene in Aschenbach's uncharacteristic surrender to a threatening but pleasurable experience. By contrast, the classic heroes positively willed their initiation into the realm of death.

Traschen's explication of Mann's parodied use of the classical labyrinth image is also persuasive. Twice, when Aschenbach pursues Tadzio through the streets of Venice, Mann echoes the plight of Theseus, who "loses his bearings in the labyrinth — not merely geographically, but also morally and spiritually." Traschen cites Robert Graves's claim that in Crete and Egypt the labyrinth served as "'a maze pattern to guide performers of an erotic spring dance.' Thus Aschenbach's sterile pursuit of Tadzio parodies the fertility rite of the earlier cultures" (Bloom 95).

Like von Gronicka, Traschen excels at showing the story's parallels to mythic material. For instance, in Aschenbach's grudging wanderlust we find a half-conscious longing for the release of death, the "underlying uneasiness" of the mythic hero and his society. When Aschenbach sees the two sculpted "apocalyptic beasts" on the mortuary temple in Munich, he is subconsciously perceiving the "apocalyptic moment" that leads the mythic hero to moral rebirth. And the fawning barber, rejuvenating Aschenbach with his two hair rinses, is the classic shaman, performing "the fertility rites of death and rebirth."

Traschen's meticulous demonstrations of myth parodied, which he shows embedded in every stage of Aschenbach's demise, enrich the essay's thesis: namely, that Mann's story is "the first to use the mythic method as a way of giving shape and significance to contemporary history by manipulating a continuous parallel between contemporaneity and antiquity" (Bloom 88). As noted in the Introduction, James Joyce rendered a similar accomplishment with his parodied Icarus myth in *A Portrait of the Artist as a Young Man* (1916).

Manfred Dierks wrote the most influential study of Mann's sources in mythology and classical literature in his book of 1972, *Studien zu Mythos und Psychologie bei Thomas Mann (Studies of Myth and Psychology in the Works of Thomas Mann)*. The textual links that Dierks traced between passages in *Death in Venice* and Nietzsche's *Birth of Tragedy* offered more concrete evidence of Mann's debt to the philosopher than anyone had shown before. But Dierks's most original discovery lies in his comparison of parallel passages in Mann and Euripides' *Bacchae* (ca. 460 B.C.). By 1972, scholars already agreed that Nietzsche had guided Mann to this text, but only Dierks demonstrated that Mann must have used the antique text as an inevitably compelling thematic and structural model. A mere synopsis of that play's action shows a haunting mythic kinship to Mann's tale. Dionysus, attempting to establish his cult in Thebes, cannot tolerate the resistance of King Pentheus. As punishment, he drives all the women of the city into the mountains, where they become raving maenads. Dionysus himself, disguised as a beautiful boy, appears to warn Pentheus of his own worse fate. When Pentheus arrests Dionysus, he takes final revenge in destroying Thebes and driving the king mad. Fleeing in women's clothes, Pentheus must witness the cannibalistic mountain orgy of the maenads. Indeed, the women devour the king himself, and his own mother finally reveals herself as his murderer.

If we read Thebes as Prussian culture, its destruction as Venice's cholera, the disguised god as Tadzio, and Pentheus' destruction as Aschenbach's death, the parallels that Dierks draws are undeniable. Mann's debt to Euripides appears most clearly in Aschenbach's climactic dream orgy, but the more subversive sociopolitical link lies in both the play's and the story's ultimate cultural message. Both writers depict the gruesome demise of a revered figure whose behavior represents a society destined to perish. Because both Pentheus and Aschenbach refuse to admit the basic human need for passion, they condemn that very culture they represent. Dierks's thesis has directed research on the classic aspect of *Death in Venice* in fruitful ways, for scholars have continued to trace other text passages to the later Greek authors Xenophon and Plutarch. And expectably enough, Freudians have picked up on Dierks's implied metaphoric clue to Aschenbach's death in Euripides' use of the hero's mother as his cannibalistic murderer.

According to the inflential Freudian analyst Heinz Kohut, the story's four foreboding male death figures — the stranger in Munich, the old fop on the boat to Venice, the menacing gondolier, and the infected street singer — refer to Aschenbach's father. In his article "Thomas Manns *Tod in Venedig:* Zerfall einer kuenstlerischen Sublimierung" ("The Collapse of an Artistic Sublimation"), Kohut reads the work's essential meaning as an oedipal conflict. Namely, Aschenbach's sexual repression stems from a longing for sexual union with his father and a concomitant fear of his mother's competition for that love. The climactic expression of this urge and its accompanying anxiety appear in the Dionysian dream orgy. In this light, Aschenbach's symbolic mother — read repressive German morality — must thwart his homosexuality. When his sexuality finally asserts itself undeniably, his mother — read his conditioning culture — must destroy him.

Influences

German critics have pursued the approach of influence studies in tracing Mann's links to the German forebears he often named: Goethe,

Schopenhauer, Wagner, and Nietzsche. Most of the criticism in this field pertains to Goethe's stylistic example and Nietzsche's revolutionary view of classic culture as a struggle between Apollonian and Dionysian forces. The critics cited earlier — especially Traschen and Dierks — seem to have settled the matter of Mann's complex debt to Nietzsche, but there is less consensus on his relation to Goethe. In this regard, American readers must first recognize the weight of so-called Goethe consciousness in any German writer's mind — what Harold Bloom calls the oedipal anxiety of influence. (It may help to compare the significance of Shakespeare for English writers.) Critics discussing Mann and Goethe had to start with Mann's early statement that he had read Goethe's *Die Wahlverwandtschaften (Elective Affinities*, 1828) five times while writing *Death in Venice*. Looking for parallels to this unlikely inspiration — a densely problematic novel of a couple's mutual adultery — critics have focused wholly on Goethe's detached, Olympian narrative tone.

In his *Thomas Mann: Fiktion, Mythos, Religion (Fiction, Myth, Religion*, 1968), Herbert Lehnert traced one particular aspect of the Mann-Goethe link: the shared dependence of their fiction on their inner worlds and their environments. Lehnert's 1993 essay "Historischer Horizont und Fiktionalität in Thomas Manns *Der Tod in Venedig*" ("Historicity and Fictionality") treats the Mann-Goethe relation as a symptom of the German craving for a *Nationaldichter*, a permanent national poet laureate. The work of such a writer signifies a sort of psychological national profile, expressing a people's major intellectual, emotional, and moral concerns. Lehnert shows how Goethe's example inevitably conditioned the intricate interplay of Mann's inner and outer worlds: fiction and history.

Werner Frizen's "Fausts Tod in Venedig" ("Faust's Death in Venice") adds specific textual evidence to the Mann-Goethe link in drawing pervasive parallels between Goethe's hero and Aschenbach. Just one example of their kinship lies in Faust's famous complaint of Romantic ambivalence: "Two souls inhabit me / which want to split apart." Frizen claims that for both men, such duality is essentially fruitful; they must constantly learn to perceive this conflict as the source of their richest life.

The Political Dimension

The most strictly political view of Mann's work appears in the Marxist treatment of Mann by Georg Lukács. This influential critic saw *Death in Venice* as Mann's self-condemnation and prophesy of the imminent collapse of Bismarck's regime. In his *Auf der Suche Nach dem Bürger* (*In Search of the Bourgeois*) of 1964, Lukács argued persuasively for Mann's own paradoxical position in that empire: he represented perfectly its middle class, whose inner corruption his work highlights. Such a perspective pertains centrally to *Death in Venice*, for it demonstrates Mann's own struggle for balance between his most intimate identity and his increasingly public persona.

Lukács calls Aschenbach's ethic "the code of composure," which characterized "the spiritual lives of the finest figures, the most sincere intellectuals in the cultural world of Wilhelmine (imperialistically Prussianized) Germany." So Lukács reads Aschenbach's collapse as portentous indeed. He claims that Mann and his forebear, the Prussian novelist Theodor Fontane (1819–1898), were "the first and only German writers to unmask the inner weakness of the Prussian behavior ethic" (Lukács 1965, 25–26). In this regard Lukács slights Nietzsche, who was already decrying the emptiness behind the mask of Bismarck's empire in the 1880s.

However, this historical slip is natural for Lukács, whose own Marxist beliefs dictated his view of Nietzsche as simply antisocialist. Lukács saw Nietzsche's philosophy as "an aggressive defensive action against the main enemy, the working class and socialism" (Foster 73). For the always complex and contradictory Nietzsche, this judgment is itself simplistic.

Narratology, Irony, Parody, Ambiguity

Mann himself pointed to an important stylistic aspect of *Death in Venice* in telling one critic that he had wanted his prose to evoke "a balance of sensuality and morality." Critics have never agreed that the work indeed does so, but they have discussed its problematic combining of several other dichotomies. Soon after the work appeared, the poet Stefan George criticized a jarring mixture of classic mythological elements with the narrator's typically cold, naturalistic treatment of Aschenbach as a clinical case. Later critics have explained this unresolved stylistic tension by referring to the text's dual birth from two different sources: Goethe's late heterosexual love affair and Mann's own "lyrical/hymnic" homosexual feelings. The novella's resulting uneven tone has led directly to several studies of Mann's narrative perspective.

In his 1954 *Das Wagnis der Sprache* (*The Feat of Language*), Fritz Martini referred to a "doubling of narrative perspective." He highlighted Mann's frequent collision of styles as the "pathetic-lyric" and the "critical-psychological." Martini read this dichotomy as Mann's deeply ironic critique of style itself. While this view does not attribute parody to the resulting product, it has sparked later investigations of Mann's particular brand of irony as an affectionate parody of Goethe's arch-classic style. Burton Pike's "Thomas Mann and the Problematic Self" (1967) went further than Martini in explaining this narrative split as a symptom of the text's growing distance between narrator and protagonist.

Mann himself inspired the title of Dorrit Cohn's acclaimed article "The Second Author of *Der Tod in Venedig*" (1983) when he wrote of narrative in a book review of 1923. Cohn quotes Mann: "Narrating is something totally different from writing, and what distinguishes them is an indirection in the former." But narration is "most slyly effective when it veils itself in directness." Cohn's separation of author and narrator rests on Mann's characteristic use of *erlebte Rede*, free indirect narration.

Generally, this style diverges from traditional third-person narration in separating a character's place in time from the time of the narrative. For instance, "He thought, 'I'll travel'" becomes "He thought he would travel," so that the character's present-tense thought gets stated in the narrative past. Thus narrator and character become entwined, with often ambivalent results. On this thorny matter, Lilian Furst's reader-response essay (included in Part Two) offers arguments to resolve such ambiguity. However, if the sentence reads "He *furtively* thought he would travel," the reader knows the narrator is supplying his or her own analysis of the character's psychology. Carefully noting such precise textual clues to the narrative intention helps us to understand what this story's third and possibly most crucial figure — the author — means to communicate. Gustave Flaubert is the most famous practitioner of this style, but Goethe used it earlier, as did Jane Austen.

In "Aspects of Parody in the Work of Thomas Mann" (1952), Hans Eichner offered one of the first studies to address Mann's specific tone: irony. The author himself had long claimed that his ambivalent treatment of his characters was not mocking but rather benign, like that of an indulgent father. Erich Heller's *The Ironic German* of 1979 finds the ultimate irony — perhaps a self-parody — in just that brilliantly polished, Apollonian style that the story proves fraudulent. Other critics of Mann's irony reveal a deeper complexity than Heller intimates in his mainly autobiographical argument. T. J. Reed, for instance, shows how an ironic tone usually saves Mann from inflicting a finally didactic message. Like all great writers, Mann transcends attacking or defending his characters and their attitudes. Instead, according to Reed, such artists render verbal portraits of individuals, their relations, their society.

However, Reed makes a notable exception to this rule in the narrator's final harsh judgment of Aschenbach: "It is a shade too emphatic for the reader accustomed to Mann's ironic temper. Where are the reservations usually felt in every inflection of his phrasing? The finality with which Aschenbach's case is finally settled is positively suspicious. . . . Is it not crudely direct beside the informed survey of Aschenbach's development in Chapter Two?" (Reed 1974, 149). Reed attributes this discrepancy to Mann's superimposing "a moral tale" on his originally "hymnic" story of a failed love. Mann himself had recognized this split in his attitude toward the story, for he told a critic he had tried to combine the sensual and the moral.

At this point, Reed's discussion of Mann's "art of ambivalence" in *Death in Venice* reaches the work's broadest significance. What may look like merely pervasive irony actually indicates the author's cultural context of decadence and its attempted reversal. In his *Considerations of an Unpolitical Man* (1918), Mann characterized himself as reaching maturity in the era of European decadence. However, far from accepting that influence as insuperable, he claimed to be "experimenting" with ways of overcoming it. (Fascism was soon to become the way favored by many Germans.) Reed maintains persuasively that *Death in Venice* is precisely that experiment, that its "ambivalent art" became Mann's hallmark: "The creation of ambivalence was the breakthrough in Mann's long-standing programme to 'elevate' the novel. It rescued the novel of ideas from the mechanical methods of simple allegory" (Reed 1974, 178).

Reed's discussion has been fruitful indeed, for several critics have replied to it. Dorrit Cohn's final argument uses Reed as a springboard, and Lilian Furst's essay in this volume also addresses this narrative problem that Reed first noticed. Russell Berman's essay here also takes up the narrator's categorical rejection of the writer. Berman argues against that judgment, noting that in choosing to leave Tadzio — just as Socrates left Phaedrus — Aschenbach saves himself morally. Hence from Reed in 1974 to Furst and Berman in 1998, critics continue to ponder the meaning of Mann's atypically un-ironic narrative treatment of Aschenbach.

AMERICAN CRITICISM

Because most of the reception just cited is in German, we can bring the criticism closer to us by noting some highlights of the specifically American treatment of *Death in Venice*. Quickly following its first American translation by Kenneth Burke in 1925, almost all the reviews praised the story. They highlighted Mann's meticulous prose style and sensitive handling of controversial material. Americans had already read his *Buddenbrooks*, translated in 1924, so some reviewers compared the story favorably with the novel. The distinctly American contribution to literary criticism in the 1950s and 1960s, New Criticism, soon appeared in its parallel German form as *werkimmanente Deutung*, "work-immanent interpretation." In fact, before the birth of linguistics, German critics had developed a strong tradition of philological criticism: a means of interpretation centered in the study of language specifically. The innovation of New Criticism lies in its radical formalist theory, first proposed by René Wellek and Austin Warren in their 1949 *Theory of Literature*. These authors urged readers to consider only the literary work in its pristine formal purity. For them, any reference to contextual conditioning factors — historical background, cultural elements, and especially the author's biography — introduces matters extraneous to the work itself. Accordingly, just as we contemplate a work of visual art as pure form, so should we interpret literature independently, without regard for the manifold factors influencing it. Perhaps the most famous title of a New Critical book, Cleanth Brooks's *The Well-Wrought Urn* (1947) explicitly and characteristically links literature to a visual art object.

With its intricate prose, its wealth of sources, and its narratological complexity, *Death in Venice* offers a meaty challenge to the formalist interpreter. Although Oskar Seidlin was a native German and thus no American New Critic, he demonstrated most impressively how deeply an exclusively stylistic analysis can interpret a work's essential meaning. His essay "Style Investigations of a Sentence by Thomas Mann" explicates only the sentence beginning chapter 2, but Seidlin reveals these sixteen lines as nothing less than verbal architecture. First of all, Mann devotes the sentence's first thirteen lines to Aschenbach's works, leaving only two lines to describe the man himself. What better indication could we have that the writing has literally oppressed him, that his life constitutes a mere appendage to his literary career? This construction linguistically illuminates the man's innermost and most problematic nature. Ignoring the significance of this construction and translating the sentence with Aschenbach's place of birth first, as Helen Lowe-Porter did, means overlooking a crucial early clue to the work's meaning.

The growing length of each phrase in the sentence reflects the gradual expanding of Aschenbach's achievement. Four periodic parts of the sentence highlight the four monumental aspects of his creativity: first factual biography in his life of Frederick the Great, then technical mastery in the "great tapestry" of his novel *Maya,* then the "ethical mission" of his story "A Study in Abjection," and finally the philosophic work *Intellect and Art.* In short, this symphonic sentence conveys Aschenbach's intellectual development from the purely material to the purely spiritual. Not accidentally, this progress takes him ever further from ordinary life. Again, a close reading of a single sentence reveals one of the work's essential ideas.

Despite Seidlin's remarkable achievement with a New Critical approach, most critics inevitably saw the all-too-obvious psychological link between Aschenbach and Mann, which precluded a New Critical reading. Accordingly, the psychoanalytic strand of the work's criticism has remained primary. As Rodney Symington's essay in Part Two shows, critics have addressed not only Aschenbach's Freudian repression, but also many other aspects of his psychology.

ADAPTATIONS

One sure sign of a work's broad and lasting appeal is its adaptation into other media. Many people know such English classics as Charles Dickens's *Great Expectations,* Emily Brontë's *Wuthering Heights,* or Jane Austen's *Sense and Sensibility* only through their filmed versions. Similarly for *Death in Venice,* its audience has expanded widely since Luchino Visconti filmed his rendition of the story in 1970. This film has immediate sensuous appeal, owing to Visconti's typically lush cinematography and to the period sets and costumes. (One whimsical reviewer called for a study of only the fantastic Edwardian hats worn by the Hotel des Bains' chic women guests.) As Aschenbach, the astute English actor Dirk Bogarde renders a memorable portrait of the aging ascetic artist who literally realizes his homosexuality too late.

Several reviews and critical essays on this film discuss Visconti's unique accomplishment in converting Aschenbach into a composer modeled unmistakably on Gustav Mahler (1860–1911). Naturally, several purist critics decried this fundamental change as not merely lacking credibility but also slighting both Mann and Mahler. Perhaps the most valid critique concerns Visconti's facile change of the artist from renowned author to controversial composer. In the film's flashback of Aschenbach conducting a symphony, the audience boos, which is surely a far cry from the writer's public acclaim. The artist figure lacking Aschenbach's universal praise loses a crucial aspect of his tragedy: the utter fall from grace. Hence Visconti reduces his plight to that of the repressed homosexual. However, a majority of film critics and Mann scholars welcomed Visconti's imaginative creation of a new work merely inspired by the novella. Perhaps the most judicious of such essays came from Hans Rudolf Vaget, that virtual dean of Mann critics, who may have surprised his fellow Germanists in praising the film's sensitivity in creating an original, independent work of art.

The other major adaptation of *Death in Venice,* the 1973 opera by Benjamin Britten (1913–1976), has brought less controversy than the film. Most reviewers marvelled at the ingenuity of Britten and his librettist, Myfanwy Piper, in transforming the cerebral Aschenbach into a fully articulate tenor. Without the internal monologue that characterizes Aschenbach for the reader, the listener must hear about his mental state through song alone.

RECENT BIOGRAPHIES

We find a particularly telling reflection of the novella's contemporary climate in its critics' neglect of the homosexual theme. Even though Mann himself had already confessed in 1918 that "everything I have written expresses my inversion," no critic took up this intriguing challenge to discuss in depth that inevitably central aspect of Mann's work (Heilbut x). What generations of critics may have understood by the term "inversion" is the dual identity that Mann constantly lamented, being both a proper middle-class citizen externally and an artist internally. In the trenchant phrase of his 1903 protagonist Tonio Kröger, Mann felt like "a bourgeois gone astray." In any case, it now seems decidedly curious that, up until the 1920s, readers all but ignored the broad cultural implications of Aschenbach's fateful condition as a repressed homosexual artist. According to Wolfgang Koeppen, "Readers of 1913 took the love for a boy instead of a girl as a sign of oddity, the whim of an artist, the wish to make desire abstract, to parody an emotion, to be original but still to remain within the bounds of bourgeois society" (Böhm 17). For such readers, Aschenbach's homosexuality had only symbolic value: they understood it as a merely cerebral symptom of his fatal repression.

Eighty-three years later, in 1996, Anthony Heilbut aptly subtitled his biography of Mann *Eros and Literature*. Heilbut speaks for most contemporary critics in finding the homoerotic aspects of Mann's oeuvre "hidden in plain sight," "too visible to be spotted." So we may owe our newly enlightening exploration of the homosexual theme to recent critics' penchant for looking at literature in new ways — ways that new history introduced.

T. J. Reed was perhaps the first critic to stress the link of homosexuality between Mann and Aschenbach in a critical edition of the work (Oxford, 1971) and in his later *The Uses of Tradition* (1974). But Reed analyzed mainly the psychological/psychoanalytic links between the two men; he did not explore in depth the relevance of Mann's own homosexuality for the story. Indeed, no critic could do so before 1980, when the death of Mann's widow Katia allowed the gradual publication of all his diaries. Here the author exposed evidence, unsuspected in his lifetime, about the depth and complexity of his sexual life.

Since about 1985 the psychosexual analysis of Mann himself has dominated the critical treatment of his oeuvre. Naturally, *Death in Venice*, as Mann's first comprehensive portrait of the homosexual artist, has taken center stage in the unfolding drama of his literary biography. In 1991, Karl Werner Böhm's *Zwischen Selbstzucht und Verlangen: Thomas Mann und das Stigma Homosexualität* (*Between Repression and Desire: Thomas Mann and the Stigma of Homosexuality*) gave the most recent and exhaustive account of the criticism that specifically concerns Mann's treatment of homosexuality. For this "history of a theme," Böhm devotes his whole first chapter to *Death in Venice*. These twenty-three pages ground his book's discussion firmly in the context of this story as a landmark — both for Mann's own coming to terms with himself and for the prewar culture's understanding of homosexuality.

Accordingly, all four biographies from 1995 and 1996 — by Donald Prater, Ronald Hayman, Klaus Harpprecht, and Anthony Heilbut — devote much space to the homosexuality in this text particularly. What results is a new view of the author whom generations of readers considered an Olympian master. "Liberated by his diaries, [Mann] becomes no longer the magisterial titan, but a troubled, self-doubting artist attempting a spectacular form of literary transcendence" (Heilbut x).

Finally, does this critical survey help us to decide just what *Death in Venice* is? How does it help us to interpret the work? What does this novella mean for us now? Several viable answers have come from the story's major critics — von Gronicka, Traschen, Dierks, Cohn, Reed, Vaget, Lehnert — who call it primarily a psychological study, a cultural critique of prewar Europe, an autobiographical confession, or a parodistic unmasking of the Olympian writer as a fraud. Until recently, most broad interpreters of *Death in Venice* have read it as a deeply ironic moral tale. Accordingly, the work reveals the inevitable demise of an artist whose necessarily sensual nature makes both his Spartan art and life fraudulent. This "moral fable" (Mann's term) echoes Nietzsche's dictum that "Success has always been the greatest liar." Nietzsche referred to the inner ruin of the German empire; Mann's story pertains just as much to that doomed culture, which Aschenbach represents.

That view still prevails, but the publication of all Mann's diaries has forced us to highlight the crucial role that his own homosexuality played, especially in this text. So the major shift in recent criticism lies in assessing the impact of this new information. Does it affect our ultimate interpretation of the story? Perhaps not, but it does add richness to critical views of Mann's already complex relation to his own work.

Naomi Ritter

WORKS CITED

Bloom, Harold, ed. *Thomas Mann*. Modern Critical Views. New York: Chelsea, 1986.

Böhm, Karl Werner. *Zwischen Selbstzucht und Verlangen: Thomas Mann und das Stigma Homosexualität*. Würzburg: Königshausen and Neumann, 1991.

Britten, Benjamin. *Death in Venice*. Piano Score. London: Faber Music, 1973.

Cohn, Dorrit. "The Second Author of *Der Tod in Venedig*." *Probleme der Moderne*. Ed. Benjamin Bennett. Tübingen: Niemeyer, 1983. 223–45. Rpt. in Ezergailis 124–43.

Dierks, Manfred. *Studien zu Mythos und Psychologie bei Thomas Mann*. Bern: Franke, 1972. Rpt. in Koelb 130–50.

Eichner, Hans. "Aspects of Parody in the Works of Thomas Mann." *Modern Language Review* 47 (1952): 30–48. Rpt. in Bloom 93–114.

Ezergailis, Inta, ed. *Critical Essays on Thomas Mann*. Boston: G. K. Hall, 1988.

———. *Male and Female: An Approach to Thomas Mann's Dialectic*. The Hague: Nijhoff, 1975.

Foster, John Burt Jr. *Heirs to Dionysus*. Princeton: Princeton UP, 1981.

Frizen, Werner. "Fausts Tod in Venedig." Gockel et al. 231–53.

Gide, André. *The Immoralist*. Trans. Richard Howard. New York: Vintage, 1970.

Gockel, Heinz, et al., eds. *Wagner, Nietzsche, Thomas Mann*. Frankfurt: Klostermann, 1993.

Harpprecht, Klaus. *Thomas Mann: Eine Autobiographie*. Berlin: Rowohlt, 1995.

Hayman, Ronald. *Thomas Mann: A Biography*. New York: Scribner, 1995.

Heilbut, Anthony. *Thomas Mann: Eros and Literature*. New York: Knopf, 1996.

Heller, Erich. *Thomas Mann: The Ironic German*. South Bend: Regnery, 1979.

Hofmiller, Josef. "Thomas Manns *Der Tod in Venedig*." *Süddeutsche Monatshefte* (Munich) 10 (1913): 218–32.

Koelb, Clayton, ed. *Death in Venice*. New York: Norton, 1994.

Kohut, Heinz. "Thomas Manns *Tod in Venedig*: Zerfall einer kuenstlerischen Sublimierung." *Psycho-Pathographien des Alltags I: Schriftsteller und Psychoanalyse*. Ed. Alexander Mitscherlich. Frankfurt: Suhrkamp, 1972. 142–67.

Korrodi, Eduard. "Thomas Mann: *Der Tod in Venedig*." *Wissen und Leben: Schweizerische Halbmonatsschrift* (Zürich) 12 (1913): 690–94.

Kuh, Anton. "Die vorahnende Literatur." *Pester Loyd* (Budapest) 11, no. 1 (1915): n.p.

Lawrence, D. H. "German Books: Thomas Mann." *The Blue Review* 1 (July 1913): 200–206.

Lehnert, Herbert. "Historischer Horizont und Fiktionalität in Thomas Manns *Der Tod in Venedig*." Gockel et al. 254–78.

———. *Thomas Mann: Fiktion, Mythos, Religion*. Stuttgart: Metzler, 1965, 1968.

Lukács, Georg. *Auf der Suche Nach dem Bourgeois*. Neuwied: Luchterhand, 1964.

———. *Essays on Thomas Mann*. Trans. Stanley Mitchell. London: Merlin, 1965.

———. *Essays Über Realismus*. Berlin: Luchterhand, 1971.

Martini, Fritz. *"Der Tod in Venedig."* In *Das Wagnis der Sprache: Interpretationen Deutscher Prosa Von Nietzsche bis Benn*. Stuttgart: Metzler, 1954. 176–224.

Martens, Kurt. *"Der Tod in Venedig." Der Zwiebelfisch* (Munich) 5 (1913): 62–63.

Mitchell, Donald, ed. *Benjamin Britten: Death in Venice*. New York: Cambridge UP, 1978.

Pike, Burton. "Thomas Mann and the Problematic Self." *Publications of the English Goethe Society* 37 (1967): 120–41.

Piper, Myfanwy. *Death in Venice: An Opera in Two Acts*. Libretto for Benjamin Britten, Opus 88. London: Faber Music, 1973.

Prater, Donald. *Thomas Mann: A Life*. Oxford: Oxford UP, 1995.

Reed, T. J. "The Art of Ambivalence: *Der Tod in Venedig." The Uses of Tradition*. Oxford: Oxford UP, 1974. 144–78.

———. *Death in Venice: Making and Unmaking a Master*. New York: Twayne, 1994.

———. *Thomas Mann: "Der Tod in Venedig."* München: Hanser, 1983. Text, materials, and commentary, with the previously unpublished work notes.

Seidlin, Oskar. "Stiluntersuchungen zu einem Thomas-Mann Satz." In *Von Goethe zu Thomas Mann: Zwölf Versuche*. Göttingen: Vandenhoeck and Ruprecht, 1963, 1969. 148–61.

Sokel, Walter. "Demaskierung und Untergang wilhelminischer Repräsentanz." *Herkommen und Erneuerung*. Ed. Gerald Gillespie et al. Tübingen: Niemeyer, 1976. 387–412.

Traschen, Isadore. "The Uses of Myth in *Death in Venice." Modern Fiction Studies* 11.2 (Summer 1965): 165–79. Rpt. in Bloom 87–101.

Visconti, Luchino, dir. *Death in Venice*. Burbank: Warner Home Video, 1984.

Vaget, Hans Rudolf. "Film and Literature: The Case of *Death in Venice:* Luchino Visconti and Thomas Mann." *German Quarterly* 53 (1980):159–75.

———. *Thomas Mann: Kommentar zu Sämtlichen Erzählungen*. München: Winkler, 1984.

von Gronicka, André. "Myth Plus Psychology: A Stylistic Analysis of *Death in Venice." Germanic Review* 31 (1956): 191–205.

Psychoanalytic Criticism
and *Death in Venice*

WHAT IS PSYCHOANALYTIC CRITICISM?

It seems natural to think about literature in terms of dreams. Like dreams, literary works are fictions, inventions of the mind that, although based on reality, are by definition not literally true. Like a literary work, a dream may have some truth to tell, but, like a literary work, it may need to be interpreted before that truth can be grasped. We can live vicariously through romantic fictions, much as we can through daydreams. Terrifying novels and nightmares affect us in much the same way, plunging us into an atmosphere that continues to cling, even after the last chapter has been read — or the alarm clock has sounded.

The notion that dreams allow such psychic explorations, of course, like the analogy between literary works and dreams, owes a great deal to the thinking of Sigmund Freud, the famous Austrian psychoanalyst who in 1900 published a seminal essay, *The Interpretation of Dreams*. But is the reader who feels that Emily Brontë's *Wuthering Heights* is dreamlike — who feels that Mary Shelley's *Frankenstein* is nightmarish — necessarily a Freudian literary critic? To some extent the answer has to be yes. We are all Freudians, really, whether or not we have read a single work by Freud. At one time or another, most of us have referred to ego, libido, complexes, unconscious desires, and sexual repression. The premises of Freud's thought have changed the way the

Western world thinks about itself. Psychoanalytic criticism has influenced the teachers our teachers studied with, the works of scholarship and criticism they read, and the critical and creative writers *we* read as well.

What Freud did was develop a language that described, a model that explained, a theory that encompassed human psychology. Many of the elements of psychology he sought to describe and explain are present in the literary works of various ages and cultures, from Sophocles' *Oedipus Rex* to Shakespeare's *Hamlet* to works being written in our own day. When the great novel of the twenty-first century is written, many of these same elements of psychology will probably inform its discourse as well. If, by understanding human psychology according to Freud, we can appreciate literature on a new level, then we should acquaint ourselves with his insights.

Freud's theories are either directly or indirectly concerned with the nature of the unconscious mind. Freud didn't invent the notion of the unconscious; others before him had suggested that even the supposedly "sane" human mind was conscious and rational only at times, and even then at possibly only one level. But Freud went further, suggesting that the powers motivating men and women are *mainly* and *normally* unconscious.

Freud, then, powerfully developed an old idea: that the human mind is essentially dual in nature. He called the predominantly passional, irrational, unknown, and unconscious part of the psyche the *id,* or "it." The *ego,* or "I," was his term for the predominantly rational, logical, orderly, conscious part. Another aspect of the psyche, which he called the *superego,* is really a projection of the ego. The superego almost seems to be outside of the self, making moral judgments, telling us to make sacrifices for good causes even though self-sacrifice may not be quite logical or rational. And, in a sense, the superego *is* "outside," since much of what it tells us to do or think we have learned from our parents, our schools, or our religious institutions.

What the ego and superego tell us *not* to do or think is repressed, forced into the unconscious mind. One of Freud's most important contributions to the study of the psyche, the theory of repression, goes something like this: much of what lies in the unconscious mind has been put there by consciousness, which acts as a censor, driving underground unconscious or conscious thoughts or instincts that it deems unacceptable. Censored materials often involve infantile sexual desires, Freud postulated. Repressed to an unconscious state, they emerge only in disguised forms: in dreams, in language (so-called Freudian slips), in creative activity that may produce art (including literature), and in neurotic behavior.

According to Freud, all of us have repressed wishes and fears; we all have dreams in which repressed feelings and memories emerge disguised, and thus we are all potential candidates for dream analysis. One of the unconscious desires most commonly repressed is the childhood wish to displace the parent of our own sex and take his or her place in the affections of the parent of the opposite sex. This desire really involves a number of different but related wishes and fears. (A boy — and it should be remarked in passing that Freud here concerns himself mainly with the male — may fear that his father will castrate him, and he may wish that his mother would return to nursing him.) Freud referred to the whole complex of feelings by the word *oedipal*, naming the complex after the Greek tragic hero Oedipus, who unwittingly killed his father and married his mother.

Why are oedipal wishes and fears repressed by the conscious side of the mind? And what happens to them after they have been censored? As Roy P. Basler puts it in *Sex, Symbolism, and Psychology in Literature* (1975), "from the beginning of recorded history such wishes have been restrained by the most powerful religious and social taboos, and as a result have come to be regarded as 'unnatural,'" even though "Freud found that such wishes are more or less characteristic of normal human development":

> In dreams, particularly, Freud found ample evidence that such wishes persisted. . . . Hence he conceived that natural urges, when identified as "wrong," may be repressed but not obliterated. . . . In the unconscious, these urges take on symbolic garb, regarded as nonsense by the waking mind that does not recognize their significance. (14)

Freud's belief in the significance of dreams, of course, was no more original than his belief that there is an unconscious side to the psyche. Again, it was the extent to which he developed a theory of how dreams work — and the extent to which that theory helped him, by analogy, to understand far more than just dreams — that made him unusual, important, and influential beyond the perimeters of medical schools and psychiatrists' offices.

The psychoanalytic approach to literature not only rests on the theories of Freud; it may even be said to have *begun* with Freud, who was interested in writers, especially those who relied heavily on symbols. Such writers regularly cloak or mystify ideas in figures that make sense only when interpreted, much as the unconscious mind of a neurotic disguises secret thoughts in dream stories or bizarre actions that need to be interpreted by an analyst. Freud's interest in literary artists led him to make some unfortunate generalizations about creativity; for example, in the twenty-third lecture in *Introductory Lectures on Psycho-Analysis* (1922), he defined the artist as "one urged on by instinctive needs that are too clamorous" (314). But it also led him to write creative literary criticism of his own, including an influential essay on "The Relation of a Poet to Daydreaming" (1908) and "The Uncanny" (1919), a provocative psychoanalytic reading of E. T. A. Hoffmann's supernatural tale "The Sandman."

Freud's application of psychoanalytic theory to literature quickly caught on. In 1909, only a year after Freud had published "The Relation of a Poet to Daydreaming," the psychoanalyst Otto Rank published *The Myth of the Birth of the Hero.* In that work, Rank subscribes to the notion that the artist turns a powerful, secret wish into a literary fantasy, and he uses Freud's notion about the "oedipal" complex to explain why the popular stories of so many heroes in literature are so similar. A year after Rank had published his psychoanalytic account of heroic texts, Ernest Jones, Freud's student and eventual biographer, turned his attention to a tragic text: Shakespeare's *Hamlet.* In an essay first published in the *American Journal of Psychology,* Jones, like Rank, makes use of the oedipal concept: he suggests that Hamlet is a victim of strong feelings toward his mother, the queen.

Between 1909 and 1949, numerous other critics decided that psychological and psychoanalytic theory could assist in the understanding of literature. I. A. Richards, Kenneth Burke, and Edmund Wilson were among the most influential to become interested in the new approach. Not all of the early critics were committed to the approach; neither were all of them Freudians. Some followed Alfred Adler, who believed that writers wrote out of inferiority complexes, and others applied the ideas of Carl Gustav Jung, who had broken with Freud over Freud's emphasis on sex and who had developed a theory of the *collective* unconscious. According to Jungian theory, a great work of literature is not a disguised expression of its author's personal, repressed wishes; rather, it is a manifestation of desires once held by the whole human race but now repressed because of the advent of civilization.

It is important to point out that among those who relied on Freud's models were a number of critics who were poets and novelists as well. Conrad Aiken wrote a Freudian study of American literature, and poets such as Robert Graves and W. H. Auden applied Freudian insights when writing critical prose. William Faulkner, Henry James, James Joyce, D. H. Lawrence, Marcel Proust, and Toni Morrison are only a few of the novelists who have either written criticism influenced by Freud or who have written novels that conceive of character, conflict, and creative writing itself in Freudian terms. The poet H.D. (Hilda Doolittle) was actually a patient of Freud's and provided an account of her analysis in her book *Tribute to Freud*. By giving Freudian theory credibility among students of literature that only they could bestow, such writers helped to endow earlier psychoanalytic criticism with a largely Freudian orientation that has begun to be challenged only in the last two decades.

The willingness, even eagerness, of writers to use Freudian models in producing literature and criticism of their own consummated a relationship that, to Freud and other pioneering psychoanalytic theorists, had seemed fated from the beginning; after all, therapy involves the close analysis of language. René Wellek and Austin Warren included "psychological" criticism as one of the five "extrinsic" approaches to literature described in their influential book *Theory of Literature* (1942). Psychological criticism, they suggest, typically attempts to do at least one of the following: provide a psychological study of an individual writer; explore the nature of the creative process; generalize about "types and laws present within works of literature"; or theorize about the psychological "effects of literature upon its readers" (81). Entire books on psychoanalytic criticism began to appear, such as Frederick J. Hoffman's *Freudianism and the Literary Mind* (1945).

Probably because of Freud's characterization of the creative mind as "clamorous" if not ill, psychoanalytic criticism written before 1950 tended to psychoanalyze the individual author. Poems were read as fantasies that allowed authors to indulge repressed wishes, to protect themselves from deep-seated anxieties, or both. A perfect example of author analysis would be Marie Bonaparte's 1933 study of Edgar Allan Poe. Bonaparte found Poe to be so fixated on his mother that his repressed longing emerges in his stories in images such as the white spot on a black cat's breast, said to represent mother's milk.

A later generation of psychoanalytic critics often paused to analyze the characters in novels and plays before proceeding to their authors. But not for long, since characters, both evil and good, tended to be seen by these critics as the author's potential selves or projections of various repressed aspects of his or her psyche. For instance, in *A*

Psychoanalytic Study of the Double in Literature (1970), Robert Rogers begins with the view that human beings are double or multiple in nature. Using this assumption, along with the psychoanalytic concept of "dissociation" (best known by its result, the dual or multiple personality), Rogers concludes that writers reveal instinctual or repressed selves in their books, often without realizing that they have done so.

In the view of critics attempting to arrive at more psychological insights into an author than biographical materials can provide, a work of literature is a fantasy or a dream — or at least so analogous to daydream or dream that Freudian analysis can help explain the nature of the mind that produced it. The author's purpose in writing is to gratify secretly some forbidden wish, in particular an infantile wish or desire that has been repressed into the unconscious mind. To discover what the wish is, the psychoanalytic critic employs many of the terms and procedures developed by Freud to analyze dreams.

The literal surface of a work is sometimes spoken of as its "manifest content" and would be treated as a "manifest dream" or "dream story" treated by a Freudian analyst. Just as the analyst tries to figure out the "dream thought" behind the dream story — that is, the latent or hidden content of the manifest dream — so the psychoanalytic literary critic tries to expose the latent, underlying content of a work. Freud used the words *condensation* and *displacement* to explain two of the mental processes whereby the mind disguises its wishes and fears in dream stories. In condensation, several thoughts or persons may be condensed into a single manifestation or image in a dream story; in displacement, an anxiety, a wish, or a person may be displaced onto the image of another, with which or whom it is loosely connected through a string of associations that only an analyst can untangle. Psychoanalytic critics treat metaphors as if they were dream condensations; they treat metonyms — figures of speech based on extremely loose, arbitrary associations — as if they were dream displacements. Thus figurative literary language in general is treated as something that evolves as the writer's conscious mind resists what the unconscious tells it to picture or describe. A symbol is, in Daniel Weiss's words, "a meaningful concealment of truth as the truth promises to emerge as some frightening or forbidden idea" (20).

In a 1970 article entitled "The 'Unconscious' of Literature," Norman Holland, a literary critic trained in psychoanalysis, succinctly sums up the attitudes held by critics who would psychoanalyze authors, but without quite saying that it is the *author* that is being analyzed by the psychoanalytic critic. "When one looks at a poem psychoanalytically," he writes, "one considers it as though it were a dream or as though some ideal patient [were speaking] from the couch in iambic pentameter." One "looks for the general level or levels of fantasy associated with the language. By level I mean the familiar stages of childhood development — oral [when desires for nourishment and infantile sexual desires overlap], anal [when infants receive their primary pleasure from defecation], urethral [when urinary functions are the locus of sexual pleasure], phallic [when the penis or, in girls, some penis substitute is of primary interest], oedipal." Holland continues by analyzing not Robert Frost but Frost's poem "Mending Wall" as a specifically oral fantasy that is not unique to its author. "Mending Wall" is "about breaking down the wall which marks the separated or individuated self so as to return to a state of closeness to some Other" — including and perhaps essentially the nursing mother ("'Unconscious'" 136, 139).

While not denying the idea that the unconscious plays a role in creativity, psychoanalytic critics such as Holland began to focus more on the ways in which authors create works that appeal to *our* repressed wishes and fantasies. Consequently, they shifted their focus away from the psyche of the author and toward the psychology of the reader and the text. Holland's theories, which have concerned themselves more with the reader than with the text, have helped to establish another school of critical theory: reader-response criticism. Elizabeth Wright explains Holland's brand of modern psychoanalytic criticism in this way: "What draws us as readers to a text is the secret expression of what we desire to hear, much as we protest we do not. The disguise must be good enough to fool the censor into thinking that the text is respectable, but bad enough to allow the unconscious to glimpse the unrespectable" (117).

Holland is one of dozens of critics who have revised Freud significantly in the process of revitalizing psychoanalytic criticism. Another such critic is R. D. Laing, whose controversial and often poetical writings about personality, repression, masks, and the double or "schizoid" self have (re)blurred the boundary between creative writing and psychoanalytic discourse. Yet another is D. W. Winnicott, an "object relations" theorist who has had a significant impact on literary criticism. Critics influenced by Winnicott and his school have questioned the tendency to see reader/text as an either/or construct; instead, they have seen reader and text (or audience and play) in terms of a *relationship* taking place in what Winnicott calls a "transitional" or "potential" space — space in which binary terms such as *real* and *illusory, objective* and *subjective,* have little or no meaning.

Psychoanalytic theorists influenced by Winnicott see the transitional or potential reader/text (or audience/play) space as being *like* the space entered into by psychoanalyst and patient. More important, they also see it as being similar to the space between mother and infant: a space characterized by trust in which categorizing terms such as *knowing* and *feeling* mix and merge and have little meaning apart from one another.

Whereas Freud saw the mother-son relationship in terms of the son and his repressed oedipal complex (and saw the analyst-patient relationship in terms of the patient and the repressed "truth" that the analyst could scientifically extract), object-relations analysts see both relationships as *dyadic* — that is, as being dynamic in both directions. Consequently, they don't depersonalize analysis or their analyses. It is hardly surprising, therefore, that contemporary literary critics who apply object-relations theory to the texts they discuss don't depersonalize critics or categorize their interpretations as "truthful," at least not in any objective or scientific sense. In the view of such critics, interpretations are made of language — itself a transitional object — and are themselves the mediating terms or transitional objects of a relationship.

Like critics of the Winnicottian school, the French structuralist theorist Jacques Lacan focuses on language and language-related issues. He treats the unconscious *as* a language and, consequently, views the dream not as Freud did (that is, as a form and symptom of repression) but rather as a form of discourse. Thus we may study dreams psychoanalytically to learn about literature, even as we may study literature to learn more about the unconscious. In Lacan's seminar on Poe's "The Purloined Letter," a pattern of repetition like that used by psychoanalysts in their analyses is used to arrive at a reading of the story. According to Wright, "the new psychoanalytic structural approach to literature" employs "analogies from psychoanalysis . . . to explain the workings of the text as distinct from the workings of a particular author's, character's, or even reader's mind" (125).

Lacan, however, did far more than extend Freud's theory of dreams, literature, and the interpretation of both. More significantly, he took Freud's whole theory of psyche and gender and added to it a crucial third term — that of language. In the process, he both used and significantly developed Freud's ideas about the oedipal stage and complex.

Lacan points out that the pre-oedipal stage, in which the child at first does not even recognize its independence from its mother, is also a pre*verbal* stage, one in which the child communicates without

the medium of language, or — if we insist on calling the child's communications a language — in a language that can only be called *literal*.
("Coos," certainly, cannot be said to be figurative or symbolic.) Then,
while still in the pre-oedipal stage, the child enters the *mirror* stage.

During the mirror period, the child comes to view itself and its
mother, later other people as well, *as* independent selves. This is the
stage in which the child is first able to fear the aggressions of another,
to desire what is recognizably beyond the self (initially the mother),
and, finally, to want to compete with another for the same desired object. This is also the stage at which the child first becomes able to feel
sympathy with another being who is being hurt by a third, to cry when
another cries. All of these developments, of course, involve projecting
beyond the self and, by extension, constructing one's own self (or
"ego" or "I") as others view one — that is, as *another*. Such constructions, according to Lacan, are just that: constructs, products, artifacts — fictions of coherence that in fact hide what Lacan calls the
"absence" or "lack" of being.

The mirror stage, which Lacan also refers to as the *imaginary*
stage, is fairly quickly succeeded by the oedipal stage. As in Freud, this
stage begins when the child, having come to view itself as self and the
father and mother as separate selves, perceives gender and gender differences between its parents and between itself and one of its parents.
For boys, gender awareness involves another, more powerful recognition, for the recognition of the father's phallus as the mark of his difference from the mother involves, at the same time, the recognition
that his older and more powerful father is also his rival. That, in turn,
leads to the understanding that what once seemed wholly his and even
indistinguishable from himself is in fact someone else's: something
properly desired only at a distance and in the form of socially acceptable *substitutes*.

The fact that the oedipal stage roughly coincides with the entry of
the child into language is extremely important for Lacan. For the linguistic order is essentially a figurative or "Symbolic" order; words are
not the things they stand for but are, rather, stand-ins or substitutes
for those things. Hence boys, who in the most critical period of their
development have had to submit to what Lacan calls the "Law of the
Father" — a law that prohibits direct desire for and communicative intimacy with what has been the boy's whole world — enter more easily
into the realm of language and the Symbolic order than do girls, who
have never really had to renounce that which once seemed continuous

with the self: the mother. The gap that has been opened up for boys, which includes the gap between signs and what they substitute — the gap marked by the phallus and encoded with the boy's sense of his maleness — has not opened up for girls, or has not opened up in the same way, to the same degree.

For Lacan, the father need not be present to trigger the oedipal stage; nor does his phallus have to be seen to catalyze the boy's (easier) transition into the Symbolic order. Rather, Lacan argues, a child's recognition of its gender is intricately tied up with a growing recognition of the system of names and naming, part of the larger system of substitutions we call language. A child has little doubt about who its mother is, but who is its father, and how would one know? The father's claim rests on the mother's *word* that he is in fact the father; the father's relationship to the child is thus established through language and a system of marriage and kinship — names — that in turn is basic to rules of everything from property to law. The name of the father (*nom du père,* which in French sounds like *non du père*) involves, in a sense, nothing of the father — nothing, that is, except his word or name.

Lacan's development of Freud has had several important results. First, his sexist-seeming association of maleness with the Symbolic order, together with his claim that women cannot therefore enter easily into the order, has prompted feminists not to reject his theory out of hand but, rather, to look more closely at the relation between language and gender, language and women's inequality. Some feminists have gone so far as to suggest that the social and political relationships between male and female will not be fundamentally altered until language itself has been radically changed. (That change might begin dialectically, with the development of some kind of "feminine language" grounded in the presymbolic, literal-to-imaginary communication between mother and child.)

Second, Lacan's theory has proved of interest to deconstructors and other poststructuralists, in part because it holds that the ego (which in Freud's view is as necessary as it is natural) is a product or construct. The ego-artifact, produced during the mirror stage, *seems* at once unified, consistent, and organized around a determinate center. But the unified self, or ego, is a fiction, according to Lacan. The yoking together of fragments and destructively dissimilar elements takes its psychic toll, and it is the job of the Lacanian psychoanalyst to "deconstruct," as it were, the ego, to show its continuities to be contradictions as well.

In the essay that follows, psychoanalytic critic Rodney Symington argues that, although *Death in Venice* is a complex and multilayered work, "the psychology of the protagonist Aschenbach stands at the center of the novella." That psychology, Symington maintains, involves the type of conflicting inclinations that philosopher Friedrich Nietzsche symbolized using the gods Apollo and Dionysus. (In Nietzsche's *Birth of Tragedy*, Apollo represents the human inclination toward "form, order, clarity, reason," whereas Dionysus represents the inclination toward "disorder, chaos, sex, unreason.")

After arguing that Nietzsche influenced Mann, Symington asks whether Mann was conversant with and influenced by Freud's work. Although Mann himself wrote that *Death in Venice* "originated under the direct influence of Freud," Symington notes that scholars have regarded this statement with skepticism because it was made fourteen years after the publication of Mann's novella.

Symington's search for other evidence of Freud's influence takes him to a short story by Wilhelm Jensen, a story that Freud discussed in print several years before Mann began *Death in Venice*. Entitled "Gradiva," it is about an archaeologist who imagines that an ancient plaster cast he keeps in his room is of a woman (named Gradiva) who died during the volcanic destruction of Pompeii. Inspired to travel to Italy, the archaeologist encounters a young woman among the ruins whom he at first believes to be Gradiva reincarnated. According to Freud's interpretation of the story, repressed erotic inclinations, not archaeological curiosity, drive the protagonist to Italy; these erotic desires, long buried, must be unearthed — much as were the victims of Pompeii. Symington maintains that a "comparison of Jensen's 'Gradiva' with Mann's *Death in Venice* shows that there are close parallels between the plot of the former and its analysis by Freud, and Mann's story."

Symington, however, does not entirely rest his claim that *Death in Venice* reveals Mann's familiarity with Freud on parallels between the novella, Jensen's story, and Freud's commentary on that story. For one thing, Freud's ideas were, as Mann once said, "in the air" by 1910 and therefore could have influenced him indirectly. Nor does Symington stake his claim that Mann was a subtle and sophisticated student of psychology on his hunch that the author was directly or indirectly familiar with Freud's ideas before sitting down to write *Death in Venice*. "Perceptive writers have always had the capacity to fathom the human soul," Symington reminds us; "psychology has always played a major role in literature." Thus great writers without knowledge of Freud's work have nonetheless anticipated or paralleled his insights in their own writings. In Nietzsche, for instance, "the attempts by the Apollonian artist to suppress the Dionysian find their direct parallel in Freud's theory of how repression operates."

As Symington develops his argument, he focuses more closely on repression, citing Peter Gay's useful assertion that "the unconscious as Freud defined it resembles a maximum-security prison holding antisocial inmates . . . barely kept under control and forever attempting to escape. Their breakouts succeed only intermittently and at great cost to themselves." Symington views *Death in Venice* as a work portraying "breakouts" of Aschenbach's imprisoned desire, the first of which occurs during a dream whose images "irrupted" into his soul, broke down his intellectual and cultural "resistance," and left him feeling "devastated and destroyed."

Symington does not limit his analysis to a discussion of what Gay terms "the unconscious as Freud defined it"; rather, he also employs the theories of Jacques Lacan in psychoanalytically reexamining *Death in Venice*. In Lacan's realm of the "Imaginary," as Symington explains it, "individuals construct for themselves an image of their personality that is a defense mechanism against the truth." In Malcolm Bowie's words, the Imaginary "is the scene of a desperate delusional attempt to be and remain 'what is,'" even though "what is" is directly threatened by a reality that Lacan calls "the Other."

In the later stages of his argument, Symington relates Lacan's concept of the Imaginary to Aschenbach's self-deluding efforts "to construct a world of form and order." He also discusses two possible interpretations of Lacan's concept of the Other, arguing that the Other is "concretize[d]" in Aschenbach's consciousness as "The Stranger" who appears in several forms throughout the story. Symington further discusses how Lacan's concepts of the Symbolic and the Real relate to Aschenbach's consciousness and, ultimately, to Mann's "creative drive." In doing so, he suggests that it is possible to provide something attempted unsuccessfully by most early psychoanalytic critics: a psychoanalytic insight not only into the literary text but also into its author, via the created consciousness of a literary character. "Mann, like Aschenbach, constructed for himself a world of the Imaginary," Symington writes. "Lacan's theories allow us to reexamine Mann's works in relation to his own biography."

Ross C Murfin

PSYCHOANALYTIC CRITICISM: A SELECTED BIBLIOGRAPHY

Some Short Introductions to Psychological and Psychoanalytic Criticism

Holland, Norman. "The 'Unconscious' of Literature: The Psychoanalytic Approach." *Contemporary Criticism.* Ed. Malcolm Bradbury and David Palmer. Stratford-upon-Avon Studies 12. New York: St. Martin's, 1971. 131–53.

Natoli, Joseph, and Frederik L. Rusch, comps. *Psychocriticism: An Annotated Bibliography.* Westport: Greenwood, 1984.

Scott, Wilbur. *Five Approaches to Literary Criticism.* London: Collier-Macmillan, 1962. See the essays by Burke and Gorer as well as Scott's introduction to the section "The Psychological Approach: Literature in the Light of Psychological Theory."

Wellek, René, and Austin Warren. *Theory of Literature.* New York: Harcourt, 1942. See the chapter "Literature and Psychology" in pt. 3, "The Extrinsic Approach to the Study of Literature."

Wright, Elizabeth. "Modern Psychoanalytic Criticism." *Modern Literary Theory: A Comparative Introduction.* Ed. Ann Jefferson and David Robey. Totowa: Barnes, 1982. 113–33.

Freud, Lacan, and Their Influence

Basler, Roy P. *Sex, Symbolism, and Psychology in Literature.* New York: Octagon, 1975. See especially 13–19.

Bowie, Malcolm. *Lacan.* Cambridge: Harvard UP, 1991.

Clément, Catherine. *The Lives and Legends of Jacques Lacan.* Trans. Arthur Goldhammer. New York: Columbia UP, 1983.

Freud, Sigmund. *Introductory Lectures on Psycho-Analysis.* Trans. Joan Riviere. London: Allen, 1922.

Gallop, Jane. *Reading Lacan.* Ithaca: Cornell UP, 1985.

Hoffman, Frederick J. *Freudianism and the Literary Mind.* Baton Rouge: Louisiana State UP, 1945.

Hogan, Patrick Colm, and Lalita Pandit, eds. *Lacan and Criticism: Essays and Dialogue on Language, Structure, and the Unconscious.* Athens: U of Georgia P, 1990.

Kazin, Alfred. "Freud and His Consequences." *Contemporaries.* Boston: Little, 1962. 351–93.

Lacan, Jacques. *Écrits: A Selection.* Trans. Alan Sheridan. New York: Norton, 1977.

————. *Feminine Sexuality: Lacan and the École Freudienne.* Ed. Juliet Mitchell and Jacqueline Rose. Trans. Rose. New York: Norton, 1985.

————. *The Four Fundamental Concepts of Psychoanalysis.* Trans. Alan Sheridan. London: Penguin, 1980.

Macey, David. *Lacan in Contexts.* New York: Verso, 1988.

Meisel, Perry, ed. *Freud: A Collection of Critical Essays.* Englewood Cliffs: Prentice, 1981.

Muller, John P., and William J. Richardson. *Lacan and Language: A Reader's Guide to "Écrits."* New York: International UP, 1982.

Porter, Laurence M. *"The Interpretation of Dreams": Freud's Theories Revisited.* Twayne's Masterwork Studies. Boston: G. K. Hall, 1986.

Reppen, Joseph, and Maurice Charney. *The Psychoanalytic Study of Literature.* Hillsdale: Analytic, 1985.

Schneiderman, Stuart. *Jacques Lacan: The Death of an Intellectual Hero.* Cambridge: Harvard UP, 1983.

————. *Returning to Freud: Clinical Psychoanalysis in the School of Lacan.* New Haven: Yale UP, 1980.

Selden, Raman. *A Reader's Guide to Contemporary Literary Theory.* 2d ed. Lexington: U of Kentucky P, 1989. See "Jacques Lacan: Language and the Unconscious."

Sullivan, Ellie Ragland. *Jacques Lacan and the Philosophy of Psychoanalysis.* Champaign: U of Illinois P, 1986.

Sullivan, Ellie Ragland, and Mark Bracher, eds. *Lacan and the Subject of Language.* New York: Routledge, 1991.

Trilling, Lionel. "Art and Neurosis." *The Liberal Imagination.* New York: Scribners, 1950. 160–80.

Wilden, Anthony. "Lacan and the Discourse of the Other." In Lacan, *Speech and Language in Psychoanalysis.* Trans. Wilden. Baltimore: Johns Hopkins UP, 1981. (Published as *The Language of the Self* in 1968.) 159–311.

Zizek, Slavoj. *Looking Awry: An Introduction to Jacques Lacan through Popular Culture.* Cambridge: MIT P, 1991.

Psychoanalysis, Feminism, and Literature

Chodorow, Nancy. *The Reproduction of Mothering: Psychoanalysis and the Sociology of Gender.* Berkeley: U of California P, 1978.

Gallop, Jane. *The Daughter's Seduction: Feminism and Psychoanalysis.* Ithaca: Cornell UP, 1982.

Garner, Shirley Nelson, Claire Kahane, and Madelon Sprengnether. *The (M)other Tongue: Essays in Feminist Psychoanalytic Interpretation.* Ithaca: Cornell UP, 1985.

Grosz, Elizabeth. *Jacques Lacan: A Feminist Introduction.* New York: Routledge, 1990.

Irigaray, Luce. *The Speculum of the Other Woman.* Trans. Gillian C. Gill. Ithaca: Cornell UP, 1985.

———. *This Sex Which Is Not One.* Trans. Catherine Porter. Ithaca: Cornell UP, 1985.

Jacobus, Mary. "Is There a Woman in This Text?" *New Literary History* 14 (1982): 117–41.

Kristeva, Julia. *The Kristeva Reader.* Ed. Toril Moi. New York: Columbia UP, 1986. See especially the selection from *Revolution in Poetic Language,* 89–136.

Mitchell, Juliet. *Psychoanalysis and Feminism.* New York: Random, 1974.

Mitchell, Juliet, and Jacqueline Rose. "Introduction I" and "Introduction II." Lacan, *Feminine Sexuality: Jacques Lacan and the École Freudienne.* New York: Norton, 1985. 1–26, 27–57.

Sprengnether, Madelon. *The Spectral Mother: Freud, Feminism, and Psychoanalysis.* Ithaca: Cornell UP, 1990.

Psychological and Psychoanalytic Studies of Literature

Bettelheim, Bruno. *The Uses of Enchantment: The Meaning and Importance of Fairy Tales.* New York: Knopf, 1976. Although this book is about fairy tales instead of literary works written for publication, it offers model Freudian readings of well-known stories.

Crews, Frederick C. *Out of My System: Psychoanalysis, Ideology, and Critical Method.* New York: Oxford UP, 1975.

———. *Relations of Literary Study.* New York: MLA, 1967. See the chapter "Literature and Psychology."

Diehl, Joanne Feit. "Re-Reading *The Letter:* Hawthorne, the Fetish, and the (Family) Romance." *Nathaniel Hawthorne, "The Scarlet Letter."* Ed. Ross C Murfin. Case Studies in Contemporary Criticism Ed. Ross C Murfin. Boston: Bedford–St. Martin's, 1991. 235–51.

Hallman, Ralph. *Psychology of Literature: A Study of Alienation and Tragedy.* New York: Philosophical Library, 1961.

Hartman, Geoffrey, ed. *Psychoanalysis and the Question of the Text.*

Baltimore: Johns Hopkins UP, 1978. See especially the essays by Hartman, Johnson, Nelson, and Schwartz.

Hertz, Neil. *The End of the Line: Essays on Psychoanalysis and the Sublime.* New York: Columbia UP, 1985.

Holland, Norman N. *Dynamics of Literary Response.* New York: Oxford UP, 1968.

————. *Poems in Persons: An Introduction to the Psychoanalysis of Literature.* New York: Norton, 1973.

Kris, Ernest. *Psychoanalytic Explorations in Art.* New York: International, 1952.

Lucas, F. L. *Literature and Psychology.* London: Cassell, 1951.

Natoli, Joseph, ed. *Psychological Perspectives on Literature: Freudian Dissidents and Non-Freudians: A Casebook.* Hamden: Archon Books–Shoe String, 1984.

Phillips, William, ed. *Art and Psychoanalysis.* New York: Columbia UP, 1977.

Rogers, Robert. *A Psychoanalytic Study of the Double in Literature.* Detroit: Wayne State UP, 1970.

Skura, Meredith. *The Literary Use of the Psychoanalytic Process.* New Haven: Yale UP, 1981.

Strelka, Joseph P. *Literary Criticism and Psychology.* University Park: Pennsylvania State UP, 1976. See especially the essays by Lerner and Peckham.

Weiss, Daniel. *The Critic Agonistes: Psychology, Myth, and the Art of Fiction.* Ed. Eric Solomon and Stephen Arkin. Seattle: U of Washington P, 1985.

Lacanian Psychoanalytic Studies of Literature

Collings, David. "The Monster and the Imaginary Mother: A Lacanian Reading of *Frankenstein.*" *Mary Shelley, "Frankenstein."* Ed. Johanna M. Smith. Case Studies in Contemporary Criticism. Ed. Ross C Murfin. Boston: Bedford–St. Martin's, 1992. 245–58.

Davis, Robert Con, ed. *The Fictional Father: Lacanian Readings of the Text.* Amherst: U of Massachusetts P, 1981.

————. "Lacan and Narration." *Modern Language Notes* 5 (1983): 848–59.

Felman, Shoshana, ed. *Jacques Lacan and the Adventure of Insight: Psychoanalysis in Contemporary Culture.* Cambridge: Harvard UP, 1987.

————. *Literature and Psychoanalysis: The Question of Reading: Otherwise.* Baltimore: Johns Hopkins UP, 1982.

Froula, Christine. "When Eve Reads Milton: Undoing the Canonical Economy." *Canons.* Ed. Robert von Hallberg. Chicago: U of Chicago P, 1984. 149–75.

Homans, Margaret. *Bearing the Word: Language and Female Experience in Nineteenth-Century Women's Writing.* Chicago: U of Chicago P, 1986.

Mellard, James. *Using Lacan, Reading Fiction.* Urbana: U of Illinois P, 1991.

Muller, John P., and William J. Richardson, eds. *The Purloined Poe: Lacan, Derrida, and Psychoanalytic Reading.* Baltimore: Johns Hopkins UP, 1988. Includes Lacan's seminar on Poe's "Purloined Letter."

Psychoanalytic Readings of *Death in Venice*

Beharriell, Frederick J. "Never without Freud: Freud's Influence on Mann." *Thomas Mann in Context: Papers of the Clark University Centennial Colloquium.* Ed. Kenneth Hughes. Worcester: Clark UP, 1978. 1–15.

Davidson, Leah. "Mid-Life Crisis in Thomas Mann's *Death in Venice.*" *Journal of the American Academy of Psychoanalysis* 4 (1976): 203–14.

Jofen, Jean. "A Freudian Commentary on Thomas Mann's *Death in Venice.*" *Journal of Evolutionary Psychology* 6 (1985): 238–47.

Kohut, Heinz. "*Death in Venice* by Thomas Mann: A Story about the Disintegration of Artistic Sublimation." *Psychoanalysis and Literature.* Ed. Hendrik M. Ruitenbeck. New York: Dutton, 1964. 282–302.

Newton, Caroline. "Thomas Mann and Sigmund Freud." *Princeton University Library Chronicle* 24 (1963): 135–39.

Slochower, Harry. "Thomas Mann's *Death in Venice.*" *American Imago* 26 (1969): 91–122.

Tarbox, Raymond. "*Death in Venice:* The Aesthetic Object as Dream Guide." *American Imago* 26 (1969): 123–44.

A PSYCHOANALYTIC PERSPECTIVE

RODNEY SYMINGTON

The Eruption of the Other: Psychoanalytic Approaches to *Death in Venice*

It does not seem possible to be an artist and not to be sick.
                                        –NIETZSCHE, *The Will to Power*

One critic has rightfully described Thomas Mann's artistic technique as "the art of ambivalence" (Reed 1974, 235). This ambivalence derives not merely from his all-pervasive relativizing irony, but also from the deliberate multilayering of motifs and ideas in his works. As with most great works of world literature, it is therefore impossible to reach definitive and final conclusions about this work's meaning. A semiotician would say that every decoding is a further encoding — that is, every attempt at explicating a work of art merely translates it into words (a new "code"), which in turn need further explanation. Likewise, each interpretation of *Death in Venice*, while capturing one or more aspects of the work, cannot possibly exhaust all the interpretive possibilities. The inherent complexity of the work and its connotative implications seem inexhaustible, and thus invite repeated attempts at explication.

That *Death in Venice* exists on many levels is incontrovertible; that the psychology of the protagonist Aschenbach stands at the center of the novella is likewise indisputable. Thus, in attempting to understand the novella, we must strive to understand the protagonist. And because the struggle occurs within him, we must examine his character, thoughts, and actions if we are to fathom the meaning of the work. *Death in Venice* deals with the moral and psychological collapse of the main character. From the heights of apparent ethical purity and public fame, Aschenbach plunges to the depths of moral degradation. What causes this collapse?

One conventional interpretation of *Death in Venice* relates Aschenbach's tragedy to the clash of the twin poles of Apollo and Dionysus. Representing form, order, clarity, and reason ("the power to create harmonious and measured beauty"), Apollo, symbolizes in myth all that Aschenbach's life and works represent, whereas Dionysus, the mythical symbol of disorder, chaos, sex, and unreason ("the symbol of

drunken frenzy that threatens to destroy all forms and codes"), sum-
marizes the unsatisfied and suppressed inclinations of Aschenbach's
darker side (Kaufmann 128). Despite all the defenses that Apollo
erects, Dionysus is finally triumphant.

Mann adopted this fundamental opposition from Nietzsche's *Birth
of Tragedy*, where the philosopher sees the two forces as indispensable
to the development of culture: the Dionysian, in the form of disease
and hardship, spurs the artist on to create things of beauty. Hence
Apollo triumphs — at least for the moment — over Dionysus. Thus
Aschenbach's creative success, his cultivation of form and beauty, are
conscious attempts to construct a bulwark against, if not to conquer,
the Dionysian elements that threaten, albeit unconsciously, both his
life in particular and civilized culture in general.

Nietzsche plays a major role in Thomas Mann's thinking and thus
constitutes a significant presence in *Death in Venice*. But there is also
evidence that Thomas Mann felt some influence from the theories of
Sigmund Freud as he wrote the novella. Thus we will first examine
how Freud's view of the psyche might have found its way into the
work, and how Freud's theories might help us to understand Aschenbach's downfall. Then we will reexamine the text in light of the more
recent theories of the personality as developed by Jacques Lacan
(1901–81). His ideas will help us move to a different plane of interpretation — one that also implies much about Thomas Mann himself.

The question of what Mann knew of Sigmund Freud's theories in
1911 has occupied scholars for a long time. In writing this novella, it
appears that he might have not only consulted but also drawn on psy-
choanalytical concepts — notably, Freud's theory of repression. Although earlier works, such as *Little Herr Friedemann* and *Royal Highness*, show traces of Freudian elements, Mann could have found these
ideas in Schopenhauer and Nietzsche. In a 1925 interview with the
Italian newspaper *La Stampa*, however, he stated, "In my own case, at
least one of my works, the novella 'Death in Venice,' originated under
the direct influence of Freud. Without Freud I would never have
thought of treating this erotic motif, or at least I would have treated it
differently" (Dierks 1990, 284).[1]

Of course, this interview took place fourteen years after the publication of the novella, and we know that Thomas Mann is seldom the
most reliable source for information or commentary on his own works.
Consequently, several commentators have regarded this statement

---

[1] All translations from German are by the author.

with some skepticism. We need not rely on this piece of information alone, however. There is some evidence that Mann might have known a work of Freud that could have affected his writing of *Death in Venice*. In his 1907 essay "Illusion and Dreams in W. Jensen's 'Gradiva,'" Freud analyzed (and indeed psychoanalyzed) a short story by Wilhelm Jensen (1837–1911) that shows remarkable parallels with *Death in Venice*. (What follows relies in part on Dierks 1990, 284–86; Dierks 1991, 114–16; and Berlin).

Norbert Hanold, a young archaeologist, is fascinated by a plaster cast that he keeps in his room, a Roman relief of a young woman, to whom he gives the name Gradiva. During one winter he imagines her life: he decides that she really looks Greek, and he places her in Pompeii in A.D. 79, when the erupting volcano covered the city in ash. Later, he dreams that he was present on the day of Pompeii's destruction and witnessed Gradiva's burial by the volcanic ash. Shortly thereafter he feels the urge to travel south — ostensibly for a scientific reason but actually as the result of "an unnameable sensation" (Freud 18). After stops in Rome and Naples, he arrives in Pompeii, where he realizes that he has come there with the unconscious purpose of seeking traces of Gradiva.

In Pompeii his fantasy about Gradiva intensifies: he comes to believe that she has come to life again and is walking about the ruined city. He follows the woman he believes is Gradiva and speaks to her, first in Greek and then in Latin; she answers him in German. In fact, the figure he identifies with Gradiva is a young woman, Zoë, with whom he had a close friendship when they were children. But since his fascination with archaeology had taken hold of him, he had scarcely looked at women, so he does not even recognize her. After several meetings with Zoë in Pompeii, he finally comes to his senses, and his and Zoë's love for each other is "unearthed" and flourishes.

Freud's interpretation of the story depends on his theory of sexual repression: through his single-minded devotion to archaeology, Hanold has repressed the sexual feelings he has had toward Zoë since childhood. His obsession with the Roman relief and his fantasies about it are the outward evidence of this repression. His urge to travel in the service of archaeology is, in fact, mistaken, as his erotic feelings for Zoë are the real motivation. Furthermore, Freud interprets the image of Pompeii — once covered by ash and now laid bare — as a symbol of Hanold's psyche. He too was "covered in ash," and his visit to Pompeii lays bare his true feelings. Hanold displaces his true feelings toward Zoë onto the mythical Gradiva until Zoë can convince him that

she is real. Freud comments: "There is really no better analogy for repression, which at the same time makes something inaccessible and yet
preserves it, than the covering of ash that was Pompeii's fate, and from
which the city reappeared through the work of the shovel" (Freud 40).

The second half of Freud's essay, constituting his analysis of the
story, contains several key elements of his psychoanalytic theory. A
comparison of Jensen's "Gradiva" with Mann's *Death in Venice* shows
that there are close parallels between the plot of the former and its
analysis by Freud, and Mann's story. For example, striking similarities
exists between the structure of Jensen's and Mann's works: the archaeologist, devoted to the discipline of science, follows the urge to travel
and finds his goal in an ancient southern place rich in cultural associations. The use of historical elements as symbolical devices (for example, the destruction of Pompeii by volcanic ash) foreshadows Mann's
employment of myth as both the typical and the embodiment of psychological truth. Furthermore, Dierks discusses some linguistic parallels between Freud's essay and Mann's novella (1990, 284–86; 1991,
114–16).

It would be a gross oversimplification, however, to assume that
Mann simply took some fundamental principles of Freud's theory of
psychoanalysis and based a novella on them. *Death in Venice,* like all of
Mann's works, is an amalgam of motifs and ideas that he culled from a
multiplicity of sources that happened to accord with his views of life
and art as he wished to express them. In fact, there is almost nothing
in the depiction of Aschenbach's psychology that we could not also
trace to the influence of Schopenhauer and Nietzsche on Mann.

In the general intellectual and artistic climate around 1910, when
the new theories of psychoanalysis were, in Mann's phrase, "in the air"
(Hoffmann 209), it was inevitable that he would in some measure be
affected by them, or would feel their effect, or at least have an opinion
about them. (We also know of his sometimes critical views of psychoanalysis.) As one critic has stated, "a survey of literary and intellectual
journals reveals that by 1910 serious discussions of Freud's ideas were
commonplace, and that it would have required an abnormal vigilance
to remain in ignorance of them" (Beharriell 12).

It is also clear that perceptive writers have always had the capacity
to fathom the human soul: psychology has always played a major role
in literature (Gay 129–31). As Freud wrote to Arthur Schnitzler in
1922, "I have the impression that you know through intuition — actually the result of astute self-perception — all the things that I have
discovered through laborious work with other people" (Wysling 205).

Mann's "knowledge" of the mental states of human beings had a similar basis and was enriched through his reading of Schopenhauer and Nietzsche, whose works gave him all that he needed to know about psychology without any reference to Freud. All of the considerable circumstantial evidence, however, points to Mann's having more than a passing familiarity with psychoanalysis by 1911 (Wysling 201–206, Beharriell).

In fact, Freud's ideas about repression fitted closely with Nietzsche's description of the clash between Apollo and Dionysus. The attempts by the Apollonian artist to suppress the Dionysian find their direct parallel in Freud's theory of how repression operates. And there is a direct line of thought that runs from Schopenhauer's all-pervasive "Will," constantly threatening and undermining civilization, through Nietzsche's Dionysus in *The Birth of Tragedy* to Freud's concept of repression that will inevitably avenge itself. Consider Freud's quote from Horace: "You may drive out nature with a hay-fork, but it will always return" (Freud 35).

All in all, we can conclude that Mann's use of psychology in *Death in Venice* sprang from a number of sources: Schopenhauer, Nietzsche, perhaps through one or more of Freud's works directly, the intellectual climate of the age, and above all his own perceptions as a writer. In this regard, he followed his usual practice of assimilating and exploiting any materials that he found appropriate for his artistic goals.

For our interpretation of *Death in Venice,* we can apply first Freud's theory of repression, which Peter Gay has well defined as follows:

Most of the unconscious consists of repressed materials. This unconscious, as Freud conceptualized it . . . resembles a maximum-security prison holding antisocial inmates languishing for years or recently arrived, inmates harshly treated and heavily guarded, but barely kept under control and forever attempting to escape. Their breakouts succeed only intermittently and at great cost to themselves and to others. (Gay 128)

It should be clear to any reader of *Death in Venice* that this description of repression closely parallels the mental state — and the resulting tragedy — of Aschenbach. Although the story gives us plenty of hints that Aschenbach has lived his life so far under the principle of repression, only near the end (and near his end) does Mann overtly portray the "breakout" of the passions that Aschenbach has kept imprisoned for so long:

That night he had a terrible dream, if dream is the right word for a bodily and mental experience which did indeed overtake him during deepest sleep, in complete independence of his will and with complete sensuous vividness, but with no perception of himself as present and moving about in any space external to the events themselves; rather, the scene of the events was his own soul, and they irrupted into it from outside, violently defeating his resistance — a profound, intellectual resistance — as they passed through him, and leaving his whole being, the culture of a lifetime, devastated and destroyed. (254–55)

The opening sentence of the description of Aschenbach's terrible yet fascinating dream illustrates vividly the fundamental psychological principle on which *Death in Venice* rests: repression, and its inevitable, ultimate effect on the psyche. The vocabulary leaves no doubt about the process: Aschenbach's mental opposition to the experience, "a profound, intellectual resistance," is no match for the forces that have "irrupted" into his soul, which is the "scene of the events" that he witnesses. That eruption is the revenge of repression that inexorably breaks down the barriers of culture erected over many years, leaving him "devastated and destroyed."

Freud's theory of repression as an interpretive device thus lends itself quite nicely to an interpretation of *Death in Venice*. Aschenbach's whole life has been lived under the sway of discipline and renunciation. From his morning ablutions in cold water to the elimination of all that is vulgar from his diction, Aschenbach has controlled his character and literary career by the conscious cultivation of form and intellect and the studious repression of all that did not fit in with his classicistic concept of art and life. One could hardly imagine a better image of Aschenbach's personality and existence than the tightly clenched fist that an acquaintance uses to symbolize his way of life: the closed fist stands for the hermetic nature of his rational mind. The unconscious is held fast (for the moment), trapped by an act of conscious will. Ironically, the opposite of this image — the relaxed and open hand — is precisely the form that Aschenbach's life is about to take on, with fateful consequences.

Of course, the undermining of Aschenbach's secure world has already begun long before the story opens. Years of self-discipline, self-sacrifice, and devotion to his art have so sapped his physical strength that he needs a "daily siesta which was now so necessary to him as he became increasingly subject to fatigue" (23). But the physical symptoms are merely the outward reflection of an inner weakness, the bodily fatigue the harbinger of spiritual collapse.

Mann indicates the innate fragility of Aschenbach's facade in the first sentence, where he informs us of the artist's having been awarded the ennobling title "von": in other words, Aschenbach is not what he seems; his name does not describe his true identity. Behind the false front of his title lurks the being who is itching to emerge. Fittingly, the equally false front of the building opposite the tram stop where he waits causes the first cracks in the civilized veneer of the revered artist: it is a mortuary chapel with "Byzantine styling," whose facade is "adorned with Greek crosses and brightly painted hieratic motifs." Although Aschenbach is in Munich, here are already hints of Venice. Thus Mann foreshadows Aschenbach's death, hidden, of course, like Aschenbach's true character, behind an ornamental facade. The mystery of what he sees here makes him pause, spending "some minutes" attempting to decipher "selected scriptural passages about the life to come" and "letting his mind wander in contemplation of the mystic meaning that suffused them" (24). This contemplation of death signifies the start of his abandonment of form and his embrace of dissolution.

Of course, these images do not *cause* Aschenbach's demise; they are only the immediate real objects stimulating the unconscious process that is already under way. The coincidence of stopping near the North Cemetery and contemplating the front of the mortuary chapel (presumably not for the first time) conjoins with a heightened psychological receptivity that unconsciously absorbs and interprets the various objects of Aschenbach's gaze in a way that sparks his "sudden" urge to travel. The additional apocalyptic beasts and the stranger with "an exotic air, as of someone who had come from distant parts" (24), complete a picture and the interpretation of it that has sprung from Aschenbach's interior. The physical reality of the scene has no meaning until Aschenbach's psychological state infuses the literal details with a coherence that they do not innately possess. Many works of the eighteenth and nineteenth centuries anthropomorphize nature; here concrete objects acquire a transferred significance through the medium of Aschenbach's psyche. On a merely biographical level, Thomas Mann's statement that he invented nothing in the story, which contained what he termed "an innate symbolism," shows that the process taking place in Aschenbach originated in the author's habit of giving cohesive form and meaning to the discrete elements of life.

In Freudian terms, Aschenbach's id, his suppressed urges, is about to break through the barriers that his ego, his self-constructed persona, has erected both by itself and under the influence of the superego, which is society. As Mann commented later, "The Ego lives out its predetermined character; in addition, it is a plaything of 'Will,' which seeks to achieve its ends by means of the intellect, which isn't even aware of those ends" (*Briefe* 3:335). Here again we see Mann's typical creative method: he has amalgamated Schopenhauer's notion of "Will" with Freud's idea of the ego.

Moreover, we should note that by the time of his fateful dream, Aschenbach is not only susceptible to the invasion of his psyche by repressed forces; he is even open to this inroad and eager for it: "It began with fear, fear and joy and a horrified curiosity about what was to come" (81).

While accepting the validity of the preceding possibilities for interpretation, we must be careful not to embroil ourselves in the "intentional fallacy": it would be wrong to assume that Thomas Mann narrowly focused on psychoanalysis when writing *Death in Venice*. On the contrary, several times he expressed his reservations about the dangers of psychoanalysis for art, as he found its principles too limiting. Whereas art was inherently connotative, suggesting manifold possibilities and never achieving or even desiring closure, psychoanalysis strove to be a science, whose ultimate goal was to reveal finite truths. In a notebook entry, Mann described Freud as: "progressively undermining: like all psychology. Art becomes impossible when one sees through it" (*Notizbücher* 269).

The wealth of connotative possibilities suggested by all great works of art infuses them with a timelessness that speaks to all ages. On the other hand, such works wait, so to speak, for their interpreters and for new interpretive methods that will throw new light on them. The theories of Jacques Lacan, while attempting primarily to revise those of Freud, have coincidentally also given new impetus to the psychoanalytic interpretation of literature. Lacan himself pointed the way with his interpretation of Edgar Allan Poe's "Purloined Letter."

For our purposes, the three central concepts of Lacan — the Imaginary, the Symbolic, and the Real — will prove most productive for a reexamination of *Death in Venice*. For Lacan, individuals construct for themselves an image of their personality that is a defense mechanism against the truth. Because we cannot encompass the entirety of being, we take refuge behind the fortified walls of a manufactured view of ourselves, a view that needs and seeks repeated confirmation of its validity. These attempts at self-validation are merely measures of avoidance, however, unacknowledged admissions of a realm of being that is present yet unknowable. Lacan's term for this other realm is the

"Other," a somewhat vague concept that corresponds to some degree with Freud's "unconscious." It represents the unconscious forces affecting our personalities, despite our denials of their existence. To start with, let us see how Lacan's concept of the Imaginary applies to Aschenbach:

> The Imaginary is the order of mirror-images, identifications and reciprocities. It is the dimension of experience in which the individual seeks not simply to placate the Other but to dissolve his otherness by becoming his counterpart. By way of the Imaginary, the original identificatory procedures which brought the ego into being are repeated and reinforced by the individual in his relationship with the external world of people and things. The Imaginary is the scene of a desperate delusional attempt to be and remain "what one is" by gathering to oneself ever more instances of sameness, resemblance and self-replication; it is the birthplace of the narcissistic "ideal ego" (*Idealich, moi idéal*). . . . The term has a strong pejorative force and suggests that the subject is seeking, in a willful and blameworthy fashion, to remove himself from the flux of becoming. (Bowie 92)

The preceding description of Lacan's concept of the Imaginary reads as if tailored to the particular case of Aschenbach. The latter's "delusional attempt" to construct a world of form and order about himself — his single-minded adherence to classicistic, Apollonian ideals — provides us with a near-perfect case history to illustrate Lacanian theory.

It is, indeed, a *constructed* world with which Aschenbach surrounds himself. The description of his mode of writing as an act of conscious effort, a battle against all the forces that conspire to prevent the creative act, merely reflects his general philosophy of life. The narrator's comment that "nearly all the great things that exist owe their existence to a defiant despite" (30) could be applied both to Aschenbach's own works as described in the novella, but even more so to his life. He lives it according to the slogan of Frederick the Great: *"durchhalten!"* (29; "endure"). The depiction of Aschenbach's life "before the Fall" illustrates the quintessential Lacanian Imaginary realm. Aschenbach's mental discipline and orderly existence is a self-directed facade, as rotten as the pilings that support the beauty of Venice: "The apparent coherence of the Imaginary, its fullness and grandiosity, is always false, a *mis*recognition that the ego (or 'me') tries to deny by imagining itself as coherent and capable" (Sullivan 488).

Lacan's central concept of the Other poses a direct threat to the individual's Imaginary construct. Commentators and interpreters of Lacan have pointed out the ambiguities in his use of the term:

> Lacan's "Other" is a pliable and sometimes confusing notion. For it designates now one member of the dialectical couple "Subject-Other" and now the limitless field and overriding condition in which both members find themselves — "alterity," "otherness." . . . The oracular power of such sentences as "the unconscious is the discourse of the Other" comes, in large part, from the hesitation they encourage in the reader between these long-range and short-range definitions. What does the sentence mean? That the unconscious is where the Other performs his darkest deeds, as an occupying force or a fifth column, or that the unconscious is otherness pure and simple, the "other scene" by which our conscious thought and action are constantly shadowed? (Bowie 82–83)

In the case of Aschenbach, it seems initially that the first definition of Lacan's Other is most appropriate. The Other lurks in his unconscious for all the years he submits himself to the discipline of Apollonian art, and this Other begins its breakthrough and drive for dominance on the fateful day that Aschenbach takes his afternoon stroll. The "Stranger God" who appears to Aschenbach in his terible dream toward the end of the novella represents the culmination of various manifestations of the Other that have been present since the beginning of the story. For instance, the stranger appearing on the steps of the mortuary chapel above the "apocalyptic beasts" concretizes the Other in Aschenbach's unconscious. The figure might even be a figment of Aschenbach's imagination, for when a few moments later he boards the tram and looks for the stranger, "the man's whereabouts remained a mystery, for he was no longer standing where he had stood, nor was he to be seen anywhere else at the stop or in the tramcar itself" (28). (Frizen likewise comments that the figure "'appears' in the truest sense of the word" [28].)

The Stranger, as a precursor of death, will reappear to Aschenbach in the course of his journey: notably, as the old fop on the ferry to Venice and the gondolier, but also by suggestive association, as the ticket agent in the bowels of the ferry and the wandering musician at the hotel. Accompanying the obvious parallels between these figures we find a much more subtle stylistic device that connects Aschenbach with them — and thus with the Other — from beginning to end. The motif of strangeness — expressed in German by the adjective *fremd* and its many variations as adjectives, nouns, and verbs — interweaves

the text so that what starts as something apparently outside of Aschenbach (as for example the Stranger on the mortuary steps) gradually becomes his own defining quality. Aschenbach slowly but inexorably assumes the motif, and thus the characteristic, of "strangeness," as the
Other takes possession of his life. In other words, the Other within
him asserts its inevitable right to dominance. Thus we might observe
that Aschenbach in fact exemplifies *both* aspects of Lacan's Other: the
realm of the Other first impinges on his Imaginary construct, undermining and fragmenting it, and then it becomes the battleground for
the struggle as Aschenbach's character assumes "Otherness." This
process also accords with Lacanian theory: "the individual seeks not
simply to placate the Other, but to dissolve his otherness by becoming
his counterpart" (Bowie 92).

For Lacan, language, a symbolic system, structures the unconscious: hence a Symbolic order governs it. Because this order exists before we are born, our birth thrusts us into the Symbolic with our having no choice in the matter. Our attempt to construct an Imaginary
image of ourselves constantly conflicts with the Symbolic order striving to dominate it.

Aschenbach's life and literary career reflect this Lacanian model of
the psyche. Even Mann's own rather simplistic, and often repeated,
view of the artist's birth through the combined discipline of the father
and the bohemian spirit of the mother acknowledges the effect of
being born *into* a Symbolic order that one cannot control. Mann was
simply putting it another way when he had Tonio Kröger declare that
"literature isn't a profession at all . . . — it is a curse!"

For Lacan, however, the problem is much more complex. In his
terms, the Symbolic order molds Aschenbach's outward life and career. The latter's Imaginary construct submits to this order, but suffers
from an inherent instability caused by the conflict between the necessity imposed on it by the Symbolic order and its own innate desires.
Even Aschenbach's accomplishments are not immune from the instability of his internal state: his short story "A Study in Abjection"
demonstrated "the possibility of moral resolution even for those who
have plumbed the depths of knowledge" (28). That is, Aschenbach
subconsciously suppresses in his art the knowledge of the Lacanian
Other, of the clash between the Symbolic and the Imaginary, in order
to erect a temporary moral bastion. Just as Schopenhauer's "Will" inevitably asserts its hegemony, so the Other will inevitably destroy all
the superb ethical rationalizing that Aschenbach has constructed in his
works.

Furthermore, Lacan's view that "signifiers" — that is, words — are merely metaphorical reflections of reality (and therefore unreliable) condemns a priori not only the ethical constructs of Aschenbach's writing but also all of his rationalizations about beauty and his objective contemplation of it in the form of Tadzio. On the surface, Aschenbach may be performing a purely intellectual exercise in regarding Tadzio as the embodiment of objective, nonsexual beauty. But because the Other also invades language itself, even apparently disinterested statements represent the conflict between what the speaker would like to believe as true and the reality behind the mask of language:

> [The Other] is that which insinuates itself between the individual and the objects of "his" desire; which traverses those objects and makes them unstable; and which makes desire more unsatiable by continuously moving its target. And as language is the site of desire – the supreme mechanism for its production and transformation, the complete tease — the Other takes language as its field of action. Where "natural" analogies and symbolism based upon them, offer the promise of completion, fullness, symmetry and repose at the end of the signifying process, the Other keeps the signifier perpetually on the move. (Bowie 83–84)

Thus even Aschenbach's use of Plato's dialogues on beauty is misguided and erroneous: the intrinsic unreliability of signifiers and their constant undermining by the Other nullifies all of his attempts to rationalize his motivation. His self-delusion about the motive for his fascination with Tadzio's beauty — which many commentators stress — is not merely a function of his own moral duplicity but rather is also inherent and unavoidable. The human psyche, as the scene of the constant struggle between the Imaginary and the Symbolic (mediated by the Other), is ipso facto the realm of uncertainty and duplicity.

For Lacan, this is the domain of the Real, the unknowable orbit that we attempt to comprehend and even master by means of our Imaginary and Symbolic constructs. But all our efforts are to no avail: "Dance as one may in the chequered shade of the signifier, parade as one may the plumage of one's own literary style, there yet exists a world that falls entirely and irretrievably outside the signifying dimension" (Bowie 94). While the three concepts of the Imaginary, the Symbolic, and the Real are inherently interrelated, feeding off one another, only the Real finally decides the course of our life. In that "the real is the irruption of the unrepresentable," however, it remains clouded in mystery (Ellmann 105).

Thus the Real ultimately determines Aschenbach's fate. His vacillation between the Imaginary and the Symbolic is a temporary stage, a waiting for the eventual and unavoidable eruption of the Other from within. Aschenbach's demise is all the more poignant because he has placed such a faith in language: form and clarity condition his worldview and the pattern of his life. The grammar of his weltanschauung bespeaks the Symbolic order, while his philosophical syntax is that of the Imaginary. In Lacanian terms, however, whoever places so much trust in these two realms as constituting the whole of existence has constructed an existential house of cards, whose collapse is inevitable. The incomprehensibility of Aschenbach's decline and fall only reflects the fundamental dilemma of life: we can never know the Real.

In sum, Lacan's theory of language and the Other suggests new interpretive possibilities for Mann's works. His mining of Schopenhauer, Nietzsche, Wagner, and Freud to create a new amalgam of philosophical, cultural, and artistic elements in order to give aesthetic form to experience has led scholars to an extensive and intensive analysis and appraisal of his sources. By applying Lacan's ideas, we now possess a fresh, hermeneutic method that permits us to move beyond the limits of conventional explication into a new realm of suggestive interpretation. Furthermore, Lacan's theories allow us to reexamine Mann's works in relation to his biography. Accordingly, we might discover new insights into the relationship between the artist and his work. Ellie Ragland Sullivan has analyzed Edith Wharton's *House of Mirth* in this way as a reflection of the author's search for identity.

One may subscribe to the conventional view that Mann's creative drive stemmed mainly from the tension between being both bourgeois and an artist. Or one may locate the source of his creativity in his ambivalent sexual nature. Lacan offers us yet another explanation: that Mann, like Aschenbach, constructed for himself a world of the Imaginary. In any case, one must draw the conclusion that the problematic existence of Thomas Mann was the wellspring of his work.

WORKS CITED

Beharriell, Frederick J. "'Never without Freud': Freud's Influence on Mann." *Thomas Mann in Context*. Ed. Kenneth Hughes. Worcester: Clark UP, 1978. 1–15.

Berlin, Jeffrey B. "Psychoanalysis, Freud, and Thomas Mann." *Approaches to Teaching Thomas Mann's "Death in Venice" and Other Short Fiction.* Ed. Jeffrey B. Berlin. New York: MLA, 1992. 105–18.

Bowie, Malcolm. *Lacan.* Cambridge, Mass., and London: Harvard UP, 1991.

Dierks, Manfred. *Studien zu Mythos und Psychologie bei Thomas Mann.* Bern and München: Francke, 1972.

———. "Thomas Mann und die Teifenpsychologie." *Thomas-Mann-Handbuch.* Ed. Helmut Koopmann. Stuttgart: Kröner, 1990. 284–300.

———. "Traumzeit und Verdichtung: Der Einfluß der Pschoanalyse auf Thomas Manns Erzählweise." *Thomas Mann und seine Quellen. Festschrift für Hans Wysling.* Ed. Eckhard Heftrich and Helmut Koopmann. Frankfurt: Klostermann, 1991. 111–37.

Ellmann, Maud, ed. *Psychoanalytic Literary Criticism.* London and New York: Longman, 1994.

Freud, Sigmund. "Der Wahn und die Träume in W. Jensens *Gradiva.*" *Sigmund Freud. Studienausgabe. Band X. Bildende Kunst und Literatur.* London: Imago, 1941. 13–85.

Frizen, Werner. *Thomas Mann: "Der Tod in Venedig."* München: Oldenbourg, 1993.

Gallop, Jane. *Reading Lacan.* Ithaca: Cornell UP, 1985.

Gay, Peter. *Freud: A Life for Our Time.* New York and London: Norton, 1988.

Hoffmann, Frederick. *Freudianism and the Literary Mind.* Baton Rouge: Louisiana State UP, 1945.

Kaufmann, Walter. *Nietzsche: Philosopher, Psychologist, Antichrist.* Princeton: Princeton UP, 1968.

Lacan, Jacques. *Écrits: A Selection.* Trans. Alan Sheridan. New York: Norton, 1977.

———. *The Four Fundamental Concepts of Psycho-Analysis.* Trans. Alan Sheridan. London: Penguin, 1980.

Mann, Thomas. *Briefe.* Vol. 3. Ed. Erika Mann. Frankfurt: Fischer, 1965.

———. *Notizbücher 7–14.* Ed. Hans Wysling and Yvonne Schmidlin. Frankfurt: Fischer, 1992.

Neu, Jerome. *The Cambridge Companion to Freud.* Cambridge: Cambridge UP, 1991.

Sullivan, Ellie Ragland. "The Daughter's Dilemma: Psychoanalytic Interpretation and Edith Wharton's *The House of Mirth.*" *Edith*

Wharton, "The House of Mirth." Case Studies in Contemporary Criticism. Ed. Shari Benstock. Boston: Bedford Books–St. Martin's, 1994. 464–81.

Reed, T. J., ed. *Thomas Mann: "Der Tod in Venedig."* München and Wien: Hanser, 1983.

———. *Thomas Mann: The Uses of Tradition.* Oxford: Oxford UP, 1974.

Slochower, Harry. "Thomas Mann's *Death in Venice.*" *American Imago* 26 (1969): 99–122.

Wysling, Hans. "Thomas Manns Rezeption der Psychoanalyse." *Probleme der Moderne: Studien zur deutschen Literatur von Nietzsche bis Brecht.* Ed. Benjamin Bennett, Anton Kaes, William J. Lillyman. Tübingen: Niemeyer, 1983. 210–22.

Reader-Response Criticism
and *Death in Venice*

WHAT IS READER-RESPONSE CRITICISM?

Students are routinely asked in English courses for their reactions to the texts they are reading. Sometimes there are so many different reactions that we may wonder whether everyone has read the same text. And some students respond so idiosyncratically to what they read that we say their responses are "totally off the wall." This variety of response interests reader-response critics, who raise theoretical questions about whether our responses to a work are the same as its meanings, whether a work can have as many meanings as we have responses to it, and whether some responses are more valid than others. They ask what determines what is and what isn't "off the wall." What, in other words, is the wall, and what standards help us define it?

In addition to posing provocative questions, reader-response criticism provides us with models that aid our understanding of texts and the reading process. Adena Rosmarin has suggested that a literary text may be likened to an incomplete work of sculpture: to see it fully, we must complete it imaginatively, taking care to do so in a way that responsibly takes into account what exists. Other reader-response critics have suggested other models, for reader-response criticism is not a monolithic school of thought but rather an umbrella term covering a variety of approaches to literature.

Nonetheless, as Steven Mailloux has shown, reader-response critics *do* share not only questions but also goals and strategies. Two of the basic goals are to show that a work gives readers something to do and to describe what the reader does by way of response. To achieve those goals, the critic may make any of a number of what Mailloux calls "moves." For instance, a reader-response critic might typically (1) cite direct references to reading in the text being analyzed, in order to justify the focus on reading and show that the world of the text is continuous with the one in which the reader reads; (2) show how other non-reading situations in the text nonetheless mirror the situation the reader is in ("Fish shows how in *Paradise Lost* Michael's teaching of Adam in Book 11 resembles Milton's teaching of the reader throughout the poem"); and (3) show, therefore, that the reader's response is, or is analogous to, the story's action or conflict. For instance, Stephen Booth calls *Hamlet* the tragic story of "an audience that cannot make up its mind" (Mailloux, "Learning" 103).

Although reader-response criticism is often said to have emerged in the United States in the 1970s, it is in one respect as old as the foundations of Western culture. The ancient Greeks and Romans tended to view literature as rhetoric, a means of making an audience react in a certain way. Although their focus was more on rhetorical strategies and devices than on the reader's (or listener's) response to those methods, the ancients by no means left the audience out of the literary equation. Aristotle thought, for instance, that the greatness of tragedy lies in its "cathartic" power to cleanse or purify the emotions of audience members. Plato, by contrast, worried about the effects of artistic productions, so much so that he advocated evicting poets from the Republic on the grounds that their words "feed and water" the passions!

In our own century, long before 1970, there were critics whose concerns and attitudes anticipated those of reader-response critics. One of these, I. A. Richards, is usually associated with formalism, a supposedly objective, text-centered approach to literature that reader-response critics of the 1970s roundly attacked. And yet in 1929 Richards managed to sound surprisingly *like* a 1970s-vintage reader-response critic, writing in *Practical Criticism* that "the personal situation of the reader inevitably (and within limits rightly) affects his reading, and many more are drawn to poetry in quest of some reflection of their latest emotional crisis than would admit it" (575). Rather than deploring this fact, as many of his formalist contemporaries would have done, Richards argued that the reader's feelings and experiences provide a kind of reality check, a way of testing the authenticity of emotions and events represented in literary works.

Approximately a decade after Richards wrote *Practical Criticism,* an American named Louise M. Rosenblatt published *Literature as Exploration* (1938). In that seminal book, now in its fourth edition (1983), Rosenblatt began developing a theory of reading that blurs the boundary between reader and text, subject and object. In a 1969 article entitled "Towards a Transactional Theory of Reading," she sums up her position by writing that "a poem is what the reader lives through under the guidance of the text and experiences as relevant to the text" (127). Rosenblatt knew her definition would be difficult for many to accept: "The idea that a *poem* presupposes a *reader* actively involved with a *text,*" she wrote, "is particularly shocking to those seeking to emphasize the objectivity of their interpretations" ("Transactional" 127).

Rosenblatt implicitly and generally refers to formalists (also called the New Critics) when she speaks of supposedly objective interpreters shocked by the notion that a "poem" is something cooperatively produced by a "reader" and a "text." Formalists spoke of "the poem itself," the "concrete work of art," the "real poem." They had no interest in what a work of literature makes a reader "live through." In fact, in *The Verbal Icon* (1954), William K. Wimsatt and Monroe C. Beardsley defined as fallacious the very notion that a reader's response is relevant to the meaning of a literary work:

> The Affective Fallacy is a confusion between the poem and its *results* (what it *is* and what it *does*). . . . It begins by trying to derive the standards of criticism from the psychological effects of a poem and ends in impressionism and relativism. The outcome . . . is that the poem itself, as an object of specifically critical judgment, tends to disappear. (21)

Reader-response critics have taken issue with their formalist predecessors. Particularly influential has been Stanley Fish, whose early work is seen by some as marking the true beginning of contemporary reader-response criticism. In "Literature in the Reader: Affective Stylistics" (1970), Fish took on the formalist hegemony, the New Critical establishment, by arguing that any school of criticism that would see a work of literature as an object, claiming to describe what it *is* and never what it *does,* is guilty of misconstruing the very essence of literature and reading. Literature exists when it is read, Fish suggests, and its force is an affective force. Furthermore, reading is a temporal process. Formalists assume it is a spatial one as they step back and survey the literary work as if it were an object spread out before them. They may find elegant patterns in the texts they examine and reexamine, but they fail to take into account that the work is quite different to a reader who is turning the pages and being moved, or affected, by lines that appear and disappear as the reader reads.

In a discussion of the effect that a sentence penned by the seventeenth-century physician Thomas Browne has on a reader reading, Fish pauses to say this about his analysis and also, by extension, about his critical strategy: "Whatever is persuasive and illuminating about [it] is the result of my substituting for one question — what does this sentence mean? — another, more operational question — what does this sentence do?" He then quotes a line from John Milton's *Paradise Lost,* a line that refers to Satan and the other fallen angels: "Nor did they not perceive their evil plight." Whereas more traditional critics might say that the "meaning" of the line is "They did perceive their evil plight," Fish relates the uncertain movement of the reader's mind *to* that half-satisfying interpretation. Furthermore, he declares that "the reader's inability to tell whether or not 'they' do perceive and his involuntary question . . . are part of the line's *meaning,* even though they take place in the mind, not on the page" (*Text* 26).

The stress on what pages *do* to minds (and what minds do in response) pervades the writings of most, if not all, reader-response critics. Stephen Booth, whose book *An Essay on Shakespeare's Sonnets* (1969) greatly influenced Fish, sets out to describe the "reading experience that results" from a "multiplicity of organizations" in a sonnet by Shakespeare (*Essay* ix). Sometimes these organizations don't make complete sense, Booth points out, and sometimes they even seem curiously contradictory. But that is precisely what interests reader-response critics, who, unlike formalists, are at least as interested in fragmentary, inconclusive, and even unfinished texts as in polished, unified works, for it is the reader's struggle to *make sense* of a challenging work that reader-response critics seek to describe.

The German critic Wolfgang Iser has described that sense-making struggle in his books *The Implied Reader* (1972) and *The Act of Reading: A Theory of Aesthetic Response* (1976). Iser argues that texts are full of "gaps" (or "blanks," as he sometimes calls them). These gaps powerfully affect the reader, who is forced to explain them, to connect what they separate, to create in his or her mind aspects of a poem or novel or play that aren't *in* the text but that the text incites. As Iser

puts it in *The Implied Reader*, the "unwritten aspects" of a story "draw
the reader into the action" and "lead him to shade in the many outlines suggested by the given situations, so that these take on a reality
of their own." These "outlines" that "the reader's imagination ani-
mates" in turn "influence" the way in which "the written part of the
text" is subsequently read (276).

In *Self-Consuming Artifacts: The Experience of Seventeenth-Century
Literature* (1972), Fish reveals his preference for literature that makes
readers work at making meaning. He contrasts two kinds of literary
presentation. By the phrase "rhetorical presentation," he describes literature that reflects and reinforces opinions that readers already hold;
by "dialectical presentation," he refers to works that prod and provoke. A dialectical text, rather than presenting an opinion as if it were
truth, challenges readers to discover truths on their own. Such a text
may not even have the kind of symmetry that formalist critics seek. Instead of offering a "single, sustained argument," a dialectical text, or
self-consuming artifact, may be "so arranged that to enter into the
spirit and assumptions of any one of [its] . . . units is implicitly to reject the spirit and assumptions of the unit immediately preceding"
(*Artifacts* 9). Whereas a critic of another school might try to force an
explanation as to why the units are fundamentally coherent, the
reader-response critic proceeds by describing how the reader deals
with the sudden twists and turns that characterize the dialectical text,
returning to earlier passages and seeing them in an entirely new light.

"The value of such a procedure," Fish has written, "is predicated
on the idea of meaning as *an event*," not as something "located (presumed to be embedded) *in* the utterance" or "verbal object as a thing
in itself" (*Text* 28). By redefining meaning as an event rather than as
something inherent in the text, the reader-response critic once again
locates meaning in time: the reader's time. A text exists and signifies
while it is being read, and what it signifies or means will depend, to no
small extent, on *when* it is read. (*Paradise Lost* had some meanings for
a seventeenth-century Puritan that it would not have for a twentieth-
century atheist.)

With the redefinition of literature as something that exists meaningfully only in the mind of the reader, with the redefinition of the literary work as a catalyst of mental events, comes a concurrent redefinition of the reader. No longer is the reader the passive recipient of
those ideas that an author has planted in a text. "The reader is *active*,"
Rosenblatt insists ("Transactional" 123). Fish begins "Literature in
the Reader" with a similar observation: "If at this moment someone

were to ask, 'what are you doing,' you might reply, 'I am reading,' and thereby acknowledge that reading is . . . something *you do*" (*Text* 22). Iser, in focusing critical interest on the gaps in texts, on what is not expressed, similarly redefines the reader as an active maker.

Amid all this talk of "the reader," it is tempting and natural to ask, "Just who *is* the reader?" (Or, to place the emphasis differently, "Just who is *the* reader?") Are reader-response critics simply sharing their own idiosyncratic responses when they describe what a line from *Paradise Lost* does in and to the reader's mind? "What about my responses?" you may want to ask. "What if they're different? Would reader-response critics be willing to say that my responses are equally valid?"

Fish defines "the reader" in this way: "*the* reader is the *informed* reader." The informed reader (whom Fish sometimes calls "the *intended* reader") is someone who is "sufficiently experienced as a reader to have internalized the properties of literary discourses, including everything from the most local of devices (figures of speech, etc.) to whole genres." And, of course, the informed reader is in full possession of the "semantic knowledge" (knowledge of idioms, for instance) assumed by the text (*Artifacts* 406).

Other reader-response critics define "*the* reader" differently. Wayne C. Booth, in *A Rhetoric of Irony* (1974), uses the phrase "the implied reader" to mean the reader "created by the work." (Only "by agreeing to play the role of this created audience," Susan Suleiman explains, "can an actual reader correctly understand and appreciate the work" [8].) Gerard Genette and Gerald Prince prefer to speak of "the narratee, . . . the necessary counterpart of a given narrator, that is, the person or figure who receives a narrative" (Suleiman 13). Like Booth, Iser employs the term "the implied reader," but he also uses "the educated reader" when he refers to what Fish called the "informed reader."

Jonathan Culler, who in 1981 criticized Fish for his sketchy definition of the informed reader, set out in *Structuralist Poetics* (1975) to describe the educated or "competent" reader's education by elaborating those reading conventions that make possible the understanding of poems and novels. In retrospect, however, Culler's definitions seem sketchy as well. By "competent reader," Culler meant competent reader of "literature." By "literature," he meant what schools and colleges mean when they speak of literature as being part of the curriculum. Culler, like his contemporaries, was not concerned with the fact that curricular content is politically and economically motivated. And "he did not," in Mailloux's words, "emphasize how the literary competence he described was embedded within larger formations and traversed by political ideologies extending beyond the academy" ("Turns" 49). It remained for a later generation of reader-oriented critics to do those things.

The fact that Fish, following Rosenblatt's lead, defined reader-response criticism in terms of its difference from and opposition to the New Criticism or formalism should not obscure the fact that the formalism of the 1950s and early 1960s had a great deal in common with the reader-response criticism of the late 1960s and early 1970s. This has become increasingly obvious with the rise of subsequent critical approaches whose practitioners have proved less interested in the close reading of texts than in the way literature represents, reproduces, or resists prevailing ideologies concerning gender, class, and race. In the retrospective essay entitled "The Turns of Reader-Response Criticism" (1990), Mailloux has suggested that, from the perspective of hindsight, the "close reading" of formalists and "Fish's early 'affective stylistics'" seem surprisingly similar. Indeed, Mailloux argues, the early "reader talk of . . . Iser and Fish enabled the continuation of the formalist practice of close reading. Through a vocabulary focused on a text's manipulation of readers, Fish was especially effective in extending and diversifying the formalist practices that continued business as usual within literary criticism" (48).

Since the mid-1970s, however, reader-response criticism (once commonly referred to as the "School of Fish") has diversified and taken on a variety of new forms, some of which truly *are* incommensurate with formalism, with its considerable respect for the integrity and power of the text. For instance, "subjectivists" like David Bleich, Norman Holland, and Robert Crosman have assumed what Mailloux calls the "absolute priority of individual selves as creators of texts" (*Conventions* 31). In other words, these critics do not see the reader's response as one "guided" by the text but rather as one motivated by deep-seated, personal, psychological needs. What they find in texts is, in Holland's phrase, their own "identity theme." Holland has argued that as readers we use "the literary work to symbolize and finally to replicate ourselves. We work out through the text our own characteristic patterns of desire" ("UNITY" 816). Subjective critics, as you may already have guessed, often find themselves confronted with the following question: If all interpretation is a function of private, psychological identity, then why have so many readers interpreted, say,

Shakespeare's *Hamlet* in the same way? Different subjective critics have answered the question differently. Holland simply has said that common identity themes exist, such as that involving an oedipal fantasy.

Meanwhile, Fish, who in the late 1970s moved away from reader-response criticism as he had initially helped define it, came up with a different answer to the question of why different readers tend to read the same works the same way. His answer, rather than involving common individual identity themes, involved common *cultural* identity. In "Interpreting the *Variorum*" (1976), he argues that the "stability of interpretation among readers" is a function of shared "interpretive strategies." These strategies, which "exist prior to the act of reading and therefore determine the shape of what is read," are held in common by "interpretive communities" such as the one constituted by American college students reading a novel as a class assignment (*Text* 167, 171). In developing the model of interpretive communities, Fish truly has made the break with formalist or New Critical predecessors, becoming in the process something of a social, structuralist, reader-response critic. Recently, he has been engaged in studying reading communities and their interpretive conventions in order to understand the conditions that give rise to a work's intelligibility.

Fish's shift in focus is in many ways typical of changes that have taken place within the field of reader-response criticism — a field that, because of those changes, is increasingly being referred to as "reader-*oriented*" criticism. Less and less common are critical analyses examining the transactional interface between the text and its individual reader. Increasingly, reader-oriented critics are investigating reading communities, as the reader-oriented cultural critic Janice A. Radway has done in her study of female readers of romance paperbacks (*Reading the Romance*, 1984). They are also studying the changing reception of literary works across time (see, for example, Mailloux in his "pragmatic readings" of American literature in *Interpretive Conventions* [1982] and *Rhetorical Power* [1989]).

An important catalyst of this gradual change was the work of Hans Robert Jauss, a colleague of Iser's whose historically oriented reception theory (unlike Iser's theory of the implied reader) was not available in English book form until the early 1980s. Rather than focusing on the implied, informed, or intended reader, Jauss examined actual past readers. In *Toward an Aesthetic of Reception* (1982), he argued that the reception of a work or author tends to depend upon the reading public's "horizons of expectations." He noted that, in the morally conservative climate of mid-nineteenth-century France, *Madame Bo-vary* was literally put on trial, its author Flaubert accused of glorifying adultery in passages representing the protagonist's fevered delirium via free indirect discourse, a mode of narration in which a third-person narrator tells us in an unfiltered way what a character is thinking and feeling.

As readers have become more sophisticated and tolerant, the popularity and reputation of *Madame Bovary* have soared. Sometimes, of course, changes in a reading public's horizons of expectations cause a work to be *less* well received over time. As American reception theorists influenced by Jauss have shown, Mark Twain's *Adventures of Huckleberry Finn* has elicited an increasingly ambivalent reaction from a reading public increasingly sensitive to demeaning racial stereotypes and racist language. The rise of feminism has prompted a downward revaluation of everything from Andrew Marvell's "To His Coy Mistress" to D. H. Lawrence's *Women in Love.*

Some reader-oriented feminists, such as Judith Fetterley, Patrocinio Schweickart, and Monique Wittig, have challenged the reader to become what Fetterley calls "the resisting reader." Arguing that literature written by men tends, in Schweickart's term, to "immasculate" women, they have advocated strategies of reading that involve substituting masculine for feminine pronouns and male for female characters in order to expose the sexism inscribed in patriarchal texts. Other feminists, such as Nancy K. Miller in *Subject to Change* (1988), have suggested that there may be essential differences between the way women and men read and write.

That suggestion, however, has prompted considerable disagreement. A number of gender critics whose work is oriented toward readers and reading have admitted that there is such a thing as "reading like a woman" (or man), but they have also tended to agree with Peggy Kamuf that such forms of reading, like gender itself, are cultural rather than natural constructs. Gay and lesbian critics, arguing that sexualities have been similarly constructed within and by social discourse, have argued that there is a homosexual way of reading; Wayne Koestenbaum has defined "the (male twentieth-century first world) gay reader" as one who "reads resistantly for inscriptions of his condition, for texts that will confirm a social and private identity founded on a desire for other men. . . . Reading becomes a hunt for histories that deliberately foreknow or unwittingly trace a desire felt not by author but by reader, who is most acute when searching for signs of himself" (in Boone and Cadden, 176–77).

Given this kind of renewed interest in the reader and reading, some students of contemporary critical practice have been tempted to conclude that reader-oriented theory has been taken over by feminist, gender, gay, and lesbian theory. Others, like Elizabeth Freund, have suggested that it is deconstruction with which the reader-oriented approach has mixed and merged. Certainly, all of these approaches have informed and have been informed by reader-response or reader-oriented theory. The case can be made, however, that there is in fact still a distinct reader-oriented approach to literature, one whose points of tangency are neither with deconstruction nor with feminist, gender, and so-called queer theory but rather with the new historicism and cultural criticism.

This relatively distinct form of reader theory is practiced by a number of critics but is perhaps best exemplified by the work of scholars such as Mailloux and Peter J. Rabinowitz. In *Before Reading: Narrative Conventions and the Politics of Interpretation* (1987), Rabinowitz identifies four conventions or rules of reading, which he calls the rules of "notice," "signification," "configuration," and "coherence" — rules telling us which parts of a narrative are important, which details have a reliable secondary or special meaning, which fit into which familiar patterns, and how stories fit together as a whole. He then proceeds to analyze the misreadings and misjudgments of critics and to show that politics governs the way in which those rules are applied and broken. ("The strategies employed by critics when they read [Raymond Chandler's] *The Big Sleep*," Rabinowitz writes, "can teach us something about the structure of misogyny, not the misogyny of the novel itself, but the misogyny of the world outside it" [195].) In subsequent critical essays, Rabinowitz proceeds similarly, showing how a society's ideological assumptions about gender, race, and class determine the way in which artistic works are perceived and evaluated.

Mailloux, who calls his approach "rhetorical reception theory" or "rhetorical hermeneutics," takes a similar tack, insofar as he describes the political contexts of (mis)interpretation. In his 1993 essay "Misreading as a Historical Act," he shows that a mid-nineteenth-century review of Frederick Douglass's slave *Narrative* by proto-feminist Margaret Fuller seems to be a misreading until we situate it "within the cultural conversation of the 'Bible politics' of 1845" (Machor 9). Woven through Mailloux's essay on Douglass and Fuller are philosophical pauses in which we are reminded, in various subtle ways, that all reading (including Mailloux's and our own) is culturally situated and likely to seem like *mis*reading someday. One such reflective pause, however, accomplishes more; in it Mailloux reads the map of where reader-oriented criticism is today, affords a rationale for its being there, and plots its likely future direction. "However we have arrived at our present juncture," Mailloux writes,

> the current talk about historical acts of reading provides a welcome opportunity for more explicit consideration of how reading is historically contingent, politically situated, institutionally embedded, and materially conditioned; of how reading any text, literary or nonliterary, relates to a larger cultural politics that goes well beyond some hypothetical private interaction between an autonomous reader and an independent text; and of how our particular views of reading relate to the liberatory potential of literacy and the transformative power of education. (5)

In the essay that follows, Lilian R. Furst argues that "reading" is "central" to *Death in Venice*, "partly because its main protagonist is a writer." Aschenbach is, moreover, a writer whose career Mann describes at length, so much so that "readers, especially first-time readers, often balk at the length of the retrospective survey of Aschenbach's output and its reception." Ultimately, however, it proves important for readers to know not only about the "formal" nature of Aschenbach's works but also about the "effect" those works have on Aschenbach's fictional readers.

Aschenbach's readers, Furst reminds us, have typically found in his writings models of purpose, constancy, and control. They assume that his heroes, who exemplify the virtues of purity and simplicity, represent not only the conservative values of their age and culture but also Aschenbach's own values and ideals. "Are his readers misinterpreting him?" Furst asks. "The answer has to be equivocal." Furst points out that as *Death in Venice* unfolds, its writer-protagonist begins to abandon those very principles that have served him as "a bulwark against the self-indulgent flirtation with the abyss that is a danger to his age." Given the connection that readers believe to exist between Aschenbach's personal values and the values espoused in his works, this abandonment or "reversal" does, to a certain extent, "turn his writings into a sort of deception."

Having identified "the possibility that reading may unwittingly be a self-deceptive activity" as a "theme" of *Death in Venice*, Furst goes on to show that the theme "recurs" in Aschenbach's "reading of Plato's *Phaedrus*" — that is, in his manner of "adopting [Plato's] message as he perceives it." In order to "validate his emotions and actions," Aschenbach recalls Plato's phrase that "only Beauty is at one and the same time visible and divine," thereby "misreading Plato by free paraphrase and Tadzio by transforming him into a god." Aschenbach's misreadings, Furst maintains, have "implications for our own act of reading this story," prompting a "wariness, a suspiciousness toward a text that portrays twice over the potential deceptiveness of reading." At the same time, Furst argues, "for us to become aware of this potential deceptiveness through its illustration within the text is the beginning of a protective amendment in our own reading."

In developing her argument, Furst identifies several points at which Mann's text "gives us identifiable clues whereby to make correctives" — that is, it provides us with "telling details" that empower "alert readers to construct the latent subtext beneath the surface." For instance, juxtaposing Aschenbach's "startling dream of a tropical landscape" with the narrator's statement that Aschenbach's internal turbulence reflects "simply a desire to travel" leads readers to take the narrator's comment ironically. Indeed, Furst argues that "this passage about the dream shows how the narratorial voice stands between Aschenbach and readers, offering us his edited version of what is happening ('simply a desire to travel', while we, on the evidence of the lurid dream, advance quite another interpretation." Furst thus argues that Mann's narrator differs from those employed by most eighteenth- and nineteenth-century novelists, for he does not "stand beside us," "guiding" our "responses" with "addresses, exhortations, and explanations of what is happening. Mann eschews such forthright glosses, leaving readers instead to construct their interpretations from the episodic events themselves."

Furst's analysis reflects and adapts the thinking of earlier reader-oriented theorists and critics. For instance, she maintains that the successful reader — or at least the successful reader of Mann's fiction — must be an *active* rather than a passive reader. (In implying that Mann's texts require readers to be more active than do earlier works by other writers, Furst implicitly makes a distinction something like the one Fish makes between dialectical and rhetorical presentations.) Furthermore, like many reader-response critics who have preceded her, Furst broadly defines readers and reading; having done so, she finds readers, instances of reading, and even the very theme of reading threaded throughout the text she "reads" (that is, interprets). We are, in Furst's view, among the readers implicated by *Death in Venice,* for if Aschenbach's readers misread Aschenbach, and if Aschenbach misreads Plato, how are we to avoid misreading Mann — or any equally challenging writer?

Furst's interest in readers and reading prompts her interest in the narrator. Although the narrator-protagonist relationship contains "the potential for deceptiveness if readers are unable to reconstruct the [narrator's] implied other meaning," it also provides — if recognized and understood — a means of avoiding the kind of deception and self-deception that leads Aschenbach first to Venice, then to his death. "The uncertainty injected by the presence of irony in *Death in Venice*," Furst writes, "obliges readers to read with utmost care, to read between the lines, with an ear always cocked for the subversive insinuation." What Iser called "blanks" or "gaps," in other words, pervade Mann's novella, permitting the "alert reader" to creatively construct meaning via what Furst terms "secret communicative collusion" with the text.

Ross C Murfin

READER-RESPONSE CRITICISM: A SELECTED BIBLIOGRAPHY

Some Introductions to Reader-Response Criticism

Beach, Richard. *A Teacher's Introduction to Reader-Response Theories.* Urbana: NCTE, 1993.

Fish, Stanley E. "Literature in the Reader: Affective Stylistics." *New Literary History* 2 (1970): 123–61. Rpt. in Fish, *Text* 21–67, and in Primeau 154–79.

Freund, Elizabeth. *The Return of the Reader: Reader-Response Criticism.* London: Methuen, 1987.

Holub, Robert C. *Reception Theory: A Critical Introduction.* New York: Methuen, 1984.

Leitch, Vincent B. *American Literary Criticism from the Thirties to the Eighties.* New York: Columbia UP, 1988.

Mailloux, Steven. "Learning to Read: Interpretation and Reader-Response Criticism." *Studies in the Literary Imagination* 12 (1979): 93–108.

———. "Reader-Response Criticism?" *Genre* 10 (1977): 413–31.

———. "The Turns of Reader-Response Criticism." *Conversations: Contemporary Critical Theory and the Teaching of Literature.* Ed. Charles Moran and Elizabeth F. Penfield. Urbana: NCTE, 1990. 38–54.

Rabinowitz, Peter J. "Whirl without End: Audience-Oriented Criticism." *Contemporary Literary Theory.* Ed. G. Douglas Atkins and Laura Morrow. Amherst: U of Massachusetts P, 1989. 81–100.

Rosenblatt, Louise M. "Towards a Transactional Theory of Reading." *Journal of Reading Behavior* 1 (1969): 31–47. Rpt. in Primeau 121–46.

Suleiman, Susan R. "Introduction: Varieties of Audience-Oriented Criticism." Suleiman and Crosman 3–45.

Tompkins, Jane P. "An Introduction to Reader-Response Criticism." Tompkins ix–xxiv.

Reader-Response Criticism in Anthologies and Collections

Flynn, Elizabeth A., and Patrocinio P. Schweickart, eds. *Gender and Reading: Essays on Readers, Texts, and Contexts.* Baltimore: Johns Hopkins UP, 1986.

Garvin, Harry R., ed. *Theories of Reading, Looking, and Listening.* Lewisburg: Bucknell UP, 1981. Essays by Cain and Rosenblatt.

Machor, James L., ed. *Readers in History: Nineteenth-Century American Literature and the Contexts of Response.* Baltimore: Johns Hopkins UP, 1993. Contains Mailloux essay "Misreading as a Historical Act: Cultural Rhetoric, Bible Politics, and Fuller's 1845 Review of Douglass's *Narrative.*"

Primeau, Ronald, ed. *Influx: Essays on Literary Influence.* Port Washington: Kennikat, 1977. Essays by Fish, Holland, and Rosenblatt.

Suleiman, Susan R., and Inge Crosman, eds. *The Reader in the Text: Essays on Audience and Interpretation.* Princeton: Princeton UP, 1980. See especially the essays by Culler, Iser, and Todorov.

Tompkins, Jane P., ed. *Reader-Response Criticism: From Formalism to Post-Structuralism.* Baltimore: Johns Hopkins UP, 1980. See especially the essays by Bleich, Fish, Holland, Prince, and Tompkins.

Reader-Response Criticism: Some Major Works

Bleich, David. *Subjective Criticism.* Baltimore: Johns Hopkins UP, 1978.

Booth, Stephen. *An Essay on Shakespeare's Sonnets.* New Haven: Yale UP, 1969.

Booth, Wayne C. *A Rhetoric of Irony.* Chicago: U of Chicago P, 1974.

Eco, Umberto. *The Role of the Reader: Explorations in the Semiotics of Texts.* Bloomington: Indiana UP, 1979.

Fish, Stanley Eugene. *Doing What Comes Naturally: Change, Rhetoric, and the Practice of Theory in Literary and Legal Studies.* Durham: Duke UP, 1989.

———. *Is There a Text in This Class? The Authority of Interpretive Communities.* Cambridge: Harvard UP, 1980. This volume contains most of Fish's most influential essays, including "Literature in the Reader: Affective Stylistics," "What It's Like to Read *L'Allegro* and *Il Penseroso*," "Interpreting the *Variorum*," "Is There a Text in This Class?," "How to Recognize a Poem When You See One," and "What Makes an Interpretation Acceptable?"

———. *Self-Consuming Artifacts: The Experience of Seventeenth-Century Literature.* Berkeley: U of California P, 1972.

———. *Surprised by Sin: The Reader in "Paradise Lost."* 2d ed. Berkeley: U of California P, 1971.

Holland, Norman N. *5 Readers Reading.* New Haven: Yale UP, 1975.

———. "UNITY IDENTITY TEXT SELF." *PMLA* 90 (1975): 813–22.

Iser, Wolfgang. *The Act of Reading: A Theory of Aesthetic Response.* Baltimore: Johns Hopkins UP, 1978.

———. *The Implied Reader: Patterns of Communication in Prose Fiction from Bunyan to Beckett.* Baltimore: Johns Hopkins UP, 1974.

Jauss, Hans Robert. *Toward an Aesthetic of Reception.* Trans. Timothy Bahti. Intro. Paul de Man. Brighton, Eng.: Harvester, 1982.

Mailloux, Steven. *Interpretive Conventions: The Reader in the Study of American Fiction.* Ithaca: Cornell UP, 1982.

———. *Rhetorical Power.* Ithaca: Cornell UP, 1989.

Messent, Peter. *New Readings of the American Novel: Narrative Theory and Its Application.* New York: Macmillan, 1991.

Prince, Gerald. *Narratology.* Hawthorne, N.Y.: Mouton, 1982.

Rabinowitz, Peter J. *Before Reading: Narrative Conventions and the Politics of Interpretation.* Ithaca: Cornell UP, 1987.

Radway, Janice A. *Reading the Romance: Women, Patriarchy, and Popular Literature.* Chapel Hill: U of North Carolina P, 1984.

Rosenblatt, Louise M. *Literature as Exploration.* 4th ed. New York: MLA, 1983.

———. *The Reader, the Text, the Poem: The Transactional Theory of the Literary Work.* Carbondale: Southern Illinois UP, 1978.

Slatoff, Walter J. *With Respect to Readers: Dimensions of Literary Response.* Ithaca: Cornell UP, 1970.

Steig, Michael. *Stories of Reading: Subjectivity and Literary Under-standing.* Baltimore: Johns Hopkins UP, 1989.

Exemplary Short Readings of Major Texts

Anderson, Howard. *"Tristram Shandy* and the Reader's Imagination." *PMLA* 86 (1971): 966–73.

Berger, Carole. "The Rake and the Reader in Jane Austen's Novels." *Studies in English Literature, 1500–1900* 15 (1975): 531–44.

Booth, Stephen. "On the Value of *Hamlet.*" *Reinterpretations of English Drama: Selected Papers from the English Institute.* Ed. Norman Rabkin. New York: Columbia UP, 1969. 137–76.

Easson, Robert R. "William Blake and His Reader in *Jerusalem.*" *Blake's Sublime Allegory.* Ed. Stuart Curran and Joseph A. Wittreich. Madison: U of Wisconsin P, 1973. 309–28.

Kirk, Carey H. *"Moby-Dick:* The Challenge of Response." *Papers on Language and Literature* 13 (1977): 383–90.

Leverenz, David. "Mrs. Hawthorne's Headache: Reading *The Scarlet Letter.*" *Nathaniel Hawthorne, "The Scarlet Letter."* Ed. Ross C Murfin. Case Studies in Contemporary Criticism. Boston: Bedford–St. Martin's, 1991. 263–74.

Lowe-Evans, Mary. "Reading with a 'Nicer Eye': Responding to *Frankenstein.*" *Mary Shelley, "Frankenstein."* Ed. Johanna M. Smith. Case Studies in Contemporary Criticism. Boston: Bedford–St. Martin's, 1992. 215–29.

Rabinowitz, Peter J. "'A Symbol of Something': Interpretive Vertigo in 'The Dead.'" *James Joyce, "The Dead."* Ed. Daniel R. Schwarz. Case Studies in Contemporary Criticism. Boston: Bedford–St. Martin's, 1994. 137–49.

Treichler, Paula. "The Construction of Ambiguity in *The Awakening.*" *Kate Chopin, "The Awakening."* Ed. Nancy A. Walker. Case Studies in Contemporary Criticism. Boston: Bedford–St. Martin's, 1993. 308–28.

Other Works Referred to in "What Is Reader-Response Criticism?"

Booth, Wayne C. *A Rhetoric of Irony.* Chicago: U of Chicago P, 1974.

Culler, Jonathan. *Structural Poetics: Structuralism, Linguistics, and the Study of Literature.* Ithaca: Cornell UP, 1975.

Koestenbaum, Wayne. "Wilde's Hard Labor and the Birth of Gay Reading." *Engendering Men: The Question of Male Feminist*

Criticism. Ed. Joseph A. Boone and Michael Cadden. New York: Routledge, 1990.

Richards, I. A. *Practical Criticism.* New York: Harcourt, 1929. Rpt. in *Criticism: The Major Texts.* Ed. Walter Jackson Bate. Rev. ed. New York: Harcourt, 1970. 575.

Wimsatt, William K., and Monroe C. Beardsley. *The Verbal Icon.* Lexington: U of Kentucky P, 1954. See especially the discussion of "The Affective Fallacy," with which reader-response critics have so sharply disagreed.

OTHER READER-RESPONSE APPROACHES TO *DEATH IN VENICE*

Furst, Lilian R. "The Ethics of Reading *Death in Venice.*" *LIT.* 1 (1990): 265–74.

———. "Reading 'Nasty' Great Books." *Through the Lens of the Reader.* Albany: State U of New York P, 1992. 39–50.

A READER-RESPONSE PERSPECTIVE

LILIAN R. FURST

The Potential Deceptiveness of Reading in *Death in Venice*

A reader-response perspective takes us to the very heart of *Death in Venice* by making us confront the challenging issue of the potential deceptiveness of reading. The story contains two quite discrete instances of readers being misled by their interpretations of texts. In what ways and to what extent do these examples of reading as deception affect our own reading of the narrative?

Reading is so central to *Death in Venice* partly because its main protagonist is himself a writer. Aschenbach has achieved not only fame but also eminence and respect: on his fiftieth birthday, we are told in the story's opening sentence, he had been honored by the dignity of a title of nobility that made him Gustav "von" Aschenbach.[1] Indeed, he

---

[1]In the democratic American system there is no equivalent to this kind of social elevation. In Britain a distinction such as a knighthood — that is, the title "Sir" — may be conferred, or very rarely "C.H." for "Companion of Honour," a highly select group of artists and thinkers. The French counterpart to "von" is "de."

has become something of a cultural icon, excerpts from whose writings are included in the prescribed school readers. By middle age he has adopted "an educator's stance" (32) in a style that is "exemplary and definitive," "fastidiously conventional," "conservative and formal and even formulaic" (32), eschewing audacities or eccentricities. Aschenbach's thrust to control, to orderliness, and to a certain noble grandeur as fundamental to his entire life and work needs to be emphatically established at the beginning of this story about his gradual but radical forfeiture of those guiding qualities.

The impact of Aschenbach's writings on his readers is elaborated in the second section. Readers, especially first-time readers, often balk at the length of the retrospective survey of Aschenbach's output and its reception. The review of his career at this point tends to provoke impatience because it retards the plot development. Aschenbach has already decided to take a break somewhere in the south, and we would naturally like to see him set off and learn how he fares instead of being held back by an account of his attainments so ample as to be one and one-half times the length of the opening section. Such expansiveness is, however, absolutely essential to the narrative, for not only is his whole past introduced here, but also his effect on his readers is recorded. His works, "lucid and massive," "powerful," and "passionate" (28), "had a native capacity to inspire confidence in the general public and to win admiration and encouragement from the discriminating connoisseur" (29). They hold a special appeal to his contemporaries on account of "something imponderable, a sense of sympathy" (30). Aschenbach, it is suggested, holds up a model to his audience, and, significantly, it is a model of "constancy of will and tenacity of purpose" (30). His position is obviously in keeping with his whole cultivation of stoic devotion to duty. The life he has hitherto led, which had been compared by one critic to a clenched fist (29), is presented as the immediate basis for the powerful influence of his writings, which are the fictionalized expression of his attitude to living. "*Durchhalten*," "staying the course" (29), is his favorite, admittedly dour motto, and his success has been achieved by building "from layer upon layer of daily opuscula, from a hundred or a thousand inspirations" (30). His determined effort and sheer willpower are underscored here, not the facility often attributed to writers. Mann himself is reputed to have commented that a writer is one to whom writing is particularly difficult.

Aschenbach's greatness is therefore rooted in an admired act of self-control and self-assertion, "a defiant despite" (30), "an ascent to dignity" (31) that springs from "renunciation of all moral skepticism" (32) to rise to a kind of "'rebirth'" in "noble purity, simplicity and symmetry" (32). The heroes of his writings, invested with these same virtues, are recognized by his readers as "the heroes of our age" (31). On the strength of his works he is regarded as an ideal, the voice of a generation combating "ethical whimsicality" (32) in order to uphold the loftiest values.

Are his readers misinterpreting him? The answer has to be equivocal. At one level, certainly not. There can be no doubt about Aschenbach's wholehearted commitment to his chosen mission, his repudiation, on the conscious level, "of every kind of sympathy with the abyss" (32). He is definitely not engaging in a deliberate deception as he struggles day by day to sustain and express his own moral and aesthetic principles. His self-image and the image that he projects of his work represents opposition to — indeed, a bulwark against — the self-indulgent flirtation with the abyss that is a danger to his age. But in the long run he himself is unable to control or suppress subconscious impulses that first surface quite harmlessly in his desire to travel. Little by little, he lets himself be an open rather than a clenched fist; he drifts into an adventure in Venice, which represents a wholesale abandonment of his stern principles as he yields to a primordial passion, to a disorderliness totally alien to his previous standards. In some sense, because of the integral connection between his life and his work, his reversal does turn his writings into a sort of deception. At the very least, the course of the development he undergoes in *Death in Venice* reveals the precariousness and latent peril of his earlier position. His exemplary perseverance is uncovered as a posture that can be undermined and overturned by the subterranean forces in his self. He has managed to repress and apparently conquer these drives for a while; but eventually they erupt, as if in revenge for the hypercontrol he had exercised. In this light, his readers' interpretations are deceptions, the fulfillment of Aschenbach's own and their wished self-image, or at most, the product of an only temporary and ultimately untenable "heroism." The second section of *Death in Venice* is thus of paramount importance in the economy of the narrative, as it initiates the possibility that reading may unwittingly be a self-deceptive activity.

This theme recurs subsequently in Aschenbach's "reading" of Plato's *Phaedrus*. The word "reading" appears in quotes here because Aschenbach is not actually reading from a book but rather adopting its message as he perceives it. The text of *Death in Venice*, especially its latter half, resonates with allusions to and echoes of Greek mythology, specifically its esteem of perfection of form in the young male body. Already infected with the cholera that will shortly kill him, Aschenbach paraphrases from the *Phaedrus* while he sits on the beach watching Tadzio at play: "'For Beauty, Phaedrus, mark well! only Beauty is at one and the same time divine and visible; and so indeed it is the sensuous lover's path, little Phaedrus, it is the artist's path to the spirit'" (85). These words float through his mind in a "strange dream-logic" (85). To paraphrase in this way is to restate, usually for the sake of clarification; however, such adapted reading may, too, involve distortion, as in this instance when Aschenbach invokes Greek precedents to validate his emotions and his actions. His quest for beauty, traditional to the creative artist, is equated here with his "sensuous lover's" pursuit of Tadzio on the grounds that in him beauty is "at one and the same time visible and divine." That Tadzio is far from divine is clearly signalled by his defective teeth, which denote a physical imperfection and a symbolic diminution of his vitality. Healthy teeth are the instruments for eating, and so signify the continued sustenance of life, and they also carry overtones of sexual potency, of the capacity to consume figuratively. In misreading Plato by free paraphrase and Tadzio by transforming him into a god, Aschenbach is engaging in self-deception. Yet it is essential to realize that his misprision derives from his very center, his being as an artist, which leads — and mis-leads — him to extol beauty as the highest desideratum.

The slipperiness inherent in Aschenbach's tendentious reading of the *Phaedrus* is foreshadowed in the story's second section in an interpolated comment by the narrator:

> And is form not two-faced? Is it not at one and the same time moral and immoral — moral as the product and expression of discipline, but immoral and even antimoral inasmuch as it houses within itself an innate moral indifference, and indeed essentially strives for nothing less than to bend morality under its proud and absolute scepter? (32–33)

The formulation in rhetorical questions is designed to leave the issue open at this early stage. Nevertheless, the dangerous duality of form is here already articulated in explicit terms. While these remarks may seem cryptic at the point where they occur, they assume resounding significance in the context of Aschenbach's interpretation of the *Phaedrus* to suit his own immediate purpose. Beauty of form, which he had embraced as the positive structuring ethos of his writing, asserts its other "immoral and even antimoral" facet as he becomes enthralled by its human incarnation. Aschenbach's "reading" is a vehicle for self-deception, allowing him to reassure himself that his adulation of Tadzio is no more than a continuation, or perhaps an extension, of the ideal he had always sought in his prose. The doubleness — and duplicity — of the text lets Aschenbach highlight those aspects that suit his own desires, and so to deceive himself. It is one of the supreme ironies of *Death in Venice* that no other than the writer protagonist should be shown as himself enmeshed in the deceptiveness of reading.

What implications do our recognition of these skewed interpretations within *Death in Venice* have for our own approach to the act of reading this story? They must surely prompt a certain wariness, a suspicion toward a text that portrays twice over the potential deceptiveness of reading. How are we to avoid the misreadings we see in the internal readers? Are they in fact unavoidable? If reading is seen as construction, a completion of the text by each reader, there are bound to be divergent interpretations, dependent on individual responses. But the multiple readings produced by different readers are variations, not deceptions. A fundamental distinction has to be drawn between the diversity of responses to *Death in Venice* among any set of readers and the deceptiveness in which Aschenbach implicates himself and his audience, for that deceptiveness is the direct result of his own consistent self-deception, which is one of the narrative's main themes. For us to become aware of this potential deceptiveness through its illustration within the text is the beginning of a protective amendment in our own reading.

In practice, much, though not all of *Death in Venice* gives us identifiable clues whereby to make correctives by enabling alert readers to construct the latent subtext beneath the surface. An obvious example occurs in the opening section, where the discrepancies between the narrator's statements about Aschenbach and what we register of his actual state are readily apparent. The stolid image of a settled Aschenbach that the narrator sets forth and that Aschenbach himself endorses is contravened by a succession of details that juxtapose to the scenario of successful mastery a perturbing alternative. In the first sentence, Aschenbach's secure position, consolidated by the bestowal of the honorific "von," is undermined by the insecurity of the world in the grave threat of war hanging over Europe at that time. The metaphorically gathering clouds of war are represented on the physical plane by the storm brewing that afternoon, which makes Aschenbach cut short his walk, perhaps in a prefiguration of the imminent foreshortening of his life. The hints, however slight, create a vague but distinct sense of disturbance: all is by no means well with Aschenbach. His writing has "reached a difficult and dangerous point," and he has become "increasingly subject to fatigue." So his approaching life crisis is contextualized and objectified in the instability of the weather and the ominous political constellation.

This technique of using telling details, so pronounced in the opening section, is characteristic of Mann's oblique narrative strategy throughout. It is worth looking closely at this section as a paradigm of his tactics. The derangement of the normal tenor of life occasioned by the approach of a storm and possibly of war is reiterated by the bizarre man who suddenly stands beside Aschenbach at the tram stop, springing mysteriously as if from nowhere. The description of his appearance fills more than half a page. This is a prime instance of seeming redundancy, of overinsistence on a minor figure, until we realize that his head suggests a skull. As a harbinger of death, he evokes the slaughter associated with war. So, without categoric mention, the idea of death is insinuated into the reader's mind in the first pages through a mosaic of details, each relatively small in itself but cumulatively coalescing to indicate the story's direction. It is typical of the indirect narrative mode of *Death in Venice* to challenge readers to the task of linking and interpreting the discrete details into a cohesive meaning that is implicit in the words printed on the page yet must be constructed through the active reader's attentiveness.

The same demand is made on readers by Aschenbach's strange dream. Jaded and exhausted by the strain of his work, he suddenly feels a longing for change, which he intends to satisfy by a trip to the south. But the form in which his longing manifests itself in his startling dream of a tropical landscape, at once seductive and frightening, alerts readers to the fact that his commotion is much more than "simply a desire to travel" (25). This comment by the narrator is sharply ironic; we can immediately recognize in Aschenbach's hallucinatory vision something far more troubled than a mere wish for a short trip. This passage about the dream shows how the narratorial voice stands between Aschenbach and readers, offering us his edited version of what is happening ("simply a desire to travel"), while we, on the evidence of the lurid dream, advance quite another interpretation. We are led to suspect that Aschenbach yearns to break out of his rigidly structured existence, but we don't yet fully trust our own reading, for, like Aschenbach, we are held in check by the narrator. Nonetheless, it is hardly possible to miss the turbulent connotations of Aschenbach's hallucinatory vision of "a kind of primeval wilderness," "moist and lush and monstrous," with "strangely misshapen trees," "stagnant shadowy-green glassy water where milk-white blossoms floated as big as plates," with "exotic birds with grotesque beaks" and "the glittering eyes of a crouching tiger" (25–26).

This scene of strength and sensuality, but also of decay, decadence, and chaos, is violently at odds with Aschenbach's customary, well-regulated, highly controlled daily existence. It exposes the terrifying, destructive undercurrents in his mind, the stratum of what Freud called the id, the subconscious, in contrast — and complement — to the conscious level of the carefully maintained ego. The seething turmoil of Aschenbach's id makes us intuit the desperate forcefulness of his urge to break loose from the restrictiveness of the life he has fashioned for himself in the service of his art. When he does accept his need for change and relaxation, he envisages an innocuous "three or four weeks at some popular holiday resort in the south" (27).

The suspension points at the end of that reverie are an open invitation to readers to further speculation. And it is easy enough for us to do so, to fathom the hidden meaning behind Aschenbach's self-consolatory defusing of his wild dream. In the phrase immediately preceding the one just cited, he himself refers to the dream when he resolves to "travel. Not all that far, not quite to where the tigers were" (27). He acknowledges and dismisses the tigers in the same breath. But the images from the dream are too vivid and compelling to be so quickly dislodged from the minds of readers. The tigers crouching within himself are precisely what Aschenbach has to face in the course of the story. To those who have read the opening section with due heed to the suggestiveness of its subtext, that comes as much less of a surprise than it does to Aschenbach.

The narration by directed indirection, apparent in the first section, prevails through most of *Death in Venice*. The narrator does not function like many eighteenth- and early-nineteenth-century novelists who openly stand beside their readers, guiding their responses with addresses, exhortations, and explanations of what is happening. Mann eschews such forthright glosses, leaving readers instead to construct their interpretations from the episodic events themselves. Good examples of his method are the two figures whom Aschenbach encounters on his way to Venice: on the boat from Pola "the dandified old man" (38), and on his arrival at his destination, the sinister gondolier. Both these men, like the mysterious apparition at the cemetery, are perceived through Aschenbach's eyes without any narratorial comment. Both also are described with a primary emphasis on the physical body:

His old head could not carry the wine as his sturdy youthful companions had done, and he was lamentably drunk. Eyes glazed, a cigarette between his trembling fingers, he stood swaying, tilted to and fro by inebriation and barely keeping his balance. Since he would have fallen at his first step he did not move from the spot, and was nevertheless full of wretched exuberance, clutching at everyone who approached him, babbling, winking, sniggering, lifting his ringed and wrinkled forefinger as he uttered some bantering inanity, and licking the corners of his mouth with the tip of his tongue in a repellently suggestive way. (38)

Likewise the gondolier:

He was a man of displeasing, indeed brutal appearance, wearing blue seaman's clothes, with a yellow scarf round his waist and a shapeless, already fraying straw hat tilted rakishly on his head. To judge by the cast of his face and the blond curling moustache under his snub nose, he was quite evidently not of Italian origin. Although rather slightly built, so that one would not have thought him particularly well suited to his job, he plied his oar with great energy, putting his whole body into every stroke. Occasionally the effort made him retract his lips and bare his white teeth. (40)

The precise notation of features and movements in these two portraits produces a lively image. Yet it does considerably more by conjuring up a psychological aura as well, a presentiment of an indefinably uncanny turn of events through the incursion of peculiar, aberrant creatures. Aschenbach admits to himself his unease as he watches the old man masquerading as a youngster: "a sense of numbness came over him, a feeling that the world was somehow, slightly yet uncontrollably, sliding into some kind of bizarre and grotesque derangement" (38). At this point he looks at the garish travesty of youthfulness "with frowning disapproval" (38) as an affront. What seems like a casual though unsettling experience, however, comes to assume additional significance for readers later in the story, when Aschenbach lets the barber color his hair and improve his appearance cosmetically. Again, narratorial comment is absent, but readers cannot fail to make the connection between the previously despised "dandified old man" and Aschenbach's new incarnation. Without voicing it in so many words, the text *shows* how Aschenbach has turned into what he had recently abhorred. A parallel connection is suggested to readers between the man at the cemetery and the gondolier, another avatar of death with his skull-like bare teeth. Aschenbach's doom is adumbrated in the repetition of his confrontation with warning figures.

These examples illustrate not only the detail-packed density of *Death in Venice* but also the necessity of reading in a supralinear manner. The text is a web of strands, closely interwoven with one another, constantly referring self-reflexively forward and backward. It is so intricately shaped a whole that only at a second reading can the full import of its various parts be grasped. Nor is meaning always as transparent as in the case of the three strange men I have discussed. Meaning is complicated by the presence of narratorial irony to varying degrees, and, in the later parts of the story, by the modulation of the narrator's stance toward his protagonist.

The problems usually posed by irony are exacerbated by the intervention of translation, for it is extraordinarily difficult to capture the nuances of tone, sentence structure, and verbal associations on which irony often depends. A cardinal instance is the phrase in the opening section: "It was simply a desire to travel" (25). An alternative version, "It was wanderlust and nothing more" (Koelb 5), is closer to the German although less colloquially smooth. The original, *"Es war Reiselust, nichts weiter,"* has just a comma, no conjunction between its two parts, so that the "nothing more" is made to seem like merely a completing afterthought. But precisely the confident proclamation that it was "nothing more" attracts extra attention to the phrase it qualifies, thereby leading readers to consider further and to come up with the hypothesis that it might well be something more, or even opposite to what is stated.

Saying the opposite to what is meant is, of course, the classical definition of irony in exactly the way it operates here. And readers' suspicion is immediately confirmed by Aschenbach's astonishing dream, which itself is the discordant opposite of his normative existence. Such use of irony is a concomitant of the narration by indirection that prevails in *Death in Venice*. It also encompasses a tendency to deceptiveness, however, or at least it entails the potential for deceptiveness if readers are unable to reconstruct the implied other meaning. There is no intention to deceive in irony; on the contrary, the narrator is drawing readers into a secret communicative collusion. Insofar as anyone is deceived, it is the protagonist who remains unaware of the possible reversal, and so becomes the butt of irony. The verdict that "it was simply a desire to travel" seems to emanate from Aschenbach's mind, although it could also be the narrator's voice. The uncertainty injected by the presence of irony in *Death in Venice* obliges readers to read with utmost care, to read between the lines, with an ear always cocked for the subversive insinuation.

Yet despite their heedfulness, readers may at times become quite unsure of their interpretation, for apart from its simplest form of saying the opposite, irony may be implicit in under- or overstatement. What, for instance, are readers to make of the way Aschenbach is presented in the second section? The encomium is such as to amount to "almost an obituary" (Reed 146). Is the excessiveness of the phraseology to be taken as a sly critique of the excessiveness of Aschenbach's life, or is it a straightforward expression of admiration — the admiration, incidentally, felt by Aschenbach's readers? It is virtually impossible to opt exclusively for one reading or the other, for both can be supported. The ambiguity at the outset, which makes Aschenbach command regard rather than liking, serves perhaps to prepare for his subsequent development. Certainly it warrants T. J. Reed's apt characterization of Mann's method as "the art of ambivalence." Reed's postulate, based on the evidence of Mann's letters and notebooks, is that the author changed his attitude toward his protagonist, reworking his first positive conception of him into a more negative view. This, he adds, would "account perfectly for the strange mixture *Der Tod in Venedig* actually is, of enthusiasm and criticism, classical beauty and penetration, elevation and sordidness" (Reed 167). Mann's own wavering about Aschenbach could well underlie the irony at his expense and the consequent dilemmas created for readers.

What is beyond doubt is the palpable change in the narrator's stance toward his protagonist in the course of the narrative. The growth of distance between them has been mentioned by many critics. Dorrit Cohn, for instance, characterizes the relationship as "essentially sympathetic, respectful, even reverent in the early phases of the story," but "in the later phases a deepening rift develops, building an increasingly ironic narratorial stance" (Koelb 180). Yet as Cohn, too, points out, "the narrator maintains his intimacy with Aschenbach's sensations, thoughts, and feelings, even as he distances himself more and more on the ideological level" (Koelb 181). This dualism results in the closing parts of the narrative in an unusual combination of closeness and detachment between the protagonist and the narrator. The immediate textual indication of the change in the narrator's stance is a greater distinctiveness of voice separating the two. Whereas it is hard to know whether the comment "it was simply a desire to travel" comes from Aschenbach or from the narrator, toward the end of *Death in Venice* the two perspectives are divorced, although the narrator continues to have inside access to Aschenbach's emotional and cognitive processes.

The disjunction is most apparent in the final pages, where the contrast with the opening section is also most striking. At the beginning, the narrator shows an understanding empathy for Aschenbach; toward the end, this is transformed into scoffing criticism. Aschenbach's paraphrasing from Plato toward the end of the story is introduced by this paragraph:

> There he sat, the master, the artist who had achieved dignity, the author of *A Study in Abjection*, he who in such paradigmatically pure form had repudiated intellectual vagrancy and the murky depths, who had proclaimed his renunciation of all sympathy with the abyss, who had weighed vileness in the balance and found it wanting; he who had risen so high, who had set his face against his own sophistication, grown out of all his irony, and taken on the commitments of one whom the public trusted; he, whose fame was official, whose name had been ennobled, and on whose style young boys were taught to model their own — there he sat, with his eyelids closed, with only an occasional mocking and rueful sideways glance from under them which he hid again at once; and his drooping, cosmetically brightened lips shaped the occasional word of the discourse his brain was delivering, his half-asleep brain with its tissue of strange dream-logic. (85)

On the one hand, such a passage raises fewer difficulties for readers than the earlier habit of ambiguity that fosters doubts and uncertainties. On the other hand, the narrator's patent and wanton gloating over his fallen "hero" opens up a wholly different kind of problem, centered on readers' relationship to the narrator. Hitherto, he had acted as an intermediary between Aschenbach and readers, chronicling his career and actions, admittedly in an often slippery manner, but from a base of more or less amicable insight. Now he distances himself from Aschenbach, whom he designates as in a "state of distraction" (70), "gripped by his adventure" (70), "beguiled" and "stricken" (72, 82).[2]

The narrator's lacerating cruelty toward Aschenbach must affect readers, too, by making them question his integrity. Most readers never really feel warm toward Aschenbach — probably because he is portrayed as himself a detached person without close human ties. Nev-

---

[2]The German text is much more strongly condemnatory in a series of harshly judgmental terms: "*der Verwirrte*" (the man gone astray), "*der Betörte*" (the bewitched man), "*der Heimgesuchte*" (the man destined for an ill fate), and "*der Berückte*" (the ensnared man).

ertheless, at the beginning he is shown as having won the admiration of his readership for the mastery he has attained by dint of his perseverance and self-discipline. At the same time, readers are encouraged to develop a trusting rapport with the narrator, who presents himself as a close associate of Aschenbach and as a trustworthy "friend"[3] to readers. His avowal of certain hesitations in regard to Aschenbach does not impinge on our confidence in him; we share his reservations. But his reiterated censure of Aschenbach in the final phases of the story, culminating in his overt taunting in the passage just cited, will likely alienate us more from the narrator than from Aschenbach, who comes to be seen as a victim of the narrator's changed attitude as well as of his own id. How much trust can readers invest in a narrator who shows malice toward his "hero"? His viciousness may have the effect of prompting readers to recoil, dissociating themselves from his harsh judgment.

The narrator's outbursts against Aschenbach at the end of *Death in Venice* have further repercussions. By becoming critical of Aschenbach, the narrator aggravates the duplicitousness immanent in his earlier, ambivalent statements. So the theme of betrayal and deception crystallizes as the central issue of *Death in Venice* at a variety of levels. Aschenbach is betrayed and deceived by his aesthetic ideal of beauty of form, which is two-faced and misleads him into an adulation of the beauty incarnated in Tadzio. He is likewise severely betrayed by the narrator's blatant treachery. And readers, too, experience a vicarious sense of betrayal through the unexpected conduct of a narrator whom they had taken to be honorable and who suddenly behaves in a distasteful manner. Far from just going along with his denigration of Aschenbach, readers become suspicious of the narrator for his deceitfulness and tend to retreat from the complicity into which he is trying to draw them.[4] So readers come eventually to distrust the narrator, too. The potential deceptiveness of reading, which has been shown within the story, comes ultimately to represent a threat to readers as they wrestle with an enigmatic text without the assured and assuring guidance of a reliable narratorial voice.

[3]For the concept of friendship between narrators and readers see Booth.

[4]For a more detailed analysis of this changed relationship between the narrator and reader, see my article "The Ethics of Reading in *Death in Venice*" and the chapter "Reading 'Nasty' Great Books" in *Through the Lens of the Reader*.

WORKS CITED

Booth, Wayne C. *The Company We Keep: An Ethics of Reading.* Berkeley: U of California P, 1988.

Cohn, Dorrit. "The Second Author of *Death in Venice.*" In *Probleme der Moderne: Studien zur deutschen Literatur von Nietzsche bis Brecht: Festschrift für Walter Sokel.* Ed. Benjamin Bennett et al. Tübingen: Niemeyer, 1983. 223–45. Rpt. in Thomas Mann, *Death in Venice.* Ed. Clayton Koelb. New York: Norton, 1994. 178–95.

Furst, Lilian R. "The Ethics of Reading *Death in Venice.*" *LIT.* 1 (1990): 265–74.

———. "Reading 'Nasty' Great Books." *Through the Lens of the Reader.* Albany: State U of New York P, 1992. 39–50.

Koelb, Clayton, ed. and trans. *Thomas Mann: "Death in Venice."* New York: Norton, 1994.

Reed, T. J. "The Art of Ambivalence." *Thomas Mann: The Uses of Tradition.* Oxford: Clarendon, 1974. 144–78.

Cultural Criticism
and
Death in Venice

WHAT IS CULTURAL CRITICISM?

What do you think of when you think of culture? The opera or ballet? A performance of a Mozart symphony at Lincoln Center or a Rembrandt show at the De Young Museum in San Francisco? Does the phrase "cultural event" conjure up images of young people in jeans and T-shirts — or of people in their sixties dressed formally? Most people hear "culture" and think "high culture." Consequently, when they first hear of cultural criticism, most people assume it is more formal than, well, say, formalism. They suspect it is "highbrow," in both subject and style.

Nothing could be further from the truth. Cultural critics oppose the view that culture refers exclusively to high culture, Culture with a capital C. Cultural critics want to make the term refer to popular, folk, urban, and mass (mass-produced, -disseminated, -mediated, and -consumed) culture, as well as to that culture we associate with the so-called classics. Raymond Williams, an early British cultural critic whose ideas will later be described at greater length, suggested that "art and culture are ordinary"; he did so not to "pull art down" but rather to point out that there is "creativity in all our living. . . . We create our human world as we have thought of art being created" (*Revolution* 37).

Cultural critics have consequently placed a great deal of emphasis on what Michel de Certeau has called "the practice of everyday life." Rather than approaching literature in the elitist way that academic literary critics have traditionally approached it, cultural critics view it more as an anthropologist would. They ask how it emerges from and competes with other forms of discourse within a given culture (science, for instance, or television). They seek to understand the social contexts in which a given text was written, and under what conditions it was — and is — produced, disseminated, read, and used.

Contemporary cultural critics are as willing to write about *Star Trek* as they are to analyze James Joyce's *Ulysses,* a modern literary classic full of allusions to Homer's *Odyssey.* And when they write about *Ulysses,* they are likely to view it as a collage reflecting and representing cultural forms common to Joyce's Dublin, such as advertising, journalism, film, and pub life. Cultural critics typically show how the boundary we tend to envision between high and low forms of culture — forms thought of as important on one hand and relatively trivial on the other — is transgressed in all sorts of exciting ways within works on both sides of the putative cultural divide.

A cultural critic writing about a revered classic might contrast it with a movie or even a comic-strip version produced during a later period. Alternatively, the literary classic might be seen in a variety of other ways: in light of some more common form of reading material (a novel by Jane Austen might be viewed in light of Gothic romances or ladies' conduct manuals); as the reflection of some common cultural myths or concerns (*The Adventures of Huckleberry Finn* might be shown to reflect and shape American myths about race and concerns about juvenile delinquency); or as an example of how texts move back and forth across the alleged boundary between "low" and "high" culture. For instance, one group of cultural critics has pointed out that although Shakespeare's history plays probably started off as popular works enjoyed by working people, they were later considered "highbrow" plays that only the privileged and educated could appreciate. That view of them changed, however, due to later film productions geared toward a national audience. A film version of *Henry V* produced during World War II, for example, made a powerful, popular, patriotic statement about England's greatness during wartime (Humm, Stigant, and Widdowson 6–7). More recently, cultural critics have analyzed the "cultural work" accomplished cooperatively by Shakespeare and Kenneth Branagh in the latter's 1992 film production of *Henry V.*

In combating old definitions of what constitutes culture, of course, cultural critics sometimes end up contesting old definitions of what constitutes the literary canon — that is, the once-agreed-upon honor roll of Great Books. They tend to do so, however, neither by adding books (and movies and television sitcoms) *to* the old list of texts that every "culturally literate" person should supposedly know nor by substituting some kind of counterculture canon. Instead, they tend to critique the very *idea* of canon.

Cultural critics want to get us away from thinking about certain works as the "best" ones produced by a given culture. They seek to be more descriptive and less evaluative, more interested in relating than in rating cultural products and events. They also aim to discover the (often political) reasons *why* a certain kind of aesthetic or cultural product is more valued than others. This is particularly true when the product in question is one produced since 1945, for most cultural critics follow Jean Baudrillard (*Simulations,* 1981) and Andreas Huyssen (*The Great Divide,* 1986) in thinking that any distinctions that may once have existed between high, popular, and mass culture collapsed after the end of World War II. Their discoveries have led them beyond the literary canon, prompting them to interrogate many other value hierarchies. For instance, Pierre Bourdieu in *Distinction: A Social Critique of the Judgment of Taste* (1984 [1979]) and Dick Hebdige in *Hiding the Light: On Images and Things* (1988) have argued that definitions of "good taste" — which are instrumental in fostering and reinforcing cultural discrimination — tell us at least as much about prevailing social, economic, and political conditions as they do about artistic quality and value.

In an article entitled "The Need for Cultural Studies," four groundbreaking cultural critics have written that "Cultural Studies should . . . abandon the goal of giving students access to that which represents a culture." A literary work, they go on to suggest, should be seen in relation to other works, to economic conditions, or to broad social discourses (about childbirth, women's education, rural decay, and so on) within whose contexts it makes sense. Perhaps most important, critics practicing cultural studies should counter the prevalent notion of culture as some preformed whole. Rather than being static or monolithic, culture is really a set of interactive *cultures,* alive and changing, and cultural critics should be present- and even future-oriented. They should be "resisting intellectuals," and cultural studies should be "an emancipatory project" (Giroux et al. 478–80).

The preceding paragraphs are peppered with words like *oppose,* *counter, deny, resist, combat, abandon,* and *emancipatory.* What these words quite accurately suggest is that a number of cultural critics view themselves in political, even oppositional, terms. Not only are they likely to take on the literary canon, but they are also likely to oppose the institution of the university, for that is where the old definitions of culture as high culture (and as something formed, finished, and canonized) have been most vigorously preserved, defended, and reinforced.

Cultural critics have been especially critical of the departmental structure of universities, which, perhaps more than anything else, has kept the study of the "arts" relatively distinct from the study of history, not to mention from the study of such things as television, film, advertising, journalism, popular photography, folklore, current affairs, shoptalk, and gossip. By maintaining artificial boundaries, universities have tended to reassert the high/low culture distinction, implying that all the latter subjects are best left to historians, sociologists, anthropologists, and communication theorists. Cultural critics have taken issue with this implication, arguing that the way of thinking reinforced by the departmentalized structure of universities keeps us from seeing the aesthetics of an advertisement as well as the propagandistic elements of a work of literature. Cultural critics have consequently mixed and matched the analytical procedures developed in a variety of disciplines. They have formed — and encouraged other scholars to form — networks and centers, often outside of those enforced departmentally.

Some initially loose interdisciplinary networks have, over time, solidified to become cultural studies programs and majors. As this has happened, a significant if subtle danger has arisen. Richard Johnson, who along with Hebdige, Stuart Hall, and Richard Hoggart was instrumental in developing the Center for Contemporary Cultural Studies at Birmingham University in England, has warned that cultural studies must not be allowed to turn into yet another traditional academic discipline — one in which students encounter a canon replete with soap operas and cartoons, one in which belief in the importance of such popular forms has become an "orthodoxy" (39). The only principles that critics doing cultural studies can doctrinally espouse, Johnson suggests, are the two that have thus far been introduced: the principle that "culture" has been an "inegalitarian" concept, a "tool" of "condescension," and the belief that a new, "interdisciplinary (and even antidisciplinary)" approach to *true* culture (that is, to the forms in which culture currently lives) is required now that history, art, and the communications media are so complex and interrelated (42).

themselves Marxist critics as well. It is important, therefore, to have some familiarity with certain Marxist concepts — those that would have been familiar to Foucault, Thompson, and Williams, plus those espoused by contemporary cultural critics who self-identify with Marxism. That familiarity can be gained from an introduction to the works of four important Marxist thinkers: Mikhail Bakhtin, Walter Benjamin, Antonio Gramsci, and Louis Althusser.

Bakhtin was a Russian, later a Soviet, critic so original in his thinking and wide ranging in his influence that some would say he was never a Marxist at all. He viewed literary works in terms of discourses and dialogues *between* discourses. The narrative of a novel written in a society in flux, for instance, may include an official, legitimate discourse, plus others that challenge its viewpoint and even its authority. In a 1929 book on Dostoyevsky and the 1940 study *Rabelais and His World*, Bakhtin examined what he calls "polyphonic" novels, each characterized by a multiplicity of voices or discourses. In Dostoyevsky, the independent status of a given character is marked by the difference of his or her language from that of the narrator. (The narrator's language may itself involve a dialogue involving opposed points of view.) In works by Rabelais, Bakhtin finds that the (profane) languages of Carnival and of other popular festivities play against and parody the more official discourses of the magistrates and the church. Bakhtin's relevance to cultural criticism lies in his suggestion that the dialogue involving high and low culture takes place not only between classic and popular texts but also between the "dialogic" voices that exist within all great books.

Walter Benjamin was a German Marxist who, during roughly the same period, attacked fascism and questioned the superior value placed on certain traditional literary forms that he felt conveyed a stultifying "aura" of culture. He took this position in part because so many previous Marxist critics (and, in his own day, Georg Lukács) had seemed to prefer nineteenth-century realistic novels to the modernist works of their own time. Benjamin not only praised modernist movements, such as dadaism, but also saw as promising the development of new art forms utilizing mechanical production and reproduction. These forms, including photography, radio, and film, promised that the arts would become a more democratic, less exclusive, domain. Anticipating by decades the work of those cultural critics interested in mass-produced, mass-mediated, and mass-consumed culture, Benjamin analyzed the meanings and (defensive) motivations behind words like *unique* and *authentic* when used in conjunction with mechanically reproduced art.

The object of cultural study should not be a body of works assumed to comprise or reflect a given culture. Rather, it should be human consciousness, and the goal of that critical analysis should be to understand and show how that consciousness is itself forged and formed, to a great extent, by cultural forces. "Subjectivities," as Johnson has put it, are "produced, not given, and are . . . objects of inquiry" inevitably related to "social practices," whether those involve factory rules, supermarket behavior patterns, reading habits, advertisements, myths, or languages and other signs to which people are exposed (44–45).

Although the United States has probably contributed more than any other nation to the *media* through which culture is currently expressed, and although many if not most contemporary practitioners of cultural criticism are North American, the evolution of cultural criticism and, more broadly, cultural studies has to a great extent been influenced by theories developed in Great Britain and Europe.

Among the continental thinkers whose work allowed for the development of cultural studies are those whose writings we associate with structuralism and poststructuralism. Using the linguistic theory of Ferdinand de Saussure, structuralists suggested that the structures of language lie behind all human organization. They attempted to create a *semiology* — a science of signs — that would give humankind at once a scientific and holistic way of studying the world and its human inhabitants. Roland Barthes, a structuralist who later shifted toward poststructuralism, attempted to recover literary language from the isolation in which it had been studied and to show that the laws that govern it govern all signs, from road signs to articles of clothing. Claude Lévi-Strauss, an anthropologist who studied the structures of everything from cuisine to villages to myths, looked for and found recurring, common elements that transcended the differences within and between cultures.

Of the structuralist and poststructuralist thinkers who have had an impact on the evolution of cultural studies, Jacques Lacan is one of three whose work has been particularly influential. A structuralist psychoanalytic theorist, Lacan posited that the human unconscious is structured like a language and treated dreams not as revealing symptoms of repression but rather as forms of discourse. Lacan also argued that the ego, subject, or self that we think of as being natural (our individual human nature) is in fact a product of the social order and its symbolic systems (especially, but not exclusively, language). Lacan's thought has served as the theoretical underpinning for cultural critics seeking to show the way in which subjectivities are produced by social discourses and practices.

Jacques Derrida, a French philosopher whose name has become synonymous with poststructuralism, has had an influence on cultural criticism at least as great as that of Lacan. The linguistic focus of structuralist thought has by no means been abandoned by poststructuralists, in spite of their opposition to structuralism's tendency to find universal patterns instead of textual and cultural contradictions. Indeed, Derrida has provocatively asserted that *"there is nothing outside the text" (Grammatology* 158), by which he means something like the following: we come to know the world through language, and even our most worldly actions and practices (the Gulf War, the wearing of condoms) are dependent upon discourses (even if they deliberately contravene those discourses). Derrida's "deconstruction" of the world/text distinction, like his deconstruction of so many of the hierarchical oppositions we habitually use to interpret and evaluate reality, has allowed cultural critics to erase the boundaries between high and low culture, classic and popular literary texts, and literature and other cultural discourses that, following Derrida, may be seen as manifestations of the same textuality.

Michel Foucault is the third continental thinker associated with structuralism and/or poststructuralism who has had a particularly powerful impact on the evolution of cultural studies — and perhaps *the* strongest influence on American cultural criticism and the so-called new historicism, an interdisciplinary form of cultural criticism whose evolution has often paralleled that of cultural criticism. Although Foucault broke with Marxism after the French student uprisings of 1968, he was influenced enough by Marxist thought to study cultures in terms of power relationships. Unlike Marxists, however, Foucault refused to see power as something exercised by a dominant class over a subservient class. Indeed, he emphasized that power is not just repressive power — that is, a tool of conspiracy by one individual or institution against another. Power, rather, is a whole complex of forces; it is that which produces what happens.

Thus even a tyrannical aristocrat does not simply wield power but is empowered by "discourses" — accepted ways of thinking, writing, and speaking — and practices that embody, exercise, and amount to power. Foucault tried to view all things, from punishment to sexuality, in terms of the widest possible variety of discourses. As a result, he traced what he called the "genealogy" of topics he studied through

texts that more traditional historians and literary critics would ha overlooked, examining (in Lynn Hunt's words) "memoirs of deviant diaries, political treatises, architectural blueprints, court records, doc tors' reports — appl[ying] consistent principles of analysis in search o moments of reversal in discourse, in search of events as loci of the conflict where social practices were transformed" (Hunt 39). Foucault tended not only to build interdisciplinary bridges but also, in the process, to bring into the study of culture the "histories of women, homosexuals, and minorities" — groups seldom studied by those interested in Culture with a capital C (Hunt 45).

Of the British influences on cultural studies and criticism, two stand out prominently. One, the Marxist historian E. P. Thompson, revolutionized the study of the industrial revolution by writing about its impact on human attitudes, even consciousness. He showed how a shared cultural view, specifically that of what constitutes a fair or just price, influenced crowd behavior and caused such things as the "food riots" of the eighteenth and nineteenth centuries (during which the women of Nottingham repriced breads in the shops of local bakers, paid for the goods they needed, and carried them away). The other, even more important early British influence on contemporary cultural criticism and cultural studies was Raymond Williams, who coined the phrase "culture is ordinary." In works like *Culture and Society: 1780–1950* (1958) and *The Long Revolution* (1961) Williams demonstrated that culture is not fixed and finished but rather living and evolving. One of the changes he called for was the development of a common socialist culture.

Although Williams dissociated himself from Marxism during the period 1945–58, he always followed the Marxist practice of viewing culture in relation to ideologies, which he defined as the "residual," "dominant," or "emerging" ways of viewing the world held by classes or individuals holding power in a given social group. He avoided dwelling on class conflict and class oppression, however, tending instead to focus on people as people, on how they experience the conditions in which they find themselves and creatively respond to those conditions through their social practices. A believer in the resiliency of the individual, Williams produced a body of criticism notable for what Stuart Hall has called its "humanism" (63).

As is clearly suggested in several of the preceding paragraphs, Marxism is the background to the background of cultural criticism. What isn't as clear is that some contemporary cultural critics consider

Antonio Gramsci, an Italian Marxist best known for his *Prison Notebooks* (first published in 1947), critiqued the very concept of literature and, beyond that, of culture in the old sense, stressing the importance of culture more broadly defined and the need for nurturing and developing proletarian, or working-class, culture. He argued that all intellectual or cultural work is fundamentally political and expressed the need for what he called "radical organic" intellectuals. Today's cultural critics urging colleagues to "legitimate the notion of writing reviews and books for the general public," to "become involved in the political reading of popular culture," and more generally to "repoliticize" scholarship have viewed Gramsci as an early precursor (Giroux et al. 482).

Gramsci related literature to the ideologies — the prevailing ideas, beliefs, values, and prejudices — of the culture in which it was produced. He developed the concept of "hegemony," which refers at once to the process of consensus formation and to the authority of the ideologies so formed — that is to say, their power to shape the way things look, what they would seem to mean, and therefore what reality *is* for the majority of people. But Gramsci did not see people, even poor people, as the helpless victims of hegemony, as ideology's pathetic robots. Rather, he believed that people have the freedom and power to struggle against and shape ideology, to alter hegemony, to break out of the weblike system of prevailing assumptions and to form a new consensus. As Patrick Brantlinger has suggested in *Crusoe's Footprints: Cultural Studies in Britain and America* (1990), Gramsci rejected the "intellectual arrogance that views the vast majority of people as deluded zombies, the victims or creatures of ideology" (100).

Of those Marxists who, after Gramsci, explored the complex relationship between literature and ideology, the French Marxist Louis Althusser had a significant impact on cultural criticism. Unlike Gramsci, Althusser tended to portray ideology as being in control of people, and not vice versa. He argued that the main function of ideology is to reproduce the society's existing relations of production, and that that function is even carried out in literary texts. In many ways, though, Althusser is as good an example of how Marxism and cultural criticism part company as he is of how cultural criticism is indebted to Marxists and their ideas. For although Althusser did argue that literature is relatively autonomous — more independent of ideology than, say, church, press, or state — he meant literature in the high-cultural sense, certainly not the variety of works that present-day cultural critics routinely examine alongside those of Tolstoy and Joyce, Eliot and Brecht.

Popular fictions, Althusser assumed, were mere packhorses designed (however unconsciously) to carry the baggage of a culture's ideology, or mere brood mares destined to reproduce it.

Thus, while a number of cultural critics would agree both with Althusser's notion that works of literature reflect certain ideological formations and with his notion that, at the same time, literary works may be relatively distant from or even resistant to ideology, they have rejected the narrow limits within which Althusser and some other Marxists (such as Georg Lukács) have defined literature. In "Marxism and Popular Fiction" (1986), Tony Bennett uses *Monty Python's Flying Circus* and another British television show, *Not the 9 o'clock News*, to argue that the Althusserian notion that all forms of culture belong "among [all those] many material forms which ideology takes . . . under capitalism" is "simply not true." The "entire field" of "popular fiction" — which Bennett takes to include films and television shows as well as books — is said to be "replete with instances" of works that do what Bennett calls the "work" of "distancing." That is, they have the effect of separating the audience from, not rebinding the audience to, prevailing ideologies (249).

Although Marxist cultural critics exist (Bennett himself is one, carrying on through his writings what may be described as a lovers' quarrel with Marxism), most cultural critics are not Marxists in any strict sense. Anne Beezer, in writing about such things as advertisements and women's magazines, contests the "Althusserian view of ideology as the construction of the subject" (qtd. in Punter 103). That is, she gives both the media she is concerned with and their audiences more credit than Althusserian Marxists presumably would. Whereas they might argue that such media make people what they are, she points out that the same magazines that, admittedly, tell women how to please their men may, at the same time, offer liberating advice to women about how to preserve their independence by not getting too serious romantically. And, she suggests, many advertisements advertise their status as ads, just as many people who view or read them see advertising as advertising and interpret it accordingly.

The complex sort of analysis that Beezer has brought to bear on women's magazines and advertisements has been focused on paperback romance novels by Tania Modleski and Janice A. Radway in *Loving with a Vengeance* (1982) and *Reading the Romance* (1984), respectively. Radway, a feminist cultural critic who uses but ultimately goes beyond Marxism, points out that many women who read romances do so in order to carve out a time and space that is wholly their own, not to be intruded upon by husbands or children. Although many such novels end in marriage, the marriage is usually between a feisty and independent heroine and a powerful man she has "tamed" — that is, made sensitive and caring. And why do so many of these stories involve such heroines and end as they do? Because, as Radway demonstrates through painstaking research into publishing houses, bookstores, and reading communities, their consumers *want* them to. They don't buy — or, if they buy they don't recommend — romances in which, for example, a heroine is raped: thus, in time, fewer and fewer such plots find their way onto the racks by the supermarket checkout.

Radway's reading is typical of feminist cultural criticism in that it is *political* but not exclusively about oppression. The subjectivities of women may be "produced" by romances — the thinking of romance readers may be governed by what is read — but the same women also govern, to a great extent, what gets written or produced, thus performing "cultural work" of their own. Rather than seeing all forms of popular culture as manifestations of ideology, soon to be remanifested in the minds of victimized audiences, cultural critics tend to see a sometimes disheartening but always dynamic synergy between cultural forms and the culture's consumers. Their observations have increasingly led to an analysis of consumerism, from a feminist but also from a more general point of view. This analysis owes a great deal to the work of de Certeau, Hall, and, especially, Hebdige, whose 1979 book *Subculture: The Meaning of Style* paved the way for critics like John Fiske (*Television Culture*, 1987), Greil Marcus (*Dead Elvis*, 1991), and Rachel Bowlby (*Shopping with Freud*, 1993). These later critics have analyzed everything from the resistance tactics employed by television audiences to the influence of consumers on rock music styles to the psychology of consumer choice.

The overlap between feminist and cultural criticism is hardly surprising, especially given the recent evolution of feminism into various feminisms, some of which remain focused on "majority" women of European descent, others of which have focused instead on the lives and writings of minority women in Western culture and of women living in Third World (now preferably called postcolonial) societies. The culturalist analysis of value hierarchies within and between cultures has inevitably focused on categories that include class, race, national origin, gender, and sexualities; the terms of its critique have proved useful to contemporary feminists, many of whom differ from their predecessors insofar as they see *woman* not as a universal category but rather as one of several that play a role in identity- or subject-formation. The influence of cultural criticism (and, in some cases, Marxist class analysis) can be seen in the work of contemporary feminist critics such as Gayatri Spivak, Trinh T. Minh-ha, and Gloria Anzaldúa, each of whom has stressed that while all women are female, they are something else as well (such as working-class, lesbian, Native American, Muslim Pakistani) and that that something else must be taken into account when their writings are read and studied.

The expansion of feminism and feminist literary criticism to include multicultural analysis, of course, parallels a transformation of education in general. On college campuses across North America, the field of African-American studies has grown and flourished. African American critics have been influenced by and have contributed to the cultural approach by pointing out that the white cultural elite of North America has tended to view the oral-musical traditions of African Americans (traditions that include jazz, the blues, sermons, and folktales) as entertaining but nonetheless inferior. Black writers, in order not to be similarly marginalized, have produced texts that, as Henry Louis Gates has pointed out, fuse the language and traditions of the white Western canon with a black vernacular and traditions derived from African and Caribbean cultures. The resulting "hybridity" (to use Homi K. Bhabha's word), although deplored by a handful of black separatist critics, has proved both rich and complex — fertile ground for many cultural critics practicing African American criticism.

Interest in race and ethnicity at home has gone hand in hand with a new, interdisciplinary focus on colonial and postcolonial societies abroad, in which issues of race, class, and ethnicity also loom large. Edward Said's book *Orientalism* (1978) is generally said to have inaugurated postcolonial studies, which in Bhabha's words "bears witness to the unequal and uneven forces of cultural representation involved in the contest for political and social authority within the modern world order" ("Postcolonial Criticism" 437). *Orientalism* showed how Eastern and Middle Eastern peoples have for centuries been systematically stereotyped by the West, and how that stereotyping facilitated the colonization of vast areas of the East and Middle East by Westerners. Said's more recent books, along with postcolonial studies by Bhabha and Patrick Brantlinger, are among the most widely read and discussed works of literary scholarship. Brantlinger focuses on British literature of the Victorian period, examining representations of the colonies in works written during an era of imperialist expansion. Bhabha complements Brantlinger by suggesting that modern Western culture is best understood from the postcolonial perspective.

Thanks to the work of scholars like Brantlinger, Bhabha, Said, Gates, Anzaldúa, and Spivak, education in general and literary study in particular is becoming more democratic, decentered (less patriarchal and Eurocentric), and multicultural. The future of literary criticism will owe a great deal indeed to those early cultural critics who demonstrated that the boundaries between high and low culture are at once repressive and permeable, that culture is common and therefore includes all forms of popular culture, that cultural definitions are inevitably political, and that the world we see is seen through society's ideology. In a very real sense, the future of education *is* cultural studies.

Cultural critic John Burt Foster Jr. begins the essay that follows by pointing out that, in *Death in Venice,* Thomas Mann refers to "'culture' at both a high and a low point in his protagonist's destiny" and by arguing that "an adequate reading of the story must come to terms with this many-faceted word." Citing Raymond Williams's assertion that "culture" is "one of the two or three most complex words in the English language," Foster maintains that it is even more problematic when it appears in an English translation of Mann's novella such as this one. Here "culture" is used in place of a German word (*Kultur*) that has been variously translated as "culture," "art," and even "culmination of effort."

The meaning of *Kultur,* Foster points out, has changed several times since the 1700s. Whereas in the eighteenth century it referred to "the language, religion, and set of customs" shared by any group of people, in the nineteenth century it became "a special marker of German identity" — that is, a word denoting what Germans believed they held in common and what other peoples — such as the German empire's Polish inhabitants — sorely lacked. Mann, Foster maintains, began his career using the term in this chauvinistic German manner. As the Nazis gained power, however, he came to "suggest that [*Kultur*] no longer meant 'culture' . . . but 'rebarbarization.'" Preferring words meaning "civilization," Mann became a critic of "culture" in the chauvinistic German sense.

When Mann wrote *Death in Venice,* Foster goes on to argue, he was in a transitional period; the novella consequently depicts "cultural attitudes" that Mann held while moving "along his path" toward belief in the value of "diversity" and "interaction." Foster also maintains that *Death in Venice* represents one aspect of Europe's "cultural geography" — which consisted of Latinate, Anglo-Saxon, Teutonic or German, and Slavic components — in "each of the story's four more memorable characters." As Mann "moved from the chauvinism of *Kultur*" toward an appreciative "awareness of cultural multiplicity," he came to a new understanding of the German sense of "being in the middle" of Europe's cultural geography. "The middle," which had traditionally suggested to Germans their culture's centrality or "pre-eminence," for Mann came to have "another meaning. It was a cultural site that allowed for interaction in many directions."

Having explored Mann's assessment of *Kultur* in general, Foster turns to *Death in Venice* more specifically. He interrelates a variety of subjects, ranging from Tadzio's sickness as a cause of Aschenbach's fascination, to Aschenbach's writing vis-à-vis the literary canon, to the role of Venice in the cultural geography of *Death in Venice*, to Mann's use of mythic materials in the novella. (In discussing myth, Foster focuses on the passage representing Aschenbach's "Dionysian dream," in which Dionysus is referred to as "*the stranger-god*".) Students reading all five of the critical approaches to literature represented in this edition may find particularly interesting Foster's use of cultural criticism not to dispute Robert Tobin's view (see "What Is Gender Criticism?") that repressed homosexuality plays a role in Aschenbach's attraction to Tadzio but rather to argue that "the longing gaze" Aschenbach casts on the Polish youth may *also* be seen in terms of "German-Slavic boundaries." Aschenbach, Foster maintains, "comes from an ethnically mixed background. Not only did he grow up in the German-Polish border province of Silesia, but through his mother he may be partly Slavic himself." Foster thus views "Aschenbach's infatuation with Tadzio" as potentially including "a belated recognition of his [own] mixed heritage," a background "previously suppressed owing to his single-minded pursuit of German *Kultur*."

Foster's essay exemplifies contemporary cultural criticism in several ways. First, it interrogates ethnic and class-based definitions of human difference (what some cultural critics have called "the Other"). Second, Foster critiques exclusionary definitions of (high) culture — in this case, as manifested in the nineteenth-century German definition of *Kultur*. Third, he focuses on a text that, in and of itself, reflects critically on the subject of cultural formation.

Although Foster's essay indicates the extent to which cultural geopolitics determines Aschenbach's — and Mann's — experiences and even subjectivity, it also shows the power of the imagination to revisit, resist, and even *alter* cultural formations — that is, old ways of seeing and being. Aschenbach's struggle to resist cultural imperatives ends in death. Mann's, however, culminates with "a sharpness of insight about the myth-driven politics of Hitler and other fascists that many Anglo-American modernists would lack." Although Foster admits that *Death in Venice* "anticipate[s] some of the most daring works of early-twentieth-century modernism" — works exemplifying "the 'mythical method' of T. S. Eliot's *The Waste Land* and James Joyce's *Ulysses*" — he also insists that Mann was "in several important ways" *ahead* of the writers whose work he seems to anticipate. *Death in Venice,* for instance, "begins to look beyond the elite English and American literature of the period, glimpsing possibilities for cultural multiplicity and interaction that avoid the shackles of grandiose, self-imposed mythologies."

Ross C Murfin

CULTURAL CRITICISM:
A SELECTED BIBLIOGRAPHY

General Introductions to
Cultural Criticism, Cultural Studies

Bathrick, David. "Cultural Studies." *Introduction to Scholarship in Modern Languages and Literatures.* Ed. Joseph Gibaldi. New York: MLA, 1992.

Brantlinger, Patrick. *Crusoe's Footprints: Cultural Studies in Britain and America.* New York: Routledge, 1990.

————. "Cultural Studies vs. the New Historicism." *English Studies/ Cultural Studies: Institutionalizing Dissent.* Ed. Isaiah Smithson and Nancy Ruff. Urbana: U of Illinois P, 1994. 43–58.

Brantlinger, Patrick, and James Naremore, eds. *Modernity and Mass Culture.* Bloomington: Indiana UP, 1991.

Brummett, Barry. *Rhetoric in Popular Culture.* New York: St. Martin's, 1994.

Desan, Philippe, Priscilla Parkhurst Ferguson, and Wendy Griswold. "Editors' Introduction: Mirrors, Frames, and Demons: Reflections on the Sociology of Literature." *Literature and Social Practice.* Ed. Desan, Ferguson, and Griswold. Chicago: U of Chicago P, 1989. 1–10.

During, Simon, ed. *The Cultural Studies Reader.* New York: Routledge, 1993.

Eagleton, Terry. "Two Approaches in the Sociology of Literature." *Critical Inquiry* 14 (1988): 469–76.

Easthope, Anthony. *Literary into Cultural Studies.* New York: Routledge, 1991.

Fisher, Philip. "American Literary and Cultural Studies since the Civil War." *Redrawing the Boundaries: The Transformation of English and American Literary Studies.* Ed. Stephen Greenblatt and Giles Gunn. New York: MLA, 1992. 232–50.

Giroux, Henry, David Shumway, Paul Smith, and James Sosnoski. "The Need for Cultural Studies: Resisting Intellectuals and Oppositional Public Spheres." *Dalhousie Review* 64.2 (1984): 472–86.

Graff, Gerald, and Bruce Robbins. "Cultural Criticism." *Redrawing the Boundaries: The Transformation of English and American Literary Studies.* Ed. Stephen Greenblatt and Giles Gunn. New York: MLA, 1992. 419–36.

Grossberg, Lawrence, Cary Nelson, and Paula A. Treichler, eds. *Cultural Studies.* New York: Routledge, 1992.

Gunn, Giles. *The Culture of Criticism and the Criticism of Culture.* New York: Oxford UP, 1987.

Hall, Stuart. "Cultural Studies: Two Paradigms." *Media, Culture and Society* 2 (1980): 57–72.

Humm, Peter, Paul Stigant, and Peter Widdowson, eds. *Popular Fictions: Essays in Literature and History.* New York: Methuen, 1986.

Hunt, Lynn, ed. *The New Cultural History: Essays.* Berkeley: U of California P, 1989.

Johnson, Richard. "What Is Cultural Studies Anyway?" *Social Text: Theory/Culture/Ideology* 16 (1986–87): 38–80.

Pfister, Joel. "The Americanization of Cultural Studies." *Yale Journal of Criticism* 4 (1991): 199–229.

Punter, David, ed. *Introduction to Contemporary Critical Studies.* New York: Longman, 1986. See especially Punter's "Introduction: Culture and Change" 1–18, Tony Dunn's "The Evolution of Cultural Studies" 71–91, and the essay "Methods for Cultural Studies Students" by Anne Beezer, Jean Grimshaw, and Martin Barker 95–118.

Storey, John. *An Introductory Guide to Cultural Theory and Popular Culture.* Athens: U of Georgia P, 1993.

Turner, Graeme. *British Cultural Studies: An Introduction.* Boston: Unwin Hyman, 1990.

Cultural Studies:
Some Early British Examples

Hoggart, Richard. *Speaking to Each Other*. 2 vols. London: Chatto, 1970.

————. *The Uses of Literacy: Changing Patterns in English Mass Culture*. Boston: Beacon, 1961.

Thompson, E. P. *The Making of the English Working Class*. New York: Harper, 1958.

————. *William Morris: Romantic to Revolutionary*. New York: Pantheon, 1977.

Williams, Raymond. *Culture and Society, 1780–1950*. 1958. New York: Harper, 1966.

————. *The Long Revolution*. New York: Columbia UP, 1961.

Cultural Studies:
Continental and Marxist Influences

Althusser, Louis. *For Marx*. Trans. Ben Brewster. New York: Pantheon, 1969.

————. "Ideology and Ideological State Apparatuses." *Lenin and Philosophy*. Trans. Ben Brewster. New York: Monthly Review P, 1971. 127–86.

Althusser, Louis, and Étienne Balibar. *Reading Capital*. Trans. Ben Brewster. New York: Pantheon, 1971.

Bakhtin, Mikhail. *The Dialogic Imagination: Four Essays*. Ed. Michael Holquist. Trans. Caryl Emerson. Austin: U of Texas P, 1981.

————. *Rabelais and His World*. Trans. Hélène Iswolsky. Cambridge: MIT P, 1968.

Baudrillard, Jean. *Simulations*. Trans. Paul Foss, Paul Patton, and Philip Beitchnan. 1981. New York: Semiotext(e), 1983.

Benjamin, Walter. *Illuminations*. Ed. with intro. Hannah Arendt. Trans. Harry H. Zohn. New York: Harcourt, 1968.

Bennett, Tony. "Marxism and Popular Fiction." Humm, Stigant, and Widdowson 237–65.

Bourdieu, Pierre. *Distinction: A Social Critique of the Judgment of Taste*. Trans. Richard Nice. Cambridge: Harvard UP, 1984.

de Certeau, Michel. *The Practice of Everyday Life*. Trans. Steven F. Rendall. Berkeley: U of California P, 1984.

Foucault, Michel. *Discipline and Punish: The Birth of the Prison*. Trans. Alan Sheridan. New York: Pantheon, 1978.

——— . *The History of Sexuality.* Trans. Robert Hurley. Vol. 1. New York: Pantheon, 1978.

Gramsci, Antonio. *Selections from the Prison Notebooks.* Ed. Quintin Hoare and Geoffrey Nowell Smith. New York: International, 1971.

Modern Cultural Studies:
Selected British and American Examples

Bagdikian, Ben H. *The Media Monopoly.* Boston: Beacon, 1983.

Bowlby, Rachel. *Shopping with Freud.* New York: Routledge, 1993.

Chambers, Iain. *Popular Culture: The Metropolitan Experience.* New York: Methuen, 1986.

Colls, Robert, and Philip Dodd, eds. *Englishness: Politics and Culture, 1880–1920.* London: Croom Helm, 1986.

Denning, Michael. *Mechanic Accents: Dime Novels and Working-Class Culture in America.* New York: Verso, 1987.

Fiske, John. "British Cultural Studies and Television." *Channels of Discourse: Television and Contemporary Criticism.* Ed. Robert C. Allen. Chapel Hill: U of North Carolina P, 1987.

——— . *Television Culture.* New York: Methuen, 1987.

Hebdige, Dick. *Hiding the Light: On Images and Things.* New York: Routledge, 1988.

——— . *Subculture: The Meaning of Style.* London: Methuen, 1979.

Huyssen, Andreas. *After the Great Divide: Modernism, Mass Culture, Postmodernism.* Bloomington: Indiana UP, 1986.

Marcus, Greil. *Dead Elvis: A Chronicle of a Cultural Obsession.* New York: Doubleday, 1991.

——— . *Lipstick Traces: A Secret History of the Twentieth Century.* Cambridge: Harvard UP, 1989.

Modleski, Tania. *Loving with a Vengeance: Mass-Produced Fantasies for Women.* Hamden: Archon, 1982.

Poovey, Mary. *Uneven Developments: The Ideological Work of Gender in Mid-Victorian England.* Chicago: U of Chicago P, 1988.

Radway, Janice A. *Reading the Romance: Women, Patriarchy, and Popular Literature.* Chapel Hill: U of North Carolina P, 1984.

Reed, T. V. *Fifteen Jugglers, Five Believers: Literary Politics and the Poetics of American Social Movements.* Berkeley: U of California P, 1992.

Ethnic and Minority Criticism, Postcolonial Studies

Anzaldúa, Gloria. *Borderlands: La Frontera = The New Mestiza*. San Francisco: Spinsters/Aunt Lute, 1987.

Baker, Houston. *Blues, Ideology, and Afro-American Literature: A Vernacular Theory*. Chicago: U of Chicago P, 1984.

———. *The Journey Back: Issues in Black Literature and Criticism*. Chicago: U of Chicago P, 1980.

Bhabha, Homi K. *The Location of Culture*. New York: Routledge, 1994.

———, ed. *Nation and Narration*. New York: Routledge, 1990.

———. "Postcolonial Criticism." *Redrawing the Boundaries: The Transformation of English and American Literary Studies*. Ed. Stephen Greenblatt and Giles Gunn. New York: MLA, 1992. 437–65.

Brantlinger, Patrick. *Rule of Darkness: British Literature and Imperialism, 1830–1914*. Ithaca: Cornell UP, 1988.

Gates, Henry Louis Jr. *Black Literature and Literary Theory*. New York: Methuen, 1984.

———, ed. *"Race," Writing, and Difference*. Chicago: U of Chicago P, 1986.

Gayle, Addison. *The Black Aesthetic*. Garden City: Doubleday, 1971.

———. *The Way of the New World: The Black Novel in America*. Garden City: Doubleday, 1975.

JanMohamed, Abdul. *Manichean Aesthetics: The Politics of Literature in Colonial Africa*. Amherst: U of Massachusetts P, 1983.

JanMohamed, Abdul, and David Lloyd, eds. *The Nature and Context of Minority Discourse*. New York: Oxford UP, 1991.

Kaplan, Amy, and Donald E. Pease, eds. *Cultures of United States Imperialism*. Durham: Duke UP, 1983.

Neocolonialism. Special issue, *Oxford Literary Review* 13 (1991).

Said, Edward. *After the Last Sky: Palestinian Lives*. New York: Pantheon, 1986.

———. *Culture and Imperialism*. New York: Knopf, 1993.

———. *Orientalism*. New York: Pantheon, 1978.

———. *The World, the Text, and the Critic*. Cambridge: Harvard UP, 1983.

Spivak, Gayatri Chakravorty. *In Other Worlds: Essays in Cultural Politics*. New York: Methuen, 1987.

Stepto, Robert B. *From Behind the Veil: A Study of Afro-American Narrative.* Urbana: U of Illinois P, 1979.

Young, Robert. *White Mythologies: Writing, History, and the West.* London: Routledge, 1990.

Modern Cultural Studies: Selected German Examples

Adorno, Theodor. *The Culture Industry: Selected Essays on Mass Culture.* Ed. and intro. J. M. Bernstein. London: Routledge, 1991.

Benjamin, Walter. *Charles Baudelaire: A Lyric Poet in the Era of High Capitalism.* Trans. Harry Zohn. London: NLB, 1973.

Berman, Russell A. *Cultural Studies of Modern Germany: History, Representation, and Nationhood.* Madison: U of Wisconsin P, 1993.

Burns, Rob, ed. *German Cultural Studies: An Introduction.* Oxford: Oxford UP, 1995.

Czaplicka, John, guest ed. *Cultural History/Cultural Studies.* Special issue, *New German Critique* 65 (Spring–Summer 1995): 3–187.

Gilman, Sander L. *Inscribing the Other.* Lincoln and London: U of Nebraska P, 1991.

Habermas, Jürgen. *The New Conservatism: Cultural Criticism and the Historians' Debate.* Ed. and trans. Shierry Weber Nicholson. Cambridge: MIT P, 1989.

Hartman, Geoffrey, ed. *Bitburg in Moral and Political Perspective.* Bloomington: Indiana UP, 1986.

Kacandes, Irene, and Scott Denham. *A User's Guide to German Cultural Studies.* Ann Arbor: U Michigan P, 1997.

Luetzeler, Paul Michael, advisory ed. "Multiculturalism in Contemporary German Literature." *World Literature Today* 69. 3 (Summer 1995): 453–546.

Translation Studies and Intercultural Relations (Emphasizing Thomas Mann and the English-Speaking World)

Bassnett-McGuire, Susan. *Translation Studies.* New York: Methuen, 1980.

Benjamin, Walter. "The Task of the Translator." *Illuminations.* Ed. Hannah Arendt. Trans. Harry Zohn. New York: Harcourt, 1968.

Even-Zohar, Itamar, and Gideon Toury, eds. *Translation Theory and Intercultural Relations.* Special issue, *Poetics Today* 2.4 (1981): v–xi, 1–239.

Gillespie, Gerald. "Thomas Mann in komparatistischer Sicht: Die angloamerikanische Auffassung seiner weltliterarischen Geltung." *Deutsche Literatur in der Weltliteratur: Kulturnation statt politischer Nation?* Ed. Franz Norbert Mennemeier and Conrad Wiedemann. Tübinge: Niemeyer, 1986. 122–26.

Gross, Harvey. "Parody, Reminiscence, Critique: Aspects of Modernist Style." *Modernism: Challenges and Perspectives.* Ed. Monique Chefdor, Ricardo Quinones, and Albert Wachtel. Urbana: U of Illinois P, 1986.

Mann, Thomas. *The Story of a Novel: The Genesis of "Doctor Faustus."* Trans. Richard and Clara Winston. New York: Knopf, 1961. An autobiographical account of Mann's experiences in the United States while he wrote his most "German" novel.

Steiner, George. *After Babel: Aspects of Language and Translation.* 2d ed. New York: Oxford UP, 1992.

Thirlwall, John C. *In Another Language: A Record of the Thirty-Year Relationship between Thomas Mann and His English Translator, Helen Tracy Lowe-Porter.* New York: Knopf, 1966.

Cultural Studies of Thomas Mann and *Death in Venice*

Hayes, Tom, and Lee Quinby. "The Aporia of Bourgeois Art: Desire in Thomas Mann's *Death in Venice.*" *Criticism: A Quarterly for Literature and the Arts* 3. 2 (Spring 1989): 159–77.

Koopmann, Helmut. "Aufklärung als Forderung des Tages: Zu Thomas Manns kulturphilosophischer Position in den 20er Jahren und im Exil." *Deutschsprächige Exilliteratur: Studien zu ihrer Bestimmung im Kontext der Epoche 1930 bis 1960.* Ed. Wulf Koepke and Michael Winkler. Bonn: Bouvier, 1984. 75–91.

———. "'German Culture Is Where I Am': Thomas Mann in Exile." *Studies in Twentieth Century Literature* 7. 1 (Fall 1982): 5–20.

Levenson, Alan. "Thomas Mann's 'Walsungenblut' in the Context of the Intermarriage Debate and the 'Jewish Question.'" *Insiders and Outsiders: Jewish and Gentile Culture in Germany and Austria.* Ed. Dagmar C. G. Lorenz and Gabriele Weinberger. Intro. Lorenz. Detroit: Wayne State UP, 1994.

Nicholls, Roger A. "Thomas Mann and Spengler." *German Quarterly* 58. 3 (Summer 1985): 361–74.

Smith, Duncan. "The Education to Despair: Some Thoughts on *Death in Venice*." *Praxis: A Journal of Radical Perspectives on the Arts* 1. 1 (1975): 73–80.

Sommer, Doris. "Thomas Mann's Gentle Prophetic Voice." *Poetic Prophecy in Western Literature*. Ed., pref., intro. Jan Wojcik and Jean-Raymond Frontain. Rutherford and London: Fairleigh Dickinson UP, 1984. 143–56.

Stock, Irvin. "Ironic Conservatism: Thomas Mann's *Reflections of a Non-Political Man*." *Salmagundi* 68–69 (Fall–Winter 1985–86): 166–85.

Tanner, Tony. *Venice Desired*. Cambridge: Harvard UP, 1992.

A CULTURAL PERSPECTIVE

JOHN BURT FOSTER JR.

Why Is Tadzio Polish? *Kultur* and Cultural Multiplicity in *Death in Venice*

1

Aschenbach is already obsessed with Tadzio when, in chapter 4 of *Death in Venice*, the writer's block that sent him on his trip to Venice unexpectedly lifts. Responding, as David Luke puts it in the translation chosen for this volume, to "a certain important cultural problem, a burning question of taste," he finds that he is able to write a short essay (62). But this moment of inspiration soon proves delusive. By chapter 5, the narrator tells us, Aschenbach's nightmarish vision of Dionysian rites in ancient Greece has left his "whole being, the culture of a lifetime, devastated and destroyed" (80). Mann's references to "culture" at both a high and low point in his character's destiny is significant. It suggests that an adequate reading of the story must come to terms with this many-faceted word — must weigh its broader implications and then try to understand their meaning for the narrative. It reveals, in short, the need for a cultural approach to *Death in Venice*.

Before we can undertake such a reading, however, we need to remember that the very word "culture" cannot be taken for granted. It is, as Raymond Williams remarked when summarizing his impressive work on its changing meanings, "one of the two or three most complicated words in the English language" (87). At different times and in varied contexts, as he has shown, "culture" has bridged a startling array of contrasts, from hard agricultural labor to subtle intellectual cultivation, from the zeal of religious cults to the apparent skepticism of secular humanism, from elite exclusivity to the habits of everyday life. Nevertheless, when we read *Death in Venice,* we need to take into account yet another layer of complexity — the fact that the word we read has been translated from the German. Of course, in both of the passages just cited, Mann originally wrote *Kultur,* and it was David Luke who decided on "culture" as the best English equivalent.

Given the barriers that often face translators, who could quarrel with this choice? After all, both the German and English words come from the same Latin root, and this ancient link has been reinforced by a great deal of social and intellectual exchange between the German- and English-speaking worlds ever since. Yet other English versions of *Death in Venice* have sometimes used other words. For H. T. Lowe-Porter, the authorized translator during Mann's lifetime, it is "a great and burning question of art and taste" that renews Aschenbach's creativity in chapter 4, and in Clayton Koelb's recent version, the Dionysian dream leaves the hero's "whole being, the culmination of a lifetime of effort, ravaged and destroyed" (Lowe-Porter 45; Koelb 56). Whether *Kultur* is redefined as "art" or as the "culmination of effort," these translations can be defended, with each choice giving further proof of the lexical richness of "culture." But comparing Luke's version with others also reveals that no translator can avoid interpretive decisions, however small, when putting literature into another language.

As a result, every translation becomes a cultural event in its own right. Even as translators try to bridge the gap between two different worlds, the texts they produce still bear traces of the distances crossed, as the founders of the new field of translation studies (André Lefèvere and Susan Bassnett) have stressed. Indeed, because one basic meaning of the word is "movement," we need to enlarge our sense of how often we read literature "in translation." It is not just a matter of joining different places, such as Mann's Germany with our own English-speaking world; it is also a question of different times. From this perspective, the translator's choice of the best equivalent for *Kultur* resembles the information we find, for example, in footnotes to Shakespeare's plays. Often even literature in our own language comes to us with interpretive assistance from third parties.

But whatever word the translators of *Death in Venice* use, once we consider Mann's German more carefully, it becomes clear that nobody could convey all the relevant implications of *Kultur*. Over the past two centuries of German history this highly charged word has witnessed a shift just as far-reaching as the ones that Williams has described in English. Understanding one special set of tensions embedded in the German word will prove essential for a fruitful cultural reading of *Death in Venice*.

2

In the later eighteenth century, in the writings of the historical thinker and theologian Johann Gottfried Herder (1744–1803), *Kultur* gained some of the overtones of current multiculturalism. Herder was one of the first figures in the Western tradition to insist that every people had its own *Kultur* — a language, religion, and set of customs that deserved respect as the basis for that people's identity. In particular, from having lived in the city of Riga on the Baltic borderlands between Germans and Slavs, Herder defended the worth of both peoples against the French elite culture that dominated Europe before the French Revolution.

During the nineteenth century, however, this generous plea for cultural diversity produced ironic results. Among both Germans and Slavs, it led to ever greater stridency and chauvinism, since each group began celebrating its culture to the exclusion of others, as Hans Kohn has discussed (12–18, 21–22). Moreover, because Germany did not exist as a nation-state until its partial unification under Bismarck in 1871, culture itself (rather than the more prosaic notion of a shared citizenship that did not yet exist) could become a special marker of German identity. In this spirit, Germans saw themselves as the *Kulturvolk*, as the people who took culture seriously. This sense of national selfhood was bolstered by major German achievements in philosophy, music, and literature from 1770 to 1830, as suggested by names such as Kant, Beethoven, and Goethe. A somewhat later source of cultural prestige was the German university system, with its major breakthroughs in scientific and humanistic research. Once the German empire was formed, this national pride intensified and turned harsher, most notably during the so-called *Kulturkampf*, or period of "culture combat." Mann was born in 1875, at the height of this controversy, which fed on fears about the potential divisiveness of religious differences between Protestants and Catholics. In this climate, issues of cultural affiliation could become a pretext for doubting someone's loyalty and claims to citizenship. For readers of *Death in Venice*, an even more telling conflict during this period was the effort to "Germanize" the empire's Polish inhabitants, who had come under German rule a century earlier, following the partition of Poland. In this context, *Kultur* no longer evoked Herder's Germano-Slavic multiculturalism but rather an aggressive German policy of cultural domination in the East.

More than the English word "culture," *Kultur* can run the gamut from cosmopolitan open-mindedness to rigid chauvinism. Mann's own career after *Death in Venice* bears witness to these fluctuations in meaning, for if he was known mainly as a fiction writer when the story appeared in 1912, he would soon become a culture critic in his own right. The outbreak of World War I in 1914 brought a crisis in his career: he stopped working on fiction almost entirely and poured his energies into *Reflections of a Nonpolitical Man,* a series of essays on cultural topics. At times these writings could suggest the more strident implications of *Kultur* — for example, when Mann tried to define the real meaning of the war. How else, he argued, could the depth and seriousness of the German *Kulturvolk* be defended against the frivolity and superficial political posturing of the French and English, neither of whom were cultured but merely "civilized"? Far from being an endowment of every people, *Kultur* here became a tool for scoring points against non-Germans, especially Western Europeans. From today's postcolonial viewpoint, to be sure, Mann's rhetorical strategy can seem quite ironic. For in defining "civilization" as culture's negative counterpart, he fastens on the very term so often used to justify the "civilizing mission" of the British and the French, whose overseas empires depended on similar invidious distinctions about the cultures of colonized peoples.

By the early 1920s, however, Mann's stance as a culture critic changed dramatically, partly in response to early Nazi-style terrorism and partly to genuine discomfort with some of his wartime positions. Instead of trying to defend an imperiled national essence, he began stressing intercultural communication; he took part in activities such as conferring in Paris with French intellectuals, or writing about German cultural life in *The Dial,* then a major literary journal in the United States. As a result, new terms such as "democracy," "humanism," "world-openness," and even "civilization" entered his vocabulary. All these words are consistent with the older, more cosmopolitan sense of *Kultur,* but by now this keyword no longer had the same overwhelming importance for Mann, probably because events in Germany were rapidly making its meaning so problematic. Indeed, on considering the sharper chauvinistic edge that the Nazis had given to *Kultur,* Mann could even suggest that the word no longer meant "culture" at all but "rebarbarization" (*Doctor Faustus* 370).

After Hitler came to power, of course, opinions such as these made Germany too dangerous for Mann, and in 1933 he went into exile. In sharp contrast to his stance during World War I, he spent World War II in the United States, where, like the Russian novelist Aleksandr Solzhenitsyn thirty years later, he was welcomed as a heroic literary opponent to tyranny. The 1940s would mark the high point of Mann's culture criticism, for along with warning against Hitlerism in speeches and radio broadcasts, he explored the disasters of modern German history in *Doctor Faustus* (1947). This major novel tells the life story of an imaginary composer whose career, like Aschenbach's, raises the issue of how an artist's creativity relates to its historical setting. Among the work's many strands of culture criticism, Mann's collaboration with Theodor Adorno in describing the composer's music and its social implications stands out as especially fruitful. Adorno, a younger exile from Hitler's regime who was both a leader of the so-called Frankfurt School of German intellectuals and a friend of Walter Benjamin (discussed above in Ross Murfin's headnote), has by now become an important influence on culture criticism in the United States (Berman).

3

As the foregoing survey suggests, *Death in Venice* opens a period of three decades in which Mann would actually live through the perils that merely "seemed to hang over the peace of Europe" when the story begins (23). At the same time, however, the story itself stands out as a breakthrough for Mann as a writer — one that, after a period of some frustration in his career, gave him a much stronger feeling of creative release than Aschenbach ever experiences. For this reason, *Death in Venice* can seem uncannily prophetic of Mann's later development: it touches depths in his authorship that would only come to the surface between 1914 and 1945, as he lived through the extremities of German history. In his first enthusiasm for World War I, for example, Mann could imitate Aschenbach by writing an admiring portrait of Frederick the Great, Prussia's national hero during an earlier European war (28). Two decades later, on the other hand, like the British travel agent who breaks the conspiracy of silence about the cholera epidemic (77–79), Mann would become a lone voice warning against Hitler.

Because *Death in Venice* pulls together so many of its author's cultural attitudes along his path toward a hard-earned reaffirmation of diversity and interaction, no single interpretive framework can do justice to Mann's meanings. To unpack just some of the story's varied implications will require instead a deliberately multiple approach — one that is alert to several distinct cultural options within the narrative. This multiplicity, which recalls Mikhail Bakhtin's idea of polyphonic narration as a "world of consciousnesses mutually illuminating each other", corresponds to what Murfin calls a sense of culture as "a set of interactive cultures" rather than "some wholeness that has already been formed" (Bakhtin 97). We should not, however, equate cultural multiplicity of this kind with present-day multiculturalism. As Charles Taylor has indicated, the core meaning of the latter term involves issues of public policy, educational philosophy, and curricular choice. But the cultural multiplicity of Mann's story implies something more private: the feelings of both unexpected affinity and buried tension that can arise from living among several cultural options, internalizing their diversity to some extent, and attempting to negotiate the differences in one's day-to-day experience.

Cultural multiplicity in *Death in Venice* challenges one common but hasty assumption of American multiculturalism. That is the charge of Eurocentrism, which is often valid when it criticizes traditional Western education for misrepresenting or slighting other cultures in the world. A brief trace of such misrepresentation surfaces early in the story, when Aschenbach's sudden urge to travel rises up in his imagination as a feverish vision of a South Asian jungle. In this passage the world has momentarily divided into two regions — a European "safe zone" and a realm of danger beyond. The Eurocentric critique goes too far, however, if it leaves the impression (perhaps encouraged by contemporary efforts at European unification) that the various European cultures have always worked together as a monolithic totality, with no major fissures or conflicts among the parts. It is this simplistic sense of identity that, as our exploration of cultural multiplicity in *Death in Venice* will show, simply did not exist in the early twentieth century. In fact, as already noted, the proponents of *Kultur* in its harshest forms tried to draw sharp boundaries *within* Europe, thereby instituting the same hierarchical distinctions that separated Europeans and native peoples in the colonial empires.

W. E. B. Du Bois has usefully highlighted the divisions within Europe when Mann wrote *Death in Venice*. As an African American living in Germany in the 1890s, Du Bois could observe, with a certain sardonic impartiality, the obstacles to placing the hypernationalistic Europeans of that time in any one cultural category. Many years later, accordingly, when he proposed eight major groups of global humanity, no fewer than four of them were European — the Teutonic, the Anglo-Saxon, the Latinate, and the Slavic, each group walled off from the others almost as much as black and white in Du Bois's United States (76–77).[1] Here, in a nutshell, we find the cultural geography of *Death in Venice*. In a story whose narrator can sum up Aschenbach's career by listing the vivid human portraits he has created (30–31), it is fitting that each of the story's four most memorable characters should personify one aspect of this geography. Most important, of course, is the return to Herder's original paradigm for cross-cultural contact, to what Du Bois would have called the Teutonic-Slavic tension: the border region suggested by the German writer's silent but avidly observant love for a Polish boy. Nonetheless, in the furious crescendo of events that marks chapter 5, other cultural realms play important roles as well, beginning with the Latinate and Anglo-Saxon domains of the Neapolitan street singer and the tourist agent. But then beyond the human world of the characters there appears the "stranger-god" of the Dionysian dream and his disturbing counterpart, the old-young man on the boat to Venice who anticipates Aschenbach's appearance just before his death.

This cultural geography depends on the idea of Germany as a land in the middle, expressed in the term *Mitteleuropa,* or Central Europe. Germans are not the only people who make such claims of centrality for themselves; consider the Chinese name for their country, which means "Middle Kingdom," or the overtones of "Mediterranean," from the Latin for "middle" and "earth." Nor does the conviction that one inhabits a place in the middle have to lead to an exclusionary sense of cultural preeminence. Ironically, within a larger entity that is called Western, a culture of the middle might find itself at one edge, the very place where a Germany divided by the iron curtain found itself during the cold war.

[1]We should realize that in German, as in English, the words for "Slav" and "slave" are closely related, reflecting the fact that before the rise of the African slave trade in the Renaissance, the medieval European experience of slavery had centered on the sale of Slavs to the Muslim world. Mann's text is more explicit than Luke's translation in reminding readers of this historical linkage. Thus in describing the Russian family's servant in chapter 3, he emphasizes her *"Sklavenmanieren"* ("slavish manners" instead of "the manner of the born serf" [48]). Similarly, when Jashu fights with Tadzio near the end, he does so in retaliation for what is called *"eine lange Sklaverei"* ("a long period of slavery" rather than a "long servitude" [87]).

For Mann, however, as he moved from the chauvinism of *Kultur* to a renewed awareness of cultural multiplicity, being in the middle had another meaning. It was a cultural site that allowed for interaction in many directions. His postwar novel *The Magic Mountain* (1924) is perhaps the supreme expression of this outlook, but it already figures in his earlier stories. Thus a northerly impulse, along with a humorous critique of the Nordic racial mystique that would play a fatal role in Nazi ideology, is one major theme of "Tonio Kröger" (1903), whose hero harbors an impossible nostalgia for Scandinavian origins. In *Death in Venice*, other options come to the fore. When Aschenbach, a privileged voice of modern German culture, meets Tadzio, the street singer, and the travel agent, he encounters influences that come mainly from the East, but also from the South and West.

4

In both this volume and his earlier essay "Why Is Tadzio a Boy?," Robert Tobin has stressed the undeniable role of homosexuality in *Death in Venice*, or, to be more specific, the role of what might be called a visually fixated pederastic yearning. In insisting on certain cultural overtones to Aschenbach's fascination with Tadzio, I do not mean to dispute the substance of Tobin's findings. Still, lifting the taboos surrounding the discussion of homosexuality in literature can also obscure other issues that deserve attention.

Thus despite the many Greek motifs that Aschenbach's overheated imagination heaps upon Tadzio, the fact that the boy is Polish never disappears from view. In chapter 4, Aschenbach hears Tadzio's family call him (59), using what we have already been told is the Polish vocative (50), and this "long-drawn-out *u* at the end" becomes a vivid feature of his Dionysian dream (81). Similarly, when he follows the boy's family into the Cathedral of San Marco in chapter 5, we are reminded that, like most Poles, they are devout Catholics (69). Perhaps the most telling incident occurs in chapter 3, when Tadzio, "glaring forth a black message of hatred," shows his anger at the vacationing Russians (48–49). Along with the two German powers, Prussia and Austria, Russia had helped to dismantle Poland in the late eighteenth century, and at the time of *Death in Venice*, it ruled the largest portion of the formerly independent country. By stressing tensions between Poles and Russians, however, Mann avoids a more controversial topic for his contemporary readers: Germany's quasi-colonial rule over Poles in areas such as West Prussia and Silesia — areas that would revert to

Poland after World Wars I and II. Even at Aschenbach's first stopping
place, an Istrian island where the inhabitants' "wild unintelligible dialect" confronts "a self-enclosed Austrian clientele" (34), the Germano-
Slavic tensions remain discreetly veiled.

Not that *Death in Venice* usually presents Germano-Slavic boundaries in the stark either-or manner of territorial disputes. In other
works, Mann often brought members of the two groups into close
contact. For example, in "Tonio Kröger," the hero unburdens himself
to his friend Lisaveta Ivanovna, a Russian artist living in Munich. In
The Magic Mountain, the main character's boyhood fascination with a
Slavic classmate named Pribislav Hippe forms the basis for his adult infatuation with a Russian woman. In *Death in Venice,* however, this in-
termingling is even closer, for like Mann (one of whose grandmothers
was Portuguese-Creole) and like Mann's wife (whose parents were
converted Jews), Aschenbach comes from an ethnically mixed background. Not only did he grow up in the German-Polish border
province of Silesia, but through his mother he may be partly Slavic
himself. Because his mother was "the daughter of a director of music
in Bohemia," however, it is probably a Czech element that accounts
for "certain exotic racial characteristics in his external appearance"
(28). Not only does this passage confirm Du Bois's insight that
around 1900 the Germano-Slavic boundary amounted to a racial divide; it also artfully mimics Aschenbach's repressive personality by failing to give a name to his "exotic" facial traits. Despite the silence here,
however, there are other hints that Aschenbach's infatuation with
Tadzio includes a belated recognition of his mixed heritage. Especially
striking is the fact that the boy's father never appears in the story, only
his mother — who mirrors the source of "foreign" influence in Aschenbach himself.

Equally important in assessing Aschenbach's attraction to Tadzio is
his repeated delight in noticing that the boy may suffer from poor
health (51, 77). At first this attitude may seem odd and even ghoulish.
But in fact it reveals the intensity of the man's identification with the
boy, for Aschenbach, too, had been ill when young and has lived his
entire life believing he would die prematurely. The extent to which
Tadzio reflects aspects of Aschenbach himself thus becomes clear, and
once we recognize this link, we must allow for cultural dimensions to
this story of homosexual attraction. Indeed, the text itself insists on
the complexity of the man's motives at this point, stating that "he
made no attempt to explain to himself a certain feeling of satisfaction
or relief" (51). Beyond an erotic element, which Aschenbach soon

recognizes easily enough, this vaguely defined feeling leaves room for other, more obscure urges. Aschenbach's delight in watching Tadzio is thus multifaceted; it includes (along with a certain relaxation of his very will to live) the "satisfaction or relief" of acknowledging a mixed heritage previously suppressed owing to his single-minded pursuit of German *Kultur*.

Nowhere does this element of potential multiplicity emerge more clearly than in the fateful scene in which Aschenbach tries to talk to Tadzio but fails. One might have expected the forging of direct personal relations to mark a deepening of Aschenbach's infatuation. Such is the case, for example, with the growing homosexual bond between Michel and Moktir in André Gide's *The Immoralist* (1901), a story that otherwise has many affinities with Mann's (Foster). In Mann, however, it is the *refusal* of speech that is decisive, because it prevents what the narrator says could have been "a wholesome disenchantment" (63). Instead, across the now-definitive silence of a linguistic-cultural barrier, the staring man and the Polish boy experience the "uneasiness and overstimulated curiosity, the nervous excitement of an unsatisfied, unnaturally suppressed need to know and to communicate" (65). This comment closely echoes the accounts of life in racially segregated or colonial societies, where members of different groups might see each other daily but could rarely speak. So in the end, Aschenbach's growing infatuation requires that he uphold and maintain the Germano-Slavic boundary that he refused to cross when he proved incapable of talking with Tadzio. In chapter 5, this refusal continues to resonate in the peremptory "I shall say nothing" with which Aschenbach reacts to the cholera epidemic (80). In Aschenbach's case, the erotic depends on a carefully nourished but entirely artificial exoticism.

5

The flip side to what might fairly be called a troubled flirtation with cultural multiplicity is Aschenbach's dedication to *Kultur*, his emphatic but ultimately questionable commitment to German literature as a form of public service. When the story opens, he has recently been ennobled for his writings, and we later learn that certain passages from his books have even appeared in school readers (33). He has become a classic — or, in current parlance, he has achieved canonization. In thus winning official recognition, Aschenbach reveals that he is far from being an aesthete, the writer as "arty" individualist and seeming rebel who is often a conformist in reverse, a type that Mann pilloried with gusto. Instead, Aschenbach conceives of authorship in the mold of his dominant heritage, as the child of "military officers, judges, government administrators, men who had spent their disciplined, decently austere life in the service of the king and the state" (28). Literature, in this view, is not a spontaneous and unpredictable product of poetic inspiration but the expression in another, purportedly "higher" sphere of the basic habits and attitudes of his society's recognized authorities. Not for nothing is it said that Aschenbach writes as if he were Frederick the Great fighting the Seven Years' War (30).

What emerges from the story, however, is the cost of this attitude: a dangerous and probably untenable narrowing of one's sympathies. In the sketch of Aschenbach's career in chapter 2, the fateful turning point comes with "A Study in Abjection" (in German, "Ein Elender"),[2] the story that repudiates "the laxity of that compassionate principle which holds that to understand all is to forgive all" (32). In his rise to fame, it is clear, Aschenbach has started to advocate a certain hardness of heart, though the full significance of this choice is cloaked by a vague and euphemistic slogan, the "miracle of reborn naiveté" (32). Indeed, given the affinities that the story explores between the "heroism of weakness" of Aschenbach's earlier works and the society at large, this change hints at a corresponding development in official German culture (31). Has Aschenbach's society also begun to lose patience with the ideals of fellow feeling or humane understanding? The full consequences of this shift in attitude lie far in the future, with a statement such as Heinrich Himmler's in a notorious speech to the men who ran the Nazi death camps: "To have stuck this out and — excepting cases of human weakness — to have kept our integrity, this is what has made us hard" (Dawidowicz 200). "Human weakness" toward Jews and other people cast into situations of total ostracism and abjection, or (to use Mann's strong German word) into worlds of

---

[2]If translating *Kultur* as "culture" seems deceptively easy, this title shows how translators can be baffled by a word with no obvious English equivalent. In German "Ein Elender" is simple and vigorous, but choices like "The Wretch" (Burke), "The Abject" (Lowe-Porter), and "A Man of Misery" (Koelb) show no consensus about how to put it into English. Given the German word's root connection with social ostracism, something like "An Outcast" or "Beyond the Pale" might be preferable. The latter choice would bring out the ironic analogies between Aschenbach's story and his own scandalous infatuation with Tadzio, which would certainly place him beyond the bounds of respectability if the infatuation became known. It would also suggest the point I argue later, that the story obliquely addresses moral issues later raised by the Holocaust, as Jews in Eastern Europe were not supposed to leave the so-called Pale of Settlement.

Elend, means letting one's heartfelt instincts of human solidarity interfere with the Holocaust.

Although far from foreseeing Himmler's brand of "integrity," *Death in Venice* does take great pains to reveal how Aschenbach's new hardness turns against him with a vengeance. Thus his well-honed invectives against moral "laxity" fail utterly to prevent his own collapse — indeed, may even encourage it. As the narrator pointedly asks in chapter 2, Does not "moral resoluteness at the far side of knowledge . . . signify a simplification, a morally simplistic view of the world and of human psychology, and thus also a resurgence of energies that are evil, forbidden, morally impossible?" (32). Near the end as well, when Aschenbach sits in the deserted square, exhausted from following Tadzio, and eats the infected strawberries that will kill him, the narrator hails him with sarcastic venom as "the author of 'A Study in Abjection'" (85). A similar but more subtle criticism emerges from the reading experience itself: people who get involved in the story will probably grant Mann's character at least some of the sympathy that he so vigorously denied to his own abject hero. Consequently, not only does Aschenbach's path as a writer lead to a literal dead end, but by refusing to approach his own creations with the same understanding spirit that we take in responding to him, he forges his career on principles that clash ironically with the very method of Mann's story.

Aschenbach's scandalous fate, moreover, raises larger questions about the process of canonization itself. At one level, there is the sardonic discrepancy between his edifying image before the world at large and the disreputable facts. The narrator remarks, "It is well that the world knows only a fine piece of work and not also its origins" (62). More broadly, there is Aschenbach's confused memory, toward the end, of Plato's recommendation that poets should be banished from the ideal republic. This condemnation he now endorses from personal experience, insisting that "the use of art to educate the nation and its youth is a reprehensible undertaking" (86). *Kultur,* as a state-sponsored program to exploit the arts for moral uplift and communal glorification, seems to be flawed from the start.

Even more dubious, however, is the role that classical Greek culture as a whole plays in the story. Without the euphoric glow of Greek myth and the alluring contours of Greek statues, would Aschenbach have ever become so obsessed with Tadzio? Indeed, in a crowning irony, even Plato has a hand in his seduction, for earlier in *Death in Venice,* in two playful passages that contrast sharply with the later rejection of poetry and art, Aschenbach could fondly recall Socratic dialogues alluding to man-boy love in ancient Greece (50, 61–62). Like the cholera epidemic that insidiously attacks the famous city of art that is Venice, an unrelenting "canonization anxiety" infects Mann's story, placing in doubt the cultural process that selects a few human artifacts for special veneration. It is not only Aschenbach's role as a major German writer or just the value of literature and art in a nation's system of education that come into question: even the prime model for Western ideals of classical achievement has fallen prey to a treacherous duplicity.

6

The longing gaze of an elderly German writer at a Polish boy: this basic situation in *Death in Venice* has raised a host of cultural issues. They range from experiences of multiplicity in border regions to the attempted repression of a mixed heritage, from the simplifications and falsifications of celebrity to anxieties about the real effectiveness of both German and broader Western traditions and values.

Within this array of concerns, Aschenbach's fascination with Tadzio puts a special premium on the Slavic East. From today's more worldwide perspective, and especially after the work of Edward Said, this version of the East may seem limited. But when *Death in Venice* was written, Germany's eastern border did seem to mark a major cultural divide, one whose full meaning would become apparent in the 1940s, with the catastrophic events that occurred during Hitler's war across Poland into Russia. To this East, Mann then adds a wider, more free-floating "Orientalizing" cultural geography, which includes the South Asian jungle already noted along with some Greek motifs, as we shall see. Another major item on this imaginary map would be Venice's historic role as a gateway to the Middle East, emphasized as early as chapter 1 by the Byzantine mortuary chapel where Aschenbach sees the stranger with a rucksack. All these "Eastern worlds" eventually merge in the cholera epidemic, which takes two routes from India to Europe — a Venetian one by sea from Syria to Italy and a Slavic one by land into Russia (77–78).

The present-day Venice of Mann's story, however, introduces several other cultural options, for it does not suggest the East so much as an uneasy blend of well-bred European cosmopolitanism and inflamed Italian nationalism. The first option is suggested by Aschenbach's elegant resort hotel, a site where many cultures can meet with a minimum of friction. Unlike the Adriatic island, it offers a "large horizon . . . tolerantly embracing many elements" (43). Yet these elements, said to include "the major world languages," turn out to be limited to representatives of Du Bois's four European groups: the English, German, French, and Slavic. Still, it is a telling sign of German cultural narrowness that Aschenbach must leave his own country to encounter this variety, even though Germany is closer than Venice to all these peoples. On the nationalistic side, there are Aschenbach's traveling companions from Pola to Venice. These young Italians still live in Austria, the country that dominated northern Italy from 1815 until the unification of Italy in the 1860s, and are taking an excursion to their homeland. Pleasure is foremost on their minds, but when a delay in passing through customs reminds them of their displaced status, they show their patriotism by cheering a squadron of *bersaglieri*, the crack Italian troops training for possible war against Austria (38). This moment of insistent nationalism looks ahead to "Mario and the Magician" (1929), Mann's great story of manipulated and corrupted loyalties in Fascist Italy.

In chapter 5 of *Death in Venice*, both the stubbornly local and the cosmopolitan aspects of the Venetian setting become vivid secondary characters. First the Neapolitan street singer defies the international realm of the resort hotel, which is set apart from the city on a separate island, and where even the employees speak French. His performance, though not actually Venetian, represents an "exhibition of folk culture," two sides of which are explored in Mann's wonderfully precise account (73). Along with recalling traditions of traveling musicians, of market-place mountebanks, and of Naples as a city of song, the passage evokes a present-day Italy of hit tunes and ambiguous feelings about foreign tourists. This last trait leaves the strongest impression, owing to the disturbing vacillation in the lead singer's behavior. Humble and even cringing while taking money from the audience, he turns insolent in performance, especially in his mocking but infectious last song, which tricks the guests into laughing at themselves. Class and ethnic tensions have forced their way into the leisured and carefree atmosphere of an exclusive hotel. As a vivid reminder of the tenacity of popular culture, moreover, this scene points up the elitist implications of Aschenbach's *Kultur*. This elitism had also conditioned his preference for Tadzio over Jashu, the other, less aristocratic Polish boy who in the end rebels against Tadzio (87).

As a character, the British travel agent who embodies European cosmopolitanism and who tells Aschenbach the real meaning of the city's "routine precautionary measures" seems rather dull. The contrast between his "sober, honest demeanor" and the "glib knaveries of the south" (77) comes close to a facile stereotype, while praise of his English as "a straightforward comfortable language" borders on condescension. The phrase suggests good common sense and even the power of articulate speech to dissolve error, but little glamour, passion, or charisma. There is also something hollow about the man's criticisms of the Venetian tourist trade, given that he makes his living from it himself. Such ambivalences help explain why Mann could criticize both English and French "civilization" so strongly during World War I.

The travel agent's speech, however, is arguably the climactic moment in *Death in Venice*. At long last we get one possible explanation for the mystery with which the story began, the abrupt hallucinatory vision of the Asian swamp that launched Aschenbach on his travels. In his plain, matter-of-fact English, the travel agent provides a scientific, even starkly medical interpretation of the event: it was a premonition of the cholera epidemic that will strike Venice, traced back to its point of origin. Equally striking is the fact that this key passage depends on information in a foreign language. The British travel agent thus reaffirms the vital importance of cross-cultural communication and cultural multiplicity, but (because Aschenbach disregards his advice) he does so at a level beyond the protagonist's limited point of view. In the process, this scene hints at Mann's own path, during the 1920s and 1930s, beyond the national exclusivity of German *Kultur*.

7

For many readers, however — and perhaps especially for English-speaking readers of modern literature — the most significant moment in Mann's story does not come when the travel agent reveals the truth but a bit later, when the Dionysian dream overwhelms Aschenbach. This powerful passage moves the reader abruptly to a new plane, away from the harsh medical facts of contemporary Venice into a realm of myth, specifically of the same ancient Greek myths that have already entranced Aschenbach. Such abrupt transitions have often been seen as paradigmatic for the so-called modernist literature of the early twentieth century (Eysteinsson 9). Thus, in an influential discussion of James Joyce's use of Greek materials in *Ulysses*, T. S. Eliot could speak of the "mythical method" and its potential for "manipulating a continuous parallel between contemporaneity and antiquity" (Eliot 177). By a telling coincidence, this statement appeared in *The Dial* in November 1923, just months before Kenneth Burke's version of *Death in Venice* came out in the same American journal in March, April, and May of 1924. Readers who had seen Eliot's comparison of Joyce's new

literary technique with a major scientific discovery would thus find
Mann's use of a similar approach in a story written more than a decade
earlier. This convergence between *Death in Venice* and two major
modern writers in English undoubtedly helped to make Mann's story a
classic in translation.

Beyond the mythical method as a literary technique, however, and
even beyond the central role that myths play in defining specific cultures, Aschenbach's Dionysian dream should interest the cultural critic
for several specific reasons. First there is the key phrase, which Mann
italicizes for further emphasis, that refers to Dionysus as "*the stranger-
god!*" (81). The historical Dionysus cult was in fact foreign to ancient
Greece — indeed, was sometimes thought to have come originally
from India, just like the cholera epidemic. But the phrase also bears directly on Aschenbach's character. For "his culture of a lifetime," based
on his sense of Germanic uniqueness and exclusivity, has been shaken
throughout the story by a variety of overfamiliar or aggressive
strangers. Beginning with the traveler at the mortuary chapel in Munich, the series continues with the young-old man on the boat, the
unlicensed gondolier whom Aschenbach encounters in Venice, and
the street singer at the resort hotel. But the most unsettling stranger of
them all has been Tadzio. As we have seen, he exposes the falsity of
Aschenbach's public persona, not just as a morally edifying figure who
could never indulge in a scandalous sexual adventure but as the voice
of a German *Kultur* that felt itself utterly distinct from the Slavic East.
This boundary, so powerful in the official discourse of the time, turns
out in Aschenbach's case to be artificial and untenable. As the
Dionysian dream reveals with utmost clarity precisely because it is a
dream, the cultural stranger is in fact no stranger; he is lodged deep
within Aschenbach himself.

In making this point, and here is the second key feature of the
Dionysian dream, Mann's story overlaps with the cultural analysis in
Nietzsche's *Birth of Tragedy* (1870). Nietzsche is still a highly controversial figure, whose full significance cannot be explored in this essay.
But by the time of the composition of *Death in Venice,* Mann had
been reading Nietzsche with intense fascination and ambivalence for
twenty years. The *Birth of Tragedy,* Nietzsche's first book, had focused
on issues drawn from his original training in the Greek classics, especially the meaning of the Dionysus cult for ancient Greek drama and,
by extension, for the general interpretation of culture. Mann often disagreed with Nietzsche, but, for both of them, an interest in the
Dionysian led to similar views on several basic issues: that culture was

mixed and multiple, not pure and single; that it was open in major
ways to outside influence, not closed off in splendid isolation; and that
it was psychologically complex, not morally simplistic.

All of these points, we have seen, enter into Mann's portrayal of
Aschenbach's infatuation with Tadzio. They are rounded off, moreover, by one further convergence with Nietzsche. In his last year of
sanity, at the height of efforts to Germanize the Poles, Nietzsche
declared (probably with no basis in fact, but certainly with the desire
to goad German hypernationalists) that his family name was Polish
(Nietzsche 1968b, 681). With Aschenbach and Tadzio, Mann returns
to this polemic but presents it from a different angle. Rather than hy-
perbolically proclaiming the fact of cultural connection across a rigid
boundary, Mann portrays an abrupt, overwhelming outbreak of hidden links — an outbreak whose very force depends on a prior situation of stern repression. This outbreak is all the more important because it anticipates Mann's own route, over the next thirty years of
turmoil and disaster, beyond the confines of cultural chauvinism. Indeed, at our present moment of heightened and often polarized views
of cultural identity, this affirmation of cultural multiplicity is well
worth recalling.

For English-language readers, however, Mann has one further
twist in store. If Burke's translation of *Death in Venice* invites us to
place the story in close proximity to the "mythical method" of Eliot's
The Waste Land and Joyce's *Ulysses*, Mann nonetheless differs from
these two classics of Anglo-American modernism, for he responds
more critically to myth. One notable expression of this critique is the
jarring image of the young-old man who welcomes Aschenbach to
Venice and whose outer appearance Aschenbach later mimics (36,
82–83). This figure is, of course, a vivid reminder of age differences
both in Aschenbach's man-boy love and in similar heterosexual relationships. (Before writing *Death in Venice*, Mann had toyed with the
idea of retelling the elderly Goethe's infatuation with a young
woman.) Yet just as the barber's cosmetics have turned the aging
writer into a stylish, young-looking dandy, so the present-day cholera
epidemic and the ancient Dionysian orgy dissolve into each other in
the last pages of the story. Aschenbach's uncanny masquerade thus
functions as a disquieting analogy for the mythical method and its startling juxtapositions of the antique and the contemporary.

Indeed, because the young-old image is so discordant — at its first
appearance, it could even awaken "a spasm of distaste" in Aschenbach
(36) — *Death in Venice* conveys a deeply ironic attitude toward the

mythical merging of different time layers. Although Mann himself exploits the method, he refuses to present it as a purely positive breakthrough for modern art. This ambivalence persists in Aschenbach's final vision of Tadzio as a mythlike "pale and lovely soul-summoner" (88), even as we know from the travel agent that he is experiencing the final symptoms of the gentler, less virulent form of cholera (78–79). In the years to come, the space opened up by this mixed attitude toward myth would give Mann a sharpness of insight about the myth-driven politics of Hitler and other fascists that many Anglo-American modernists would lack. As a major work of world fiction translated into English, *Death in Venice* does anticipate some of the most daring works of early-twentieth-century modernism. In several important ways, however, it also begins to look beyond the elite English and American literature of the period, glimpsing possibilities for cultural multiplicity and interaction that avoid the shackles of grandiose, self-imposed mythologies.

WORKS CITED

Bakhtin, Mikhail. *Problems of Dostoevsky's Poetics.* Ed. and trans. Caryl Emerson. Intro. Wayne C. Booth. Minneapolis: U Minnesota P, 1984.

Bassnett, Susan. *Translation Studies.* London: Methuen, 1980.

Berman, Russell A. "Cultural Criticism and Cultural Studies: Reconsidering the Frankfurt School." *Cultural Studies of Modern Germany: History, Representation, and Nationhood.* Madison: U Wisconsin P, 1993. 11–25.

Burke, Kenneth, trans. *Death in Venice.* With a critical essay by Erich Heller. New York: Modern Library, 1970. (Reprints the English translation that appeared in *The Dial* in 1924.)

Dawidowicz, Lucy. *The War against the Jews, 1933–45.* New York: Holt, 1975.

Du Bois, W. E. B. "The Conservation of Races." *W. E. B. Du Bois Speaks: Speeches and Addresses, 1890–1919.* Ed. Philip S. Foner. New York: Pathfinders, 1970. 73–85.

Eliot, T. S. "Ulysses, Order, and Myth." *Selected Prose of T. S. Eliot.* Ed. and intro. Frank Kermode. London: Faber, 1975. 175–78.

Eysteinsson, Astradur. *The Concept of Modernism.* Ithaca: Cornell UP, 1990.

Foster, John Burt Jr. "From Nietzsche to the Savage God: An Early Appropriation by the Young Gide and Mann." *Heirs to Dionysus:*

A Nietzschean Current in Literary Modernism. Princeton: Princeton UP, 1981. 145–79.

Koelb, Clayton, ed. and trans. *"Death in Venice": A Norton Critical Edition.* New York: Norton, 1994.

Kohn, Hans. *Political Ideologies of the Twentieth Century.* 3d ed. New York: Harper, 1966.

Lefèvere, André. *Translating Literature: Practice and Theory in a Comparative Literature Context.* New York: MLA, 1992.

Lowe-Porter, H. T., trans. *"Death in Venice" and Seven Other Stories.* New York: Vintage, 1989.

Mann, Thomas. *Doctor Faustus: The Life of the German Composer Adrian Leverkühn as Told by a Friend.* Trans. H. T. Lowe-Porter. New York: Modern Library, 1966.

——. *Reflections of a Nonpolitical Man.* Trans. and intro. Walter D. Morris. New York: Ungar, 1983.

Nietzsche, Friedrich. *The Birth of Tragedy. Basic Writings of Friedrich Nietzsche.* Ed. and trans. Walter Kaufmann. New York: Modern Library, 1968a. 15–194.

——. *Ecce Homo. Basic Writings of Friedrich Nietzsche.* Ed. and trans. Walter Kaufmann. New York: Modern Library, 1968b. 673–791.

Said, Edward. *Orientalism.* New York: Pantheon, 1978.

Taylor, Charles. *Multiculturalism and "The Politics of Recognition."* An essay with commentary by Amy Gutmann, editor, and by Steven C. Rockefeller, Michael Walzer, and Susan Wolf. Princeton: Princeton UP, 1992.

Tobin, Robert. "Why Is Tadzio a Boy? Perspectives on Homoeroticism in *Death in Venice.*" In Koelb 207–32.

Williams, Raymond. *Keywords: A Vocabulary of Culture and Society.* Rev. ed. New York: Oxford UP, 1983.

Gender Criticism and
Death in Venice

WHAT IS GENDER CRITICISM?

Feminist criticism was accorded academic legitimacy in American universities "around 1981," Jane Gallop claims in her book *Around 1981: Academic Feminist Literary Theory*. With Gallop's title and amusing approximation in mind, Naomi Schor has since estimated that, "around 1985, feminism began to give way to what has come to be called gender studies" (Schor 275).

In explaining her reason for saying that feminism began to give way to gender studies "around 1985," Schor says that she chose that date "in part because it marks the publication of *Between Men*," a book whose author, the influential gender critic Eve Kosofsky Sedgwick, "articulates the insights of feminist criticism onto those of gay-male studies, which had up to then pursued often parallel but separate courses (affirming the existence of a homosexual or female imagination, recovering lost traditions, decoding the cryptic discourse of works already in the canon by homosexual or feminist authors)" (Schor 276). Today, gay and lesbian criticism is so much a part of gender criticism that some people equate "sexualities criticism" with the gender approach.

Many would quarrel with the notion that feminist criticism and women's studies have been giving way to gender criticism and gender studies — and with the either/or distinction that such a claim implies. Some would argue that feminist criticism is by definition gender criticism. (When Simone de Beauvoir declared in 1949 that "one is not born a woman, one becomes one" [301], she was talking about the way in which individuals of the female sex assume the feminine gender — that is, that elaborate set of restrictive, socially prescribed attitudes and behaviors that we associate with femininity.) Others would point out that one critic whose work *everyone* associates with feminism (Julia Kristeva) has problems with the feminist label, while another critic whose name, like Sedgwick's, is continually linked with the gender approach (Teresa de Lauretis) continues to refer to herself and her work as feminist.

Certainly, feminist and gender criticism are not polar opposites but, rather, exist along a continuum of attitudes toward sex and sexism, sexuality and gender, language and the literary canon. There are, however, a few distinctions to be made between those critics whose writings are inevitably identified as being toward one end of the continuum or the other.

One distinction is based on focus: as the word implies, "feminists" have concentrated their efforts on the study of women and women's issues. Gender criticism, by contrast, has not been woman centered. It has tended to view the male and female sexes — and the masculine and feminine genders — in terms of a complicated continuum, much as we are viewing feminist and gender criticism. Critics like Diane K. Lewis have raised the possibility that black women may be more like white men in terms of familial and economic roles, like black men in terms of their relationships with whites, and like white women in terms of their relationships with men. Lesbian gender critics have asked whether lesbian women are really more like straight women than they are like gay (or for that matter straight) men. That we refer to gay and lesbian studies as gender studies has led some to suggest that gender studies is a misnomer; after all, homosexuality is not a gender. This objection may easily be answered once we realize that one purpose of gender criticism is to criticize gender as we commonly conceive of it, to expose its insufficiency and inadequacy as a category.

Another distinction between feminist and gender criticism is based on the terms "gender" and "sex." As de Lauretis suggests in *Technologies of Gender* (1987), feminists of the 1970s tended to equate gender with sex, gender difference with sexual difference. But that equation doesn't help us explain "the differences among women, . . . the differences *within women*." After positing that "we need a notion of gender that is not so bound up with sexual difference," de Lauretis provides just such a notion by arguing that "gender is not a property of bodies or something originally existent in human beings"; rather, it is "the product of various social technologies, such as cinema" (2). Gender is, in other words, a construct, an effect of language, culture, and its institutions. It is gender, not sex, that causes a weak old man to open a door for an athletic young woman. And it is gender, not sex, that may cause one young woman to expect old men to behave in this way, another to view this kind of behavior as chauvinistic and insulting, and still another to have mixed feelings (hence de Lauretis's phrase "differences *within women*") about "gentlemanly gallantry."

Still another, related distinction between feminist and gender criticism is based on the *essentialist* views of many feminist critics and the *constructionist* views of many gender critics (both those who would call themselves feminists and those who would not). Stated simply and perhaps too reductively, the term "essentialist" refers to the view that women are essentially different from men. "Constructionist," by contrast, refers to the view that most of those differences are characteristics not of the male and female sex (nature) but, rather, of the masculine and feminine genders (nurture). Because of its essentialist tendencies, "radical feminism," according to Sedgwick, "tends to deny that the meaning of gender or sexuality has ever significantly changed; and more damagingly, it can make future change appear impossible" (*Between Men* 13).

Most obviously essentialist would be those feminists who emphasize the female body, its difference, and the manifold implications of that difference. The equation made by some avant-garde French feminists between the female body and the *maternal* body has proved especially troubling to some gender critics, who worry that it may paradoxically play into the hands of extreme conservatives and fundamentalists seeking to reestablish patriarchal family values. In her book *The Reproduction of Mothering* (1978), Nancy Chodorow, a sociologist of gender, admits that what we call "mothering" — not having or nursing babies but mothering more broadly conceived — is commonly associated not just with the feminine gender but also with the female sex, often considered nurturing by nature. But she critically interrogates the common assumption that it is in women's nature or biological destiny to "mother" in this broader sense, arguing that the separation of home and workplace brought about by the development of capitalism and the ensuing industrial revolution made mothering *appear* to be essentially a woman's job in modern Western society.

If sex turns out to be gender where mothering is concerned, what differences *are* grounded in sex — that is, nature? *Are* there *essential* differences between men and women — other than those that are purely anatomical and anatomically determined (for example, a man can exclusively take on the job of feeding an infant milk, but he may not do so from his own breast)? A growing number of gender critics would answer the question in the negative. Sometimes referred to as "extreme constructionists" and "postfeminists," these critics have adopted the viewpoint of philosopher Judith Butler, who in her book *Gender Trouble* (1990) predicts that "sex, by definition, will be shown to have been gender all along" (8). As Naomi Schor explains their position, "there is nothing outside or before culture, no nature that is not always and already enculturated" (278).

Whereas a number of feminists celebrate women's difference, postfeminist gender critics would agree with Chodorow's statement that men have an "investment in difference that women do not have" (Eisenstein and Jardine 14). They see difference as a symptom of oppression, not a cause for celebration, and would abolish it by dismantling gender categories and, ultimately, destroying gender itself. Because gender categories and distinctions are embedded in and perpetuated through language, gender critics like Monique Wittig have called for the wholesale transformation of language into a nonsexist, and nonheterosexist, medium.

Language has proved the site of important debates between feminist and gender critics, essentialists and constructionists. Gender critics have taken issue with those French feminists who have spoken of a feminine language and writing and who have grounded differences in language and writing in the female body.[1] For much the same reason, they have disagreed with those French-influenced Anglo-American critics who, like Toril Moi and Nancy K. Miller, have posited an essential relationship between sexuality and textuality. (In an essentialist sense, such critics have suggested that when women write, they tend to break the rules of plausibility and verisimilitude that men have created to evaluate fiction.) Gender critics like Peggy Kamuf posit a relationship only between *gen-*

---

[1]Because feminist/gender studies, not unlike sex/gender, should be thought of as existing along a continuum of attitudes and not in terms of simple opposition, attempts to highlight the difference between feminist and gender criticism are inevitably prone to reductive overgeneralization and occasional distortion. Here, for instance, French feminism is made out to be more monolithic than it actually is. Hélène Cixous has said that a few men (such as Jean Genet) have produced "feminine writing," although she suggests that these are exceptional men who have acknowledged their own bisexuality.

der and textuality, between what most men and women *become* after they are born and the way in which they write. They are therefore less interested in the author's sexual "signature" — in whether the author was a woman writing — than in whether the author was (to borrow from Kamuf) "Writing like a Woman."

Feminists such as Miller have suggested that no man could write the "female anger, desire, and selfhood" that Emily Brontë, for instance, inscribed in her poetry and in *Wuthering Heights* (*Subject* 72). In the view of gender critics, it is and has been possible for a man to write like a woman, a woman to write like a man. Shari Benstock, a noted feminist critic whose investigations into psychoanalytic and poststructuralist theory have led her increasingly to adopt the gender approach, poses the following question to herself in *Textualizing the Feminine* (1991): "Isn't it precisely 'the feminine' in Joyce's writings and Derrida's that carries me along?" (45). In an essay entitled "Unsexing Language: Pronomial Protest in Emily Dickinson's 'Lay This Laurel,'" Anna Shannon Elfenbein has argued that "like Walt Whitman, Emily Dickinson crossed the gender barrier in some remarkable poems," such as "We learned to like the Fire/By playing Glaciers — when a Boy — " (Berg 215).

It is also possible, in the view of most gender critics, for women to read as men, men as women. The view that women can, and indeed have been forced to, read as men has been fairly noncontroversial. Everyone agrees that the literary canon is largely "androcentric" and that writings by men have tended to "immasculate" women, forcing them to see the world from a masculine viewpoint. But the question of whether men can read as women has proved to be yet another issue dividing feminist and gender critics. Some feminists suggest that men and women have some essentially different reading strategies and outcomes, while gender critics maintain that such differences arise entirely out of social training and cultural norms. One interesting outcome of recent attention to gender and reading is Elizabeth A. Flynn's argument that women in fact make the best interpreters of imaginative literature. Based on a study of how male and female students read works of fiction, she concludes that women come up with more imaginative, open-ended readings of stories. Quite possibly the imputed hedging and tentativeness of women's speech, often seen by men as disadvantages, are transformed into useful interpretive strategies — receptivity combined with critical assessment of the text — in the act of reading (Flynn and Schweickart 286).

In singling out a catalyst of gender studies, many historians of criticism have pointed to Michel Foucault. In his *History of Sexuality*
(1976, trans. 1978), Foucault distinguished sexuality from sex, calling
the former a "technology of sex." De Lauretis, who has deliberately
developed her theory of gender "along the lines of . . . Foucault's
theory of sexuality," explains his use of "technology" this way: "sexuality, commonly thought to be a natural as well as a private matter, is
in fact completely constructed in culture according to the political
aims of the society's dominant class" (*Technologies* 2, 12).

Foucault suggests that homosexuality as we now think of it was to
a great extent an invention of the nineteenth century. In earlier peri-
ods there had been "acts of sodomy" and individuals who committed
them, but the "sodomite" was, according to Foucault, "a temporary
aberration," not the "species" he became with the advent of the modern concept of homosexuality (42–43). According to Foucault, in
other words, sodomitic acts did not define people so markedly as the
word *homosexual* tags and marks people now. Sodomitic *acts* have
been replaced by homosexual *persons,* and in the process the range of
acceptable relationships between individuals of the same gender has
been restrictively altered. As Sedgwick writes, "to specify someone's
sexuality [today] is not to locate her or him on a map teeming with
zoophiles, gynecomasts, sexoesthetic inverts, and so forth. . . . In the
late twentieth century, if I ask you what your sexual orientation or sexual preference is, you will understand me to be asking precisely one
thing: whether you are homosexual or heterosexual" ("Gender" 282).

By historicizing sexuality, Foucault made it possible for his succes-
sors to consider the possibility that all of the categories and assumptions that currently come to mind when we think about sex, sexual difference, gender, and sexuality are social artifacts, the products of
cultural discourses. Following Foucault's lead, some gay and lesbian
critics have argued that the heterosexual/homosexual distinction is as
much a cultural construct as is the masculine/feminine dichotomy.

Arguing that sexuality is a continuum, not a fixed and static set of
binary oppositions, a number of gay and lesbian critics have critiqued
heterosexuality arguing that it has been an enforced corollary and consequence of what Gayle Rubin has referred to as the "sex/gender system" ("Traffic"). Acording to this system, persons of the male sex are
assumed be masculine, masculine men are assumed to be attracted to
women, and therefore it is supposedly natural for men to be attracted
to women and unnatural for them to be attracted to men. Lesbian

critics have also taken issue with some feminists on the grounds that they proceed from fundamentally heterosexual and even heterosexist assumptions. Particularly offensive to lesbians have been those feminists who, following Doris Lessing, have implied that to affirm a lesbian identity is to act out feminist hostility against men. According to poet-critic Adrienne Rich,

> The fact is that women in every culture throughout history have undertaken the task of independent, nonheterosexual, women-centered existence, to the extent made possible by their context, often in the belief that they were the "only ones" ever to have done so. They have undertaken it even though few women have been in an economic position to resist marriage altogether; and even though attacks against [them] have ranged from aspersions and mockery to deliberate gynocide.

Rich goes on to suggest, in her essay entitled "Compulsory Heterosexuality," that "heterosexuality [is] a beachhead of male dominance," and that, "like motherhood, [it] needs to be recognized and studied as a political institution" (141, 143, 145).

If there is such a thing as reading like a woman and such a thing as reading like a man, how then do lesbians read? Are there gay and lesbian ways of reading? Many would say that there are. Rich, by reading Emily Dickinson's poetry as a lesbian — by not assuming that "heterosexual romance is the key to a woman's life and work" — has introduced us to a poet somewhat different from the one heterosexual critics have made familiar (*Lies* 158). As for gay reading, Wayne Koestenbaum has defined "the (male twentieth-century first world) gay reader" as one who "reads resistantly for inscriptions of his condition, for texts that will confirm a social and private identity founded on a desire for other men. . . . Reading becomes a hunt for histories that deliberately foreknow or unwittingly trace a desire felt not by author but by reader, who is most acute when searching for signs of himself" (Boone and Cadden 176–77).

Lesbian critics have produced a number of compelling reinterpretations, or in-scriptions, of works by authors as diverse as Emily Dickinson, Virginia Woolf, and Toni Morrison. As a result of these provocative readings, significant disagreements have arisen between straight and lesbian critics and among lesbian critics as well. Perhaps the most famous and interesting example of this kind of interpretive controversy involves the claim by Barbara Smith and Adrienne Rich that Morrison's novel *Sula* can be read as a lesbian text — and author Toni Morrison's counterclaim that it cannot.

Gay male critics have produced a body of readings no less revisionist and controversial, focusing on writers as staidly classic as Henry James and Wallace Stevens. In Melville's *Billy Budd* and *Moby-Dick,* Robert K. Martin suggests, a triangle of homosexual desire exists. In the latter novel, the hero must choose between a captain who represents "the imposition of the male on the female" and a "Dark Stranger" (Queequeg) who "offers the possibility of an alternate sexuality, one that is less dependent upon performance and conquest" (5).

Masculinity as a complex construct producing and reproducing a constellation of behaviors and goals, many of them destructive (like performance and conquest) and most of them injurious to women, has become the object of an unprecedented number of gender studies. A 1983 issue of *Feminist Review* contained an essay entitled "Anti-Porn: Soft Issue, Hard World," in which B. Ruby Rich suggested that the "legions of feminist men" who examine and deplore the effects of pornography on women might better "undertake the analysis that can tell us why men like porn (not, piously, why this or that exceptional man does *not*)" (Berg 185). The advent of gender criticism makes precisely that kind of analysis possible. Stephen H. Clark, who alludes to Ruby Rich's challenge, reads T. S. Eliot "as a man." Responding to "Eliot's implicit appeal to a specifically masculine audience — 'You! hypocrite lecteur! — mon semblable, — mon *frère!*'" — Clark concludes that poems such as "Sweeney among the Nightingales" and "Gerontion," rather than offering what they are usually said to offer — "a social critique into which a misogynistic language accidentally seeps" — instead articulate a masculine "psychology of sexual fear and desired retaliation" (Berg 173).

Some gender critics focusing on masculinity have analyzed "the anthropology of boyhood," a phrase coined by Mark Seltzer in an article in which he comparatively reads, among other things, Stephen Crane's *Red Badge of Courage,* Jack London's *White Fang,* and the first *Boy Scouts of America* handbook (Boone and Cadden 150). Others have examined the fear men have that artistry is unmasculine, a guilty worry that surfaces perhaps most obviously in "The Custom-House," Hawthorne's lengthy preface to *The Scarlet Letter.* Still others have studied the representation in literature of subtly erotic disciple-patron relationships, relationships like the ones between Nick Carraway and Jay Gatsby, Charlie Marlow and Lord Jim, Doctor Watson and Sherlock Holmes, and any number of characters in Henry James's stories. Not all of these studies have focused on literary texts. Because the movies have played a primary role in gender construction during our lifetimes, gender critics have analyzed the dynamics of masculinity (vis-à-vis femininity and androgyny) in films from *Rebel without a Cause* to *Tootsie* to last year's Best Picture. One of the "social technologies" most influential in (re)constructing gender, film is one of the media in which today's sexual politics is most evident.

Necessary as it is, in an introduction such as this one, to define the difference between feminist and gender criticism, it is equally necessary to conclude by unmaking the distinction, at least partially. The two topics just discussed (film theory and so-called queer theory) give us grounds for undertaking that necessary deconstruction. The alliance I have been creating between gay and lesbian criticism on the one hand and gender criticism on the other is complicated greatly by the fact that not all gay and lesbian critics are constructionists. Indeed, a number of them (Robert K. Martin included) share with many feminists the *essentialist* point of view; that is, they believe homosexuals and heterosexuals to be essentially different, different by nature, just as a number of feminists believe men and women to be different.

In film theory and criticism, feminist and gender critics have so influenced one another that their differences would be difficult to define based on any available criteria, including the ones just outlined. Cinema has been of special interest to contemporary feminists like Minh-ha (herself a filmmaker) and Spivak (whose critical eye has focused on movies including *My Beautiful Laundrette* and *Sammie and Rosie Get Laid*). Teresa de Lauretis, whose *Technologies of Gender* (1987) has proved influential in the area of gender studies, continues to publish film criticism consistent with earlier, unambiguously feminist works in which she argued that "the representation of woman as spectacle — body to be looked at, place of sexuality, and object of desire — so pervasive in our culture, finds in narrative cinema its most complex expression and widest circulation" (*Alice* 4).

Feminist film theory has developed alongside a feminist performance theory grounded in Joan Riviere's recently rediscovered essay "Womanliness as a Masquerade" (1929), in which the author argues that there is no femininity that is *not* masquerade. Marjorie Garber, a contemporary cultural critic with an interest in gender, has analyzed the constructed nature of femininity by focusing on men who have apparently achieved it — through the transvestism, transsexualism, and other forms of "cross-dressing" evident in cultural productions from

Shakespeare to Elvis, from "Little Red Riding Hood" to *La Cage aux Folles*. The future of feminist and gender criticism, it would seem, is not one of further bifurcation but one involving a refocusing on femininity, masculinity, and related sexualities, not only as represented in poems, novels, and films but also as manifested and developed in video, on television, and along the almost infinite number of waystations rapidly being developed on the information highways running through an exponentially expanding cyberspace.

In the essay that follows, Robert Tobin establishes the centrality of homosexual desire in Thomas Mann's life by quoting from the author's diaries, which record his infatuation with several young men. Tobin then draws parallels between individuals described in the diaries and fictional characters in numerous works by Mann, works such as "Tonio Kröger," *The Magic Mountain*, and *Doctor Faustus*. Turning to *Death in Venice*, Tobin identifies Tadzio as "the product of an immediate, real-life inspiration": Wladislow Moes, a young Polish nobleman whom Mann met in Venice on travels with his wife, Katia. Mann's wife, who in her memoirs states that her husband "immediately had a weakness for the youth," explicitly connects that weakness to the writing of *Death in Venice:* "My husband transferred the pleasure that he indeed had from this very charming youth to Aschenbach, and stylized it to most extreme passion."

Having shown the existence of "a clear historical and biographical basis for the presence of homosexuality in Mann's works," Tobin argues that Mann embeds subtle "codes," "tones," and "signifiers" throughout *Death in Venice* in order to suggest that "Western society . . . is far gayer" than is commonly acknowledged. Today's reader, instead of "suppressing the story's homosexual tones, as generations of previous critics have done," can "augment them, bring them out. Such a search for the homosexual signifiers of the story," Tobin writes, "will put Aschenbach into a clearer context and provide for a much richer reading of the novella and its understanding of society."

Tobin finds homosexual signifiers, tones, and codes subtly present even in the novella's opening chapter. As Aschenbach strolls through a public garden in Munich (a city in which consensual adult sex had recently been decriminalized), he runs into an exotic-looking foreigner — one of a number of "vaguely threatening" male strangers he is to come upon during the course of his journey. As a result of this encounter, Aschenbach envisions a sexually suggestive jungle that makes him want to travel.

In the novella's second chapter, Tobin identifies Aschenbach's writings as another thread in the subtly "gay pattern" of *Death in Venice*. Readers "conversant in the lore of the European homosexual subculture," Tobin maintains, would have found "something gay in almost every element" of Aschenbach's work, from the type of hero he favored to the philosophers and other writers he cited. Even Venice — the place to which Aschenbach's jungle vision leads him — functions as a kind of gay code word, for in Mann's time the city was, in Tobin's words, "the epitome of queer Italy." As for the interest Aschenbach develops in Tadzio on arriving in Venice, it "is also marked as homosexual in ways that might escape the uninitiated reader."

Tobin's essay amounts to what Tobin acknowledges is "a queer reading" of Mann's *Death in Venice*. "Rather than hiding homosexuality," Tobin admits that he has "sought it out in the subtlest nuances, which can enrich everyone's understanding of the novella." Tobin sees *Death in Venice*, as "a foundational text for gay and lesbian studies," a work that shows how art can be produced by "fearful repression" yet also dramatizes the point at which writing can no longer be "fuel[ed]" by "sublimated passions." "Eros" and "logos" — erotic passion and the word — must ultimately come together, Tobin argues; "if narration is comparable to sexuality, then a hidden, closeted sexuality will produce a narration of secrets."

Tobin's essay exemplifies gay and lesbian reading specifically but also gender criticism more generally insofar as it views sexuality both as "a basic component of creativity" and as "a construct of creative and social forces." Aschenbach is "prepare[d] for his encounter with Tadzio," Tobin maintains, by the "male-male erotic subtext" of Western literary tradition dating back to Socrates, who felt "physical desire for his pupil" Phaedrus. Eve Sedgwick, as Tobin points out, has identified "the link between Phaedrus and Tadzio, Aschenbach and Socrates, as indicating that 'the history of Western thought is importantly constituted and motivated by . . . male-male . . . relations.'" Tobin expands on Sedgwick's argument by suggesting that *Death in Venice* "establishes the foundation for a powerful critique of the exclusion of women from the educational system that transmits Western values."

In making this argument, Tobin effectively reveals not only the difference but also the link between gender and feminist criticism. Although Tobin acknowledges that certain feminists believe that Mann and other male homosexuals have reinforced patriarchal views and institutions, he argues that "*Death in Venice* presents the dead end of misogynistic male homosexuality, perhaps more clearly than its author knew. It allows the reader to see that the man excited by male beauty shares the perspective of the woman excited by that beauty. Even as Aschenbach equates his kind of eros with supermanliness, he must admit that 'though we may be heroes in our own fashion and disciplined warriors, yet we are like women, for it is passion that exalts us.'"

Ross C Murfin

GENDER CRITICISM:
A SELECTED BIBLIOGRAPHY

Studies of Gender and Sexuality

Boone, Joseph A., and Michael Cadden, eds. *Engendering Men: The Question of Male Feminist Criticism.* New York: Routledge, 1990.

Butler, Judith. *Gender Trouble: Feminism and the Subversion of Identity.* New York: Routledge, 1990.

Chodorow, Nancy. *The Reproduction of Mothering: Psychoanalysis and the Sociology of Gender.* Berkeley: U of California P, 1978.

Claridge, Laura, and Elizabeth Langland, eds. *Out of Bounds: Male Writing and Gender(ed) Criticism.* Amherst: U of Massachusetts P, 1990.

de Lauretis, Teresa. *Technologies of Gender: Essays on Theory, Film, and Fiction.* Bloomington: Indiana UP, 1987.

Doane, Mary Ann. "Masquerade Reconsidered: Further Thoughts on the Female Spectator." *Discourse* 11 (1988–89): 42–54.

Flynn, Elizabeth A., and Patrocinio P. Schweickart, eds. *Gender and Reading: Essays on Readers, Texts, and Contexts.* Baltimore: Johns Hopkins UP, 1986.

Foucault, Michel. *The History of Sexuality.* Vol. 1. Trans. Robert Hurley. New York: Random, 1978.

Kamuf, Peggy. "Writing like a Woman." *Women and Language in Literature and Society.* New York: Praeger, 1980. 284–99.

Laqueur, Thomas. *Making Sex: Body and Gender from the Greeks to Freud.* Cambridge: Harvard UP, 1990.

Riviere, Joan. "Womanliness as a Masquerade." 1929. Rpt. in *Formations of Fantasy.* Ed. Victor Burgin, James Donald, and Cora Kaplan. London: Methuen, 1986. 35–44.

Rubin, Gayle. "Thinking Sex: Notes for a Radical Theory of the Politics of Sexuality." *The Lesbian and Gay Studies Reader.* Abelove et al. New York: Routledge, 1993. 3–44.

_____. "The Traffic in Women: Notes on the 'Political Economy' of Sex." *Toward an Anthropology of Women.* Ed. Rayna R. Reiter. New York: Monthly Review, 1975. 157–210.

Schor, Naomi. "Feminist and Gender Studies." *Introduction to Scholarship in Modern Languages and Literatures.* Ed. Joseph Gibaldi. New York: MLA, 1992. 262–87.

Sedgwick, Eve Kosofsky. *Between Men: English Literature and Male Homosocial Desire.* New York: Columbia UP, 1988.

_____. "Gender Criticism." *Redrawing the Boundaries: The Transformation of English and American Literary Studies.* Ed. Stephen Greenblatt and Giles Gunn. New York: MLA, 1992. 271–302.

Lesbian and Gay Criticism

Abelove, Henry, Michèle Aina Barale, and David Halperin, eds. *The Lesbian and Gay Studies Reader.* New York: Routledge, 1993.

Butters, Ronald, John M. Clum, and Michael Moon, eds. *Displacing Homophobia: Gay Male Perspectives in Literature and Culture.* Durham: Duke UP, 1989.

Craft, Christopher. *Another Kind of Love: Male Homosexual Desire in English Discourse, 1850–1920.* Berkeley: U of California P, 1994.

de Lauretis, Teresa. *The Practice of Love: Lesbian Sexuality and Perverse Desire.* Bloomington: Indiana UP, 1994.

Dollimore, Jonathan. *Sexual Dissidence: Augustine to Wilde, Freud to Foucault.* Oxford: Clarendon, 1991.

Fuss, Diana, ed. *Inside/Out: Lesbian Theories, Gay Theories.* New York: Routledge, 1991.

Garber, Marjorie. *Vested Interests: Cross-Dressing and Cultural Anxiety.* New York: Routledge, 1992.

Halperin, David M. *One Hundred Years of Homosexuality and Other Essays on Greek Love.* New York: Routledge, 1990.

"The Lesbian Issue." Special issue, *Signs* 9 (1984).

Martin, Robert K. *Hero, Captain, and Stranger: Male Friendship, Social Critique, and Literary Form in the Sea Novels of Herman Melville.* Chapel Hill: U of North Carolina P, 1986.

Munt, Sally, ed. *New Lesbian Criticism: Literary and Cultural Readings.* New York: Harvester Wheatsheaf, 1992.

Rich, Adrienne. "Compulsory Heterosexuality and Lesbian Existence."

The "Signs" Reader: Women, Gender, and Scholarship. Ed. Elizabeth
   Abel and Emily K. Abel. Chicago: U of Chicago P, 1983. 139–68.
Smith, Barbara. "Toward a Black Feminist Criticism." The New Femi-
   nist Criticism. Ed. Elaine Showalter. New York: Pantheon, 1985.
   168–85.
Stimpson, Catherine R. "Zero Degree Deviancy: The Lesbian Novel
   in English." Critical Inquiry 8 (1981): 363–79.
Weeks, Jeffrey. Sexuality and Its Discontents: Meanings, Myths, and
   Modern Sexualities. London: Routledge, 1985.
Wittig, Monique. "The Mark of Gender." The Poetics of Gender. Ed.
   Nancy K. Miller. New York: Columbia UP, 1986. 63–73.
_____. "One Is Not Born a Woman." Feminist Issues 1.2 (1981):
   47–54.
_____. The Straight Mind and Other Essays. Boston: Beacon, 1992.

Queer Theory

Butler, Judith. Bodies That Matter: On the Discursive Limits of "Sex."
   New York: Routledge, 1993.
Cohen, Ed. Talk on the Wilde Side: Towards a Genealogy of Discourse
   on Male Sexualities. New York: Routledge, 1993.
de Lauretis, Teresa, ed. Issue on queer theory, Differences 3.2 (1991).
Sedgwick, Eve Kosofsky. Epistemology of the Closet. Berkeley: U of Cal-
   ifornia P, 1991.
_____. Tendencies. Durham: Duke UP, 1993.
Sinfield, Alan. Cultural Politics — Queer Reading. Philadelphia: U of
   Pennsylvania P, 1994.
_____. The Wilde Century: Effeminacy, Oscar Wilde, and the Queer
   Moment. New York: Columbia UP, 1994.

Other Works Referred to in
"What Is Gender Criticism?"

Beauvoir, Simone de. The Second Sex, ed. and trans. H. M. Parshley.
   New York: Modern Library, 1952.
Gallop, Jane. Around 1981: Academic Feminist Literary Theory. New
   York: Routledge, 1992.
Miller, D. A. The Novel and the Police. Berkeley: U of California P,
   1988.

Miller, Nancy K. *Subject to Change: Reading Feminist Writing.* New York: Columbia UP, 1988.

Rich, Adrienne. *On Lies, Secrets, and Silence: Selected Prose, 1966–1979.* New York: Norton, 1979.

Tate, Claudia. *Black Women Writers at Work.* New York: Continuum, 1983.

Gendered and Gay/Lesbian Approaches to *Death in Venice*

Feuerlicht, Ignace. "Thomas Mann and Homoeroticism." *Germanic Review* 57.3 (Summer 1982):89–97.

Gullette, Margaret Morganroth. "The Exile of Adulthood Pedophilia in the Midlife Novel." *Novel: A Forum on Fiction* 17.3 (Spring 1984):215–32.

Hayes, Tom, and Lee Quinby. "The Aporia of Bourgeois Art Desire in Thomas Mann's *Death in Venice.*" *Criticism: A Quarterly for Literature and the Arts* 31.2 (Spring 1989):159–77.

Jofen, Jean. "A Freudian Commentary on Thomas Mann's *Death in Venice.*" *Journal of Evolutionary Psychology* 6.3–4 (August 1985):238–47.

Martin, Robert. "Gender, Sexuality, and Identity in Mann's Short Fiction." *Approaches to Teaching Mann's "Death in Venice" and Other Short Fiction.* Ed. Jeffrey B. Berlin. New York: MLA, 1992. 57–67.

A PERSPECTIVE ON GENDER AND SEXUALITY

ROBERT TOBIN

The Life and Work of Thomas Mann: A Gay Perspective

The publication of Thomas Mann's diaries in the last twenty years has brought to the fore once again the question of the relationship between an author's lived experience and his or her writings. These diaries have made more explicit than ever that homoerotic feelings were an important component of Mann's personal life. Indeed, when Mann

concludes his reflections on his profound personal relationship with
Paul Ehrenberg, he writes, "Yes, I have lived and loved" (Tagebücher
1933–34, 411), implying that "living" is closely related to male-male
love. How does this conception of Mann's "life" fit into his works?
How would it fit into any author's works? *Death in Venice* provinces a
particularly salient answer to this old question, not so much because its
author had homosexual inclinations, nor solely because its subject
matter is male-male desire, but because it addresses in particular the
relationship between erotic desire and artistic production. Mann's
notebooks for *Death in Venice* include the phrase "eros and *the word*"
("Working Notes" 83). *Death in Venice* itself is more specific: it both
declares that "eros dwells in language" and suggests that language is in
eros as well (239).

Over the years, *Death in Venice* has been the scene of battles over
the question of the relationship between Mann's homosexuality and
his writing. Many critics have downplayed the issue of homosexuality
in Mann's work. As one recent reviewer writes, "For generations,
readers were taught that the homoerotic passages in Thomas Mann's
fiction were never to be taken literally. Aschenbach's falling in love
with Tadzio, the beautiful Polish boy, in 'Death in Venice'? Merely
symbolic of the fistlike Teutonic artist declining into Mediterranean
disease and death" (Lehmann-Haupt). According to Ronald Hayman,
in most biographies, Mann's homosexuality has been "depicted with a
discretion that borders on dishonesty" (Hayman 63). To be fair, some
of those who have discussed the matter include Ignace Feuerlicht, Jeffrey Meyers, and T. J. Reed. And from the beginning, Mann and his
more honest readers have seen "life," including sexuality, as a tremen-
dously important component of *Death in Venice*. In an early review of
the novella, Thomas Mann's elder brother, the novelist Heinrich
Mann, claims that the central question of *Death in Venice* is, "What is
earlier, reality or poetry?" (Bahr 136). Thomas Mann frequently made
clear what this "reality" that possibly preceded his "poetry" might be:
in 1918 he declared, "Everything I have written expresses my inversion," using an early word for homosexuality (Heilbut 313). Near the
end of his life, in his diaries, he asserts again that "the insane and passionately maintained enthusiasm for the attraction of male youth, un-
surpassed by anything in the world, . . . lies at the basis of everything"
(*Tagebücher* 1950, 239). In *Death in Venice,* Mann gives a clearer picture of how this foundational desire for other men grounds everything
else — including his texts.

"In the Life"

Although it has always been obvious that male-male desire plays a prominent role in Mann's writings, and gay readers have often leaped to the conclusion that only another gay person could write so fluently about such topics, it has only been in the last twenty years, with the posthumous publication of Mann's diaries, that readers have become aware of just how homosexual Mann was. Diaries, of course, are as prone to fabrication and misinterpretation as any other text, but nonetheless, it is worth dwelling on Mann's a moment in order to situate the representation of sexuality in *Death in Venice* in the life of its author. The goal here is not to pass on mere gossip, but rather to suggest the great importance of Mann's homosexual affections for his life. With a bit of cross-cultural imagination, these diary entries could even be taken as evidence that Mann was "in the life," a phrase used by some gay African Americans to describe their culture (Beam 12). And if Mann was perhaps not strictly speaking *in* the gay life of early-twentieth-century Germany, his many recorded homosexual adventures suggest that he was at least *near* it.

Repeatedly in the diaries, Mann sums up his love life, always in terms of a string of young men whom he had known. Never does his lifelong wife, Katia, born Pringsheim, show up on these lists. It must be added that Mann lived contentedly with Katia and had six children with her. Katia claimed to have married only to have children. She came from a broadminded, tolerant and progressive family; her grandmother, Hedwig Dohm, was one of the most prominent feminist writers in nineteenth-century Germany. Accordingly, Mann acknowledged that Katia was very understanding of his desires that "went the other way." In any case, the erotic life of his fantasy circled exclusively around young men.

The first of these young men who appear in Mann's diaries and his fictional works is Armin Martens, with whom Mann fell in love as a schoolboy in 1890. The story of Mann's infatuation for Martens shows up in Tonio Kröger's crush on Hans Hansen in the story "Tonio Kröger." The next is Willri Tempe, who caught Mann's eye sometime between 1890 and 1892. He became Pribislav Hippe, Hans Castorp's schoolboy crush in *The Magic Mountain*. But, as Mann writes on May 6, 1934, both "the A.M. and the W.T. experiences recede far into childishness" when compared with the relationship with Paul Ehrenberg (*Tagebücher* 1933–34, 411). About this passion,

which developed between 1899 and 1903, Mann wrote on September
13, 1919, "I loved him and [it] was something like a happy love"
(*Tagebücher* 1918–21, 301). In the 1940s, he wrote, "One cannot experience love more strongly" (*Tagebücher* 1940–43, 551). Calling it
"that central experience of the heart," he concludes that he, too, has
"'paid' for being human," suggesting that the sufferings of love are
what make one a human being (*Tagebücher* 1933–34, 411). Ehrenberg gets his immortality, among other places, as Rudi Schwerdtfeger,
the charming and handsome violinist who seduces Adrian Leverkühn
in *Doctor Faustus*.

After publication of *Death in Venice*, other infatuations and loves
appeared in Mann's diaries — Klaus Heuser and Franz Westermayer
being the most celebrated — along with countless young men (including Mann's own son, Klaus) who attracted the attention of the author.
Tadzio of *Death in Venice* was also the product of an immediate, real-
life inspiration, Wladislaw Moes, a young Polish nobleman. In 1911,
Thomas and Katia Mann met Thomas's brother Heinrich in Venice,
where Thomas became entranced with the Polish youth, as Katia
records in her memoirs: "He immediately had a weakness for the
youth, he liked him inordinately, and he always watched him on the
beach with his friends. He did not follow him through all of Venice,
but the youth did fascinate him, and he thought about him often" (K.
Mann 70). She goes on to explain how her husband turned his flirtation into a text: "My husband transferred the pleasure that he indeed
had from this very charming youth to Aschenbach, and stylized it to
most extreme passion (K. Mann 72). Thus, like many other of Mann's
infatuations and loves, Wladislaw Moes ended up a literary figure.
There is, then, a clear historical and biographical basis for the presence
of homosexuality in Mann's works.

Bringing Out the Text

"Even in a personal sense, after all, art is an intensified life," declares the narrator of *Death in Venice*. If Mann was at least near the life
of early-twentieth-century German homosexuals, it would not be surprising to find the ever-observant Mann using elements of that subculture in his writings, given his penchant for turning reality into literature. And, indeed, a new generation of readers is now beginning to
realize that the novella is "a virtual Baedekker's guide to homosexual
love" (Heilbut 261). Like all the strange male loners in the story who
seem to be telling Aschenbach that he is one of them, the novella of-

fers a perverse mirror to modern Western society, suggesting that it is far gayer than people had realized. One of these loners, the guitar-playing leader of the troupe who entertains the hotel society with the Italian song near the end of *Death in Venice,* mocks his audience while causing it to laugh. Hence, he plays the same role that the novella does, captivating a heterosexual audience that does not understand its gay codes. In order to avoid being in the position of that audience, it is worthwhile for the reader to submerge him- or herself into "the life" and to develop a sensitivity to the gay themes that reverberate throughout the novella. Rather than suppressing the story's homosexual tones, as generations of previous critics have done, the reader can augment them, bring them out. Such a search for the homosexual signifiers of the story will put Aschenbach into a clearer context and provide for a much richer reading of the novella and its understanding of society.

The novella's initial setting suggests, at the very least, a gay-friendly story. It takes place in Munich, capital of Bavaria, which in the nineteenth century could lay claim to a certain social liberalism. Anselm Feuerbach's legal theories and Bavaria's adoption of the Napoleonic Code had resulted in a fairly serious attempt to separate the realm of law from that of morality. As a result, consensual sexual acts between adults (including homosexual ones) became decriminalized, although police harassment of sodomites still continued (Hull 333–70). Even after the recriminalization of homosexuality in the second half of the nineteenth century (Derks 161–63), Bavaria remained comparatively liberal, compared with other German states — perhaps because its ruler, King Ludwig II, was rumored to have been homosexual himself (Mayer 210–12). Mann knew of these rumors, referring to Ludwig as a "type of homosexual" in his letter on homosexuality and *Death in Venice* to Carl Maria Weber on July 4, 1920 (*Letters,* 104).

Aschenbach's decision to go for a walk in the English Garden is also intriguing when viewed from the gay perspective, for that public park, especially those "less and less frequented paths" that Aschenbach seeks out, has been a meeting place for male homosexuals since its construction at the end of the eighteenth century. Nowadays, when a single male author goes for a walk in that park by himself, there's a good chance that he's looking for a romantic adventure, possibly of the homosexual sort — and things weren't all that different a century ago. Mann's reference to the "traffic" in the park suggests a possible double entendre, for that word in German ("Verkehr") can also mean sexual intercourse.

Although Aschenbach might not completely understand the sexual implications of his stroll through the English Garden, he soon runs into someone who does: a man with a "slightly unusual appearance" and an "exotic air." At least one critic has seen something vaguely homosexual in his description: "beardless," "snub-nosed," "red-haired," "freckled" (Traschen 90). These characteristics, as well as his unusual hat, his "yellowish" clothing, and his large Adam's apple, while not in and of themselves evidence for homosexuality, are all part of a network of signifiers that link this man with all the other vaguely threatening men whom Aschenbach meets on his journey (Venable 27). Of these characteristics, the most salient consists in being "someone who had come from distant parts." Homosexuality is often viewed as a vice that comes from other cultures; in any case, the homosexual is one of the paradigmatic "outsiders," as the critic Hans Mayer has noted. In *Death in Venice,* all of these strangers diverge somewhat from the norm: they are unusual, even queer, if not in the sense of modern American slang, at least in the sense of being "other."

The possible homosexuality of the stranger in the cemetery becomes more plausible when one reads the narrator's report on the visual encounter between Aschenbach and the stranger. Aschenbach begins the confrontation, perhaps unintentionally, with his "half absent-minded, half intended scrutiny" (25), which the other understands as a form of "cruising," a visual invitation or challenge to a sexual meeting. In any case, the narrator reports that "the man was in fact staring at him so aggressively, so straight in the eye, with so evident an intention to make an issue of the matter and outstare him" (25). Here a look at the German helps to strengthen the case for a sexual understanding of this gaze: David Luke has accurately rendered as "to make an issue of the matter" the German phrase, *"die Sache aufs Äußerste zu treiben"* (literally, "to drive the thing to the extreme"). The word *treiben,* related to English "drive," can have sexual connotations: *"es mit jemandem treiben"* means roughly "to do it (i.e. to have sex) with someone." Set in Munich's English Garden, this direct visual challenge between two solitary men is very likely to have the sexual component that the word *treiben* implies.

Even more evidence for the sexual nature of this encounter is what it provokes: "an extraordinary expansion of his inner self, a kind of roving restlessness" (25). The subsequent vision hints that this initial expansion is a release of a previously repressed sexuality. It is, as Jofen notes (62), obviously sexual, filled with phallic symbols such as "hairy palm trunks thrusting upwards . . . thick fleshly plants . . . strangely misshapen trees with roots that arched through the air . . . and . . . exotic birds with grotesque beaks" (25–26). The jungles of ferns are "rank," in German *geil*, a word that can also be translated as "lewd," as it is in Aschenbach's final dream of the Dionysian orgy (81–82). This vision of the jungle causes Aschenbach to throb with "mysterious longing," reinforcing the importance of sexuality as the motivation behind Aschenbach's "desire to travel" (25).

If the opening of *Death in Venice* alerts the reader with many signals to a possible gay aspect of Aschenbach's lived experience, the second chapter suggests a homosexual subtext to his writings. Aschenbach's subject matter, like Thomas Mann's, consistently revolves, once again, if not *in* the life of homosexuality, then *around* it. And we must remember that most of Aschenbach's works are those that Mann himself wanted to write. The narrator concludes his summary of Aschenbach's works by using a passage from the literary critic Samuel Lublinsky's actual description of Mann's prose, comparing "the new hero-type favoured by Aschenbach and recurring in his books in a multiplicity of individual variants" to the figure of St. Sebastian (30). Sebastian, that often erotically charged and aesthetically beautiful icon of the penetrated male, rumored to have been the beloved of Diocletian before his conversion to Christianity, has been a favorite of homosexual men for generations. Oscar Wilde took his name while in Parisian exile, and Yukio Mishima famously posed as the pierced saint. The use of Lublinsky's observations about Mann for the narrator's critique of Aschenbach strengthens the tie between Aschenbach and Mann. This device puts Mann into a kind of intercourse with another male author who understood him, and it enacts on the level of the text, the consensual penetration of one man's prose by another man's (Böhm 339).

Looking more closely Aschenbach's writings, a gay pattern emerges. The "tapestry of the novel called *Maya*" (30) is inspired by the German philosopher Arthur Schopenhauer, who had made speculations on male homosexuality that Mann quoted in his essay "On the German Republic" (*Von deutscher Republik* 154).[1] "That powerful tale entitled *A Study in Abjection*" (28) actually has the German title of *"Ein Elender,"* which defies translation. *Elend* ("abject") has the meaning of "banned" or "homeless" and thus connects its main character to all those queer, exotic, foreign strangers whom Aschenbach

---

[1]Unfortunately, but typically, the translator has omitted the passage in question from the English edition of this essay. It should be in *Order of the Day,* on p. 42.

meets en route to Venice. The connection between his "passionate treatise *Intellect and Art* and Schiller's disquisition *On Naive and Reflective Literature*" (28) brings to mind Mann's appropriation of Schiller as homoerotic. Tonio Kröger, for instance, uses Schiller's *Don Carlos* as a homoerotic love offering to Hans Hansen. The first and last work by Aschenbach mentioned in the second chapter, however, is his "lucid and massive prose epic about the life of Frederic of Prussia." In his notebooks to his own Frederick project, Mann noted that the Prussian king was rumored to have been homosexual. Indeed, "the flashing exchange of the dialogue between Voltaire and the King" concerned not only the "subject of war"; it also contained accusations and counter-accusations of sodomy and buggery (Böhm 278–87). A reader conversant in the lore of the European homosexual subculture finds something gay in almost every element of Aschenbach's writing.

A closer look at the Sebastian-like characteristics that unite all these characters reveals the late-nineteenth-century homosexual. The "elegant self-control concealing from the world's eyes until the very last moment a state of inner disintegration and biological decay" (31) reminds one of Oscar Wilde's Dorian Gray, another figure instantly recognized by homosexual readers as one of their own (Mayer 224–29). "The false, dangerous life of the born deceiver" was the life that any cultured homosexual led in trying to pass as straight; it was dangerous, among other reasons, because of the constant threat of exposure or blackmail. Yet this very falseness could become "gracious poise and composure in the empty austere service of form," as the homosexual became a master of heterosexual rites. Passing as straight, constructing the closet, equipped the homosexual with such social and theatrical skills that he or she could become a remarkably proficient actor or dissimulator. And thus the "sallow ugliness" that Mann saw in homosexual desire was "able to fan its smoldering concupiscence to a pure flame, and even to exalt itself to mastery in the realm of beauty" (31). Aschenbach therefore consistently writes about the artistic benefits of the repression or sublimation of homosexuality; he sings the productivity of the closet. The narrator's observation that Aschenbach "has uncovered what is better kept hidden, made talent seem suspect, betrayed the truth about art" confirms the suspicion that the writer underscores the productivity of homosexuality in his work. So does his reference to Aschenbach's "breathtaking cynicisms about the questionable nature of art and of the artist himself" (32).

Given that Aschenbach's desire to travel is sparked by the cruising gaze of the queer man in the cemetery, it makes sense that his travels lead him to more male-male encounters. Since the eighteenth century, Europeans who could afford it had traveled to Italy, as well as other Mediterranean destinations such as North Africa, in search of homosexual encounters (Aldrich). In the German tradition, the art historian Winckelmann moved to Italy in order to live something like a gay life, while Goethe made note of the open expression of male-male love. In a letter to Grautoff, his confidant from boyhood days on matters concerning sexuality, Mann had also noted male prostitution in Italy (*Briefe an Otto Grautoff* 80). For Mann and many other upper-class Germans, Venice was the epitome of queer Italy (Jones 282, Weeks). The nineteenth-century German poet August von Platen, about whose homosexuality Mann wrote an essay, composed sonnets about Venice, to which the narrator of *Death in Venice* alludes: Aschenbach "recalled that poet of plangent inspiration who long ago had seen the cupolas and bell-towers of his dream rise before him out of these same waters" (37). Platen, by the way, like Aschenbach, died of cholera (Aldrich 58–59). Mann himself wrote a short story, set in Venice, "Disappointment," in which two solitary men converse in an attempted pickup on the Piazza San Marco; here we see the cynicism and depression resulting from the clandestine lives of upper-class homosexuals in the late nineteenth century (Härle 168). Thus it seems likely that, in wanting the "strange" Venice, Aschenbach wants the queer Venice. As the text says, in Venice he hopes to find "a fantastic mutation of normal reality," which brings to mind Mann's assessment of his love of Klaus Heuser: "happiness, as it stands in the book of humanity, although not normalcy" (*Tagebücher* 1933–34, 296). Aschenbach desires a kind of abnormal happiness, the kind that early-twentieth-century homosexual Europeans knew they could find in Italy. Again, a look at the German lends further support to the suggestion that Venice has a sexual connotation, for the word translated as "mutation" is *Abweichendes*, literally, "the deviant," including the sexually deviant.

On Aschenbach's path to his fantastic goal he meets more of those loners who all have something homosexual about them. It begins with a sailor, wearing the same kind of uniform that Tadzio does. Quickly, the ticket salesman appears, with that "smooth facility" of movement and that "glib empty talk" that so perversely mirrors Aschenbach's own elegant formalism. But more seriously, Aschenbach glimpses the aging, made-up fop, with his "rakishly tilted hat" and "yellowish" false teeth. His cosmetics and flamboyant behavior mark him as sexually suspect. When he screams out compliments to Aschenbach's "sweetheart," he remains suspiciously vague about the gender of that sweetheart. Before he reaches his destination, Aschenbach has a final encounter with a homosexual type: the gondolier, with his "seamen's clothes," his "yellow scarf," his "hat tilted rakishly on his head," his "snub nose, and his reddish eyebrows." Psychoanalysis has seen a homosexual element in this man, plying "his oar with great energy, putting his whole body into every stroke" behind another man (Jofen 242). Aschenbach's almost unwilling pleasure in the trip would confirm such a reading — as does his anxiety that he might have "fallen into the hands of a criminal" whose real goal was "extorting money from him." The hint of blackmail is strengthened in Aschenbach's desire to "pay off" the gondolier, once he has finally landed. It is a hint that would have resonated in homosexual circles of early-twentieth-century Germany. The early homosexual rights activist Magnus Hirschfeld reported that 3,000 of the 10,000 homosexuals he had interviewed had been blackmailed (Karlen 248). Moreover, one of the first German film treatments of homosexuality, a 1918 piece entitled *Different from the Others*, empathetically depicts the plight of the blackmailed homosexual (Dyer 1990, 10–17). In any case, the gondolier, like any chance homosexual trick who wanted money, flees when he sees the police. He is "a bad man, a man without a license . . . the only gondolier who has no license"(42).

Aschenbach's passion for Tadzio is also marked as homosexual in ways that might escape the uninitiated reader. The educated early-twentieth-century homosexual would respond to the allusions to Greco-Roman myth — for instance, the statue of the beautiful *Boy Extracting a Thorn,* Hyacinthus, the beloved of Apollo and Zephyr, and "that Trojan shepherd boy," Ganymede, as well as the references to Greek philosophers and writers, especially Socrates and Plato. In addition, the visual element of the relationship reflects Mann's personal experience, which consisted primarily of admiring men from afar, visually. The narrator remarks on the visual exchanges between Tadzio and Aschenbach: "Nothing is stranger, more delicate, than the relationship between people who know each other only by sight . . . and yet are compelled by the constraint of convention or by their own temperament to keep up the pretense of being indifferent strangers" (65). Mann might just as well have said, "nothing is queerer . . . ," for members of the early-twentieth-century homosexual subculture were highly dependent on the kind of cruising, or visual communication, that takes place between Aschenbach and his male partners, including the stranger in the cemetery and Tadzio. The members of that subculture would know all about "the constraint of convention" that prevented them from coming together in a more articulate manner.

In addition, Tadzio is marked as "sick." From the beginning, Aschenbach wonders whether Tadzio is "in poor health" (44). He subsequently reassures himself that "he's sickly" (51), and then concludes
once again, "he's sickly, he'll probably not live long" (77). This kind
of thinking would also resonate profoundly with anyone familiar with
the gay subculture of the early twentieth century. To begin with,
Mann uses the word *leidend* in the passage translated as "poor health,"
bringing together the semantic complexes of *leiden* ("to suffer") and
Leidenschaft ("passion") in a way that points directly to sexuality. But
more generally, Tadzio's sickliness could easily be his sexuality, given
that nineteenth-century medicine viewed homosexuality as an illness
to be cured.

A queer reading of this text, rather than hiding homosexuality, has
sought it out in the subtlest nuances, which can enrich everyone's understanding of the novella. This reading demonstrates that everything
about Aschenbach is heading for a homosexual encounter of some
kind. Nevertheless, one cannot say that his sexuality goes unchanged
as the story proceeds, for Aschenbach does develop. At the beginning
of the novella, the hideous fop on the ferry wears a red tie, a marker of
homosexuality at the turn of the century. One historian of sexuality reports that male prostitutes often wore such ties (Karlen 243–54). At
the end of the novella, Aschenbach has donned the red tie, along with
all the makeup. Aschenbach's sexuality emerges and develops. The
queer reading, however, suggests that it doesn't come out of nothing.
Marc Weiner has shown that Aschenbach's attitude toward music, that
vague amorphous zone into which nineteenth-century Europeans
poured so much queer sexuality, became ever more open, bringing
him back to his mother's side of the family tree, which had consisted
of foreign musicians. "A development is a destiny," asserts the narrator
enigmatically. Perhaps he implies that Aschenbach's development signifies a return to his roots (biological or cultural), an opening up of his
core — or even a coming out.

Along with Aschenbach's return to his roots comes — at least for a
while — a freeing of his creativity. The relationship to Tadzio is not entirely wordless and visual. Admittedly, at first, while Aschenbach watches
Tadzio on the beach, he cannot write: "after no more than a quarter of
an hour he felt that it was a great pity to turn his mind away from this
present situation. . . . He threw his writing materials aside . . . and before long . . . he turned his head . . . to investigate once more the whereabouts and doings of the excellent Adgio" (49). Later, when Aschenbach learns Tadzio's full name, he can write the "page and a half of

exquisite prose" (62). Perhaps Aschenbach learns, if not to desublimate, at least a more refined form of sublimation that lets him enjoy the physical beauty aroused by his homosexual desire as well as to create. Does this development stand in contrast to his earlier writing style, his writing "despite" his underlying homosexuality? Having established the presence of homosexuality in the character of Aschenbach, it is now time to examine the relationship between Aschenbach's love, his eros, and his word, his logos.

Eros and Logos

The interaction between eros and logos makes *Death in Venice* a foundational text for gay and lesbian studies. *Death in Venice* begins with a description of an artist's difficulties in writing one spring afternoon. In discussing Aschenbach's creative process, the text argues that fearful repression has produced his artworks. But it also suggests that his sublimated passions can no longer fuel his writings: "Could it be that the enslaved emotion was now avenging itself by deserting him, by refusing from now on to bear up his art on his wings . . . ?" (27). At the height of Aschenbach's passion for Tadzio, he senses a possibility of a world in which the bodily, passionate realm of "emotion" can fuse with the intellectual, textual world of "thought": "The writer's joy is the thought that can become emotion, the emotion that can wholly become a thought" (62). In this brief epiphany, Aschenbach is able to experience a unity of eros and logos that contrasts with the rigid sublimation that had characterized his writing before: "Never had he felt the joy of the word more sweetly, never had he known so clearly that Eros dwells in language" (62). After describing "that page and a half of exquisite prose," the narrator exclaims, "How mysterious this act of intercourse and begetting between a mind and a body" (62). The "intercourse" is, incidentally, the same *Verkehr* ("traffic") that filled the English Garden at the beginning of the novella. The sexual nature of this intercourse becomes clear when the narrator describes Aschenbach's feelings after the writing in terms of postcoital depression: "he felt worn out, even broken, and his conscience seemed to be reproaching him as if after some kind of debauch" (62).

If narration is comparable to sexuality, then a hidden, closeted sexuality will produce a narration of secrets. And indeed, in describing Aschenbach's writing, the narrator interjects, "It is well that the world knows only a fine piece of work and not also its origins, the conditions under which it came into being; for the knowledge of a source of an artist's inspiration would often confuse readers and shock them" (62). Aschenbach himself returns to this mentality once cholera enters the scene:

> Thus Aschenbach felt an obscure sense of satisfaction at what was going on in the dirty alleyways of Venice, cloaked in official secrecy — this guilty secret of the city, which merged with his own innermost secret and which it was also so much in his own interests to protect. . . . "They want to keep it silent!" he whispered vehemently. "I shall say nothing!" The consciousness of his complicity in the secret, of his share in the guilt, intoxicated him as small qualities of wine intoxicate a weary brain. (68–69, 80)

Aschenbach, however, doesn't want to hide the truth of the disease completely. Because he is "conscious of having a special claim to participation in this secret . . . he took a perverse pleasure in putting embarrassing questions to those in possession of the facts" (72). Not for nothing does Heilbut call Mann "the poet of the half-open closet." "Closeting," the hiding and coy exposure of sexuality, becomes one of the main forces, both in the creation of Mann's and Aschenbach's literature and in its reception.

If, however, sexual desire and its repression, sublimation, hiding, or "closeting," as well as its occasionally flirtatious revelation, is often at the root of creativity in *Death in Venice*, what is at the root of sexual desire? In the latter part of the twentieth century, the truly revolutionary aspect of *Death in Venice* is not the by now relatively comfortable notion that sexuality is a basic component of creativity but the suggestion that sexuality itself is a construct of creative and social forces. Here Mann anticipates Michel Foucault, author of *The History of Sexuality*, and all those thinkers who in his wake have seen sexuality as constantly changing and historically conditioned.

The very conflation of Aschenbach's homosexual desire, Tadzio's sickliness, and Venice's cholera suggest Mann's awareness of the historical determinants of sexuality, for in fact the vocabulary of sexuality is a product of nineteenth-century central European medicine. The date 1869 is a crucial one. In that year, the Hungarian Karoly Maria Benkert, writing under the name Kertbeny, first coined the word "homosexual." Benkert's piece languished in obscurity until Hirschfeld reprinted it in 1905, but, also in 1869, the Berlin psychiatrist Carl Westphal mobilized medical energies in the sexual wars with a seminal article on what he called "contrary sexual feelings" (Bullough 7–8; see also Faderman 239–53). Early homosexual readers were sometimes disturbed by the equation of homosexuality and cholera in *Death in Venice*, but Mann consistently distanced himself from medical perspectives. In a letter to Grautoff dated April 6, 1897, he cast aspersions specifically on medical experts who treated sexual disorders (*Briefe an Otto Grautoff* 85). And in his famous letter to Weber, he clearly distanced himself from the "medical" and "pathological" approach to literature (*Letters* 103). Hence we may see Mann's use of cholera in the novella not as an equation of homosexuality with sickness but as an awareness of the importance of medical discourses in creating modern notions of sexuality.

Mann's understanding of the construction of sexuality becomes quite clear in a fascinating diary passage in which he laments the lack of unclothed men in non-German films: "German films give me something that those of other nationalities scarcely offer. . . . This is connected with German 'homosexuality' . . . the showing of young male nudity in flattering, indeed loving photographic lighting, wherever the opportunity presents itself. . . . The Germans, or the German Jews, who do this are certainly right: there is basically nothing 'more beautiful'" (*Tagebücher* 1933–34, 309). By putting both "homosexuality" and "more beautiful" in quotation marks, Mann implies that both sexuality and aesthetics are constructs. In associating "homosexuality" with Germans and German Jews, Mann takes seriously the notion of a socially constructed sexuality and looks specifically at the society he knows best. Mann's attention to film in this matter suggests the importance of cultural and specifically visual artifacts in recording, or even delimiting, sexuality.

Not just in Mann's diaries, but also in *Death in Venice*, the notion of the artistic construction of sexuality emerges. In Aschenbach's case, a poem contributes to the development of his sexuality. Platen's homoerotic poetry first puts Aschenbach in the mood: "inwardly he recited a few lines of the measured music that had been made from that reverence and joy and sadness, and effortlessly moved by a passion already shaped into language, he questioned his grave and weary heart, wondering whether . . . some late adventure of the emotions might yet be in store for him on his leisured journey" (37). If Platen's passions were already shaped into language, that language is now shaping Aschenbach's passions.

When Aschenbach speculates that "the kind of love that had taken possession of him" (that is, male-male love) had "been honored by the most valiant of peoples" (71), he implies a priority of culture before sexuality: "Numerous warrior-heroes of older times had willingly borne its yoke" (71). Rather than the sexuality creating a certain culture — militaristic and formal, according to Mann's way of thinking — that culture brings about, or chooses, a certain sexuality. Aschenbach is specifically thinking of certain elements of Greek culture that were both militaristic and open to forms of same-sex desire. Greek culture, a center for Aschenbach's European education, is still understood in the United States as the cradle of democracy, the birthplace of Western culture, and the origin of our political, theatrical, and philosophical institutions. This same culture is equally well known for its predilection for "Greek love" — male-male erotic interaction. The double legacy of the Greek tradition is neatly encapsulated by the varied fates of the Greek word *gymnasion*. In Germany, the word *Gymnasium* designates the most intellectual secondary schools, those that prepare pupils for higher education, while in the United States, the word *gymnasium* denotes the physical, to describe a place where athletic events take place. In Venice, Aschenbach learns the truth of both developments of the word; he learns that mind and body are one. When Aschenbach sees Tadzio, his vision of the youthful boy activates the repository of Western thought going back to this ancient Greek culture: "His mind was in labor, its store of culture was in ferment, his memory threw up thoughts from ancient tradition which he had been taught as a boy, but which had never yet come alive in his own fire" (60). The notion of a mind in the presence of truth going into labor harks back to Plato's *Symposium*. But the more sweeping assertion is that Aschenbach's mind might never have gone into labor in the presence of Tadzio if his entire cultural tradition had not made him a fertile bed for such beautiful inseminations.

The educational system bears a large responsibility for passing on this tradition that prepares Aschenbach for his encounter with Tadzio. The male-male erotic subtext of the pedagogical tradition is central to *Death in Venice,* as it is to other works by Mann. It appears in Socrates' desire in the pedagogical scene of the *Phaedrus,* which *Death in Venice* expresses as Socrates' physical desire for his pupil. It also reveals itself in "the pedagogical structures" that leave Tadzio's sisters "at the point of disfigurement" and cause "any charm of figure they might have had" to be "suppressed and negated" (44). Eve Sedgwick sees the link between Phaedrus and Tadzio, Aschenbach and Socrates, as indicating that "the history of Western thought is importantly constituted and motivated by a priceless history of male-male pedagogical and pederastic relations" (Sedgwick 55). The narrator exposes Aschenbach's complicity in this chain of educational male-male links, when he repeatedly notes that Aschenbach's writings have taken their place in the canon and are taught to young schoolboys. Here, resisting whatever misogyny we may find in Mann's writings, *Death in Venice* establishes the foundation for a powerful critique of the exclusion of women from the educational system that transmits Western values. Moreover, the story points to the self-perpetuating nature of this educational system: if it is based on male-male desire, it also creates that desire.

Tadzio therefore has to be a boy: "His own sensibility and . . . the collective European psyche" point him in the direction of loving male youth (26). Here Mann foreshadows those queer theorists who have found homosexual desire in such seemingly heterosexual scenarios as nineteenth-century opera (Koestenbaum), as well as at the root of such icons as Marilyn Monroe (Dyer 1988), James Dean (Castiglia), and even Barbie dolls (Rand) — icons that help structure normative heterosexual desire. Mann anticipates this "queering" of culture when he implicates all of "us" in Aschenbach's desire: "So too the lovegod . . . loves to use the shapes and colors of young men . . . so that the sight of them will truly set us on fire with pain and hope" (61). Who constitutes this "us" — gay men and straight women? *Death in Venice* hints at the conclusion that in a patriarchal society, everyone — male or female, gay or straight — is caught up in a desire for masculinity. An entire culture responds so positively to Aschenbach's writings because the desire that goes hand in hand with these writings is at the center of that culture: "For a significant intellectual product to make a broad and immediate appeal, there must be a hidden affinity, indeed, a congruence, between the personal destiny of the author and the wider destiny of his generation" (30). The shared "destiny" that constitutes the "congruence" between author and reader is a basic pattern of adulation of masculinity at the foundation of patriarchal society. The narrator recognizes this historic pattern when he asks, concerning the protagonists in Aschenbach's writings, "what other heroism could be more in keeping with the times?" (31). Aschenbach's readers see themselves in his homosexual writings: "And they all recognized themselves in his work, they found that it confirmed them" (31). The masculinist center of the culture that produces Aschenbach, his desires, and his writing ensures the success of that desire and that writing.

All of the ideas in Mann's subsequent writings on sexuality are already present in this novella. Aschenbach's homosexual desire is specifically alloyed with his formalism, a linkage that Mann specifically underscores in his analysis of the homosexuality in the writings of Platen: "The strictly formal and form-plastic character of the verse forms [that Platen used] had an aesthetic and psychological affinity with his eros" (*Essays of Three Decades* 265). And if Aschenbach sees something military about his love, Mann does also in his essay on the German Republic, in which he asserts that many of the believers in "this eros" are militarists (*Von deutscher Republik* 154–55; once again omitted from *Order of the Day*, 42). Once the National Socialists took over Germany, Mann linked their militarism to homosexuality as well, mocking their moral campaign because, as he felt, homosexuality "belonged essentially to the movement, to warfare, yes to Germanness" (*Tagebücher* 1933–34, 470). All of these rationally expressed thoughts appeared decades after *Death in Venice*, suggesting that here again an aesthetic product prefigured and helped to construct an abstract understanding of sexuality.

   Death in Venice may in fact achieve some insights into the relationship between sexuality and gender that Mann's essays do not. In both *Death in Venice* and Mann's more essayistic statements about homosexuality from the 1920s and 1930s, a linkage of male homosexuality and misogyny seems to emerge. And, indeed, some feminists, such as Luce Irigaray, concur with Mann that a certain "hom(m)osexuality" provides the glue that keeps patriarchy together. Jane Gallop has expressed her distrust for male homosexuals, "because they choose men over women, just as do our social and political institutions" (Gallop 113). Both Irigaray and Gallop have much more complicated arguments to make about male homosexuality, but for the moment it suffices to say that they seem to conflate homosociality — close same-sex bonding that explicitly precludes actual sexual encounters — with homosexuality that does not repress its sexual side (Sedgwick). Thus National Socialism's glorification of the masculine would differ from gay male love in its rejection of actual sexual acts, as well as in its persecution of homosexual men and women. *Death in Venice* presents the dead end of misogynistic male homosexuality, perhaps more clearly than its author knew. It allows the reader to see that the man excited by male beauty shares the perspective of the woman excited by that beauty: even if Aschenbach equates his kind of eros with supermanliness, he must admit that "though we may be heroes in our own fashion and disciplined warriors, yet we are like women, for it is passion that exalts us" (85). Thus the novella implies that the gay man does not have an interest in glorifying patriarchy, but rather in breaking down the polarity between a positively expressed masculinity and a negatively viewed space inhabited by woman and the homosexual man.

Death in Venice — a novella that demonstrates the relationship between, on the one hand, the erotic life of authors, readers, and entire cultures, and, on the other hand, the texts that those authors compose, those readers read, and those cultures celebrate — continues to mediate between sexuality and textuality, suggesting to modern readers ways in which sexuality could interact with gender. Many players are involved with this interaction between desire and discourse: the man Thomas Mann; the time and place of early-twentieth-century Germany; readers of different sexualities and genders, from different cultures, epochs, and belief systems; and a text, *Death in Venice,* constructed at least in part out of a network of gay signs. In this interaction, it becomes clear that writing can emerge from erotic longing. Most profoundly, however, *Death in Venice* reveals the lexicon of sexuality to be a construct of language and culture. Mann's novella suggests that sexuality not only affects the creation of culture but that those cultural works — for instance, literature — in turn create sexuality. The circuit between culturally created sexuality and sexually created culture becomes a "motus anima continuus," a continuous motion of the spirit that unites the life and work, not only of Thomas Mann, but of culture in general.

WORKS CITED

Aldrich, Robert. *The Seduction of the Mediterranean.* New York: Routledge, 1993.

Bahr, Ehrhard. *Erläuterungen und Dokumente. Thomas Mann: "Der Tod in Venedig."* Stuttgart: Reclam, 1991.

Beam, Joseph, ed. *In the Life: A Black Gay Anthology.* Boston: Alyson, 1986.

Böhm, Klaus Werner. *Zwischen Selbstzucht und Verlangen: Thomas Mann und das Stigma Homosexualität.* Würzburg: Königshausen & Neumann, 1991.

Bullough, Vern L. *Homosexuality: A History.* New York: Meridian, 1979.

Castiglia, Christopher. "Rebel without a Closet." *Engendering Men: The Question of Male Feminist Criticism.* Ed. Joseph Boone and Michael Cadden. New York: Routledge, 1990.

Derks, Paul. *Die Schande der heiligen Päderastie. Homosexualität und Öffentlichkeit in der deutschen Literatur, 1750–1850.* Berlin: Verlag Rosa Winkel, 1990.

Dyer, Richard. "Monroe and Sexuality." *Women and Film.* Ed. Janet Todd. New York: Holmes & Meier, 1988. 69–96.

———. *Now You See It: Essays on Lesbian and Gay Film.* London: Routledge, 1990.

Faderman, Lillian. *Surpassing the Love of Men: Romantic Friendship and Love between Women from the Renaissance to the Present.* New York: Morrow, 1981.

Feuerlicht, Ignace. "Thomas Mann and Homoeroticism." *Germanic Review* 57.3 (1982): 89–97.

Foucault, Michel. *History of Sexuality.* 3 vols. Trans. Robert Hurley. New York: Vintage, 1980–88.

Gallop, Jane. *Thinking through the Body.* New York: Columbia, 1988.

Härle, Gerhard. *Männerweiblichkeit: Zur Homosexualität bei Klaus und Thomas Mann.* Frankfurt am Main: Athenäum, 1988.

Hayman, Ronald. *Thomas Mann: A Biography.* New York: Scribner, 1995.

Heilbut, Anthony. *Thomas Mann: Eros and Literature.* New York: Knopf, 1996.

Hull, Isabel. *Sexuality, State, and Civil Society in Germany, 1700–1815.* Ithaca, N.Y.: Cornell UP, 1996.

Jofen, Jean. "A Freudian Commentary on Thomas Mann's *Death in Venice.*" *Journal of Evolutionary Psychology* 6. 3–4 (August 1985): 238–47.

Jones, James W. *"We of the Third Sex": Literary Representations of Homosexuality in Wilhelmine Germany.* New York: Lang, 1990.

Karlen, Arno. *Sexuality and Homosexuality: A New View.* New York: Norton, 1971.

Kostenbaum, Wayne. *The Queen's Throat: Opera, Homosexuality, and the Mystery of Desire.* New York: Poseidon, 1993.

Lehmann-Haupt, Christopher. "Of the Homoerotic Elements in Mann's Work and Life." *New York Times,* 21 March 1996. B5.

Mann, Katia. *Meine ungeschriebenen Memoiren.* Ed. Elisabeth Plessen and Michael Mann. Frankfurt am Main: Fischer, 1974.

Mann, Thomas. *Briefe an Otto Grautoff.* Ed. Peter de Mendelssohn. Frankfurt am Main: Fischer, 1975.

———. *Essays of Three Decades.* Trans. Helen T. Lowe-Porter. New York: Knopf, 1947.

————. *Letters of Thomas Mann, 1889–1955*. Trans. Richard and Clara Winston. New York: Knopf, 1971.

————. *Order of the Day: Political and Speeches of Two Decades*. Freeport: Books for Libraries Press, 1937.

————. *Tagebücher, 1918–1943*. 5 vols. Ed. Peter de Mendelssohn. Frankfurt am Main: Fischer, 1977–82.

————. *Tagebücher, 1944–1950*. 3 vols. Ed. Inge Jens. Frankfurt am Main: Fischer, 1986–89.

————. *Von deutscher Republik: Politsche Schriften und Reden in Deutschland*. Ed. Peter de Mendelssohn. Frankfurt am Main: Fischer, 1984.

————. "Working Notes for *Death in Venice*." Trans. Lynda Hoffman Jeep. *"Death in Venice": A New Translation. Backgrounds and Contexts. Criticism*. Ed. and trans. Clayton Koelb. New York: Norton, 1994.

Mayer, Hans. *Outsiders: A Study in Life and Letters*. Trans. Dennis Sweet. Cambridge: MIT P, 1982.

Meyers, Jeffrey. *Homosexuality and Literature, 1890–1930*. London: Athlone, 1977.

Rand, Erica. *Barbie's Queer Accessories*. Durham: Duke UP, 1995.

Reed, T. J. *Thomas Mann: The Uses of Tradition*. Oxford: Clarendon, 1974.

Sedgwick, Eve. *Epistemology of the Closet*. Berkeley: U of California P, 1990.

Traschen, Isadore. "The Uses of Myth in *Death in Venice*." *Modern Critical Views of Thomas Mann*. Ed. Harold Bloom. New York: Chelsea, 1986. 87–101.

Venable, Vernon. "Structural Elements in *Death in Venice*." *Modern Critical Views of Thomas Mann*. Ed. Harold Bloom. New York: Chelsea, 1986. 23–34.

Weeks, Jeffrey. "Discourse, Desire, and Social Deviance: Some Problems in a History of Homosexuality." *The Making of the Modern Homosexual*. Ed. Kenneth Plummer. London: Hutchinson, 1981.

Weiner, Marc. "Silence, Sound, and Song in *Der Tod in Venedig*: A Study in Psycho-Social Repression." *Seminar* 23 (1987): 137–56.

The New Historicism
and
Death in Venice

WHAT IS THE NEW HISTORICISM?

The title of Brook Thomas's *The New Historicism and Other Old-Fashioned Topics* (1991) is telling. Whenever an emergent theory, movement, method, approach, or group gets labeled with the adjective "new," trouble is bound to ensue, for what is new today is either established, old, or forgotten tomorrow. Few of you will have heard of the band called New Kids on the Block. New Age bookshops and jewelry may seem "old hat" by the time this introduction is published. The New Criticism, or formalism, is just about the oldest approach to literature and literary study currently being practiced. The new historicism, by contrast, is *not* as old-fashioned as formalism, but it is hardly new, either. The term "new" eventually and inevitably requires some explanation. In the case of the new historicism, the best explanation is historical.

Although a number of influential critics working between 1920 and 1950 wrote about literature from a psychoanalytic perspective, the majority took what might generally be referred to as the historical approach. With the advent of the New Criticism, however, historically oriented critics almost seemed to disappear from the face of the earth. The dominant New Critics, or formalists, tended to treat literary works as if they were self-contained, self-referential objects. Rather than basing their interpretations on parallels between the text and historical contexts (such as the author's life or stated intentions in writing the work), these critics concentrated on the relationships *within* the text that give it its form and meaning. During the heyday of the New Criticism, concern about the interplay between literature and history virtually disappeared from literary discourse. In its place was a concern about intratextual repetition, particularly of images or symbols but also of rhythms and sound effect.

Around 1970 the New Criticism came under attack by reader-response critics (who believe that the meaning of a work is not inherent in its internal form but rather is cooperatively produced by the reader and the text) and poststructuralists (who, following the philosophy of Jacques Derrida, argue that texts are inevitably self-contradictory and that we can find form in them only by ignoring or suppressing conflicting details or elements). In retrospect it is clear that, their outspoken opposition to the New Criticism notwithstanding, the reader-response critics and poststructuralists of the 1970s were very much *like* their formalist predecessors in two important respects: for the most part, they ignored the world beyond the text and its reader, and, for the most part, they ignored the historical contexts within which literary works are written and read.

Jerome McGann first articulated this retrospective insight in 1985, writing that "a text-only approach has been so vigorously promoted during the last thirty-five years that most historical critics have been driven from the field, and have raised the flag of their surrender by yielding the title 'critic,' and accepting the title 'scholar' for themselves" (*Inflections* 17). Most, but not all. The American Marxist Fredric Jameson had begun his 1981 book *The Political Unconscious* with the following two-word challenge: "Always historicize!" (9). Beginning about 1980, a form of historical criticism practiced by Louis Montrose and Stephen Greenblatt had transformed the field of Renaissance studies and begun to influence the study of American and English Romantic literature as well. And by the mid-1980s, Brook Thomas was working on an essay in which he suggests that classroom discussions of Keats's "Ode on a Grecian Urn" might begin with questions such as the following: Where would Keats have seen such an urn? How did a Grecian urn end up in a museum in England? Some very important historical and political realities, Thomas suggests, lie behind and inform Keats's definitions of art, truth, beauty, the past, and timelessness.

When McGann lamented the surrender of "most historical critics," he no doubt realized what is now clear to everyone involved in the study of literature. Those who had *not* yet surrendered — had not yet "yield[ed] the title 'critic'" to the formalist, reader-response, and post-structuralist "victors" — were armed with powerful new arguments and intent on winning back long-lost ground. Indeed, at about the same time that McGann was deploring the near-complete dominance of critics advocating the text-only approach, Herbert Lindenberger was sounding a more hopeful note: "It comes as something of a surprise," he wrote in 1984, "to find that history is making a powerful comeback" ("New History" 16).

We now know that history was indeed making a powerful comeback in the 1980s, although the word is misleading if it causes us to imagine that the historical criticism being practiced in the 1980s by Greenblatt and Montrose, McGann and Thomas, was the same as the historical criticism that had been practiced in the 1930s and 1940s. Indeed, if the word "new" still serves any useful purpose in defining the historical criticism of today, it is in distinguishing it from the old historicism. The new historicism is informed by the poststructuralist and reader-response theory of the 1970s, plus the thinking of feminist, cultural, and Marxist critics whose work was also "new" in the 1980s. New historicist critics are less fact- and event-oriented than historical critics used to be, perhaps because they have come to wonder whether the truth about what really happened can ever be purely and objectively known. They are less likely to see history as linear and progressive, as something developing toward the present or the future ("teleological"), and they are also less likely to think of it in terms of specific eras, each with a definite, persistent, and consistent *Zeitgeist* ("spirit of the times"). Consequently, they are unlikely to suggest that a literary text has a single or easily identifiable historical context.

New historicist critics also tend to define the discipline of history more broadly than it was defined before the advent of formalism. They view history as a social science and the social sciences as being properly historical. In *Historical Studies and Literary Criticism* (1985), McGann speaks of the need to make "sociohistorical" subjects and methods central to literary studies; in *The Beauty of Inflections: Literary Investigations in Historical Method and Theory* (1985), he links sociology and the future of historical criticism. "A sociological poetics," he writes, "must be recognized not only as relevant to the analysis of poetry, but in fact as central to the analysis" (62). Lindenberger cites anthropology as particularly useful in the new historical analysis of literature, especially anthropology as practiced by Victor Turner and Clifford Geertz.

Geertz, who has related theatrical traditions in nineteenth-century Bali to forms of political organization that developed during the same period, has influenced some of the most important critics writing the new kind of historical criticism. Owing in large part to Geertz's anthropological influence, new historicists such as Greenblatt have asserted that literature is not a sphere apart or distinct from the history that is relevant to it. That is what the old criticism tended to do: present the background information you needed to know before you could fully appreciate the separate world of art. The new historicists have used what Geertz would call "thick description" to blur distinctions, not only between history and the other social sciences but also between background and foreground, historical and literary materials, political and poetical events. They have erased the old boundary line dividing historical and literary materials, showing that the production of one of Shakespeare's historical plays was a political act and historical event, while at the same time showing that the coronation of Elizabeth I was carried out with the same care for staging and symbol lavished on works of dramatic art.

In addition to breaking down barriers that separate literature and history, history and the social sciences, new historicists have reminded us that it is treacherously difficult to reconstruct the past as it really was, rather than as we have been conditioned by our own place and time to believe that it was. And they know that the job is utterly impossible for those who are unaware of that difficulty and insensitive to the bent or bias of their own historical vantage point. Historical criticism must be "conscious of its status as interpretation," Greenblatt has written (*Renaissance* 4). McGann obviously concurs, writing that "historical criticism can no longer make any part of [its] sweeping picture unselfconsciously, or treat any of its details in an untheorized way" (*Studies* 11).

Unselfconsciously and *untheorized* are the key words in McGann's statement. When new historicist critics of literature describe a historical change, they are highly conscious of, and even likely to discuss, the *theory* of historical change that informs their account. They know that the changes they happen to see and describe are the ones that their theory of change allows or helps them to see and describe. And they know, too, that their theory of change is historically determined. They seek to minimize the distortion inherent in their perceptions and representations by admitting that they see through preconceived notions;

in other words, they learn to reveal the color of the lenses in the glasses that they wear.

Nearly everyone who wrote on the new historicism during the 1980s cited the importance of the late Michel Foucault. A French philosophical historian who liked to think of himself as an archaeologist of human knowledge, Foucault brought together incidents and phenomena from areas of inquiry and orders of life that we normally regard as being unconnected. As much as anyone, he encouraged the new historicist critic of literature to redefine the boundaries of historical inquiry.

Foucault's views of history were influenced by the philosopher Friedrich Nietzsche's concept of a *wirkliche* ("real" or "true") history that is neither melioristic (that is, "getting better all the time") nor metaphysical. Like Nietzsche, Foucault didn't see history in terms of a continuous development toward the present. Neither did he view it as an abstraction, idea, or ideal, as something that began "In the beginning" and that will come to THE END, a moment of definite closure, a Day of Judgment. In his own words, Foucault "abandoned [the old history's] attempts to understand events in terms of . . . some great evolutionary process" (*Discipline and Punish* 129). He warned a new generation of historians to be aware of the fact that investigators are themselves "situated." It is difficult, he reminded them, to see present cultural practices critically from within them, and because of the same cultural practices, it is extremely difficult to enter bygone ages. In *Discipline and Punish: The Birth of the Prison* (1975), Foucault admitted that his own interest in the past was fueled by a passion to write the history of the present.

Like Marx, Foucault saw history in terms of power, but his view of power probably owed more to Nietzsche than to Marx. Foucault seldom viewed power as a repressive force. He certainly did not view it as a tool of conspiracy used by one specific individual or institution against another. Rather, power represents a whole web or complex of forces; it is that which produces what happens. Not even a tyrannical aristocrat simply wields power, for the aristocrat is himself formed and empowered by a network of discourses and practices that constitute power. Viewed by Foucault, power is "positive and productive," not "repressive" and "prohibitive" (Smart 63). Furthermore, no historical event, according to Foucault, has a single cause; rather, it is intricately connected with a vast web of economic, social, and political factors.

A brief sketch of one of Foucault's major works may help to clarify some of his ideas. *Discipline and Punish* begins with a shocking but accurate description of the public drawing and quartering of a Frenchman who had botched his attempt to assassinate King Louis XV in 1757. Foucault proceeds by describing rules governing the daily life of modern Parisian felons. What happened to torture, to punishment as public spectacle? he asks. What complex network of forces made it disappear? In working toward a picture of this "power," Foucault turns up many interesting puzzle pieces, such as the fact that in the early years of the nineteenth century, crowds would sometimes identify with the prisoner and treat the executioner as if *he* were the guilty party. But Foucault sets forth a related reason for keeping prisoners alive, moving punishment indoors, and changing discipline from physical torture into mental rehabilitation: colonization. In this historical period, people were needed to establish colonies and trade, and prisoners could be used for that purpose. Also, because these were politically unsettled times, governments needed infiltrators and informers. Who better to fill those roles than prisoners pardoned or released early for showing a willingness to be rehabilitated? As for rehabilitation itself, Foucault compares it with the old form of punishment, which began with a torturer extracting a confession. In more modern, "reasonable" times, psychologists probe the minds of prisoners with a scientific rigor that Foucault sees as a different kind of torture, a kind that our modern perspective does not allow us to see as such.

Thus, a change took place, but perhaps not as great a change as we generally assume. It may have been for the better or for the worse; the point is that agents of power didn't make the change because mankind is evolving and, therefore, more prone to perform good-hearted deeds. Rather, different objectives arose, including those of a new class of doctors and scientists bent on studying aberrant examples of the human mind. And where do we stand vis-à-vis the history Foucault tells? We are implicated by it, for the evolution of discipline as punishment into the study of the human mind includes the evolution of the "disciplines" as we now understand that word, including the discipline of history, the discipline of literary study, and now a discipline that is neither and both, a form of historical criticism that from the vantage point of the 1980s looked "new."

Foucault's type of analysis has been practiced by a number of literary critics at the vanguard of the back-to-history movement. One of them is Greenblatt, who along with Montrose was to a great extent responsible for transforming Renaissance studies in the early 1980s and revitalizing historical criticism in the process. Greenblatt follows Foucault's lead in interpreting literary devices as if they were continuous with all other representational devices in a culture; he therefore turns to scholars in other fields in order to better understand the workings of literature. "We wall off literary symbolism from the symbolic structures operative elsewhere," he writes, "as if art alone were a human creation, as if humans themselves were not, in Clifford Geertz's phrase, cultural artifacts" (*Renaissance* 4).

Greenblatt's name, more than anyone else's, is synonymous with the new historicism; his essay entitled "Invisible Bullets" (1981) has been said by Patrick Brantlinger to be "perhaps the most frequently cited example of New Historicist work" ("Cultural Studies" 45). An English professor at the University of California, Berkeley — the early academic home of the new historicism — Greenblatt was a founding editor of *Representations*, a journal published by the University of California Press that is still considered today to be *the* mouthpiece of the new historicism.

In *Learning to Curse* (1990), Greenblatt cites as central to his own intellectual development his decision to interrupt his literary education at Yale University by accepting a Fulbright fellowship to study in England at Cambridge University. There he came under the influence of the great Marxist cultural critic Raymond Williams, who made Greenblatt realize how much — and what — was missing from his Yale education. "In Williams' lectures," Greenblatt writes, "all that had been carefully excluded from the literary criticism in which I had been trained — who controlled access to the printing press, who owned the land and the factories, whose voices were being repressed as well as represented in literary texts, what social strategies were being served by the aesthetic values we constructed — came pressing back in upon the act of interpretation" (2).

Greenblatt returned to the United States determined not to exclude such matters from his own literary investigations. Blending what he had learned from Williams with poststructuralist thought about the indeterminacy or "undecidability" of meaning, he eventually developed a critical method that he now calls "cultural poetics." More tentative and less overtly political than cultural criticism, it involves what Thomas calls "the technique of montage. Starting with the analysis of a particular historical event, it cuts to the analysis of a particular literary text. The point is not to show that the literary text reflects the historical event but to create a field of energy between the two so that we come to see the event as a social text and the literary text as a social event" ("New Literary

Historicism" 490). Alluding to deconstructor Jacques Derrida's assertion that "there is nothing outside the text," Montrose explains that the goal of this new historicist criticism is to show the "historicity of texts and the textuality of history" (Veeser 20).

The relationship between the cultural poetics practiced by a number of new historicists and the cultural criticism associated with Marxism is important not only because of the proximity of the two approaches but also because one must recognize the difference between the two to understand the new historicism. Still very much a part of the contemporary critical scene, cultural criticism (sometimes called "cultural studies" or "cultural critique") nonetheless involves several tendencies more compatible with the old historicism than with the thinking of new historicists such as Greenblatt. These include the tendency to believe that history is driven by economics; that it is determinable even as it determines the lives of individuals; and that it is progressive, its dialectic one that will bring about justice and equality.

Greenblatt does not privilege economics in his analyses and views individuals as agents possessing considerable productive power. (He says that "the work of art is the product of a negotiation between a creator or class of creators . . . and the institutions and practices of a society" [*Learning* 158]: he also acknowledges that artistic productions are "intensely marked by the private obsessions of individuals," however much they may result from "collective negotiation and exchange" [*Negotiations* vii].) His optimism about the individual, however, should not be confused with optimism about either history's direction or any historian's capacity to foretell it. Like a work of art, a work of history is the negotiated product of a private creator and the public practices of a given society.

This does not mean that Greenblatt does not discern historical change, or that he is uninterested in describing it. Indeed, in works from *Renaissance Self-Fashioning* (1980) to *Shakespearean Negotiations* (1988), he has written about Renaissance changes in the development of both literary characters and real people. But his view of change — like his view of the individual — is more Foucauldian than Marxist. That is to say, it is not melioristic or teleological. And, like Foucault, Greenblatt is careful to point out that any one change is connected with a host of others, no one of which may simply be identified as cause or effect, progressive or regressive, repressive or enabling.

Not all of the critics trying to lead students of literature back to history are as Foucauldian as Greenblatt. Some even owe more to

Marx than to Foucault. Others, like Thomas, have clearly been more influenced by Walter Benjamin, best known for essays such as "Theses on the Philosophy of History" and "The Work of Art in the Age of Mechanical Reproduction." Still others — McGann, for example — have followed the lead of Soviet critic M. M. Bakhtin, who viewed literary works in terms of discourses and dialogues between the official, legitimate voices of a society and other, more challenging or critical voices echoing popular or traditional culture. In the "polyphonic" writings of Rabelais, for instance, Bakhtin found that the profane language of Carnival and other popular festivals offsets and parodies the "legitimate" discourses representing the outlook of the king, church, and socially powerful intellectuals of the day.

Moreover, there are other reasons not to consider Foucault the single or even central influence on the new historicism. First, he critiqued the old-style historicism to such an extent that he ended up being antihistorical, or at least ahistorical, in the view of a number of new historicists. Second, his commitment to a radical remapping of the relations of power and influence, cause and effect, may have led him to adopt too cavalier an attitude toward chronology and facts. Finally, the very act of identifying and labeling *any* primary influence goes against the grain of the new historicism. Its practitioners have sought to "decenter" the study of literature, not only by overlapping it with historical studies (broadly defined to include anthropology and sociology) but also by struggling to see history from a decentered perspective. That struggle has involved recognizing (1) that the historian's cultural and historical position may not afford the best purview of a given set of events and (2) that events seldom have any single or central cause. In keeping with these principles, it may be appropriate to acknowledge Foucault as just one of several powerful, interactive intellectual forces rather than to declare him the single, master influence.

Throughout the 1980s it seemed to many that the ongoing debates about the sources of the new historicist movement, the importance of Marx or Foucault, Walter Benjamin or Mikhail Bakhtin, and the exact locations of all the complex boundaries between the new historicism and other "isms" (Marxism and poststructuralism, to name only two) were historically contingent functions of the new historicism *newness*. In the initial stages of their development, new intellectual movements are difficult to outline clearly because, like partially developed photographic images, they are themselves fuzzy and lacking in definition. They respond to disparate influences and include thinkers who represent a wide range of backgrounds; like movements that are disintegrating, they inevitably include a broad spectrum of opinions and positions.

From the vantage point of the 1990s, however, it seems that the inchoate quality of the new historicism is characteristic rather than a function of newness. The boundaries around the new historicism remain fuzzy not because it hasn't reached its full maturity but because, if it is to live up to its name, it must always be subject to revision and redefinition as historical circumstances change. The fact that so many critics we label new historicist are working right at the border of Marxist, poststructuralist, cultural, postcolonial, feminist, and now even a new form of reader-response (or at least reader-oriented) criticism is evidence of the new historicism's multiple interests and motivations, rather than of its embryonic state.

New historicists themselves advocate and even stress the need to perpetually redefine categories and boundaries — whether they be disciplinary, generic, national, or racial — not because definitions are unimportant but because they are historically constructed and thus subject to revision. If new historicists like Thomas and reader-oriented critics like Steven Mailloux and Peter Rabinowitz seem to spend most of their time talking over the low wall separating their respective fields, then maybe the wall is in the wrong place. As Catherine Gallagher has suggested, the boundary between new historicists and feminists studying "people and phenomena that once seemed insignificant, indeed outside of history: women, criminals, the insane" often turns out to be shifting or even nonexistent (Veeser 43).

If the fact that new historicists all seem to be working on the border of another school should not be viewed as a symptom of the new historicism's newness (or disintegration); neither should it be viewed as evidence that new historicists are intellectual loners or divisive outriders who enjoy talking over walls to people in other fields but who share no common views among themselves. Greenblatt, McGann, and Thomas all started with the assumption that works of literature are simultaneously influenced by and influencing reality, broadly defined. Whatever their disagreements, they share a belief in referentiality — a belief that literature refers to and is referred to by things outside itself — stronger than that found in the works of formalist, poststructuralist, and even reader-response critics. They believe with Greenblatt that the "central concerns" of criticism "should prevent it from permanently sealing off one type of discourse from another or decisively separating works of art from the minds and lives of their creators and their audiences" (*Renaissance* 5).

McGann, in his introduction to *Historical Studies and Literary Criticism*, turns referentiality into a rallying cry:

What will not be found in these essays . . . is the assumption, so common in text-centered studies of every type, that literary works are self-enclosed verbal constructs, or looped intertextual fields of autonomous signifiers and signifieds. In these essays, the question of referentiality is once again brought to the fore. (3)

In "Keats and the Historical Method in Literary Criticism," he suggests a set of basic, scholarly procedures to be followed by those who have rallied to the cry. These procedures, which he claims are "practical derivatives of the Bakhtin school," assume that historicist critics will study a literary work's "point of origin" by studying biography and bibliography. The critic must then consider the expressed intentions of the author, because, if printed, these intentions have also modified the developing history of the work. Next, the new historicist must learn the history of the work's reception, as that body of opinion has become part of the platform on which we are situated when we study the work at our own particular "point of reception." Finally, McGann urges the new historicist critic to point toward the future, toward his or her *own* audience, defining for its members the aims and limits of the critical project and injecting the analysis with a degree of self-consciousness that alone can give it credibility (*Inflections* 62).

In his introduction to a collection of new historical writings on *The New Historicism* (1989), H. Aram Veeser stresses the unity among new historicists, not by focusing on common critical procedures but, rather, by outlining five "key assumptions" that "continually reappear and bind together the avowed practitioners and even some of their critics":

1. that every expressive act is embedded in a network of material practices;
2. that every act of unmasking, critique, and opposition uses the tools it condemns and risks falling prey to the practice it exposes;
3. that literary and non-literary texts circulate inseparably;
4. that no discourse, imaginative or archival, gives access to unchanging truths nor expresses inalterable human nature;
5. finally, . . . that a critical method and a language adequate to describe culture under capitalism participate in the economy they describe. (xi)

These same assumptions are shared by a group of historians practicing what is now commonly referred to as "the new cultural history."

Influenced by *Annales*-school historians in France, post-Althusserian Marxists, and Foucault, these historians share with their new historicist counterparts not only many of the same influences and assumptions but also the following: an interest in anthropological and sociological subjects and methods; a creative way of weaving stories and anecdotes about the past into revealing thick descriptions; a tendency to focus on nontraditional, noncanonical subjects and relations (historian Thomas Laqueur is best known for *Making Sex: Body and Gender from the Greeks to Freud* [1990]); and some of the same journals and projects.

Thus, in addition to being significantly unified by their own interests, assumptions, and procedures, new historicist literary critics have participated in a broader, interdisciplinary movement toward unification virtually unprecedented within and across academic disciplines. Their tendency to work along disciplinary borderlines, far from being evidence of their factious or fractious tendencies, has been precisely what has allowed them to engage historians in a conversation certain to revolutionize the way in which we understand the past, present, and future.

In the essay that follows, Russell A. Berman maintains that, "from its opening lines, *Death in Venice* invites us to reflect on the multifaceted relationship between literature and history." Gustav Aschenbach, a writer who resembles both his author and other artists of the period, is also a fictional protagonist characterized via numerous literary allusions. (Mann most famously alludes to Friedrich Nietzsche's *Birth of Tragedy,* in which Nietzsche distinguished between the Apollonian tendency toward order and reason and the competing Dionysian tendency toward disorder and unreason.) We meet Aschenbach as he sets out from his apartment for a walk during a year in which, we are told, the peace of Europe is gravely threatened. Does Aschenbach, a character whose inner peace is threatened, personify a whole continent in grave trouble? If so, can his subsequent "demise on the beach in Venice" be viewed as a foreshadowing of World War I, the historical "catastrophe that would soon befall the Continent"? In posing such questions, Berman suggests, the text forces us to consider "the relationship between the external and the personal, between the political and the private," and, ultimately, between the ethical and the aesthetic. It also invites us to practice new historicist reading, which is interested not only in "what a work might have meant in a temporally distant context" but also in "what light it sheds on what has transpired in the interim."

Much as the novella's protagonist, Aschenbach, seems at once a fictional individual and the personification of Europe, so Venice seems at once the setting of Mann's story and a symbol of his all too real and increasingly volatile continent. In Venice, Mann writes, "one saw the dry elongated visages of Americans, many-membered Russian families, English ladies, German children with French nurses." We also see ethnic Italians from the Austrian territory of Istria cheering Italian soldiers in a park, and we watch as Tadzio, a young Pole, glowers at a Russian family. "Thus," Berman writes, "the text lays the groundwork for the bitter fighting that would soon take place between Italy and Austria" and reminds us that "czarist Russia occupied large parts of what would become an independent Poland after World War I."

Having made this connection between Venice and Europe, Berman returns his focus to Aschenbach, whom he identifies as a particular kind of German, a Prussian, not only because of his Silesian background but also because of his "ethic of discipline." Aschenbach is an artist who thinks of himself as a soldier, a writer whose model is Frederick the Great. Berman even attributes to his Prussian history and heritage Aschenbach's failure to side with Tadzio against the Russians. He explains that Prussia, like Russia, had "carved out a piece of Polish territory, and Aschenbach's writings implicate him in this imperial undertaking." Connecting him not just to Prussian imperialism but to European imperialism more generally, Berman argues that Aschenbach's "vision of a tropical jungle" and, later, of a "crouching tiger" involve typical European images of "the non-European world during the age of colonialism."

As Berman develops his argument, he deals not only with the historical contexts of Mann's novella but also with the history of the novel's reception. He points out that most critics have viewed *Death in Venice*, as a "narrative of decay," a novel about abandoning the Prussian, Protestant, Apollonian work ethic and, in Erich Heller's phrase, "dying in the embrace of Dionysus." Critics taking this view have often pointed to a shift in the narrator's attitude toward Aschenbach from an essentially positive and sympathetic outlook to a basically ironic and critical one. Berman, however, questions the notion that Aschenbach succumbs, in the end, to Dionysian temptation, arguing instead that Aschenbach makes an "ultimately ethical decision to refrain from acting on a desire incompatible with social norms and 'the moral law' that the narrator has just accused him of abandoning."

By focusing on narrative structures and strategies, Berman proves himself to be a new — rather than an old-style — historicist. As he points out in the first pages of his essay, whereas historical critics of previous generations "studied the 'lives and times' of authors," eschewing questions of form and structure, "contemporary historicist criticism is hardly blind to textual complexities." Berman also shows himself to be a new historicist insofar as he is interested in his own — in our own — historically determined vantage point. He freely admits that his reading of the novella's conclusion clashes with any number of historically sanctioned readings. If he is wrong, then, as he himself points out, we may continue to read the novella both as the story of one man's moral failure and as the story of Germany's and Europe's fall into World War I (and, for that matter, World War II). But if he is right, then Aschenbach achieves a moral victory that exemplifies the ability to reject immorality "thanks to an internal strength of character derived from the . . . Prussian-Protestant tradition."

Berman makes his new historicist case for a new reading of *Death in Venice* with clarity and confidence. But he stops short of claiming the sort of objective certainty found in some old-style historical approaches to literature. Berman leaves his readers to judge both the validity of his approach and the conclusions to which that approach has led. Like other new historicists, he expects that his text, just like Mann's, will be subject to reappraisal over time.

Ross C Murfin

THE NEW HISTORICISM: A SELECTED BIBLIOGRAPHY

The New Historicism: Further Reading

Brantlinger, Patrick. "Cultural Studies vs. the New Historicism." *English Studies/Cultural Studies: Institutionalizing Dissent.* Ed. Isaiah Smithson and Nancy Ruff. Urbana: U of Illinois P, 1994. 43–58.

Cox, Jeffrey N., and Larry J. Reynolds, eds. *New Historical Literary Study.* Princeton: Princeton UP, 1993.

Dimock, Wai-Chee. "Feminism, New Historicism, and the Reader." *American Literature* 63 (1991): 601–22.

Howard, Jean. "The New Historicism in Renaissance Studies." *English Literary Renaissance* 16 (1986): 13–43.

Lindenberger, Herbert. *The History in Literature: On Value, Genre, Institutions.* New York: Columbia UP, 1990.

———. "Toward a New History in Literary Study." *Profession: Selected Articles from the Bulletins of the Association of Departments of English and the Association of the Departments of Foreign Languages.* New York: MLA, 1984. 16–23.

Liu, Alan. "The Power of Formalism: The New Historicism." *English Literary History* 56 (1989): 721–71.

McGann, Jerome. *The Beauty of Inflections: Literary Investigations in Historical Method and Theory.* Oxford: Clarendon–Oxford UP, 1985.

———. *Historical Studies and Literary Criticism.* Madison: U of Wisconsin P, 1985. See especially the introduction and the essays in the following sections: "Historical Methods and Literary Interpretations" and "Biographical Contexts and the Critical Object."

Montrose, Louis Adrian. "Renaissance Literary Studies and the Subject of History." *English Literary Renaissance* 16 (1986): 5–12.

Morris, Wesley. *Toward a New Historicism.* Princeton: Princeton UP, 1972.

New Literary History 21 (1990). "History and . . . " (special issue). See especially the essays by Carolyn Porter, Rena Fraden, Clifford Geertz, and Renato Rosaldo.

Representations. This quarterly journal, printed by the University of California Press, regularly publishes new historicist studies and cultural criticism.

Thomas, Brook. "The Historical Necessity for — and Difficulties with — New Historical Analysis in Introductory Courses." *College English* 49 (1987): 509–22.

———. *The New Historicism and Other Old-Fashioned Topics.* Princeton: Princeton UP, 1991.

———. "The New Literary Historicism." *A Companion to American Thought.* Ed. Richard Wightman Fox and James T. Klappenberg. New York: Basil Blackwell, 1995.

———. "Walter Benn Michaels and the New Historicism: Where's the Difference?" *Boundary 2* 18 (1991): 118–59.

Veeser, H. Aram, ed. *The New Historicism.* New York: Routledge, 1989. See especially Veeser's introduction, Louis Montrose's "Professing the Renaissance," Catherine Gallagher's "Marxism and the New Historicism," and Frank Lentricchia's "Foucault's Legacy: A New Historicism?"

Wayne, Don E. "Power, Politics, and the Shakespearean Text: Recent Criticism in England and the United States." *Shakespeare Reproduced: The Text in History and Ideology.* Ed. Jean Howard and Marion O'Connor. New York: Methuen, 1987. 47–67.

Winn, James A. "An Old Historian Looks at the New Historicism." *Comparative Studies in Society and History* 35 (1993): 859–70.

The New Historicism: Influential Examples

The new historicism has taken its present form less through the elaboration of basic theoretical postulates and more through certain influential examples. The works listed represent some of the most important contributions guiding research in this area.

Bercovitch, Sacvan. *The Rites of Assent: Transformations in the Symbolic Construction of America*. New York: Routledge, 1993.

Brown, Gillian. *Domestic Individualism: Imagining Self in Nineteenth-Century America*. Berkeley: U of California P, 1990.

Dollimore, Jonathan. *Radical Tragedy: Religion, Ideology, and Power in the Drama of Shakespeare and His Contemporaries*. Brighton, Eng.: Harvester, 1984.

Dollimore, Jonathan, and Alan Sinfield, eds. *Political Shakespeare: New Essays in Cultural Materialism*. Manchester, Eng.: Manchester UP, 1985. This volume occupies the borderline between new historicist and cultural criticism. See especially the essays by Dollimore, Greenblatt, and Tennenhouse.

Gallagher, Catherine. *The Industrial Reformation of English Fiction*. Chicago: U of Chicago P, 1985.

Goldberg, Jonathan. *James I and the Politics of Literature*. Baltimore: Johns Hopkins UP, 1983.

Greenblatt, Stephen J. *Learning to Curse: Essays in Early Modern Culture*. New York: Routledge, 1990.

———. *Marvelous Possessions: The Wonder of the New World*. Chicago: U of Chicago P, 1991.

———. *Renaissance Self-Fashioning from More to Shakespeare*. Chicago: U of Chicago P, 1980. See chapter 1 and the chapter on *Othello*, "The Improvisation of Power."

———. *Shakespearean Negotiations: The Circulation of Social Energy in Renaissance England*. Berkeley: U of California P, 1988. See especially "The Circulation of Social Energy" and "Invisible Bullets."

Liu, Alan. *Wordsworth, the Sense of History*. Stanford: Stanford UP, 1989.

Marcus, Leah. *Puzzling Shakespeare: Local Reading and Its Discontents*. Berkeley: U of California P, 1988.

McGann, Jerome. *The Romantic Ideology.* Chicago: U of Chicago P, 1983.

Michaels, Walter Benn. *The Gold Standard and the Logic of Naturalism: American Literature at the Turn of the Century.* Berkeley: U of California P, 1987.

Montrose, Louis Adrian. "'Shaping Fantasies': Figurations of Gender and Power in Elizabethan Culture." *Representations* 2 (1983): 61–94. One of the most influential early new historicist essays.

Mullaney, Steven. *The Place of the Stage: License, Play, and Power in Renaissance England.* Chicago: U of Chicago P, 1987.

Orgel, Stephen. *The Illusion of Power: Political Theater in the English Renaissance.* Berkeley: U of California P, 1975.

Sinfield, Alan. *Literature, Politics, and Culture in Postwar Britain.* Berkeley: U of California P, 1989.

Tennenhouse, Leonard. *Power on Display: The Politics of Shakespeare's Genres.* New York: Methuen, 1986.

Foucault and His Influence

As I point out in the introduction to the new historicism, some new historicists would question the "privileging" of Foucault implicit in this section heading ("Foucault and His Influence") and the following one ("Other Writers and Works"). They might cite the greater importance of one of those other writers or point out that to cite a central influence or a definitive cause runs against the very spirit of the movement.

Foucault, Michel. *The Archaeology of Knowledge.* Trans. A. M. Sheridan Smith. New York: Harper, 1972.

———. *Discipline and Punish: The Birth of the Prison.* 1975. Trans. Alan Sheridan. New York: Pantheon, 1978.

———. *The History of Sexuality,* Vol. 1. Trans. Robert Hurley. New York: Pantheon, 1978.

———. *Language, Counter-Memory, Practice.* Ed. Donald F. Bouchard. Trans. Donald F. Bouchard and Sherry Simon. Ithaca: Cornell UP, 1977.

———. *The Order of Things: An Archaeology of the Human Sciences.* New York: Vintage, 1973.

———. *Politics, Philosophy, Culture.* Ed. Lawrence D. Kritzman. Trans. Alan Sheridan et al. New York: Routledge, 1988.

————. *Power/Knowledge*. Ed. Colin Gordon. Trans. Colin Gordon et al. New York: Pantheon, 1980.

————. *Technologies of the Self*. Ed. Luther H. Martin, Huck Gutman, and Patrick H. Hutton. Amherst: U of Massachusetts P, 1988.

Dreyfus, Hubert L., and Paul Rabinow. *Michel Foucault: Beyond Structuralism and Hermeneutics*. Chicago: U of Chicago P, 1983.

Sheridan, Alan. *Michel Foucault: The Will to Truth*. New York: Tavistock, 1980.

Smart, Barry. *Michel Foucault*. New York: Ellis Horwood and Tavistock, 1985.

Other Writers and Works of Interest to New Historicist Critics

Bakhtin, M. M. *The Dialogic Imagination: Four Essays*. Ed. Michael Holquist. Trans. Caryl Emerson. Austin: U of Texas P, 1981. Bakhtin wrote many influential studies on subjects as varied as Dostoyevsky, Rabelais, and formalist criticism. But this book, in part due to Holquist's helpful introduction, is probably the best place to begin reading Bakhtin.

Benjamin, Walter. "The Work of Art in the Age of Mechanical Reproduction." 1936. *Illuminations*. Ed. Hannah Arendt. Trans. Harry Zohn. New York: Harcourt, 1968.

Fried, Michael. *Absorption and Theatricality: Painting and Beholder in the Works of Diderot*. Berkeley: U of California P, 1980.

Geertz, Clifford. *The Interpretation of Cultures*. New York: Basic, 1973.

————. *Negara: The Theatre State in Nineteenth-Century Bali*. Princeton: Princeton UP, 1980.

Goffman, Erving. *Frame Analysis*. New York: Harper, 1974.

Jameson, Fredric. *The Political Unconscious*. Ithaca: Cornell UP, 1981.

Koselleck, Reinhart. *Futures Past*. Trans. Keith Tribe. Cambridge: MIT P, 1985.

Said, Edward. *Orientalism*. New York: Columbia UP, 1978.

Turner, Victor. *The Ritual Process: Structure and Anti-Structure*. Chicago: Aldine, 1969.

Young, Robert. *White Mythologies: Writing History and the West*. New York: Routledge, 1990.

A NEW HISTORICIST PERSPECTIVE

RUSSELL A. BERMAN

History and Community in *Death in Venice*

During recent decades literary critics have increasingly chosen to
approach texts by scrutinizing their historical standing. This "new"
history represents a significant break with the formalist methods associated with the once "New" Criticism, which flourished during the
middle of the century and directed attention to the internal structures
of literature rather than to contextual matters. Critics treated such
contexts, somewhat derisively, as merely "extrinsic" to the work of art.
The recent historicist turn has also, however, proliferated in competition with the neoformalism of deconstructive criticism, which, when
strictly pursued, addresses only the linguistic ambivalences of literary
texts rather than their cultural or institutional embeddedness, the
purview of historical criticism.

Yet contemporary historicist criticism is hardly blind to textual
complexities. On the contrary, it continues to assimilate intellectual
questions posed by a range of critical schools, and this contributes to
its distinctiveness from the older historiographical methods of literary
scholarship of the early twentieth century. Those positivist scholars
were concerned often with the collection and ordering of manuscripts
and the determination of the historical data around the production of
works, which they thereby ensconced as elements of national literary
historical canons. In addition, scholars studied the "lives and times" of
authors with an eye to alleged "influences" that they found in the
works; the underlying vision presumed a deterministic relationship between external factors and literary facts.

In contrast, contemporary historical criticism asks much more
complex questions regarding a text's participation in wider cultural
discourses, positing a dynamic relationship between text and context.
Moreover, in the wake of reader-response theory, the historicity of the
reception process becomes urgent — that is, the text is understood as
implicated both in the context of its production (when the author
wrote it) as well as in the context of its subsequent receptions, including our current reading. Therefore a historical reading should not only
ask what a work might have meant in a temporally distant context but
also why it can continue to interest us today, and what light it sheds

on what has transpired in the interim. We now understand history to entail several concurrent temporalities rather than a uniform or universal time in which older historicism might have neatly shelved away a text. Criticism today explores the multiple and often conflicting levels of time within a text in order to understand both its position within contemporary discourses and its own history through the course of time.

From its opening lines, *Death in Venice* invites us to reflect on the multifaceted relationships between literature and history. "On a spring afternoon in 19 —— , the year in which for months on end so grave a threat seemed to hang over the peace of Europe, Gustav Aschenbach, or von Aschenbach as he had been officially known since his fiftieth birthday, had set out from his apartment on the Prinzregentenstrasse in Munich to take a walk of some length by himself" (23). Despite the conventional conceit of using an ambiguous date ("19 —— "), the novella has begun with a reference to time — indeed, to a very specific moment in time, although the text identifies this moment as standing at the intersection of two distinct temporal levels. On the one hand, the reference to a political threat, presumably one of the several foreign policy crises that led Europe into World War I very soon after the publication of the text, sets a larger historical context; on the other hand, we learn of the mundane fact — Aschenbach's starting out on a stroll. In addition, political time and personal time explicitly converge in the report that he "had been officially known since his fiftieth birthday" as von Aschenbach — that is, he had received a title of nobility. The "von," of course, is part of the characterization of Aschenbach as a representative of the cultural and political establishment, and the subsequent tale involves the steady erosion of that status. At the outset, however, the issue is the confluence of personal and political temporalities and their relationship to each other, and the same problem recurs close to the end, as Aschenbach struggles to the beach on his last morning, fraught with despair, "though he could not decide whether this [feeling of hopelessness and pointlessness] referred to the external world or to his personal existence" (86). What is the relationship between the external and the personal, between the political and the private? And if Aschenbach's individual life is set, from the beginning, in an emphatic relationship to European developments, is *Death in Venice* therefore suggesting that Aschenbach's demise on the beach in Venice stands as a prediction for the catastrophe that would soon befall the Continent? In that case, what might appear to be a story concerned with largely literary issues — a writer with a block, his abstruse aesthetic concerns, and a private infatuation — would turn into a radical reflection on highly political matters.

To ask about Aschenbach and Europe is, of course, to ask about the relationship between literature and history, as if the early-twentieth-century novella were itself already a reflection on the new historicism of the end of the century. Needless to say, *Death in Venice* and this literary-critical practice are separated by cataclysmic decades, for Europe and especially for the Germany with which Aschenbach's character is tightly intertwined. The century has also witnessed dramatic changes with regard to the status of literature and culture within society: during the past eighty years, the history of modernism, the flourishing of cinema and other new media, the growth of a commercialized culture industry, and a general secularization of values have all contributed to the near extinction of the type of author, represented by Aschenbach, who commanded respect as an arbiter of public morality. Indeed, today we think of writers and artists more often as outsiders and as adversarial critics of public values rather than as their standard-bearers. Yet our own distance from Aschenbach's world can help us explore the internal logic of *Death in Venice*, especially when we proceed from the problem posed at the outset: the relationship between the writer and society, between subjective experience and objective structures, and — this is the philosophical theme of the novella — between aesthetics and ethics.

Aesthetics, in this context, denotes the practices of the artist in the imaginative realm, whereas ethics points to the rules of life in a social community. *Death in Venice* crosses back and forth between life and art in the explicit sense that there is much in the novella, particularly in the description of Aschenbach, that draws directly from Mann's own experience. We know that Mann vacationed on the Lido and that, like Aschenbach, he penned an important short essay on the beach, and a Polish aristocrat has even offered testimony that he had been the model for Tadzio decades earlier. We know that Mann, again like Aschenbach, was concerned with questions of mastery, for the detailed list of Aschenbach's writings correspond to works already published or planned by Mann. Even a quotation attributed by the narrator to Aschenbach — "that all the great things that exist owe their existence to a defiant despite"(30) — is in fact an excerpt from a minor essay by Mann himself. Has Mann merely transformed his own life into art?

For all of this aestheticizing of autobiography, there is still much in the novella of other provenance that disallows any neat equation of author and hero (or, as we will see, even author and narrator). The detailed description of Aschenbach's physiognomy evokes another

Gustav, the composer Gustav Mahler who died in 1911, while the contemporary public readily recognized the site of the story, Venice, as the real location of the death of a further musical figure, Richard Wagner, in 1883. The extensive network of material from Greek mythology — in particular the association of Tadzio with Apollo and the appearance of Dionysus in the dream — stems from Friedrich Nietzsche's *Birth of Tragedy from the Spirit of Music* (1872), which is both a brash history of Greek culture and a manifesto of modern art. Meanwhile, behind this network lies a further layer of cultural history, an engagement with the most prominent author of German literary history, Johann Wolfgang von Goethe. At a critical moment in his career, he traveled to Italy to escape the formalism of the Weimar court and to rediscover a classical balance of beauty. Moreover, we know that the project that became *Death in Venice* began as a plan to treat the old Goethe's love for a young woman; in a similar vein, the early reference to Aschenbach's fiftieth birthday recalls Goethe's novella, *A Man of Fifty*, which describes how a mature officer falls in love with his much younger niece.

The complexity of the historical construction is beginning to become apparent. Mann appropriates and weaves his personal history into a thick intertextuality of cultural-historical references. In addition to the individual and general temporalities of the initial passage, the Nietzschean material represents the eruption of an archaic mythic time into the mundane present — a structure that bears comparison with similar archaism in the works of other modernist authors. The combination of naturalistic description with symbolic types is both a stylistic transition in Mann's own career and evidence of a radically new temporality: the past is never completely over, for ancient Greece may suddenly protrude into everyday exchanges, and the present, a dimension of potentiality fraught with dreams, is not fully present, as its mythic symbols always point to other dimensions. Meanwhile, as the novella's analysis of Aschenbach, character and soul, approaches the equally mythological realm of Freudian psychoanalysis, it draws on a larger canon of German literary history. Goethe and Schiller are also present, and the judgment on Aschenbach, as we will see, grows into a verdict on German culture and its prospects.

The first sentence of the text has asked us to pay attention to the wider historical context of continental affairs, for this story of the paradigmatic German author takes place in a larger frame of international relations. Later we find that Aschenbach is delighted by the cosmopolitan clientele at his hotel: "Discreetly muted, the sounds of the

major world languages mingled. . . . One saw the dry elongated visages of Americans, many-membered Russian families, English ladies,
German children with French nurses. The Slav component seemed to
predominate" (43). The wide horizon contrasts sharply with the insu-
lar life that Aschenbach had led in Munich or, even more so, with the
isolated Alpine retreat where he would normally have spent the summer. Yet this superficially placid internationality cannot fully muffle the
warning of an impending political crisis, announced at the beginning
as the threat hanging over Europe and lingering like a foreboding
cloud on the horizon of the narration. After all, this is the last moment
before the outbreak of World War I, and while one can hardly ascribe
to Mann prophetic powers, he was clearly astute enough to incorpo-
rate into the text explicit indications of the nationality crises that
would soon lead to a redrawing of the map of Europe.

Leaving Munich, Aschenbach first chose to vacation on an island
in the Adriatic off the Istrian coast, an Austrian territory "with colorful
ragged inhabitants speaking a wild unintelligible dialect" (34). The
imperialist character of the regime emerges clearly by the distinction
between tourists and locals and even more so by the otherwise unnec-
essary reference to a naval base (35). The European summer vacation
transpires on a militarized continent. Aschenbach quickly leaves the island and travels by boat to Venice. In this passage he encounters "the
goat-bearded man" (35), a satyr figure anticipating the later Dionysian
eruption, as well as an old man among the youths, foreshadowing Aschenbach's own pedophilic obsessions. Yet the youths themselves are
the important indicators of the historical situation. They appear at first
merely out for a pleasant trip with no further intention, innocence at
play: "The company on the upper deck consisted of a group of young
men, probably shop or office workers from Pola, a high-spirited party
about to set off on an excursion to Italy" (35). On their arrival, however, an unexpected metamorphosis takes place: "The young men
from Pola had come on deck, no doubt also patriotically attracted by
the military sound of bugle calls across the water from the direction of
the Public Garden; and elated by the Asti they had drunk, they began
cheering the *bersaglieri* as they drilled there in the park" (38). Ethnic
Italians from Istria, resentful of Hapsburg domination, arrive in
Venice, applaud the Italian soldiers, and celebrate the signs of the
newly established Italian nation. Thus the text lays the groundwork for
the bitter fighting that would soon take place between Italy and Austria during the war. Moreover, this historical material, with its weighty
political implication, interlocks with mythic time: Italian nationalism is

fully Dionysian when it emerges as music and with the help of sparkling wine.

Furthermore, another ethnic war is under way. Aschenbach watches Tadzio's reaction to a group of Russians on the beach:

> scarcely had he noticed the Russian family, as it sat there in contented concord and going about its natural business, than a storm of angry contempt gathered over his face. He frowned darkly, his lips pouted, a bitter grimace pulled them to one side and distorted his cheek; his brows were contracted in so deep a scowl that his eyes seemed to have sunk right in under their pressure, glaring forth a black message of hatred. He looked down, looked back again menacingly, then made with one shoulder an emphatic gesture of rejection as he turned his back and left his enemies behind him. (48–49)

Just as the Austro-Hungarian empire controlled much of the Balkans in 1911, czarist Russia occupied large parts of what would become an independent Poland after World War I and the establishment of new nation-states in the wake of the Versailles Treaty. Hence the Polish youth appears hateful toward the colonizing power; indeed, given the grace and beauty he radiates throughout the text, it is quite striking that Mann so underscores the nationalist enmity that distorts Tadzio's handsome features. Evidently the text is not particularly sympathetic to the representatives of national liberation, for the Italians are drunk, and Tadzio's Polish patriotism appears exaggerated, given the hardly critical account of the Russians.

Whatever the "political correctness" of those judgments, the text conveys evidence, albeit indirectly, of the tensions underlying the discreet cosmopolitanism of the hotel. The same tensions fueled the political crisis surrounding the narrative. Nevertheless it is remarkable that after the opening reference to those political tensions, neither the narrator nor Aschenbach elaborates on them, even though the author has filled the text with so much documentation of their urgency. This discrepancy highlights Aschenbach's refusal to consider politics, despite the fact that he has been introduced as a direct beneficiary of the political establishment; he is preoccupied with other matters, while a war is about to break out around him. Political indifference represents tacit support for the status quo, whatever it may be. Mann would later describe this "unpolitical" character as a constitutive element of German conservatism, part of the bourgeoisie's predemocratic accommodation with the power of the authoritarian state.

Death in Venice encodes another important aspect of the erosion of the prewar European order. Otherwise so enamored of Tadzio, Aschenbach refrains from siding with his Polish patriotism against the Russian "enemies"; in fact, in the context of the beach scene, this derogatory term ("enemies") has the rhetorical status of an overstatement that conveys an ironic distance from the boy's political passion: Mann or the narrator is holding Tadzio's politics at arm's length. This neutrality is deeply self-interested, however, for it was not only Russia that partook of the division of Poland at the end of the eighteenth century. Prussia — the core of what would later become unified Germany under Bismarck in 1871 — also carved out a piece of Polish territory, and Aschenbach's writings implicate him in this imperial undertaking. His most prominent work is, after all, a biography of Frederick II, king of Prussia, who consolidated the nation's military primacy in the middle of the eighteenth century and directed a crucial stage of the expansion into areas of Central and Eastern Europe. Aschenbach's personal genealogy compounds this ideological sympathy; born in the province of Silesia, precisely the area Frederick had conquered, he came from a family implicated in the political order: "His ancestors had been military officers, judges, government administrators; men who had spent their disciplined, decently austere life in the service of the king and the state" (28). In his own way, Aschenbach carries on this tradition; he is a German author not only by virtue of his language and public but also because of his ideological involvement with the agenda of German imperialism. Given the predominance of Prussia within prewar Germany and especially the proliferation of a historiography that ascribed German ascendancy to the legacy of Prussia and Frederick, this offspring of Prussian officials in Silesia was certainly not predisposed to sympathize with Polish independence. Hence Aschenbach notices Tadzio's political aspirations only in order to repress them. The aestheticization of Tadzio as a symbol of beauty proceeds on the basis of the displacement of the political discussion.

The imperialist horizon reaches much farther than Silesia and Istria. When Aschenbach first recognizes his desire to travel, he sinks into a vision of a tropical jungle, more exotic than anything he will encounter later. We may take the swampy landscape as an anticipation of the discovery that the cholera has spread from India. Similarly, his imagination of the "glinting eyes of a crouching tiger" (26) might point toward the iconography of Dionysus, frequently depicted on a tiger-drawn chariot. Above all, however, the passage gives significant evidence of a fascinated desire with the typical imagery of the non-European world during the age of colonialism: "his heart throbbed with terror and mysterious longing" (26) as he contemplates a primeval and barbaric landscape beyond the borders of civilizational order. Even in the provincial setting of Munich and its city park, a global process of imperialism intrudes in order to rip the author out of his repetitive routines and carry him off to confrontations with the unexpected. The text locates Venice less securely within Europe than at its border, open to foreign influences stretching far afield.

A latecomer to colonialist policies, Germany had recently acquired extensive possessions in Africa (including today's Namibia, Togo, and Tanzania) and in the South Pacific. This imperialist expansion was driven to a large extent by a competition with the other European powers, especially England, whose presence in India the text indicates in a British clerk's report on the cholera's origin in the Ganges delta. Eventually the same Versailles Treaty that would grant independence to Tadzio's Poland and push Austria out of the Adriatic also stripped defeated Germany of its colonies, redistributing them among the victorious parties in the war. The competition for colonies had certainly contributed to prewar political tensions and led some to see it as a crucial factor in unleashing the war. Writing in 1919, W. E. B. Du Bois commented on the militarization of Europe by arguing that "the only adequate cause of this preparation was conquest and conquest, not in Europe, but primarily among the darker peoples of Asia and Africa; conquest, not for assimilation and uplift, but for commerce and degradation. For this, and this mainly, did Europe gird herself at frightful cost for war" (Du Bois 46). Opponents of colonialism such as Du Bois felt bitter to see the war waged in the name of democracy leading to a redivison of colonial spoils, rather than to independence and self-government for the colonized nations. One major accomplishment of *Death in Venice* is to demonstrate the extremely labile network of national identities on the eve of World War I. The text also places this network within a contested structure of global imperialism, simultaneously analyzing a personality remarkably unwilling to reflect on precisely these political matters.

We may mine from the text still more elements of historical and political significance. For example, the class structure evident on the boat to Venice suggests that Italian nationalism was a solely middle-class phenomenon — a position quite comfortable for a German ally of the Austo-Hungarian empire. Even more critical of the Italian situation is the account of the political process associated with official efforts to deny the danger to public health just to protect the profitable tourist trade: "such corruption in high places, combined with the prevailing insecurity, the state of crisis in which the city had been plunged by the death that walked its streets, led at the lower social levels to a certain breakdown of moral standards, to an activation of the dark and antisocial forces, which manifested itself in intemperance, shameless license and growing criminality" (79). The mendacity of the state induces a cultural crisis, which in turn stands as a metaphor for a Europe ripe for collapse.

Yet as important as such a passage is to decipher the political thematics of the text, *Death in Venice* is surely not a tendentious text concerned primarily with political corruption. It is not protest fiction, and to the extent that one focuses solely on these sections, one is open to the criticism of having restricted the reading to framing material while avoiding the evident core of the story, the vicissitudes of the writer and his aesthetic concerns. Unless one would want to concede that historical matters are really only extrinsic — surely not my position — one must focus on Aschenbach himself, now that we have established the imperialist setting of the narrative.

Not only Aschenbach's Silesian background links him to Prussia; his very character as a writer epitomizes a Prussian ethic of discipline. He thinks of himself repeatedly as a soldier, and the text makes clear that Frederick is both a topic for Aschenbach and a model of rigor, order, and a willingness to endure — a man whom the artist Aschenbach strives to emulate. Despite disadvantages, "he would 'stay the course' — it was his favorite motto, he saw his historical novel about Frederic the Great as nothing if not the apotheosis of this, the king's word of command, '*durchhalten!*' which to Aschenbach epitomized a manly ethos of suffering action" (29). Therefore, the text's concern with the nature of art parallels an investigation of a Prussian legacy, epitomized by the trenchant comment of Aschenbach having always lived like a tightly closed fist, never allowing a moment of relaxation: "Aschenbach did not enjoy enjoying himself. Whenever and wherever he had to stop work, have a breathing space, take things easily, he would soon find himself driven by restlessness and dissatisfaction . . . back to his lofty travail, to his stern and sacred daily routine" (58). This perpetual effort, a never-ending labor, required a "constant harnessing of his energies [which] was something to which he had been called, but not really born" (29). This effort is a duty, like a soldier's, which he has accepted, and which he fulfills no matter what the cost. Moreover, this manner of work is also the topic of much of his fiction, concerned with heroes who carry on, despite greatest difficulty, out of sheer tenacity, rather than out of any deeply felt substantive ideal. It is a "heroism of weakness," as it lacks any internal value except the obligation to duty, and in this unwavering soldierliness — a sort of internal militarization — Aschenbach embodies the bourgeois ethic of his age: he

> was the writer who spoke for all those who work on the brink of exhaustion, who labor and are heavy-laden, who are worn out already but still stand upright, all those moralists of achievement who are slight of stature and scanty of resources, but who yet, by some ecstasy of the will and by wise husbandry, manage at least for a time to force their work into a semblance of greatness. There are many such, they are the heroes of our age. (31)

The morality of achievement means that heroism lies in the sheer fact of persistent labor, not in the substance or quality of its results. The refusal to yield in the pursuit of one's calling exemplifies the cultural structure that the German sociologist Max Weber discussed in his study *The Protestant Ethic and the Spirit of Capitalism* of 1904–1905. Weber argues that the Protestant Reformation upset traditional medieval forms of behavior by establishing a new mode of individuality dependent on the primacy of faith, election, and divine calling. The result is a mode of labor Weber describes as rational because it excludes all considerations irrelevant to its perpetuation. The point of work is not the enjoyment of its products but only further work, as evidence of a vocation — that is, one's feeling called and chosen by God. Even though explicit religious belief gradually waned, the originally Protestant structure became essential to capitalist behavior, according to which regular labor implies a refusal of pleasure and an increasing specialization in order to pursue ever greater efficiency. Yet this morality of achievement, Weber feared, would lead to an internal impoverishment and a reduction in the subjective experience of the individual:

> One of the fundamental elements of the spirit of modern capitalism, and not only of that but of all modern culture: rational conduct on the basis of the idea of the calling, was born . . . from the spirit of Christian asceticism. . . . This fundamentally ascetic trait of middle-class life, if it attempts to be a way of life at all, and not simply the absence of any, was what Goethe wanted to teach. . . . For him the realization meant a renunciation, a departure from an age of full and beautiful humanity, which can no more be repeated in the course of our cultural development than can the flower of the Athenian culture of antiquity. (Weber 1976, 180–81)

The comment is striking, as it recalls Aschenbach's anachronistic desire for the beauty of ancient Greece.

While Mann suggests the possibility of archaic elements exploding onto the modern scene, Weber asserts the irreversible separation between the two ages. Nonetheless, his further comments go straight to the heart of Aschenbach's dilemma:

> The Puritan wanted to work in a calling; we are forced to do so. For when asceticism was carried out of monastic cells into everyday life, and began to dominate world morality, it did its part in building the tremendous cosmos of the modern economic order. This order is now bound to the technical and economic conditions of machine production which to-day determine the lives of all the individuals who are born into this mechanism, not only those directly concerned with economic acquisition, with irresistible force. Perhaps it will so determine them until the last ton of fossilized coal is burnt. In [Richard] Baxter's view the care for external goods should only lie on the shoulders of the "saint like a light cloak, which can be thrown aside at any moment." But fate decreed that the cloak should become an iron cage. (Weber 1976, 181)

The metaphor of the "iron cage" implies that the rationalized structure of labor that has spread throughout society — even to writers — derives from an asceticism that simultaneously leaves little room for the naive pleasures of life and limits the scope of individual experience. This situation portrays Aschenbach trapped in a Prussian Protestant culture, which forces him to stay the course, no matter what the cost. This connection in turn leads to the conclusion that despite many critics' fixation on Mann's frequent distinction between artistic and bourgeois modes of existence, Aschenbach embodies the artist precisely as a bourgeois in the sense of the work ethic. He is a moralist of achievement, and indeed he must be so.

As Harvey Goldman has noted, "The true artist has to adopt the model of the bourgeois calling and a mode of service that demands and provides self-conquest; this model equips the self, through ascetic denial, for the 'conquest' of the world. But the adherent of the calling adopts as well, however unintentionally, the perils of the calling and the personality constructed on it" (Goldman 172). Aschenbach is trapped in an "iron cage" that is withering his creative powers; his decision to travel entails an effort to escape the cage and to find "an expansion of his inner self" that his regulated life otherwise denied him (25).

By this point in our reading, the political intertwining of *Death in Venice* with its historical context has become quite complex. In addition to the material pertaining to the international order on the eve of World War I, at least three ideologically laden constellations have emerged: the turn to aesthetics as a specific displacement of political materials, the Prussianism of the good soldier Aschenbach, and the Protestant work ethic as a description of all modern labor, including the labor of the artist. Yet before we can tie these strands together, we must evaluate the course of the narrative, Aschenbach's passage from Munich to Venice and to death. Critics typically approach *Death in Venice* as a narrative of decline, the story of the writer's fall from public acclaim to degradation and humiliating defeat. Thus, for example, Erich Heller's summation: "He, the classical writer of his age and country, who has 'rejected the abyss' and entered into a covenant with Apollo, determined as he is to let his art do service in the humanization of man, unwittingly goes out in search of Dionysus and dies in his embrace" (Heller 1958, 105). Such a reading insinuates a causal connection between Aschenbach's succumbing to Dionysus and death, which Heller takes as a disqualification of the writer's project. In other words, the critic views the writer's demise as a negative verdict on some aspect of his being. Hence the reader must consider Aschenbach implicitly guilty and condemn him. Indeed, several parts of Aschenbach's identity come into question: his Prussianism, his work ethic, his repressed homoeroticism, and his classical aesthetics. Whatever issue critics such as Heller might select, they must all cast Aschenbach as an embodiment of an order so internally flawed that the encounter with the strange god precipitates a well-deserved collapse.

This sort of moralizing judgment on Aschenbach — and on the orders of existence he supposedly represents — is, however, inadequate for reasons that the text itself makes clear. The first critic to judge the writer is of course none other than the narrator of *Death in Venice,* and, as Dorrit Cohn has shown persuasively, the relationship between the narrator and Aschenbach undergoes an important shift in the course of the text:

> In briefest summary the relationship of the narrator to his protagonist . . . may be described as one of increasing distance. In the early phases of the story it is essentially sympathetic, respectful, even reverent; in the later phases a deepening rift develops, building an increasingly ironic narratorial stance. . . . [T]he protagonist does not rise to his narrator's ethical and cultural standards but falls away from them. . . . The narrator meanwhile . . . remains

poised on the cultural pinnacle that has brought forth his protagonist's own artistic achievement. (Cohn 226)

As the writer's infatuation with Tadzio grows, the narrator becomes increasingly critical, culminating in the harsh and bitter condemnation when the exhausted Aschenbach is resting by a well in an
out-of-the-way square. Yet here, at the very latest, the overstated moralizing of the narrator — the prototype of subsequent judgments on
Aschenbach in the novella's reception history — must become questionable, even for a reader not previously put off by the earlier senten-
tiousness and pomposity. Now the narrator introduces with obvious
disgust the "strange dream-logic" of Aschenbach's second Socratic
reverie, even though precisely in this passage Aschenbach revises the
seduction scenario articulated earlier. Here he explicitly announces a
renunciation of the impermissible desire: "And now I shall go, Phaedrus, and you shall stay here; and leave this place only when you no
longer see me" (86).

The imminent separation from Tadzio, announced immediately af-
terwards, underscores the significance of this passage. It also highlights
the inadequacy of the narrator's verdict, which has ignored Aschenbach's ultimately ethical decision to refrain from acting on a desire incompatible with social norms and "the moral law" that the narrator
has just accused him of abandoning (82). Hence the text demonstrates
the inappropriateness of the narrator's evaluation of the writer. Yet if
the narrator's unfounded judgment on the writer can be appealed, we
might similarly question the interpretations that treat *Death in Venice*
primarily as a narrative of decay. In that case the evaluation of Aschenbach's death, the final scene on the beach, urgently needs reconsidera-
tion.

Heller errs in claiming that Aschenbach "dies in the embrace of
Dionysus, the wild deity of chaos, abandon, and intoxication" (Heller
1976, 178). On the contrary, Aschenbach has overcome the
Dionysian temptation, or rather, having sunk into the chaos, he has
reemerged capable of recognizing the ethical necessity of a separation
from Phaedrus/Tadzio. Far from signaling an ultimate condemnation,
the concluding passages point to a transfiguring salvation as a reversal
of the journey through degradation. Tadzio seems to share a similar
fate in his own story in the text. Just as Aschenbach's "enslaved emotion" (27) took vengeance on him, Tadzio's subordinate companion
Jaschu, "his particular vassal and friend" (50), "this lesser and servile
mortal" (60), also rebels: "as if in this hour of leave-taking the

submissiveness of the lesser partner had been transformed into cruel brutality, as if he were now bent on revenge for his long servitude, the victor did not release his defeated friend even then, but knelt on his back and pressed his face into the sand so hard and so long that Tadzio, breathless from the fight in any case, seemed to be on the point of suffocation" (87).

The marginal story of Tadzio and Jaschu provides a miniature model of Aschenbach's trajectory: the servile friend, like the enslaved emotions, rises up, overcoming the master. But — and this is precisely the important turn — in the wake of defeat, a vindication takes place, the suggestion of a final consonance between the writer and youth. Tadzio appears as a "soul-summoner," inviting Aschenbach "into an immensity rich with unutterable expectation" (88). A death both profoundly Platonic and Christian summons Aschenbach's soul: hardly the description of a humiliating demise or damnation of the sort that the narrator's verdict might have warranted. Indeed, the very term the prosecutorial narrator had earlier thrown at Aschenbach, alleged to have contemplated "monstrous things" (82) (*"das Ungeheuerliche"*), recurs now as the redemptive immensity to which Tadzio points (*"ins Verheißungsvoll-Ungeheure"*). If there is a defeat at the conclusion, it is surely not Aschenbach's but that of the authoritarian narrator, who emerges as deeply mistaken in his moralizing judgment.

The historical significance of this reversal is profound, for it shifts attention back to the problem of the iron cage, the work ethic, and the form of bourgeois life in the modern world — a form deeply rational but simultaneously devoid of meaning. Weber was enormously concerned with the consequences of this sense of meaninglessness and, interestingly in this context, he describes extramarital sexual life as one of the rare alternatives to the isolating alienation of modernity: "The lover realizes himself to be rooted in the kernel of the truly living, which is eternally inaccessible to any rational endeavor. He knows himself to be freed from the cold skeleton hands of rational orders, just as completely as from the banality of everyday routine" (Weber 1958, 347). Such a beckoning possibility of a moment of meaning is surely a strong explanation for Aschenbach's passion, given his otherwise deeply lonely life. In *Death in Venice,* Mann is exploring the alternative to loneliness in a context where it seems as if one can only choose between either empty routine or destructive chaos, between the meaningless order of Prussian rationality or the orderless meaning of Dionysian destruction. The conclusion points toward a solution without resolving the contradictions: Aschenbach and Tadzio separate, art and life part ways, as do form and content, aesthetics and ethics, but the soul-summoning coda maintains their reconciliation as a utopian hope for human community.

Reading this investigation into the mind of an imaginary writer so tightly associated with the Prussian ideology, one can surely wonder how *Death in Venice* fares in the light of subsequent German history. Mann was an outspoken critic of Hitler and spent the Nazi years in exile in the United States. But what of Aschenbach, whose repression, loyalty, orderliness, and efficiency are stereotypes often associated with Germany? Much depends on the evaluation of the conclusion. If we read the story as portraying the writer's moral failing (as the narrator suggests), then we might take Aschenbach as anticipating the psychology of the German unwilling to resist Hitler's criminal regime. The Dionysian chaos would represent the potential for an irrational revolt against civilized order. If we focus on Aschenbach's renunciation, however, then we would surely have an example of the ability to reject immorality, thanks to an internal strength of character derived from the same Prussian-Protestant tradition, which now appears in quite a different light. In this case, Aschenbach's final renunciation represents a transition beyond the "heroism of weakness" and the "ethics of achievement," beyond an emptied morality of production in order to act for the first time in the interest of a moral community.

In the wake of the considerable illiberalism of twentieth-century Germany, it is equally interesting to rethink the narrator's verdicts. We recall that the narrator condemned Aschenbach harshly, even though he had, after all, done nothing criminal; indeed, he had never even addressed Tadzio. On the contrary, the condemnation rests solely on intention, belying a confusion between intention and deed, or perhaps treating mere intent as if it were already a forbidden act. Yet that sort of proscription on imagined acts would quickly stifle all creativity, especially the artist's, for precisely such a stifling atmosphere led Aschenbach to escape his routinized life and to set off into the unknown. His trip to Dionysus is therefore not at all an escapist flight from his vocation (as the narrator would have it) but the most radical and consistent pursuit of the vocation — an orphic descent into Hades in search of the wellsprings of creativity that his heavy routine has crushed. *Death in Venice* does not show that the ethic of duty, Prussian soldierliness, is wrong; the point is rather that when duty degenerates into meaningless routine, it crushes the spirit, while the genuine and most dutiful pursuit of a calling that has not hardened into an iron cage requires not only discipline but also courage and imagination. Perhaps the good soldier Aschenbach was the best soldier only when he dared to travel to Venice, plumb the depths of his soul, and face an ultimate temptation and overcome it with grace.

The novella raises the question of the possibility of an ethical community, and it maps two equally undesirable answers: a Prussian obedience, maintaining the law no matter what the content ("moral resoluteness at the far side of knowledge" [32]), and the chaos of formless experience in the Dionysian crowd, with disregard for any "moral law" (82). Aschenbach begins with the inadequacy of the former and recoils from the violence of the latter, but the dissatisfying choice corresponds to two equally unattractive models of Germany. In *Eichmann in Jerusalem*, Hannah Arendt describes the trial of a Nazi official who played a key role in the organization of the Holocaust. A major point of his defense, and of many other Nazis, was the imperative to follow orders, without any substantive examination of these orders. Arendt labeled this behavior the "banality of evil," which has become a major paradigm to describe individuals' complicity with authoritarian regimes. More recently, Daniel Goldhagen has presented a different model of participation in the Holocaust in his study *Hitler's Willing Executioners*. Goldhagen argues that Germans supported and participated in the killing of Jews because of their heartfelt belief in an "eliminationist antisemitism" and not at all because of a blind acceptance of duty. His evidence includes descriptions of systemic cruelty to the victims that

gives lie to the perpetrators' postwar assertions that they were obliged to follow orders either because orders are to be followed or because they were in no position to evaluate the morality and legality of the orders. The systemic cruelty demonstrated to all Germans involved that their countrymen were treating Jews as they did . . . because of a set of beliefs that defined the Jews in a way that demanded Jewish suffering as retribution, a set of beliefs which inhered as profound a hatred as one people has likely ever harbored for another. (Goldhagen 389)

The two explanations cannot be further apart. For Arendt, it is a matter of formal legality blind to content, whereas for Goldhagen, it is a content of uninhibited hatred, with no appeal to legal forms. Aschenbach, representing Germany, must grapple with this same polarized alternative: rigorous ethics that exclude meaning, or chaotic desire beyond any morality.

To identify the historical ramifications of his quandary, we need to think not only of the question of German morality in the twentieth century but also of the aesthetic problem inherited from Nietzsche's *Birth of Tragedy*. The tension between Apollo and Dionysus in Aschenbach's Venice derives from Nietzsche's commentary on the history of ancient Greek culture. Greek tragedy arose originally, he argues, in musical rituals to celebrate Dionysus — rituals such as Mann evokes in the dream sequence — but these plays achieved aesthetic form through the Apollonian principle of representing individuals, the heroes of the myths. Nevertheless, the core of the work remains in the Dionysian element of the chorus, not in the brief illusion of the characters on stage. As a commentary on art, *The Birth of Tragedy* is less concerned with the polarity of the gods than with their synthesis. Nietzsche recounts how Socrates, deeply hostile to Dionysus, initiated a rationalist attack on myth. But Nietzsche also insists on claiming that a reconciliation between Socrates and Dionysus ultimately took place, leading to "the Socrates who practices music" (Nietzsche 98).

After the distinctly Apollonian imagery of the fourth chapter of *Death in Venice* and the largely Dionysian fifth chapter, the final passages, introduced by the second Socratic interlude, also point toward a reconciliation. The transfigurative conclusion suggests a community in which form and content, ethics and aesthetics, Apollo and Dionysus, could coincide. There are small hints of such a world in the "human solidarity" (48) of the Russian family or the "air of discipline, obligation, and self-respect" (45) among the Poles, indications of a good life with room for both community and dignity, pleasure and meaning, music and Socrates. These are examples, brief to be sure, but they suggest the ability to imagine a society in which people can live with order but without repression — a modest utopia, but one that has remained elusive for many. A decade after the publication of *Death in Venice*, Mann would disappoint his politically conservative public by arguing that the new democratic Germany, the Weimar Republic, could harbor such a society. Weimar ended after only a decade and a half, overthrown by the Nazis, who soon plunged the world into another war. Those German struggles with political form cast shadows backward across time onto *Death in Venice*, a text concerned perhaps even more with the form of community than with the form of art.

WORKS CITED

Arendt, Hannah. *Eichmann in Jerusalem: A Report on the Banality of Evil*. New York: Viking, 1963.

Cohn, Dorrit. "The Second Author of *Der Tod in Venedig*." *Probleme der Moderne: Studien zur deutschen Literatur von Nietzsche bis Brecht*. Ed. Benjamin Bennett, et. al. Tübingen: Niemeyer, 1983. 223–45.

Du Bois, W. E. B. *Darkwater: Voices from within the Veil*. New York: Schocken, 1969.

Goldhagen, Daniel Jonah. *Hitler's Willing Executions: Ordinary Germans and the Holocaust*. New York: Knopf, 1996.

Goldman, Harvey. *Max Weber and Thomas Mann: Calling and the Shaping of the Self*. Berkeley: U of California P, 1988.

Heller, Erich. *The Ironic German: A Study of Thomas Mann*. Boston: Little, 1958.

———. *The Poet's Self and the Poem: Essays on Goethe, Nietzsche, Rilke, and Thomas Mann*. London: Athlone, 1976.

Nietzsche, Friedrich. *Basic Writings of Friedrich Nietzsche*. Ed. and trans. Walter Kaufmann. New York: Modern Library, 1992.

Weber, Max. *From Max Weber: Essays in Sociology*. Ed. and trans. H. H. Geerth and C. Wright Mills. New York: Oxford UP, 1958.

———. *The Protestant Ethic and the Spirit of Capitalism*. Trans. Talcott Parsons. New York: Scribners, 1976.

Glossary of Critical
and Theoretical Terms

Most terms have been glossed parenthetically where they first appear in the text. Mainly, the glossary lists terms that are too complex to define in a phrase or a sentence or two. A few of the terms listed are discussed at greater length elsewhere (feminist criticism, for instance); these terms are defined succinctly and a page reference to the longer discussion is provided.

AFFECTIVE FALLACY First used by William K. Wimsatt and Monroe C. Beardsley to refer to what they regarded as the erroneous practice of interpreting texts according to the psychological responses of readers. "The Affective Fallacy," they wrote in a 1946 essay later republished in *The Verbal Icon* (1954), "is a confusion between the poem and its *results* (what it *is* and what it *does*). . . . It begins by trying to derive the standards of criticism from the psychological effects of a poem and ends in impressionism and relativism." The affective fallacy, like the intentional fallacy (confusing the meaning of a work with the author's expressly intended meaning), was one of the main tenets of the New Criticism, or formalism. The affective fallacy has recently been contested by reader-response critics, who have deliberately dedicated their efforts to describing the way individual readers and "interpretive communities" go about "making sense" of texts.
    See also: Authorial Intention, Formalism, Reader-Response Criticism.
    AUTHORIAL INTENTION Defined narrowly, an author's intention in writing a work, as expressed in letters, diaries, interviews, and conversations. Defined more broadly, "intentionality" involves unexpressed motivations, designs, and purposes, some of which may have remained unconscious.
    The debate over whether critics should try to discern an author's intentions (conscious or otherwise) is an old one. William K. Wimsatt and

Monroe C. Beardsley, in an essay first published in the 1940s, coined the term "intentional fallacy" to refer to the practice of basing interpretations on the expressed or implied intentions of authors, a practice they judged to be erroneous. As proponents of the New Criticism, or formalism, they argued that a work of literature is an object in itself and should be studied as such. They believed that it is sometimes helpful to learn what an author intended, but the critic's real purpose is to show what is actually in the text, not what an author intended to put there.

See also: Affective Fallacy, Formalism.

BASE   *See* Marxist Criticism.

BINARY OPPOSITIONS   *See* Oppositions.

BLANKS   *See* Gaps.

CANON   Since the fourth century, used to refer to those books of the Bible that the Christian church accepts as being Holy Scripture. The term has come to be applied more generally to those literary works given special status, or "privileged," by a culture. Works we tend to think of as "classics" or the "Great Books" produced by Western culture — texts that are found in every anthology of American, British, and world literature — would be among those that constitute the canon.

Recently, Marxist, feminist, minority, and postcolonial critics have argued that, for political reasons, many excellent works never enter the canon. Canonized works, they claim, are those that reflect — and respect — the culture's dominant ideology or perform some socially acceptable or even necessary form of "cultural work." Attempts have been made to broaden or redefine the canon by discovering valuable texts, or versions of texts, that were repressed or ignored for political reasons. These have been published both in traditional and in nontraditional anthologies. The most outspoken critics of the canon, especially radical critics practicing cultural criticism, have called into question the whole concept of canon or "canonicity." Privileging no form of artistic expression that reflects and revises the culture, these critics treat cartoons, comics, and soap operas with the same cogency and respect they accord novels, poems, and plays.

See also: Cultural Criticism, Feminist Criticism, Ideology, Marxist Criticism.

CONFLICTS, CONTRADICTIONS   *See* Gaps.

CULTURAL CRITICISM   A critical approach that is sometimes referred to as "cultural studies" or "cultural critique." Practitioners of cultural criticism oppose "high" definitions of culture and take seriously popular cultural forms. Grounded in a variety of European influences, cultural criticism nonetheless gained institutional force in England, in 1964, with the founding of the Centre for Contemporary Cultural Studies at Birmingham University. Broadly interdisciplinary in its scope and approach, cultural criticism views the text as the locus and catalyst of a complex network of political and economic discourses. Cultural critics share with Marxist critics an interest in the ideological contexts of cultural forms.

See also "What Is Cultural Criticism?" pp. 171–185.

DECONSTRUCTION   A poststructuralist approach to literature that is strongly influenced by the writings of the French philosopher Jacques Derrida. Deconstruction, partly in response to structuralism and formalism, posits the undecidability of meaning for all texts. In fact, as the deconstructionist critic J. Hillis Miller points out, "deconstruction is not a dismantling of the structure of a text but a demonstration that it has already dismantled itself."

DIALECTIC Originally developed by Greek philosophers, mainly Socrates and Plato, as a form and method of logical argumentation; the term later came to denote a philosophical notion of evolution. The German philosopher G. W. F. Hegel described dialectic as a process whereby a thesis, when countered by an antithesis, leads to the synthesis of a new idea. Karl Marx and Friedrich Engels, adapting Hegel's idealist theory, used the phrase "dialectical materialism" to discuss the way in which a revolutionary class war might lead to the synthesis of a new social economic order. The American Marxist critic Fredric Jameson has coined the phrase "dialectical criticism" to refer to a Marxist critical approach that synthesizes structuralist and poststructuralist methodologies.

See also: Marxist Criticism, Poststructuralism, Structuralism.

DIALOGIC *See* Discourse.

DISCOURSE Used specifically, can refer to (1) spoken or written discussion of a subject or area of knowledge; (2) the words in, or text of, a narrative as opposed to its story line; or (3) a "strand" within a given narrative that argues a certain point or defends a given value system.

More generally, "discourse" refers to the language in which a subject or area of knowledge is discussed or a certain kind of business is transacted. Human knowledge is collected and structured in discourses. Theology and medicine are defined by their discourses, as are politics, sexuality, and literary criticism.

A society is generally made up of a number of different discourses or "discourse communities," one or more of which may be dominant or serve the dominant ideology. Each discourse has its own vocabulary, concepts, and rules, the knowledge of which constitutes power. The psychoanalyst and psychoanalytic critic Jacques Lacan has treated the unconscious as a form of discourse, the patterns of which are repeated in literature. Cultural critics, following Mikhail Bakhtin, use the word "dialogic" to discuss the dialogue *between* discourses that takes place within language or, more specifically, a literary text.

See also: Cultural Criticism, Ideology, Narrative, Psychoanalytic Criticism.

FEMINIST CRITICISM An aspect of the feminist movement whose primary goals include critiquing masculine-dominated language and literature by showing how they reflect a masculine ideology; writing the history of unknown or undervalued women writers, thereby earning them their rightful place in the literary canon; and helping to create a climate in which women's creativity may be fully realized and appreciated. *See* "What Is Gender Criticism?" pp. 211–22.

FIGURE *See* Metaphor, Metonymy, Symbol.

FORMALISM Also referred to as the New Criticism, formalism reached its height during the 1940s and 1950s, but it is still practiced today. Formalists treat a work of literary art as if it were a self-contained, self-referential object. Rather than basing their interpretations of a text on the reader's response, the author's stated intentions, or parallels between the text and historical contexts (such as the author's life), formalists concentrate on the relationships *within* the text that give it its own distinctive character or form. Special attention is paid to repetition, particularly of images or symbols, but also of sound effects and rhythms in poetry.

Because of the importance placed on close analysis and the stress on the text as a carefully crafted, orderly object containing observable formal patterns, formalism has often been seen as an attack on Romanticism and impressionism, particularly impressionistic criticism. It has sometimes even been called an "objective" approach to literature. Formalists are more likely than certain other critics to believe and say that the meaning of a text can be known objectively. For instance, reader-response critics see meaning as a function either of each reader's experience or of the norms that govern a particular "interpretive community," and deconstructors argue that texts mean opposite things at the same time.

Formalism was originally based on essays written during the 1920s and 1930s by T. S. Eliot, I. A. Richards, and William Empson. It was significantly developed later by a group of American poets and critics, including R. P. Blackmur, Cleanth Brooks, John Crowe Ransom, Allen Tate, Robert Penn Warren, and William K. Wimsatt. Although we associate formalism with certain principles and terms (such as the "affective fallacy" and the "intentional fallacy" as defined by Wimsatt and Monroe C. Beardsley), formalists were trying to make a cultural statement rather than establish a critical dogma. Generally southern, religious, and culturally conservative, they advocated the inherent value of literary works (particularly of literary works regarded as beautiful art objects) because they were sick of the growing ugliness of modern life and contemporary events. Some recent theorists even suggest that the rising popularity of formalism after World War II was a feature of American isolationism, the formalist tendency to isolate literature from biography and history being a manifestation of the American fatigue with wider involvements.

See also: Affective Fallacy, Authorial Intention, Deconstruction, Reader-Response Criticism, Symbol.

GAPS   When used by reader-response critics familiar with the theories of Wolfgang Iser, refers to "blanks" in texts that must be filled in by readers. A gap may be said to exist whenever and wherever a reader perceives something to be missing between words, sentences, paragraphs, stanzas, or chapters. Readers respond to gaps actively and creatively, explaining apparent inconsistencies in point of view, accounting for jumps in chronology, speculatively supplying information missing from plots, and resolving problems or issues left ambiguous or "indeterminate" in the text.

Reader-response critics sometimes speak as if a gap actually exists in a text; a gap is, of course, to some extent a product of readers' perceptions. Different readers may find gaps in different texts, and different gaps in the same text. Furthermore, they may fill these gaps in different ways, which is why, a reader-response critic might argue, works are interpreted in different ways.

Although the concept of the gap has been used mainly by reader-response critics, it has also been used by critics taking other theoretical approaches. Practitioners of deconstruction might use "gap" when speaking of the radical contradictoriness of a text. Marxists have used the term to speak of everything from the gap that opens up between economic base and cultural superstructure to the two kinds of conflicts or contradictions to be found in literary texts. The first of these, they would argue, results from the fact that texts reflect ideology, within which certain subjects cannot be covered, things that cannot be said, contradictory views that cannot be recognized as contradictory. The second kind of conflict, contradiction, or gap within a text results from the fact that works don't just reflect ideology: they are also fictions that, consciously or unconsciously, distance themselves from the same ideology.

See also: Deconstruction, Ideology, Marxist Criticism, Reader-Response Criticism.

GENDER CRITICISM   Developing out of feminist criticism in the mid-1980s, this fluid and inclusive movement by its nature defies neat definition. Its practitioners include, but are not limited to, self-identified feminists, gay and lesbian critics, queer and performance theorists, and poststructuralists interested in deconstructing oppositions such as masculine/feminine, heterosexual/homosexual. This diverse group of critics shares an interest in interrogating categories of gender and sexuality and exploring the relationships between them, though it does not necessarily share any central assumptions about the nature of these categories. For example, some gender critics insist that all gender identities are cultural constructions, but others have maintained a belief in essential gender identity. Often gender critics are more interested in examining gender issues through a literary text than a literary text through gender issues. *See* "What Is Gender Criticism?" pp. 211–22.

GENRE   A French word referring to a kind or type of literature. Individual works within a genre may exhibit a distinctive form, be governed by certain conventions, or represent characteristic subjects. Tragedy, epic, and romance are all genres.

Perhaps inevitably, the term *genre* is used loosely. Lyric poetry is a genre, but so are characteristic *types* of the lyric, such as the sonnet, the ode, and the elegy. Fiction is a genre, as are detective fiction and science fiction. The list of genres grows constantly as critics establish new lines of connection between individual works and discern new categories of works with common characteristics. Moreover, some writers form hybrid genres by combining the characteristics of several in a single work. Knowledge of genres helps critics to understand and explain what is conventional and unconventional, borrowed and original, in a work.

HEGEMONY   Given intellectual currency by the Italian communist Antonio Gramsci, the word (a translation of *egemonia*) refers to the pervasive system of assumptions, meanings, and values — the web of ideologies, in other words — that shapes the way things look, what they mean, and therefore what reality *is* for the majority of people within a given culture.

See also: Ideology, Marxist Criticism.

IDEOLOGY   A set of beliefs underlying the customs, habits, or practices common to a given social group. To members of that group, the beliefs seem obviously true, natural, and even universally applicable. They may seem just as obviously arbitrary, idiosyncratic, and even false to outsiders or members of another group who adhere to another ideology. Within a society, several ideologies may coexist, or one or more may be dominant.

Ideologies may be forcefully imposed or willingly subscribed to. Their component beliefs may be held consciously or unconsciously. In either case, they come to form what Johanna M. Smith has called "the unexamined ground of our experience." Ideology governs our perceptions, judgments, and prejudices — our sense of what is acceptable, normal, and deviant. Ideology may cause a revolution; it may also allow discrimination and even exploitation.

Ideologies are of special interest to sociologically oriented critics of literature because of the way in which authors reflect or resist prevailing views in their texts. Some Marxist critics have argued that literary texts reflect and reproduce the ideologies that produced them; most, however, have shown how ideologies are riven with contradictions that works of literature manage to expose and widen. Still other Marxists have focused on the way in which texts themselves are characterized by gaps, conflicts, and contradictions between their ideological and anti-ideological functions.

Feminist critics have addressed the question of ideology by seeking to expose (and thereby call into question) the patriarchal ideology mirrored or inscribed in works written by men — even men who have sought to counter sexism and break down sexual stereotypes. New historicists have been interested in demonstrating the ideological underpinnings not only of literary representations but also of our interpretations of them. Fredric Jameson, an American Marxist critic, argues that all thought is ideological, but that ideological thought that knows itself as such stands the chance of seeing through and transcending ideology.

See also: Cultural Criticism, Feminist Criticism, Marxist Criticism, New Historicism.

IMAGINARY ORDER   One of the three essential orders of the psychoanalytic field (*see* Real and Symbolic Order), it is most closely associated with the senses (sight, sound, touch, taste, and smell). The infant, who by comparison to other animals is born premature and thus is wholly dependent on others for a prolonged period, enters the Imaginary order when it begins to experience a unity of body parts and motor control that is empowering. This usually occurs between six and eighteen months, and is called by Lacan the "mirror stage" or "mirror phase," in which the child anticipates mastery of its body. It does so by identifying with the *image* of wholeness (that is, seeing its own image in the mirror, experiencing its mother as a whole body, and so on). This sense of oneness, and also difference from others (especially the mother or primary caretaker), is established through an image or a vision of harmony that is both a mirroring and a "mirage of maturation" or false sense of individuality and independence. The Imaginary is a metaphor for unity, is related to the visual order, and is always part of human subjectivity. Because the subject is fundamentally separate from others and also internally divided (conscious/unconscious), the apparent coherence of the Imaginary, its fullness and grandiosity, is always false, a *mis*recognition that the ego (or "me") tries to deny by imagining itself as coherent and empowered. The Imaginary operates in conjunction with the Real and the Symbolic and is not a "stage" of development equivalent to Freud's "pre-oedipal stage," nor is it prelinguistic.

See also: Psychoanalytic Criticism, Real, Symbolic Order.

IMPLIED READER   A phrase used by some reader-response critics in place of the phrase "the reader." Whereas "the reader" could refer to any idiosyncratic individual who happens to have read or to be reading the text, "the implied reader" is *the* reader intended, even created, by the text. Other reader-response critics seeking to describe this more generally conceived reader have spoken of the "informed reader" or the "narratee," who is "the necessary counterpart of a given narrator."

See also Reader-Response Criticism.

INTENTIONAL FALLACY *See* Authorial Intention.

INTENTIONALITY *See* Authorial Intention.

INTERTEXTUALITY The condition of interconnectedness among texts. Every author has been influenced by others, and every work contains explicit and implicit references to other works. Writers may consciously or unconsciously echo a predecessor or precursor; they may also consciously or unconsciously disguise their indebtedness, making intertextual relationships difficult for the critic to trace.

Reacting against the formalist tendency to view each work as a freestanding object, some poststructuralist critics suggested that the meaning of a work emerges only intertextually, that is, within the context provided by other works. But there has been a reaction, too, against this type of intertextual criticism. Some new historicist critics suggest that literary history is itself too narrow a context and that works should be interpreted in light of a larger set of cultural contexts.

There is, however, a broader definition of intertextuality, one that refers to the relationship between works of literature and a wide range of narratives and discourses that we don't usually consider literary. Thus defined, intertextuality could be used by a new historicist to refer to the significant interconnectedness between a literary text and nonliterary discussions of or discourses about contemporary culture. Or it could be used by a poststructuralist to suggest that a work can only be recognized and read only within a vast field of signs and tropes that is *like* a text and that makes any single text self-contradictory and "undecidable."

See also: Discourse, Formalism, Narrative, New Historicism, Poststructuralism, Trope.

MARXIST CRITICISM An approach that treats literary texts as material products, describing them in broadly historical terms. In Marxist criticism, the text is viewed in terms of its production and consumption, as a product *of* work that does identifiable cultural work of its own. Following Karl Marx, the founder of communism, Marxist critics have used the terms *base* to refer to economic reality and *superstructure* to refer to the corresponding or "homologous" infrastructure consisting of politics, law, philosophy, religion, and the arts. Also following Marx, they have used the word *ideology* to refer to that set of cultural beliefs that literary works at once reproduce, resist, and revise.

METAPHOR The representation of one thing by another related or similar thing. The image (or activity or concept) used to represent or "figure" something else is known as the "vehicle" of the metaphor; the thing represented is called the "tenor." In other words, the vehicle is what we substitute for the tenor. The relationship between vehicle and tenor can provide much additional meaning. Thus, instead of saying, "Last night I read a book," we might say, "Last night I plowed through a book." "Plowed through" (or the activity of plowing) is the vehicle of our metaphor; "read" (or the act of reading) is the tenor, the thing being figured. The increment in meaning through metaphor is fairly obvious. Our audience knows not only *that* we read but also *how* we read, because to read a book in the way that a plow rips through earth is surely to read in a relentless, unreflective way. Note that in the sentence above, a new metaphor — "rips through" — has been used to explain an old one. This serves (which is a metaphor) as an example of just how thick (another metaphor) language is with metaphors!

Metaphor is a kind of "trope" (literally, a "turning," that is, a figure of speech that alters or "turns" the meaning of a word or phrase). Other tropes include allegory, conceit, metonymy, personification, simile, symbol, and synecdoche. Traditionally, metaphor and symbol have been viewed as the principal tropes; minor tropes have been categorized as *types* of these two major ones. Similes, for instance, are usually defined as simple metaphors that usually employ *like* or *as* and state the tenor outright, as in "My love is like a red, red rose." Synecdoche involves a vehicle that is a *part* of the tenor, as in "I see a sail" meaning "I see a boat." Metonymy is viewed as a metaphor involving two terms commonly if arbitrarily associated with (but not fundamentally or intrinsically related to) each other. Recently, however, deconstructors such as Paul de Man and J. Hillis Miller have questioned the "privilege" granted to metaphor and the metaphor/metonymy distinction or "opposition." They have suggested that all metaphors are really metonyms and that all figuration is arbitrary.

See also: Deconstruction, Metonymy, Oppositions, Symbol.

METONYMY   The representation of one thing by another that is commonly and often physically associated with it. To refer to a writer's handwriting as his or her "hand" is to use a metonymic "figure" or "trope." The image or thing used to represent something else is known as the "vehicle" of the metonym; the thing represented is called the "tenor."

Like other tropes (such as metaphor), metonymy involves the replacement of one word or phrase by another. Liquor may be referred to as "the bottle," a monarch as "the crown." Narrowly defined, the vehicle of a metonym is arbitrarily, not intrinsically, associated with the tenor. In other words, the bottle just happens to be what liquor is stored in and poured from in our culture. The hand may be involved in the production of handwriting, but so are the brain and the pen. There is no special, intrinsic likeness between a crown and a monarch; it's just that crowns traditionally sit on monarchs' heads and not on the heads of university professors. More broadly, *metonym* and *metonymy* have been used by recent critics to refer to a wide range of figures and tropes. Deconstructors have questioned the distinction between metaphor and metonymy.

See also: Deconstruction, Metaphor, Trope.

NARRATIVE   A story or a telling of a story, or an account of a situation or of events. A novel and a biography of a novelist are both narratives, as are Freud's case histories.

Some critics use the word "narrative" even more generally; Brook Thomas, a new historicist, has critiqued "narratives of human history that neglect the role human labor has played."

NEW CRITICISM   *See* Formalism.

NEW HISTORICISM   First practiced and articulated in the late 1970s and early 1980s in the work of critics such as Stephen Greenblatt — who named this movement in contemporary critical theory — and Louis Montrose, its practitioners share certain convictions, primarily that literary critics need to develop a high degree of historical consciousness and that literature should not be viewed apart from other human creations, artistic or otherwise. They share a belief in referentiality — a belief that literature refers to and is referred to by things outside itself — that is fainter in the works of formalist, poststructuralist, and even reader-response critics. Discarding old distinctions between literature, history, and the social sciences, new historicists agree with Greenblatt that the "central concerns" of criticism "should prevent it from permanently sealing off one type of discourse from another, or decisively separating works of art from the minds and lives of their creators and their audiences."

   See also: "What Is the New Historicism?" pp. 245–58; Authorial Intention, Deconstruction, Formalism, Ideology, Poststructuralism, Psychoanalytic Criticism.

OPPOSITIONS   A concept highly relevant to linguistics, inasmuch as linguists maintain that words (such as *black* and *death*) have meaning not in themselves but in relation to other words (*white* and *life*). Jacques Derrida, a poststructuralist philosopher of language, has suggested that in the West we think in terms of these "binary oppositions" or dichotomies, which on examination turn out to be evaluative hierarchies. In other words, each opposition — beginning/end, presence/absence, or consciousness/unconsciousness — contains one term that our culture views as superior and one term that we view as negative or inferior.

   Derrida has "deconstructed" a number of these binary oppositions, including two — speech/writing and signifier/signified — that he believes to be central to linguistics in particular and Western culture in general. He has concurrently critiqued the "law" of noncontradiction, which is fundamental to Western logic. He and other deconstructors have argued that a text can contain opposed strands of discourse and, therefore, mean opposite things: reason *and* passion, life *and* death, hope *and* despair, black *and* white. Traditionally, criticism has involved choosing between opposed or contradictory meanings and arguing that one is present in the text and the other absent.

   French feminists have adopted the ideas of Derrida and other deconstructors, showing not only that we think in terms of such binary oppositions as male/female, reason/emotion, and active/passive, but that we also associate reason and activity with masculinity and emotion and passivity with femininity. Because of this, they have concluded that language is "phallocentric," or masculine-dominated.

   See also: Deconstruction, Discourse, Feminist Criticism, Poststructuralism.

PHALLUS   The symbolic value of the penis that organizes libidinal development and which Freud saw as a stage in the process of human subjectivity. Lacan viewed the Phallus as the representative of a fraudulent power (male over female) whose "Law" is a principle of psychic division (conscious/unconscious) and sexual difference (masculine/feminine). The Symbolic order (*see* Symbolic Order) is ruled by the Phallus, which of itself has no inherent meaning *apart* *from* the power and meaning given to it by individual cultures and societies, and represented by the name of the father as lawgiver and namer.

POSTSTRUCTURALISM The general attempt to contest and subvert structuralism initiated by deconstructors and certain other critics associated with psychoanalytic, Marxist, and feminist theory. Structuralists, using linguistics as a model and employing semiotic (sign) theory, posit the possibility of knowing a text systematically and revealing the "grammar" behind its form and meaning. Poststructuralists argue against the possibility of such knowledge and description. They counter that texts can be shown to contradict not only structuralist accounts of them but also themselves. In making their adversarial claims, they rely on close readings of texts and on the work of theorists such as Jacques Derrida and Jacques Lacan.

Poststructuralists have suggested that structuralism rests on distinctions between "signifier" and "signified" (signs and the things they point toward), "self" and "language" (or "text"), texts and other texts, and text and world that are overly simplistic, if not patently inaccurate. Poststructuralists have shown how all signifieds are also signifiers, and they have treated texts as "intertexts." They have viewed the world as if it *were* a text (we desire a certain car because it *symbolizes* achievement) and the self as the subject, as well as the user, of language; for example, we may shape and speak through language, but it also shapes and speaks through us.

See also: Deconstruction, Feminist Criticism, Intertextuality, Psychoanalytic Criticism, Semiotics, Structuralism.

PSYCHOANALYTIC CRITICISM Grounded in the psychoanalytic theories of Sigmund Freud, it is one of the oldest critical methodologies still in use. Freud's view that works of literature, like dreams, express secret, unconscious desires led to criticism and interpreted literary works as manifestations of the authors' neuroses. More recently, psychoanalytic critics have come to see literary works as skillfully crafted artifacts that may appeal to *our* neuroses by tapping into our repressed wishes and fantasies. Other forms of psychological criticism that diverge from Freud, although they ultimately derive from his insights, include those based on the theories of Carl Jung and Jacques Lacan. *See* "What Is Psychoanalytic Criticism?" pp. 110–21.

READER-RESPONSE CRITICISM An approach to literature that, as its name implies, considers the way readers respond to texts, as they read. Stanley Fish describes the method by saying that it substitutes for one question, "What does this sentence mean?" a more operational question, "What does this sentence do?" Reader-response criticism shares with deconstruction a strong textual orientation and a reluctance to define a single meaning for a work. Along with psychoanalytic criticism, it shares an interest in the dynamics of mental response to textual cues. *See* "What Is Reader-Response Criticism?" pp. 142–54.

REAL One of the three orders of subjectivity (*see* Imaginary Order and Symbolic Order), the Real is the intractable and substantial world that resists and exceeds interpretation. The Real cannot be imagined, symbolized, or known directly. It constantly eludes our efforts to name it (death, gravity, the physicality of objects are examples of the Real), and thus challenges both the Imaginary and the Symbolic orders. The Real is fundamentally "Other," the mark of the divide between conscious and unconscious, and is signaled in language by gaps, slips, speechlessness, and the sense of the uncanny. The Real is not what we call "reality." It is the stumbling block of the Imaginary (which thinks it can "imagine" anything, including the Real) and of the Symbolic, which tries to bring the Real under its laws (the Real exposes the "phallacy" of the Law of the Phallus). The Real is frightening; we try to tame it with laws and language and call it "reality."

See also: Imaginary Order, Psychoanalytic Criticism, Symbolic Order.

SEMIOLOGY, SEMIOTIC   See Semiotics.

SEMIOTICS   The study of signs and sign systems and the way meaning is derived from them. Structuralist anthropologists, psychoanalysts, and literary critics developed semiotics during the decades following 1950, but much of the pioneering work had been done at the turn of the century by the founder of modern linguistics, Ferdinand de Saussure, and the American philosopher Charles Sanders Peirce.

Semiotics is based on several important distinctions, including the distinction between "signifier" and "signified" (the sign and what it points toward) and the distinction between "langue" and "parole." *Langue* (French for "tongue," as in "native tongue," meaning language) refers to the entire system within which individual utterances or usages of language have meaning; *parole* (French for "word") refers to the particular utterances or usages. A principal tenet of semiotics is that signs, like words, are not significant in themselves, but instead have meaning only in relation to other signs and the entire system of signs, or langue.

The affinity between semiotics and structuralist literary criticism derives from this emphasis placed on langue, or system. Structuralist critics, after all, were reacting against formalists and their procedure of focusing on individual words as if meanings didn't depend on anything external to the text.

Poststructuralists have used semiotics but questioned some of its underlying assumptions, including the opposition between signifier and signified. The feminist poststructuralist Julia Kristeva, for instance, has used the word *semiotic* to describe feminine language, a highly figurative, fluid form of discourse that she sets in opposition to rigid, symbolic masculine language.

See also: Deconstruction, Feminist Criticism, Formalism, Oppositions, Poststructuralism, Structuralism, Symbol.

SIMILE   See Metaphor.

SOCIOHISTORICAL CRITICISM   See New Historicism.

STRUCTURALISM   A science of humankind whose proponents attempted to show that all elements of human culture, including literature, may be understood as parts of a system of signs. Structuralism, according to Robert Scholes, was a reaction to "'modernist' alienation and despair."

Using Ferdinand de Saussure's linguistic theory, European structuralists such as Roman Jakobson, Claude Lévi-Strauss, and Roland Barthes (before his shift toward poststructuralism) attempted to develop a "semiology" or "semiotics" (science of signs). Barthes, among others, sought to recover literature and even language from the isolation in which they had been studied and to show that the laws that govern them govern all signs, from road signs to articles of clothing.

Particularly useful to structuralists were two of Saussure's concepts: the idea of "phoneme" in language and the idea that phonemes exist in two kinds of relationships: "synchronic" and "diachronic." A phoneme is the smallest consistently significant unit in language; thus, both "a" and "an" are phonemes, but "n" is not. A diachronic relationship is that which a phoneme has with those that have preceded it in time and those that will follow it. These "horizontal" relationships produce what we might call discourse or narrative and what Saussure called "parole." The synchronic relationship is the "vertical" one that a word has in a given instant with the entire system of language ("langue") in which it may generate meaning. "An" means what it means in English because those of us who speak the language are using it in the same way at a given time.

Following Saussure, Lévi-Strauss studied hundreds of myths, breaking them into their smallest meaningful units, which he called "mythemes." Removing each from its diachronic relations with other mythemes in a single myth (such as the myth of Oedipus and his mother), he vertically aligned those mythemes that he found to be homologous (structurally correspondent). He then studied the relationships within as well as between vertically aligned columns, in an attempt to understand scientifically, through ratios and proportions, those thoughts and processes that humankind has shared, both at one particular time and across time. One could say, then, that structuralists followed Saussure in preferring to think about the overriding langue or language of myth, in which each mytheme and mytheme-constituted myth fits meaningfully, rather than about isolated individual paroles or narratives. Structuralists followed Saussure's lead in believing what the poststructuralist Jacques Derrida later decided he could not subscribe to — that sign systems must be understood in terms of binary oppositions. In analyzing myths and texts to find basic structures, structuralists tended to find that opposite terms modulate until they are finally resolved or reconciled by some intermediary third term. Thus, a structuralist reading of *Paradise Lost* would show that the war between God and the bad angels becomes a rift between God and sinful, fallen man, the rift then being healed by the Son of God, the mediating third term.

See also: Deconstruction, Discourse, Narrative, Poststructuralism, Semiotics.

SUPERSTRUCTURE   *See* Marxist Criticism.

SYMBOL   A thing, image, or action that, although it is of interest in its own right, stands for or suggests something larger and more complex — often an idea or a range of interrelated ideas, attitudes, and practices.

Within a given culture, some things are understood to be symbols: the flag of the United States is an obvious example. More subtle cultural symbols might be the river as a symbol of time and the journey as a symbol of life and its manifold experiences.

Instead of appropriating symbols generally used and understood within their culture, writers often create symbols by setting up, in their works, a complex but identifiable web of associations. As a result, one object, image, or action suggests others, and often, ultimately, a range of ideas.

A symbol may thus be defined as a metaphor in which the "vehicle," the thing, image, or action used to represent something else, represents many related things (or "tenors") or is broadly suggestive. The urn in Keats's "Ode on a Grecian Urn" suggests many interrelated concepts, including art, truth, beauty, and timelessness.

Symbols have been of particular interest to formalists, who study how meanings emerge from the complex, patterned relationships between images in a work, and psychoanalytic critics, who are interested in how individual authors and the larger culture both disguise and reveal unconscious fears and desires through symbols. Recently, French feminists have also focused on the symbolic. They have suggested that, as wide-ranging as it seems, symbolic language is ultimately rigid and restrictive. They favor semiotic language and writing, which, they contend, is at once more rhythmic, unifying, and feminine.

See also: Feminist Criticism, Metaphor, Psychoanalytic Criticism, Trope.

SYMBOLIC ORDER   One of the three orders of subjectivity (*see* Imaginary Order and Real), it is the realm of law, language, and society; it is the repository of generally held cultural beliefs. Its symbolic system is language, whose agent is the father or lawgiver, the one who has the power of naming. The human subject is commanded into this preestablished order by language (a process that begins long before a child can speak) and must submit to its orders of communication (grammar, syntax, and so on). Entrance into the Symbolic order determines subjectivity according to a primary law of referentiality that takes the male sign (phallus, *see* Phallus) as its ordering principle. Lacan states that both sexes submit to the Law of the Phallus (the law of order, language, and differentiation) but that their individual relation to the law determines whether they see themselves as — and are seen by others to be — either "masculine" or "feminine." The Symbolic institutes repression (of the Imaginary), thus creating the unconscious, which itself is structured like the language of the symbolic. The unconscious, a timeless realm, cannot be known directly, but it can be understood by a kind of translation that takes place in language — psychoanalysis is the "talking cure." The Symbolic is not a "stage" of development (as is Freud's "oedipal stage") nor is it set in place once and for all in human life. We constantly negotiate its threshold (in sleep, in drunkenness) and can "fall out" of it altogether in psychosis.

See also: Imaginary Order, Psychoanalytic Criticism, Real.

SYNECDOCHE   *See* Metaphor, Metonymy.

TENOR   *See* Metaphor, Metonymy, Symbol.

TROPE   A figure, as in "figure of speech." Literally a "turning," that is, a turning or twisting of a word or phrase to make it mean something else. Principal tropes include metaphor, metonymy, personification, simile, and synecdoche.

See also: Metaphor, Metonymy.

VEHICLE   *See* Metaphor, Metonymy, Symbol.

About the Contributors

THE VOLUME EDITOR

Naomi Ritter is a professor emerita of German at the University of Missouri. She has published internationally on German and comparative literature of the nineteenth and twentieth centuries. Her most recent scholarly book, *Art as Spectacle: Images of the Entertainer since Romanticism* (1989), won the University of Missouri Curators' Prize for the outstanding book of the year by a Missouri faculty member published by the University of Missouri Press. Her essay in *Arts Indiana*, "Dance: Stepchild of the Arts Family," won the Penrod Award in 1995. She is now a freelance writer and editor in Bloomington, Indiana.

THE CRITICS

Russell A. Berman is professor of German studies and comparative literature at Stanford University. He has written extensively on modern German literature and culture. His books include *Between Fontane and Tucholsky: Literary Criticism and the Public Sphere in Imperial Germany* (1983), *The Rise of the Modern German Novel: Crisis and Charisma* (1986), *Modern Culture and Critical Theory: Art, Politics, and the Legacy of the Frankfurt School* (1989), and *Cultural Studies of Modern Germany: History, Representation, and Nationhood* (1993).

John Burt Foster Jr. is professor of English and cultural studies at George Mason University, where he also teaches literature in translation. In addition to many articles on comparative literature and cultural interchange, he has written *Heirs to Dionysus: A Nietzschean Current in Literary Modernism* (1981) and *Nabokov's Art of Memory and European Modernism* (1993). He is also an editor of the journal *The Comparatist* and is coediting two volumes of essays on cultural issues in the contemporary humanities for the International Association for Philosophy and Literature.

Lilian R. Furst, Marcel Bataillon Professor of Comparative Literature at the University of North Carolina at Chapel Hill, has applied a reader-oriented approach in her most recent book, *All Is True: The Claims and Strategies of Realist Fiction* (1995), which deals with Thomas Mann also. Her earlier books include *Romanticism in Perspective* (1969), *Romanticism* (1969), *Naturalism* (1976), *Fictions of Romantic Irony* (1984), *Through the Lens of the Reader* (1992), and a dual-voice autobiography with her father, *Home Is Somewhere Else* (1994).

Rodney Symington is professor and chair of the Department of Germanic Studies at the University of Victoria, where he has taught since 1967. He is also the editor of *Seminar: A Journal of Germanic Studies,* and author of *Brecht und Shakespeare.* He has published many articles on Bertolt Brecht, Thomas Mann, and Heimito von Doderer, and has edited numerous volumes, including *A History of Modern German Literature.*

Robert Tobin is associate professor of German at Whitman College in Walla Walla, Washington. He has published extensively on sexuality in the writings of Goethe, Moritz, Wieland, and Thomas Mann.

THE SERIES EDITOR

Ross C Murfin, general editor of Case Studies in Contemporary Criticism and volume editor of Conrad's *Heart of Darkness* and Hawthorne's *Scarlet Letter* in the series, is provost and vice president for academic affairs at Southern Methodist University. He has taught at the University of Miami, Yale University, and the University of Virginia, and has published scholarly studies on Joseph Conrad, Thomas Hardy, and D. H. Lawrence.